Artwork by Tom Romano

12-1-21

Dear Gretchen

Enjoy!

Keith Wire

The Night Birds Still Sing

Ruth Wire

Award-winning poet, playwright and short story writer

Rosalind Press – Oregon

ISBN: 978-1-95574600-7

Cover Artwork by Tom Romano

Rosalind Press - Oregon

dedicated to my mother, Irene Rodgers

TABLE OF CONTENTS

Prologue...9

HOMELESS, 1942

Chapter 1 - The Rooming House 10

Chapter 2 - Settling in; Memories.................................... 15

Chapter 3 – John; The Ebberly sisters 30

Chapter 4 - Tony, Mario and Joey.................................... 40

Chapter 5 - Grandma Feldman's...................................... 48

Chapter 6 - Mama's Wisdom 55

Chapter 7 - Charlotte 60

Chapter 8 - Bass Lake 68

Chapter 9 - Joey's Problem 86

Chapter 10 - Daddy's Offer; Mr. Green, Writer 96

Chapter 11 - Mrs. Yachinflaster 107

Chapter 12 - Flashlight.. 117

Chapter 13 – Laurie... 128

Chapter 14 - Laurie Visits the Rooming House 138

Chapter 15 - The Laurie Effect 148

Chapter 16 - The Facts of Life 160

Chapter 17 - Lisbeth's Birthday Party 174

Chapter 18 - Jack Ruchek; Heart Break.............................. 185

Chapter 19 - The Light Bulb Incident 195

Chapter 20 - The Crumpetts 199

Chapter 21 – Carmel; The Night Birds Sing.......................... 205

Chapter 22 - Rainbow 213

Chapter 23 - Night Act...219

Chapter 24 - The Artistic Code 224

Chapter 25 - Arabella Suffers; Joey's Plight...........................231

Chapter 26 - Alma Mae's Devotion 245

Chapter 27 - Bobby Carver 252

Chapter 28 - "The Turn of the Screw" 264

Chapter 29 - The Big Let Down................................268

Chapter 30 - Tony's Club; Exodus............................277

Chapter 31 - Ruchek's Business...............................292

Chapter 32 - VE Day Celebration.............................306

Chapter 33 - The End of Corville Green 315

Chapter 34 - Caught Between 320

Chapter 35 - Remek...326

Chapter 36 - The Survivors 333

Chapter 37 - Joseph, the Werewolf..........................343

GLOSSARY..360

Acknowledgements...362

About the Author 363

HOMELESS, 1942

One sees nothing
in the dawn that
follows the erasure
of swiftly packed boxes
a ticket pinned to a coat
with government haste;
alien angles tilt the world
as former neighbors
pull down their shades
to keep out the rising sun.

But their houses echo
with memory feet
ghosting time here
as the cold sun sets
to come up forever changed
tomorrow.
A sack of rice,
a scarlet poppy scarf
wait to be discovered
in a drawer.

Ruth Wire

Prologue

I've been at this novel since the 1950s, when I took a class at Venice High School in commercial writing. One assignment was to produce an autobiography in thirty pages or less. I remember the words spilling out in relief as I recalled my turbulent childhood, and especially my first encounters with artists. In this book, I have added incidents that never occurred but could have, and so it has become a novel, not a memoir.

Those years of World War II remind me how proud and patriotic we were. The whole country had only one aim: to lick the axis forces. Any military man was welcome at any table in the country. We had total strangers in for dinner, and we trusted them.

We worried about our relatives in Europe. We couldn't conceive that a government would kill innocent people just because of their religion, but we lost forty relatives.

A sign that I might one day become a writer came at age five, when I preferred to stay at home and listen to "Let's Pretend" on the radio rather than collect a bag of nuts and raisins at the Temple. I was known to love treats; the choice to listen to Nila Mack's show marked me as a fanatic for stories.

Little did I guess how hard it would be to create those stories in my head from words. It took a second workshop, run by the poet Stanly Kurnik in the 1950s, where I met a continental mix of communists to liberals, to rid me of any romantic notions of writing and get me down to the actual rendering of truth in fiction.

-Ruth Wire 2021

Chapter 1 - The Rooming House

East Hollywood, June 1942

"Gosh, it's a palace," Phoebe said as she stood on tiptoe peering over the retaining wall. She could just make out the overhanging brow of an old Victorian house the color of dusty cantaloupe.

With a sharp nudge to her arm, Mama whispered in Phoebe's ear, "You dope. What did I just tell you? You don't say nice things about the house in front of the real estate agent. I can't bargain with him now."

Her enthusiasm punctured, Phoebe shrugged.

"And get that sullen look off your face," Mama hissed into her ear.

You won't even let me be mad at you! Phoebe thought, and she ran up the fifty stone steps to the front porch of the house. Sheila, her little sister, Mama, and the real estate agent, Mr. Johnson, were right behind her. She heard Mama say to Mr. Johnson, "Please disregard my daughter. She gets carried away."

The porch stretched clear across the front of the house.

Phoebe grinned at Mama's white angry face and said, "I love porches." She knew if Mr. Johnson were not there, Mama would've smacked her.

She skipped onto the veranda and spied a glass door. "Oh look!" Inside the portal, little oak trees and little birch trees just big enough for a doll's house sat on a table. There was a drain in the floor. A pair of gardener's gloves and a small trowel lay on a bench. The sun's rays alive with dust motes slanted through a glass roof. She'd seen plants like these before. Emiko's father grew Bonsai trees. With a tightness in her chest, she thought, *where is Emiko now?* They were supposed to enter Junior High together in September.

Mama, Mr. Johnson, and Sheila came in. "This is the greenhouse, Mrs. Feldman," Mr. Johnson said. "They sure don't make houses like this anymore."

He kept looking at Mama. She'd lost thirty pounds since the divorce and the rose-colored suit outlined her slim figure. Her narrow face and fine brown hair were perfect for the short bob famous in the twenties and thirties. She'd been an executive secretary before she married and carried herself with confidence. Phoebe was so proud. Mama was courageous.

Sheila quietly looked around. "This is a house for my dollies. I'll bring my buggy here." Sheila's straight ash blonde hair shone in the sun. Phoebe had always longed for Sheila's straight hair. Her own honey blonde frizzed in front.

Mama laid her hand on Sheila's head. "Don't lay claim to it. I haven't bought anything yet." Mr. Johnson unlocked the front door, and they saw the living room spread sideways across a polished wooden surface that at one side ended in a dining room through an archway, with a lowboy of wood and glass cabinets.

Phoebe ran to the real fireplace against the opposite wall that had a hearth flanked on either side by window seats. Lifting a seat lid, she found a great place to hide should they play hide 'n go seek. "Wow. Look what I found."

Mama said, "That's for storage."

Sheila said, "We could hide in there from the lion." Sheila looked young for her six years, with dark circles under her eyes. Mama was always "building her up," with malted milk.

"There's no lion," said Mama. "You were having a bad dream."

Sheila had been having nightmares since the divorce. Phoebe had been walking in her sleep.

Off the dining room they entered a large square kitchen. Cupboards rose to the ceiling. One had shallow shelves that Mr. Johnson said held one glass-depth at a time.

"And this is the dumb waiter," he said, revealing through a push-up door, a small elevator for food trays.

Sheila said, "I can give Arabella rides up and down."

Mr. Johnson laughed. "Your kids like this house, Mrs. Feldman. Through the back kitchen door you have a laundry room with another bathroom and across from that is your breakfast room." They inspected the breakfast room that featured a bank of windows looking out on the back yard. A dried-looking wisteria drooped from the roof to the upper part of the windowpane.

"Nice," Mama said. "And where does this door lead?" She

turned the knob at the far end of the room, and they trooped in.

"This is the library," Mr. Johnson said. "Built-in bookcases, a window seat and these French doors lead you back to the living room." He opened the French doors, and they stepped down to the living room again.

"Let's see the upstairs," Mama said.

"Oh boy!" Phoebe and Sheila, holding hands, took the stairs two at a time. Off the second story landing were doors to all the bedrooms. At the extreme right, there was an old fashioned bathroom with a shower over the tub, wall tiles, and linoleum on the floor, but Phoebe was more interested in the bedrooms.

In the bedroom off the landing, wooden window boxes held a bedraggled geranium. There was an alcove to the left, with a built-in hutch, glass door framed in wood, and small window. Looking through it to the back yard, she saw one lone palm tree and tangled green and yellow weeds that stretched to a fence. On the other side of the alcove, a column of bins one above the other rose to the ceiling. Phoebe pulled a handle and revealed a shallow space that went the width of the wall. Mr. Johnson came in and said it was for linen storage. You only had to fold the sheets the long way to store them.

"I want this room," Phoebe said.

Mama, her knuckle bent beneath her nose, her eyes pensive, said, "I'm thinking. I haven't decided anything yet. Let's see, there are five actual rooms up here if you count the outside screened room attached to that bedroom across the hall."

Phoebe dashed from room to room. She discovered a bedroom with a balcony. *A balcony.* She wanted the balcony bedroom, too. Someone had left a chest of drawers. She opened the top drawer and found a blue silk scarf with one red poppy painted on it. It so reminded her of Emiko that she shut the drawer and stood there a moment fighting tears. *Who had lived here before?* She had no heart to explore the other rooms. She dragged down the stairs and into the dining room. On the bare bookshelf sat a big paper sack full of rice with Japanese writing. Whoever lived there had left a bag of rice and a poppy scarf behind.

"I don't want to live here," she told Mama.

"A moment ago you were all excited," Mama said, laughing.

"You picked out your room," Sheila said, with a giggle.

Phoebe began to fiddle with a loose thread on her blouse. "I can't leave City Terrace. I promised Daddy to water the orange trees." All she could see was Emiko's scared face on December 7. She could hear Emiko sobbing next to her. She glared at Mr. Johnson. He had that tender look grownups get when they humor a child.

His forehead wrinkled as he said, "You'll like it here. The Junior High is just a few blocks away."

"Where will Emiko go to school?" Phoebe demanded.

"What is she talking about?" Mr. Johnson asked.

Mama blushed. "We had Japanese neighbors."

"Oh."

Did Mama know they were selling Japanese homes? Phoebe began to chew on her braid. *Oh God!*

Mama said to Mr. Johnson, "This place will make a great rooming house. I'm taking it."

Chapter 2 - Settling in; Memories

Phoebe brooded in her new room. She'd promised Daddy to water the trees, and hoped whoever would buy their old house would do it. She stared out the window, afraid to enjoy even the window box where Alexander, her turtle, now lived in a glass bowl. The house really did not belong to them: it belonged to Japanese people who'd been taken away in the night by government troops. Even though her things still lay in a suitcase, she recalled how it hadn't been that hard to put aside her reluctance to live in the rooming house. After all, she loved this home.

Mama had laughed at her. They were not to blame for what happened to the Japanese. The government wanted to get rid of these houses and was selling them for cheap. It only cost $15,000. If they didn't buy it, someone else would. She had to face facts. People needed a place to live since house construction had stopped, and Mama said she didn't want to work in a war plant. She would be there for her and Sheila all day long. Now wasn't that nice? Phoebe nodded yes. She finally had to agree with Mama, feeling heavy because she was a traitor to someone whatever she did. The events of a few months ago began to reel through her mind.

She, Emiko, and Daddy had just planted purple lantana between the orange trees on December 7, 1941 when Mama burst through the screen door and asked, "Where is Pearl Harbor?"

"In Hawaii?" Daddy said.

Phoebe remembered the scent of fresh earth, of orange blossoms, how Daddy scraped mud off his shoes on the bottle cap carpet he'd made. How the sun shone off the bald place on his head. How he'd flipped one of her honey blonde braids. He always looked at her with shining eyes. He'd told her she was as good as a son. He could talk to her.

"The Japanese have attacked our base there," Mama said, drying her chapped red hands on her apron. She carried the aroma of garlic and onions with her from the kitchen. Mama was angry all the time then, picking on her, and irritable with Daddy. When Mama had flown through the door like that Phoebe thought Mama was mad at her again. She was relieved it was only that war had been declared.

Emiko's eyes widened.

Daddy said, "Those bastards. They said they came to Washington, Elaine, to make peace."

Mama said to Emiko, "They say our boys were caught sleeping."

Emiko said, "I better go home," her eyes filling with tears.

"I'll walk you," Phoebe said. She'd put her arm around

Emiko and gave Mama a look that said, *"How'd you like it if someone said something like that to you?"*

Phoebe and Emiko made their way along the gravel of Roselyn Drive. Below, they could see downtown City Terrace and the end of the E trolley car line.

Phoebe glanced at Mr. Salazar, who lived two houses away, as he stepped off the curb. He peered at Emiko, mumbling something. Big Olaf, their Swedish neighbor, lumbered down the street, his eyes fixed on Emiko. Emiko shrank from Mr. Salazar and Big Olaf and hid her face in Phoebe's shoulder, trembling.

When they'd reached the Moroto home, a scowling man from the Bulgarian family down the street joined the other men. Just before Mrs. Moroto opened the door and shooed Emiko in, Phoebe said, "Thank your dad for helping my dad with the landscaping. The back yard looks swell."

Emiko nodded, and ran in. The Venetian blinds in their living room lowered like an eye closing.

The neighbors were deadly quiet until the Bulgarian father said, "Dirty, sneaking Japs."

A growl of agreement rolled through the crowd.

Then a police car drove up and came to a stop on the unpaved street, spraying pebbles. The cop slammed the car door. "You folks go home. We'll deal with these Japs."

These Japs. Emiko hadn't done anything. Mrs. Moroto shared recipes with Mama. Mr. Moroto sold Daddy the orange trees and lantana they'd just planted. Phoebe eyed the policeman, and then bent over with sudden cramps. She ran home. When she got there, Daddy and Mama were standing over the radio. President Roosevelt's voice rang through the living room. "As of this morning, Sunday, December 7th, 1941, the United States of America and the Empire of Japan are in a state of war."

The phone rang. Mama held the receiver away from her ear as they heard Aunt Ceil's dramatic voice. "It was a sneak attack. All the boys I know are going to enlist!" She hung up with a sharp click.

Daddy sat back with his eyes closed. Mama went into the kitchen without a word. She was mad at Daddy as usual. Phoebe heard her banging pots and pans around. From the kitchen Phoebe heard her say, "That's all I need today. A sneak attack. Don't I have enough trouble?"

Phoebe put her hand on Daddy's forehead. He opened his eyes. "Are you all right, Daddy?"

"Ah, Phoebele. You did good today. You're my helper. We take care of the trees. We make oranges, ha?" He sat up, looked around, and said, "Where's Sheila? Sheila!"

Sheila came into the living room, holding her doll across her forearms as if offering her for sacrifice. Glamorous Arabella wore a red satin dress and black patent leather Mary Janes on her feet. "Arabella's sick today." Sheila was still in her pajamas, her little pale face bent to her doll.

Daddy put his cheek against Sheila's temple. "You have a little fever. Go back in bed. I'll bring you carrot coconut juice."

"What were they hollering on the radio?" Sheila asked.

"We're at war," Phoebe said.

"Like the card game?"

Phoebe snickered. Her little sister: dumb, and always sick.

***

The next day, Phoebe tried to find Emiko, but their house was empty. The gate swung back and forth in the breeze.

Phoebe roused herself from memory. A sob caught in her throat. *Wherever you are, Emiko, remember we're still friends.*

She turned her attention to the room. Mama had put up some white cotton curtains so she'd have privacy yet light would come through. Phoebe had a chest of drawers, her bed, an end table with a lamp, and a desk and chair in the alcove. Alexander, the turtle, toggled his green and black neck out of his shell. Phoebe reached through the window and picked him up. On his back it said *Venice Beach*. "Do you like your new home?" Phoebe asked, and then she poured some water for him. "Do turtles worry? Are you happy sometimes and sad others? Do you miss your turtle friends?"

She put Alexander back in his glass bowl and gazed out onto the vacant lot next door where unkempt yellow weeds looked just like their backyard.

Gloomy thoughts dripped. She'd punished Mama for laughing at her by locking herself into her room and not speaking to her. Mama didn't believe Phoebe walked in her sleep. Daddy reported she'd come in like a zombie while he was bathing, a sleepwalker. But the raw feeling of the night Daddy left was no sleepwalk. She had to go to the bathroom, got up and stopped just before she stepped into the hall. She could hear her parents' familiar bicker.

Daddy said, "What do you want from me, woman? We're gonna need every extra cent. I don't have it."

"That's a lie," Mama said. "And that's not the only way you're stingy."

"I'm trying to build a business—"

"I don't mean business. I spoke to Dr. Harris, Max. He says we should talk to him."

Daddy said, "Talk to him. I don't want to talk to him."

"He's concerned about me, about us. I told him about us," Mama said.

"What did you tell him? Why are you always *schlepping* to him with stories?"

"I did it for our marriage. Live in a modern age, Max. Face it. Dr. Harris can help. We have trouble in our life together."

"What trouble?"

"Don't you know anything? Tell me, Max, why do I have a swelling in my throat when there is nothing wrong with me? Do this for me, Max, see him, please."

"Absolutely no. Go back to my doctor. Harris is a quack. He takes money from people who can't afford it."

"You cheap—I'm gasping for air!" There was a moment of silence and then Mama went on. "I had to pawn the watch today."

Daddy's voice sounded incredulous. "You what? *Mischugena!*"

"I'm not crazy. The kids needed winter coats."

"How could you pawn the watch I gave you? I gave it to you

so you should keep it, not sell it."

Mama said, "I don't want watches from you."

Alarmed, as the argument got louder, Phoebe tried to hold her pee and crossed her thighs.

Daddy said, "You don't want watches—you know what? You're crazy like your sister, Myrna. Your whole family is crazy. Don't I work hard enough—slave in the shop? You don't want watches. So what do you want?"

"I want a man—love me, Max. I need love. I'm starving."

"You're insane."

"*I'm* insane—maybe you don't know how to love a woman. Maybe that's it. You did your duty and we have two children, but for twelve years I've been waiting for you to warm up to me. Maybe you like your business and your family better than me. Maybe you'd rather be with your mother." In Grandma Feldman's voice, she simpered, "Max, *ess a bissel,* eat a little, here's some soup. Max put your legs on the pillow. Everybody go away. My Max is working, my precious Max is busy."

"Yes, yes! My mother understands. A man has to be left alone to work."

"And a woman is left alone . . .?"

"With the children and the house you can't keep busy all day?"

Mama began to cry. "You're made of stone. I hate you—I hate you—you can't love anybody. You're a machine for making money and a sponge for your family to suck on—"

"Stop it, woman."

"Listen Max, didn't you ever think there was anything

wrong with you? You and your whole family are cold fish and you're all married to your mother, that god-damned bitch!"

Phoebe's eyes widened as Mama burst from the bedroom into the hallway. Daddy overtook her, pinned her to the wall and pounded her between the shoulder blades with his fist. *Oh, Daddy! Stop!* She sagged as if she'd received the blow. Mama screamed. Phoebe wanted to run to Mama, to stop him, but she couldn't move. Daddy quit pounding. He staggered back, staring at Mama as she sank to the floor. His back hunched. He spun around. Phoebe could see the turmoil in his brown eyes, but those eyes apparently didn't see her. He backed away into the bedroom. Phoebe heard a click, then drawers opening and closing. He burst into the hall again with a suitcase showing a shirt sleeve caught hanging outside, and he zigzagged down the hall hitting the walls with the suitcase until he was out of the house. Pee poured down Phoebe's leg.

Daddy pounding Mama stuck in her mind like a piece of shrapnel as she held her sobbing mother for hours that night.

"I'm leaving your father," Mama said. "This is no life for me. All he cares about is his business and that family of his that sucks him dry. He's old country, Phoebe. Honey, rub my back. It's so sore."

She heard herself say as if she were a grownup person, "I saw him hit you." She began to massage Mama's back.

"You weren't sleepwalking again? You saw it?"

"I saw him run after you in the hallway. I've never seen him so mad. What did you say to him?"

After a second, Mama said, "You saw him? Then you have to

testify in court."

Phoebe stopped kneading Mama's shoulder. "Against Daddy?"

Mama propped herself on one elbow and said, "You saw it. I'm only asking you to tell the truth."

"But—but—don't make me. Please." Then she said in a sharper tone, "Daddy never hit you before. Why?"

Mama answered, "I asked him for money to buy you kids winter coats, and when he wouldn't give me the money I pawned a watch he'd given to me. And he reacted like a crazy man."

Phoebe's chest tightened. "No, no! I can't do it!"

"Do you love me?" Mama asked.

Phoebe put her head on Mama's bosom. "You know I do." She sat up with her face turned away, thinking, while stomach acids churned inside. Finally, she said in a bare whisper, "Okay."

Yet that promise made her shiver when she found herself with Sheila and Mama on a bench in the Domestic Relations Court, fifteen stories up, in City Hall.

Mama said, "Now tell me again what you're gonna say, Phoebe."

Phoebe wadded a tissue in her hand, looking around, hoping Daddy wasn't there. "Uh—I saw you run out in the hall and he—he—got you against the wall, and he . . . hit you with his fist."

Mama said, "Now. Was that so hard?"

Phoebe turned her head to hide the tears trickling down her cheeks. *Why do I have to do it?*

A clerk ushered them into the courtroom where Daddy's

lawyer sat. Daddy was not there. Mr. Kornblatt, Mama's lawyer got up and made room for Mama to sit near him. Sheila and Phoebe sat in the rear. They held hands as Mama began her testimony.

"My daughter Phoebe can tell you. She witnessed him beating me."

The judge frowned. "Your testimony will be sufficient. We don't usually allow children to testify against a parent," he said, looking over the heads of people at Phoebe and Sheila.

Then it was over. Mama had her divorce. She got up with a satisfied look.

Phoebe had a stomachache. She was a skunk. *Daddy! I love you.* She left the courtroom, her head down, crying, and ran along the corridor.

Mama was just behind, dragging Sheila. "Oh my God, Phoebe. What are you doing?"

"I hate you!" Phoebe said, slumping onto a bench. "I wish I was dead."

Mama put her arm around Phoebe. "It's harder to live than to die," she said. "C'mon, let's go home."

***

The day of forbidden foods, Mama walked in with two paper bags full of groceries. They'd just received their food ration books. Phoebe named it The Day of Forbidden Foods because Daddy had been forbidden by the doctor to eat delicatessen. The bags fell over. Out tumbled *bialys* and a loaf of corn rye bread from the Jewish bakery, kosher dill pickles, mustard, a string of fat knockwurst, a bottle of beer, and a tub of white stuff that Mama said was oleomargarine, along with its coloring packet to make it look like butter. The last item was a pound of bacon.

"Hot dogs! Pickles!" Phoebe said. "I'm in heaven."

Mama said, "I had to cook plain for your father, but now we can eat anything we like. Those are not hot dogs, Phoebe. They're knockwurst. Much better." Mama unwrapped the bacon.

Sheila said, "Aren't Jews forbidden to eat bacon?"

"Who says? Your father?"

Phoebe giggled. She peered down at the brown and white strips of bacon that, even uncooked, gave off whiffs like barbeque.

Sheila stared at the bacon, her nose wrinkled.

"You don't have to eat it, Sheila. That makes more for Mama and me. Mama, how do you cook it?"

"In a frying pan. All I have is the iron skillet for *blintzes*."

With a mischievous glance, Mama dived under the counter for the blintz pan. She laid the bacon strips across its surface, placed it on the stove and soon it was sizzling and sending savory aromas into the air. The bacon shriveled to mahogany colored ripples. As soon as each strip came dripping out of the pan, Phoebe burned her tongue, gobbling it. Soon Sheila was grabbing pieces, too, and Mama washed hers down with gulps of beer. They ate the whole pound.

After feasting on the juicy knockwurst that burst their skins in boiling water, and munching garlic pickles, Phoebe groaned with a stomachache. Mama lay on the couch. She'd drunk the whole bottle of beer. Sheila still nibbled one half of a knockwurst, smeared with yellow mustard.

"God, I hope we have ration stamps for the rest of the month," Mama said, and gave a little burp. "It was worth it, wasn't it?"

Phoebe wrapped her arms around her bloated abdomen. "My first knockwurst! And my first bacon."

Mama said, "You have no idea how much fun the rest of the world has, Phoebe. This is only the beginning. We are gonna live!"

Suddenly Phoebe's stomach cramped, her mouth filled with undigested food. She made a run for the bathroom and spewed knockwurst, pickle, and bits of bacon into the toilet bowl.

Mama called after her, "You ate too much again."

Mama snored gently on the couch when she returned.

Phoebe had kissed Mama's damp forehead.

Phoebe sighed, remembering. What would Mama think of next? But that day was the past. Was she going to live in the past?

She surveyed her new bedroom and imagined how it would look if she could afford to decorate it. The walls would have pink flowered wallpaper, white organdy tieback curtains at the windows, and scalloped window shades with fringes and silver pulls. On her bed, a ruffled baby blue bedspread, with matching pillow shams, and a plush pink rug on the floor. She would comb her hair looking in a mirror on a padded stool before a blue ruffled vanity. In the alcove, she'd have a Remington typewriter with a new black ribbon next to a ream of white paper instead of her black and white notebook and stub of pencil.

She sighed and lay on her back in bed, staring at cobwebs hanging from the ceiling.

It was just a daydream. It would never come true. Not unless they struck oil. She drifted off, half-asleep, tears falling sideways, trying to block more painful memories that marched across her mind like a line of imps. Was the divorce only a few months ago? It seemed like another lifetime. The phone had rung just after the divorce. She could hardly bear to listen to her father. He sounded strange and dry. "So, Phoebe, how come you never call me? I never see you."

"I'm sorry, Daddy."

"You know what your mother is doing to me?"

"Yes."

"Do I deserve that?" He burped into the phone, then said, "What do you know? You're only a child. Look, Phoebe, do something for me. Water the trees. Young trees need lots of water or they'll die."

"Sure, Daddy. I will."

"And come and see me sometimes. All I have is you and Sheila—" His voice choked.

"Don't cry, Daddy, please."

"I have to hang up." The phone clicked in her ear.

She looked at the phone. He wasn't the only one suffering. Since her day in court, she could not control her confused thoughts. She hid in her room. She wouldn't talk to Sheila. Mama accused her of sulking. When she wouldn't eat, Mama said, "Good. You need to go on a diet. You're overweight." When she gave Mama a death-ray stare, Mama said, "Get that look off your face, Phoebe, and come back to the living."

Who could understand? Who could she talk to? Then she thought of Aunt Ceil, Daddy's sister. Aunt Ceil would have her own opinion about the divorce. She'd dialed her number.

An hour later Aunt Ceil was in their living room, her eyes shifting here and there like a spy. "Is your mother at home?"

"No."

Aunt Ceil was tall and fleshy, with a big open face. She sat cautiously on the couch, her lips pressed together. "What your mother is doing, you'll pardon me, is lousy. There has never been a divorce in our family. Your mother is a self-indulgent woman. I'm not saying this because I'm his sister, Phoebe, but Max is a good man. If he laid a hand on her, she must have driven him to it. Try to stay out of it, darling."

"How can I? They both need me."

Aunt Ceil's chubby cheeks raised in a smile. "Just be a good girl, Phoebe."

"We used to hike together. He'd tell me stuff about Mama."

"What do you know of such things? You're only a kid. Your father and Uncle Leonard are building a business. He loved her enough to slave twelve hours at a time and never took a day off."

Phoebe got up and tucked a stray hair out of Aunt Ceil's eyes. "Mama says that was wrong. We never had any fun as a family." She looked down. "He liked to be with me."

"His children mean everything to him. Your father is a prince."

Aunt Ceil didn't get it. Phoebe began to perspire. "If he could've been nicer to Mama, maybe she wouldn't have minded so much about the business. If Mama could've only made Daddy feel she was pulling for him, maybe . . ."

Aunt Ceil blew into her hankie. "Well, you said it. Phoebe—*if only*. Listen, darling, don't take it too hard. It's not your fault."

"But it is."

"How?"

"I just stood there, watching. I just stood there."

"What are you talking about?"

"Nothing. Just forget it. Thank you for coming over, Aunt Ceil."

"Wait a minute. Where's Sheila? I want to see my *babela*."

Phoebe sighed, went out and returned with Sheila. Sheila stared at Aunt Ceil, fearfully.

"*Momila*, come kiss Aunt Ceil." The woman put out her arms, smiling, but Sheila hung on to Phoebe's hand. "She doesn't know me anymore. What has your mother been saying to her about me?"

"Nothing! My mother has not said one thing about you. Sheila has nightmares lately. She thinks there's a lion in her bedroom and she can't go to sleep. She's been running to me in the middle of the night."

Sheila picked at Phoebe's dress, and said, "Doesn't Daddy like us anymore? Why doesn't he come see us?"

Aunt Ceil cried, "Oh my God, oh my God" and picked limp, dull-eyed Sheila up in her arms, rocking her.

Chapter 3 – John; The Ebberly sisters

The big house was hard to clean. With annoyance, Elaine noticed cobwebs and grease on the kitchen light fixture, but she wasn't going to climb up there. She raked the kitchen ceiling cobwebs down with a broom, and sneezed.

That damn light fixture. Phoebe could climb up on the five-foot ladder and take it down, but she'd refused to help. *Stubborn kid. Sulked for weeks.* Wearily, she stuck the broom out the window, shaking dust off. She ached from the unaccustomed work. She'd never been strong like her mother, who everyone called The General. Pleading with Max, she'd finally got him to hire a cleaning woman. How her mother-in-law had scoffed! Called her the straw lady.

Elaine could hear Phoebe crying upstairs and sighed. *I told her Emiko is okay. After all, those camps are protective isolation.* Their neighbors in City Terrace got ugly after Pearl Harbor. Phoebe had run home and told them what had happened the day before Emiko was sent to the camps.

Why persecute a peaceful family like the Morotos? Mr. Moroto had helped Max landscape the back yard, and she'd traded recipes with Mrs. Moroto.

The war had slowed the mail. Elaine had not heard from Uncle Hindl in Austria for months. What was the war doing to her family over there? She'd surely hear from one of them soon.

She should go up and make peace with Phoebe. She was cleaning a ten-room house all by herself. Her thoughts nagged as she scrubbed the woodwork. There's no time for tears over something Phoebe can do nothing about. *Give it up, Phoebe. It's unhealthy to stew.*

She got to her knees and was about to shut the window, when Elaine gave a startled cry. A brown face suddenly grinned at her through the window.

"I be John, your neighbor," he said. "If you need anything, you just ask me. I see you don't have a man around."

Her throat tightened for a moment. *This colored man lives next door?* Then, with a shrug, she thought, *so what?* She raised the window higher. He wore a plaid cotton shirt and clean denim overalls. His tight curls were going grey. A sad yet contented look in his brown eyes reassured her he was a nice man. He lifted a paper bag to the window sill. "Made some cookies for you and your daughters, Ma'am."

Elaine looked away and then back, not quite sure how to take this gesture. "You didn't have to do that." But her tired hands took the cookies. "My children will love them. Thank you. My name is Elaine and my girls are Phoebe and Sheila."

"Phoebe and Sheila. I'll remember. Soon, I'll teach them

31

how to plant a Victory garden and you can have fresh vegetables."

"Well, thank you." Elaine drew back a little. John was awfully nice, almost too nice. She should ask him to climb the ladder and get the kitchen light fixture down, but she couldn't. Something made her shut the window firmly, glad she was snug in her house with walls between them. Crossing her arms on her chest, she took shallow breaths. Was it her imagination, or had he looked at her like a man looks at a woman? No. She laughed at herself, sprang up, and rinsed the rag she planned to wash the baseboards with.

With a little shiver, she considered all that she'd done since the divorce a few months ago. She'd learned what owning a home meant. All those papers she'd had to sign. The gas company came to get the furnace working, she had the electricity and water turned on, and got the garbage pick-up started. Everything cost money. It made her eager to get the house cleaned and filled with renters. She'd prepared the bedrooms first in case she had an answer to the ad in the paper.

Phoebe had put a sign on her door saying, "No Admittance without Permission." She was probably scribbling in a notebook. Phoebe wanted to be a writer. The kid had her romantic dreams. Time would tell whether she was a writer or not. Stories! Pie in the sky waste of time. Yet Phoebe had written the sixth grade play. Her teachers were astounded. She knew her daughter could easily become a haughty do-nothing and as a mother, it was her duty to introduce the child to reality.

Elaine hung onto the railing, trudged up the stairs, and

gritted her teeth, wishing it was an escalator. Every muscle ached. She'd just have to get used to it, and think of things she needed to take along when she went up and down. No wonder they'd started building single story houses.

Sheila brightened when her mother came in to their shared master bedroom. "Did you bring me a drink of water?"

Sheila spent her days upstairs, in bed, perched next to the big window.

Elaine massaged an aching hip with her palm. "Water?" She wasn't gonna go downstairs for water. "Go into the bathroom and drink out of your toothbrush cup."

Sheila jumped out of bed. "I forgot. The bathroom!" She scooted past Elaine, yanking her doll, Arabella by the arm.

Elaine shook down the thermometer, and thought, The doctor doesn't know what's wrong with her. I've got to build her up with egg shakes. Sheila coughed up a lot of stuff and had a low grade fever. It must be bronchitis.

Sheila came running back with her mouth already open and Elaine slipped the thermometer in. As usual, her temperature was 100.4.

What a spacious place her master bedroom was! Two bureaus and two twin beds took up only a small area, but the room looked empty. She even forgot where she put things. Oh, what the hell, they'd find a way to fill it. It was good not to feel cramped. The hardwood floor of the bedroom gleamed after she'd polished it. The walk-in closet was as big as a bathroom.

A ring at the front door made Elaine start. "Get back in bed, Sheila. There's someone here."

She hung onto the railing, her thigh and leg muscles threatening to knot, and she descended to the living room. Through the small glass window in the door she saw two old women dressed in 1920's clothes. Rayon flower prints draped from their shoulders. Each wore a big straw hat with daisies around the headband.

When Elaine opened the door, the taller one, holding a newspaper, said, "Do you have a room to let?"

Suddenly full of energy, Elaine peeled off her apron, ripped off her kerchief and opened the door wide. "I do! Please come in."

The taller lady said, "I'm Adora Ebberly and this is my sister, Darlene."

"I'm Elaine Feldman."

The ladies eyed the living room, all smiles. Adora grasped Darlene's arm in joy. "I just love these old houses."

Elaine nodded with pride. "It was built a little after the turn of the century as a men's club."

"Oh my. A men's club!" Darlene said, daintily wiping her lips of spittle with a hanky.

As Elaine directed the sisters up, Phoebe appeared on the stairway with reddened eyes. "This is my eldest daughter, Phoebe," Elaine said. Behind their backs, Phoebe put her finger far into her mouth and pretended to gag herself. Elaine almost laughed but suppressed it. *I'll have words with Phoebe later.* With these moods of Phoebe's who knew what rude thing she would say to the two ladies. Elaine hurried up the stairs. "There are two bedrooms available." Elaine threw open the bedroom with the adjacent screened summer room.

Darlene chuckled. "I wouldn't mind living in the screened room, Adora."

Adora gave her a big-sister stare. "Not with your hay fever, dear. And what about the winters? It might get uncomfortably cold in there. I'm afraid not, Mrs. Feldman."

Elaine proceeded to the room with the balcony, but Phoebe got there first. "You can't have this room," she told the prospective tenants.

Elaine stamped her foot and almost slapped her. "Phoebe! Go to your room. Now." But Adora raised her eyebrows, and Elaine dropped her hand.

Phoebe strode into the bedroom with a balcony and stood against the chest of drawers as if shielding it.

Elaine closed her eyes and then opened them again, trying for patience, but Adora ignored Phoebe. The woman lifted the storage seat lid tucked between two slanted walls, peeked into the closet, squeaked open the screen door to the balcony, stuck her head outside like a chicken, and popped back in.

Elaine's lips twitched. She couldn't help but be fascinated by these old fashioned dames who reminded her of scratching hens.

Phoebe's chin jutted stubbornly, unmovable against the chest of drawers,. What was in there? Some secret manuscript with girlish wishes? Elaine took a moment to really look at Phoebe. The kid's eyes and lips struggled against tears with a rigid control she didn't think Phoebe possessed. Poor thing. *I've been paying a lot more attention to Sheila and her mysterious ailment. Phoebe is so alone. Hell, she better get used to it. I'm alone too. Anyway she reminds me of Max and I can't cuddle up to her without thinking of him. She was always Daddy's girl anyway.* Elaine came to as she heard Adora say, "This is only big enough for one person. What else do you have?"

"You can have my room!" Phoebe strode dramatically to her door and flung it open. "There's plenty of space in here."

Adora and Darlene rushed to Phoebe's room, oohing and aahing about the closet, the linen storage, the alcove, the cabinet and its drawers. "You don't want to give up your big beautiful room, sweet child," Adora said, as if she meant it, but Elaine saw her covetous eyes. Darlene nodded and smiled. "I think Phoebe is full of Christian charity."

Elaine burst out laughing. "She knows nothing about Christians or charity."

When the Ebberlys weren't looking, Phoebe stuck her tongue out at Elaine. Elaine thought, *she can't get away with that. I'll knock that sass out of her later.* Just then she felt Adora's watery blue eyes on her. Adora beckoned Darlene with a crooked finger and they mumbled something to each other. "Um, Mrs. Feldman, are you a Hebrew?" Adora asked, blushing.

"We're Jewish, if that's what you mean, Miss Ebberly."

"Oh how wonderful. People of the book."

Elaine stood on one foot and then the other. She could feel her face getting hot.

"Do you like Phoebe's room?" she finally asked.

"Well . . . I do."

"I'll move to the balcony room," Phoebe said, and ran in to pack.

"God bless you," Darlene said, to Elaine, "and your saintly daughter."

Elaine could barely keep from laughing in their faces as she gave them their receipt.

***

Delayed punishment didn't appeal to Elaine. She forgot all about Phoebe's disrespect as life with the Ebberlys began to unfold.

"They eat canned vegetables," Phoebe said. "Canned spinach. Oh I'm gonna gag. Canned washed out peas. And canned chicken. They put the can in a pot of water and heat it."

Elaine added with relish, "They fly their underwear out the window on a clothes line. Bloomers, can you imagine? Bloomers!"

Elaine grabbed Phoebe by the shoulders and they laughed until tears rolled down.

***

Adora and Darlene, their hands in white lace gloves, their billowing white and pink cotton dresses cinched at the hip by wide pink satin cummerbunds paused in the kitchen doorway. Elaine nodded hello.

Adora said, "It's Sunday, Mrs. Feldman. We're going to church."

Elaine slowly wiped her hands on a dish towel. Why were

they looking at her in that expectant way? What was she supposed to say? "Have fun."

Darlene giggled. "We don't have fun at church, Mrs. Feldman."

"Too bad," Elaine said.

Adora gently pushed Darlene aside. "We, uh, we thought you might benefit from the sermon. And your girls may come, too. We, uh, noticed you don't take them to a synagogue or Temple. What are you doing for their spiritual life?"

Elaine's hands curled into fists. Hot gastric juices began to travel up her food pipe. *Why those old biddies! How dare they?* "That is none of your business, Miss Ebberly."

"Oh dear. We've made you angry," Darlene said.

"Damn right."

Adora planted herself on a kitchen chair. "We couldn't help noticing that you're a good woman, but you seem to have a hard life, and we want to help."

"I don't need your help. Stay out of my business." Elaine turned toward the breakfast dishes. *It doesn't matter. Temple or church. Bunch of fairy-tales that do no practical good.* When she turned back, the two women were still there, looks of sticky sympathy on their smiling faces.

"I don't believe in God, ladies. And I refuse to teach your bullshit to my children."

Adora's cheeks blanched as if she'd received a physical blow. With the smile still pasted upon her lips, she rose, taking Darlene's hand, and said, "We are sorry for you, Mrs. Feldman. What a dreary grey world you inhabit without the Lord's blessing. And those poor children. Why do you deny them the happiness of faith?"

Elaine held up her fists. "Faith? I have faith in these two hands." She held out her reddened hands and then hit her temples. "And this mind. What right do you have to invade my privacy? It's your hogwash. Get out of here!"

With *ooo's* and *oh dears*, Adora and Darlene retreated to the landing. Then Darlene stuck her head into the kitchen with one last passionate plea. "*You* may not believe, but we believe in you, Mrs. Feldman. We believe in the *divinity* in you." She was pulled out of view as Adora whooshed the front door open and then shuddered it shut.

Phoebe came running into the kitchen. "Oh my God. You really gave it to them, Mama."

Elaine dropped onto a kitchen chair. "Yeah, I guess I did." She eyed Phoebe as her daughter danced across the kitchen.

Phoebe cried out, "They believe in the divinity in you! It's hilarious."

"Yeah. Hilarious." What had she done? Their first renters and she'd chased them away.

Chapter 4 - Tony, Mario and Joey

Phoebe chuckled as Chapter One of *My Life with Mother's Boarders* wrote itself under her pencil. Satisfied that she had brought the vivid Ebberly sisters to life, she straightened the pages and secured them with a paper clip. She laid the sheets into a stationery box and stretched a rubber band over it.

A knock on her door, and Mama said, "Guess what's happened?"

She didn't want to talk to Mama, but curiosity overcame Phoebe, and she opened the door. She stared at Mama. *I'm mad at you.*

Mama's blue eyes sparkled. Her mouth quivered in a nervous smile. "Are you ready for some good news?"

Phoebe shifted from foot to foot. Good news. You never knew with her mother. "What's got into you, Mama?"

Mama sailed into her room and plopped onto the overstuffed chair. "I've met somebody."

A man, Phoebe thought, watching her mother's girlish

display.

"He's a band leader. Tony Popela. He plays sax and clarinet."

Another musician. Mama had loved a band leader when she was young. "Is he like The Blue Baron?"

Mama dropped her gaze. "He's not big time." Then she grinned. "He can fix any instrument. His family wanted him to be a doctor. But he dropped out of medical school."

"So he could've been a doctor. What else do you know about him?"

"Music is his whole life. His face lights up when he talks about it." Mama put her arm around Phoebe's shoulders. "My little inquisitor. He's also a divorced father."

"He has kids? How many?"

"Two."

Maybe there was a girl her age. Phoebe asked with a hopeful voice, "Boys or girls?"

"Two boys."

What good were little boys? "Do they live with their mother?"

"No. Tony just found them after searching high and low for years. Their good-for-nothing mother dropped them off in an orphanage when they were five and seven. Can you imagine? And that bitch was the Jewish half of the marriage. I think Tony wanted to know his children. They're living with him now."

"How old are they?"

The skin around Mama's eyes crinkled with amusement. "He has two sons. Mario's fifteen. Joey's thirteen. Why do you want to know?"

"Cause I like boys!"

"Since when?"

Phoebe let out an audible breath. "Are they good looking?"

"Mario's handsome. Must take after their mother 'cause Tony's nothing to look at. Joey's a glum string-bean of a boy. Anyway, I want you and Sheila to meet them."

Phoebe smoothed a wisp of hair that had escaped her braids. *A handsome fifteen-year-old boy*! "Are they coming here?"

"No. We're going to *drop in anytime* according to Tony's invitation. They live on the east side of town."

Phoebe planted a kiss on her mother's cheek. "When do we leave?"

***

"This is a bad neighborhood," Mama said, as she parked the car. "I'm almost afraid to get out. Do you see those Pachucos leaning against the wall across the street?"

Phoebe scribbled a short description of the boys:

The Pachucos look as if they had knives hidden in their pleated zoot suits. But they don't look at me. They whistle at girls in tight dresses who wiggle past. One guy flicks his black hair over his forehead and saunters after a Pachuca. Taking a whiff of his cigarette, he then drops that hand to his side all the time calling out something in Spanish. His red satin shirt rolls like waves as it catches the sun. He's in no hurry, bending his knees a little and leaning kind of backwards as he slinks along letting his gold key chain almost touch the ground. The girl he is after glances over her shoulder and giggles. She wears high heels and wobbles down the street.

Phoebe chewed on her pencil. She hoped she'd captured how Pachucos walked, casual but menacing.

"Don't look at them," Mama said.

Sheila closed her eyes.

Mama checked the address on a pad she held. "Is this really where Tony lives? Yep. This is the place."

Phoebe didn't want to go into the brown stucco building, three stories high, adorned with chalked Spanish writing on its weathered side.

"I don't like it here," Sheila said.

"It's where Mexicans live," Phoebe informed her. She was secretly thrilled she'd seen Pachucos in action.

Mama locked the car and hurried them into the building. "Tony told me this neighborhood has changed since he was a boy. His whole family still lives near here."

They climbed a creaking staircase to the second floor. It smelled like cat poo in the hallway, and Sheila held her nose.

At Mama's knock, a thin boy with a large nose covered with blackheads opened the door. He squinted his close-set eyes at the three of them. "What do you want, Elaine?"

"Your father asked me to stop by, Joey."

What a rude boy. He held playing cards and he left the three of them standing at the door, returning to the crowded kitchen table to play solitaire at the one clear spot.

Holding Sheila by the shoulders, Mama edged them into the apartment.

Joey paid them no attention, dropping cards with a bent wrist. Under the dirty dishes, the stained table oilcloth was a relief map of dried ketchup and egg yolk.

Mama's nostrils flared and her face stiffened. Phoebe held a tissue to her nose from the sour odor as Mama dumped cigarette butts into the trash can.

Phoebe stood uncertainly in the middle of the kitchen. *Where was Mario?* She didn't want to seem too eager, so she glanced over Joey's shoulder. "Hi, Joey, I'm Phoebe. Oh-oh. You missed one." She placed a red four below a black five.

"Get lost," Joey said, not even looking up.

Who does he think he is! And what a disgusting complexion. "Pimple face."

Joey crashed the game with his fist and knocked most of the dirty dishes onto the floor. "Get her outta here. Elaine!"

Mama whirled around and Sheila's mouth opened in a silent O.

"How can you live in such filth?" Mama said. "Don't sit down, Sheila."

Joey peered around and nervously picked at a pimple on his face. "You came at a bad time. Pop cleans tomorrow."

"You're waiting for him? You should help your dad, Joey."

Joey's eyes glazed over. *Mama wasn't gonna get anywhere acting like a "you-should" parent.* But to Phoebe's surprise, Joey bent down to pick up broken cups and plates. Mama

44

provided a paper bag. A look passed between them; the nasty boy now appeared no longer nasty but hung his shoulders in dejection. Mama put her hand on his head. He turned his face away.

***

Swing music bounced from the next room. *Mario, the handsome one!* Phoebe padded toward the sound. Would he laugh at her childish braids? She mustn't be a jerk and talk too much. Boys didn't like that. Her heart thumped in her ears. Mama followed with Sheila.

Someone in a terry cloth bathrobe lay face up on a couch with one leg on the floor and one hand over his eyes, nodding to the music coming from a Victrola. When Mama lifted the needle off the record player, he jolted upright, his black curls shaking.

"Jesus Christ!" He glared at Mama. "What are you doing? That was Jack Teagarden!" He plunged his hands into the pockets of his bathrobe, staring at Mama. "Don't ever do that again," he finally said.

"Don't you talk to me like that, you big ox. Get into some clothes, get a mop and clean up this pest hole."

"Aw, be a good egg, Elaine. Pop cleans tomorrow."

"I've heard that one before," she spat. "Two of you, and you let your father do all the work? Surprise him. Make him faint. Mario, your father needs a nice surprise."

But Mario seemed only concerned with his record. He ran his fingers lovingly over the little grooves. Apparently satisfied that it wasn't scratched, he placed it in a paper sleeve. He seemed so deeply shaken by their intrusion, Phoebe wanted to say, "Mama, leave him alone." It wasn't just his dark good looks, but the real agony of his distress that she sympathized with. He smoldered. She couldn't look at him directly. It was like she was afraid she'd burn up if she touched him. Her dry tongue stuck to the roof of her mouth. Something had happened to her. In confusion, she turned back into the kitchen.

She found Mama helping Joey who was trying to clear unbroken dishes from the table.

"Not that way," Mama said, softer. "This way. Stack them together and put the silver on top."

"Pop will flip his lid if he sees the kitchen clean," Joey said.

"Where is he?" Mama asked, helping Joey to the sink with the dishes.

"He's asleep," Joey said. He worked last night until two A.M."

Mario strode into the kitchen, dressed in slacks and loafers, holding his sax case and sheets of music.

"Where are you going?" Mama asked.

"Somewhere quiet where I can play. And I'm not scrubbing floors, Elaine. I practice six hours a day, and I've got to keep my hands right." He examined his palms and fingers with their clean short fingernails. Giving Mama a defiant stare, he left the apartment.

"My brother taught himself to play sax and clarinet in the Home," Joey said.

Mama studied her shoes. "A genius, no doubt."

The bedroom door opened. A short man with Joey's large

nose and a dazed look in his soft brown eyes slowly focused on Mama. "Elaine! You brought your girls." He pointed at Sheila. "The little one. Hi, I'm Tony." He grinned in Phoebe's direction. "And this must be Phoebe."

The way he said *Phoebe* warmed her completely. It was like he was honoring her by saying her name. Like she was somebody important. It was easy to grin back and mean it. Even though he could pass for a comedian with that Jimmy Durante nose, she wasn't surprised when Tony took Mama into his arms and kissed her. *Oh bless him.*

When Mama recovered from the kiss, she had the softest look in her eyes, like a heroine in a love story. She was in love and love was in her. "Tony, your boys need a decent home. I want to take them to live with us in the rooming house. You could see them as often as you want. Would that be all right with you?"

Tony grabbed Mama again and bent her over in a deep kiss.

Sheila's icy fingers grabbed her hand, and Phoebe glanced down. Sheila's skin was drawn tight over her cheekbones and her lips pale with indignation, but her eyes were bruised flowers.

Chapter 5 - Grandma Feldman's

At Grandma Esther Feldman's door, Phoebe's stomach felt hollow. She had risen reluctantly from the car, Sheila dragging after her. It was supposed to be a celebration. It was her twelfth birthday.

The living room reminded her of haunted houses in movies: dark papered walls, draped windows, musty furniture. She heard Daddy before she saw him. Sunk in an upholstered armchair, his bald spot back, his eyes closed, Daddy groaned every once in a while.

Grandma Esther picked lint off her sweater, her weak eyes not showing that she even understood Daddy was crazy with grief. She hugged Phoebe and Sheila and lurched toward a chair. *"Kinda, Zetzin Zee."*

They sat.

Grandma kind of fell onto her chair, holding her cane for support, her heavy body wallowing like a walrus.

Phoebe nervously sucked on a braid. Next to her Sheila sunk into herself, shoulders rounded, head down, her hands in her lap.

Grandma said what she always said: "You been good goils?"

Phoebe smiled. "Yes, Grandma."

"*Zayagit.*" Grandma sighed and glanced at Daddy, who hadn't moved or said anything, not even hello.

Grandma looked like a witch in fairy-tales. Phoebe eyed Grandma's wig, a sign of an orthodox married woman. It looked like a German helmet with all the hair plastered under a heavy webbing, flanged out in back. On one eyelid, there hung a wart. In her mouth, three teeth: one in the lower jaw, and two in the upper. She was the *Ezsha-Bubbe*, the grandma who made you eat. Mama said it was because she'd not forgotten starvation in Europe that she'd forced food on Phoebe and Sheila from babyhood. Grandma Esther had broken her hip as a young woman. It had healed leaving her left leg shorter than her right. Her feet, the left fixed at a right angle to the other, impeded her walk, and even in the black leather built-up shoe, she pitched and rolled like a sailor on a heavy sea. Her voice rasped with guttural commands. "Phebeleh, the boiday goil. C'mere, *momila.*"

Phoebe rose and woodenly approached Grandma.

The Ezsha-Bubbe kissed her and the pressure of that one tooth in the lower jaw gnawed her cheek. At close range, Bubbe gave off a stale old-person odor. "Soon you'll be a *calla moit.*"

Phoebe gasped.

Sheila asked, "What did she say?"

"Soon I'll be ready for marriage."

Sheila giggled and Ezsha-Bubbe said, "Shame. Don't make fun from me. Come, Sheila *babela* give Ezsha-Bubbe a kiss."

Sheila looked to Phoebe for help.

With a laugh, Phoebe pushed Sheila toward Grandma who smothered the struggling Sheila with her breasts and landed munches on her cheek. Sheila's angry gaze promised Phoebe retaliation later. Grandma then held Sheila at arms' length and examined her straight ash blonde hair.

"Mama makes your hair *vass*? Mama put on something to make you blonda?"

"No, Grandma."

"Mama shouldn't make blonda da hair."

Sheila and Phoebe clapped hands over their mouths to keep giggles suppressed.

Grandma hiked herself up and said, "*Kind-a,* something in *mole aran?*

Phoebe interpreted. "She wants to know if we're hungry. I want matzoh and peanut butter, Bubbe."

The Ezsha-Bubbe shuddered. "You put that *chazarei* on matzoh?

"She's calling peanut butter pig food," Phoebe said with a straight face.

Sheila put her hands over her mouth and giggled.

"Bubbe, whatever you have is okay," Phoebe said.

The Ezsha-Bubbe careened to the kitchen and returned with a tray of matzoh, butter, and a glass of hot tea for Daddy. He ignored the tea. Phoebe and Sheila ate, silently.

A deep groan came from Daddy's armchair.

They became solemn again.

Daddy's voice sounded like it was coming from a cave. "Do you still practice the violin every day, Phoebe?"

She sighed. She'd given up the violin that he'd laid in her lap when she was seven. She was not musical. It was just another thing that would make Daddy sad now. Since she didn't want to answer him, Phoebe said, "I wrote a play for sixth grade graduation. They put it on."

A dreadful silence filled the room again. Suddenly, Daddy shouted, "She's insane! She ruined my life. My home! My children. My children . . . She wrecked my life. Tell me why?" His eyes didn't see her or Sheila. Phoebe squeezed Sheila's small hand.

"I worked all my life to get somewhere, but no! Nothing I do is ever good. So now what? What good is my life?" His voice broke and he sobbed.

Phoebe said, "Mama is very upset too."

"She throws me out on the garbage—so all right, I'm on the garbage. But my little girls . . . c'mere, Sheila." Sheila came close, and he stroked her hair. "I can't live like this." He started to sob again. At this point, Phoebe and Sheila began to cry too.

"Don't cry, Daddy, please don't cry. Don't blame Mama," Phoebe said.

"Look how Sheila pulls away. What has your mother said about me?"

"Nothing," Phoebe lied.

"She told you to say that. My own children. She's poisoning you against me."

Instead of replying, Phoebe went to Daddy and hugged him. "I love you, Daddy."

"It's not your fault, Phoebe. She doesn't know how to be a Jewish wife. Her family was no example!" He shuddered. "Your grandmother, Rebecca, had ten children. She lost eight of them in the New York slums. She suffered. But suffering didn't make her gentle; she was known as The General. When I met them, Elaine and her sisters, they fought like cats in a bag. The apartment was noisy with bickering. Rebecca would beat them with a skillet when it got too much for her. There was no respect, no love."

Phoebe sat down again with her head bowed, listening, sniffing back tears. Every word hit her like a rock.

Daddy seemed unaware of his effect on her, his head tilted back. "All of us immigrants have stories. When your pregnant aunt got the flu and died, Rebecca tried to throw herself off the roof. And who saved her? Not David, your saintly grandfather. The other women in the building."

"Are we going home soon?" Sheila asked.

Daddy acted as if he didn't hear Sheila and went on. "David, to give him credit, was pious. He prayed five times a day, read the Talmud, and pressed pants without complaint in a sweltering cleaning shop. You remember him, Phoebe?"

Phoebe nodded. Her beloved *Zaada* David with the white beard and tender red lips who drank the *Shabbos* wine. Mama looked like him with a narrow aquiline nose, faded blue eyes.

Phoebe recalled the delicate lines around his eyes.

"I thought your mother would be like David, but no. She dressed like a flapper, danced to American jazz, rouged her knees and flattened her breasts. She called me old fashioned. Still, she didn't stop me when I helped her family out. Instead, she looked at me with scorn. I was surprised. That look of scorn coming out of David's face. I should have known then, but I needed a wife, a sense of completeness. Besides it was good for business to be married." He sighed roughly and lowered his face into his hands.

This is too much. With a trembling finger, Phoebe tapped her father on the shoulder. "Take us home, Daddy."

He looked up with wild grief in his eyes. "Women aren't meant to be loud and boisterous. Women are meant to be looked after, protected, decorated with furs and beautiful clothes. They should be tender with the children, understanding about men's work—" He dropped his gaze abruptly. "They should run the house quietly and be efficient." He stroked Phoebe's hand. "She wanted a washing machine. I got it for her. She wanted a cleaning woman. She got it. Grandma Esther still thinks it was terrible to use my money that way. That's when Elaine decided we should move away from my family. Blood ties meant nothing to her." He shook his head. "Nothing."

Ezsha-Bubbe sighed. "Oy! Oy!"

After a while he reached into his pocket and removed a ring case. "I bought you a little present for your birthday, Phoebe." It was a fire opal.

Although the ring was beautiful, Phoebe didn't want it.

Daddy was scaring her. She'd never seen him so miserable. What she wanted was Daddy smiling, kidding her, building things, and making corny jokes the way he used to. That would be a good birthday present.

Daddy stared at her with bloodshot eyes. Phoebe knew she should accept the ring. She put it on her finger. "It's beautiful, Daddy. Thank you."

He reached into his pocket again and brought out another ring case. "Sheila, here, for you."

Sheila accepted the case but didn't open it. "It's Phoebe's birthday, not mine."

Daddy said to Phoebe, "Why does she look on me like that? She doesn't know me anymore." He pounded the arm of the chair. "See what that woman has done."

Sheila hid her face in Phoebe's dress.

Daddy took them home shortly afterwards.

Chapter 6 - Mama's Wisdom

Phoebe and Sheila dragged into the rooming house after their visit.

Mama sat in a chair, waiting for them, her lips twitching.

Sheila produced the ring case and out tumbled the story of how Daddy had cried and then given them both presents. "I don't want a present on Phoebe's birthday," Sheila said, bursting into tears, as if getting the ring on the wrong day made the world suddenly strange and frightening.

"Why did you take it then?"

Sheila sobbed louder.

"All right, Sheila. Calm down. Your father is so blind."

Mama spoke to Phoebe. "Can't you see he's trying to buy you? If it had been me, I'd have thrown that ring in his face."

Phoebe pulled her ring off and threw it on the floor. "There. Does that make you feel better?"

"You fresh kid!" Mama raised her hand to slap Phoebe, but Phoebe dodged.

She saw Mama eyeing the phone for a few seconds, and she said, "What are you going to do?"

"This is his way of getting back at me, but it's not gonna work," Mama said, and began to dial.

"No! No! Don't call him. He's so unhappy." Phoebe tore at a hangnail and it bled.

While waiting for the connection, Phoebe caught Mama's bleak stare.

Mama said, "I don't know how you could take his part after what he did to me." Mama turned abruptly to the phone. "Who is this? I want to talk to Max." Mama's mouth dropped open. "Just his ex-wife, Elaine." Mama held the phone out and looked at it in surprise. With her hand over the mouthpiece, she said to Phoebe and Sheila, "He didn't waste any time. There's a woman over there, and she sure isn't his mother." Then twisting the phone cord in her fingers, she said, "Max, this is Elaine. The kids are crying. If this is the way you're gonna act on your visitations—what? You were always too busy working on the Sabbath. You hypocrite! That's what I said. Hypocrite." Mama began to circle the rug, dragging the long cord.

Phoebe's cheeks heated up. *Oh God! Stop it.*

Mama went on. "You want to fill their heads with all that phony baloney? I've already told the kids that God didn't part the waters of the Red Sea. It was low tide. They waded across. Then a flash flood drowned the Egyptians."

Mama stopped circling and put the phone back. "He hung up on me."

Phoebe picked the ring up off the rug. She and Sheila started to climb the stairs to their rooms, but Mama called after them. "Religion. People like your father made up fairy-tales because they wanted to have a hold over people. They wanted people to fear God. You know, Jews don't get divorced very often; you're supposed to stay married and suffer. But I've done it anyway, and I feel better already."

Phoebe stopped climbing, shooed Sheila upstairs and looked down at her mother. Wasn't Mama scared of going against the rules? How did she know she was right? Making fun of the whole way they had been taught to believe? Fascinated, Phoebe descended to the living room again.

"Come sit beside me, Phoebe," Mama said. "You have to be untaught some things. Your father, he loves all that stuff."

Phoebe sat next to Mama, a little in awe of what she was hearing. If her mother was right, then she was a heroine, fighting for the truth. If not, she was what Daddy called her, *insane*. Phoebe felt Mama stroking her hand. Her mother's eyes were filled with passion. "And you know what, Phoebe? The Ten Commandments didn't come from God. Burning bush—hooey!"

"They didn't?"

"Don't look so shocked, Phoebe. Let me tell you something about the history of the times. Jews were just as bad as the Babylonians. They had wars, they killed people, they stole, and they were promiscuous. Yes, Phoebe, Jews did all those things, and it wasn't working out so well for them. To have civilization you need more cooperation between people. Jews had begun to worship Baal and had huge orgies. It was chaos."

"Promiscuous? Orgies?"

Mama smiled. "My student. Promiscuous is when men and women do it any old time with anybody. It's even worse if they're married."

"Oh. You mean sex!"

"Sure. Like I told you when you were ten, and orgies are when they do it in a big group."

"Wow."

"Well, there were babies galore being born and nobody wanted to take care of them. The people were running wild. So some smart Rabbis got together and made up a few rules and told Moses to give them to the people saying they were from God. See, back then people could kill a real person they disagreed with, like they did Jesus, but the Jews were smarter—they used the word, God. You can't kill a word. That's the reason we Jews survived all this time."

Phoebe was bewildered. "Because we used the word God?"

"No, silly. Because we're smarter."

"But what's that have to do with—"

"I'm getting to that. You worry me, Phoebe. I don't know how you'll make it. You're not smart enough. You're too soft. I decided to go against the rules. I'm smart enough to do it. Your father is a slave to the rules. You're a lot like him."

Phoebe blinked. *Does she think I'm dumb?* Mama had Daddy pegged for religion's fool. But just saying she was smarter didn't make it true. It was a cynical take on something people believed with all their hearts and souls.

She rolled *cynical* around in her mind, one of the new words she had just learned. Was Mama happier because she'd junked religion? Or did she make fun of it because Daddy said he believed in it? Yet Mama was daring and brave. She wasn't afraid of divorcing Daddy. She'd struck out into the world and bought the rooming house so she wouldn't have to work in a war plant and leave them alone all day. A rush of feeling for Mama overcame her. But then she remembered her shattered father. "Daddy thinks we're being poisoned against him."

Mama grinned. "You can already see how limited he is. Let me tell you, Phoebe. All he can think of is how I hurt him. The big baboon. He doesn't see what he's doing to you. What a way to treat you, blubbering like a child. You don't have to sit over there and listen to that."

"I hate to see him so broken up."

Mama leaned forward. "Phoebe listen to me. He has no love for anything but his business."

He loves me, Phoebe thought.

Sheila's quavering voice came from upstairs. "I can't go into my room. There's a lion in my bedroom."

Mama called upstairs. "There are no lions in my house, Sheila. They wouldn't dare." Mama sighed and took Phoebe's hand. "I know you're having a time adjusting to this new life, Phoebe, and you miss Emiko. There's a long summer ahead. Would you like to join the local Girl Scouts?"

"I guess so."

"Good," said Mama. "I'll sign you up."

The phone rang. Phoebe beat Mama to it. "Hello? Daddy? Uh, okay. Uh. That sounds like fun. Okay, I'll tell Mama." Phoebe put the phone into the cradle slowly. He was Daddy again. Something had happened to make him stop crying.

Mama stood before her with arms crossed. "Well?"

"Daddy says he's bought a cabin at Lake Arrowhead and he wants Sheila and me to come with him for the weekend."

Chapter 7 - Charlotte

Phoebe was shocked to find that Charlotte Goren was joining them on their trip to Arrowhead with Daddy. Phoebe and Sheila, packed for the trip, waited in the car outside an apartment building as Daddy brought out his big surprise. A woman, probably the same woman Mama had talked to, leaned into the car window and said in a fake-sweet voice, "I'm Mrs. Goren. May I kiss you?"

Kiss me? I don't even know you. But the look on Daddy's face—he was *qvelling* from her, and smiling! So Phoebe allowed the kiss, marveling at Daddy's relaxed expression.

Charlotte's greater insult was rushing to kiss Sheila. Sheila froze, and gave Charlotte a scathing look. Charlotte jerked back as if she'd seen a snake.

Phoebe noticed apprehensively how Mrs. Goren's glasses hung from a cord like a school principal. Daddy announced Charlotte had been a teacher. She looked like an owl with a puffed breast. You couldn't help but look down from there to her skinny legs. The glint in her hazel eyes showed she was absolutely delighted with her and Sheila.

Phoebe and Sheila exchanged horrified looks when Charlotte examined their dresses with probing eyes before she sat on the front seat where Phoebe usually sat. She said to
60

Daddy right in front of them, "What lovely children. It's a pity they look so shabby. Let's buy them some nice clothes."

And what was Daddy's reaction to that? His eyes sparkled as if he'd never heard anything so wonderful.

"My mother sewed our dresses," Phoebe said, fingering loose threads and painfully aware of her uneven hem. Hurt for Mama burned Phoebe's cheeks.

What did Daddy see in Charlotte? A heavy corset probably was why she took such shallow breaths. You could see her fat bulging above the corset line. Phoebe clenched her fist, but said nothing as they started to drive.

That was Friday afternoon.

***

A second shock awaited Phoebe as they reached the new cabin. Phoebe had been picturing a rustic structure like a hunting lodge, with stacks of cordwood piled against the log walls and a fireplace. Instead, the cabin turned out to be a prefabricated model like others on the dusty road. There wasn't even a view of the lake, but the air smelled piney and Daddy said there was a brook not far away.

The inside of the cabin was one big room with a small bathroom. They stepped onto linoleum. Phoebe ran to the aluminum bunk beds and said, "I get the top one."

"I didn't want the top one anyway," Sheila said in a cranky voice.

The grownups had twin beds near them. The kitchen area housed a refrigerator, stove, and metal table and chairs with the seats upholstered in fake blue leather. The whole thing was brand new. Phoebe tried for Daddy's sake to be cheerful, but Charlotte Goren and this too clean un-woodsy cabin made her glum.

Phoebe crawled between clean sheets and a padded quilt under a metal ceiling. She wanted to feel like Heidi on the Alm, to look out the small round window from her hay-tick mattress, but there was no window near the top bunk. She couldn't see the fir trees waving in the wind . . . .

***

The smell of frying eggs woke her. Charlotte sang out, "Wake up, you sleepy heads."

Charlotte wore an apron over brown tailored slacks and a white blouse. She'd set the table, and orange juice sat in small glasses at each place. Toast popped up from a chrome toaster, and Charlotte said, "Phoebe, dear, please butter the toast before it gets cold."

Phoebe yawned and stretched. What time was it? Then she saw the wall clock. It was seven thirty. *Who in the world ever gets up before eight o'clock? Charlotte does, with her irritating cheer.* Phoebe hopped down in her pajamas and began to butter the toast.

"Please get dressed before you come to the table, Phoebe."

It was going to be a long weekend.

***

When Daddy and Sheila got up due to Charlotte's sing-song-y nag, they put on clothes and sat at the table. Charlotte's sunny-side-up eggs tasted good: crisp brown on the white edges and the round yolks broke by a fork into an orange stream that could be mopped up with toast. Phoebe and Sheila drank hot cocoa that Charlotte made with floating white marshmallows. Phoebe gave the woman credit. She was a good cook.

Sheila ate like a fugitive, keeping her eyes down on the plate. Daddy tipped his chair back and seemed to admire Charlotte's efficiency. Every plate was washed, and the kitchen area swept up before she was ready for the day.

"We'll take a ride to the lake," Daddy said.

"How far is it?" Phoebe asked.

"About a mile."

"We could walk." Trees along the path. Maybe they'd see a squirrel.

"No. Charlotte isn't supposed to exert herself. Doctor's orders, right Charlotte?"

Charlotte blushed as much as an owl could blush. It was obvious. She was trying to look helpless and feminine for Daddy. So fake. Phoebe closed her eyes. *Give me strength.*

Again Charlotte sat in the front seat with Phoebe and Sheila in the back. Phoebe set her jaw. *That's my seat.* In profile, Phoebe could see the powder line where she'd stopped applying makeup. Phoebe added up demerits: Charlotte was fat, she didn't put on makeup correctly, she was sugary sweet, probably to impress Daddy, and she was a snob about clothes. Phoebe decided not to give her any good points. The sooner this weekend was over, the better.

At the lake, small sailboats skimmed the little blue waves. Oh how she would love to sail away. One look at Charlotte heading for the tourist shop, and she knew they were in for it. Charlotte was a browser.

Daddy said, "I don't want to look at things. We'll see you later, Charlotte." To Phoebe and Sheila, he said, "Let's take a walk."

Phoebe gratefully grabbed Daddy's hand and matched his stride. "Remember when we were poor and we walked a mile to the movies?"

Daddy said, "And we put Mama and Sheila on the streetcar. You were my little soldier, Phoebe. We laughed at those people in cars."

Sheila sat down on a bench, looking winded.

Daddy said, "Sheila, you feel tired?"

Sheila nodded. Her face was pale and her expression pinched. *That darn bronchitis.*

Now they wouldn't walk near the lake. Daddy sat next to Sheila, his arm around her. Darn it!

Pretty soon Charlotte came back with packages. She'd bought a tee shirt that said *Lake Arrowhead* for Phoebe, and a bracelet with beads that said the same for Sheila. She placed a straw fedora on Daddy's head. "The air's thinner up here. You shouldn't get your head sunburned. They say you could get skin cancer."

The rest of the day Charlotte fussed with them. She shampooed their hair while Daddy was talking with other cabin owners.

Sitting with a towel around her shoulders, Phoebe watched Charlotte comb Sheila's wet locks. Charlotte acted as if it was the most fun she'd ever had. With scissors Charlotte began to cut her hair.

Sheila squirmed and shook with indignation. "I don't want my hair cut."

Charlotte said, "Hold still, dear. I don't want to poke you with this scissors. Wait 'til you see the transformation. You'll love it."

Daddy told them Charlotte didn't have children of her own. *Now this would-be mother had them in her claws.*

Charlotte put Sheila's fallen hair in an envelope. "Maybe you want to keep this." She cut Sheila's front hair into bangs and feathered the rest. As soon as Charlotte let her go, Sheila ran to her bunk and crawled under the covers.

And now, Charlotte beckoned to Phoebe.

"Why can't I wear braids? They keep the hair out of my eyes."

"You don't know what's best for you." Charlotte said, and combed Phoebe's hair out. It went down her back. "You're a young lady. Don't you want to be as attractive as you can?"

"Why?"

Charlotte chuckled. "What a silly question. Every girl wants to be pretty."

"I don't care."

"Don't you want to be pretty for someone?"

Mario swam in front of her eyes. If Mario would only look at her. She sighed. "I've only put my hair up once and it wound so tight I couldn't get a comb through it. If I leave it alone, it's frizzy. I always end up with braids."

Charlotte's fingers passed through Phoebe's honey-colored hair. "Naturally curly, huh?"

Phoebe shut her eyes tight. This woman was determined. Well, maybe Charlotte could work with her hair. Mama had given up. Charlotte clipped away, but only took off a few inches. Phoebe relaxed. She kind of enjoyed the attention. Mama never talked about her hair, or her being attractive, or anything. Then Charlotte revealed a box full of curlers. Soon, Phoebe's head was heavy with metal tubes.

"When your hair is dry, we'll see how it looks. You need to be a young lady, not a tomboy."

Daddy came in then. "These houses are going like hot cakes," he said. "It's a good thing I bought when I did." He laughed at Phoebe's head full of metal. "The things women do to themselves."

"For men," Phoebe said.

"It's worth it. Wait 'til you see her." Charlotte pulled a portable dryer out of her bag and began to blow it on Phoebe's head.

For the first time, Daddy didn't applaud something Charlotte did. Maybe he was getting tired of her bossy ways. Phoebe smiled to herself. *Just wait.*

When the rollers came off, Phoebe felt tight curls next to her scalp. "I told you what would happen," she said to Charlotte.

"Don't be so silly. I have to comb it out now." Charlotte produced a stiff brush and began yanking and pulling.

"Ow! That hurts."

"Hold still. I can't do anything with you jumping around."

Sheila's hair had dried straight and Charlotte's shaping gave Sheila a pixie look.

For the millionth time Phoebe wished she had Sheila's sleek hair. Phoebe slumped in the chair while Charlotte fought to comb it. Charlotte would not give up. Tears formed in Phoebe's eyes. It took all of Charlotte's strength to civilize Phoebe's tangled nest. Charlotte finally put the brush down and gave Phoebe a mirror.

Phoebe cried, "I look like George Washington! I told you this would happen! Why didn't you listen to me?"

Charlotte took refuge in frosty dignity. "You look like a nice young lady."

"It's worse than Little Orphan Annie!"

Daddy never said a word.

Sheila grinned like a Halloween pumpkin.

Phoebe pulled a kerchief over her hair, tied it in a knot under her chin and climbed into her bunk, her back to the world.

***

When they arrived home, Mama had a big surprise waiting for her.

Chapter 8 - Bass Lake

Phoebe flew downstairs in her new Girl Scout "greenies" which were camp shorts and tee shirt. Bass Lake! It was to be a water sports' two weeks. Diving lessons, snorkeling, water skiing, campfires. "How do I look?" she asked Mama and Sheila.

Mama chuckled. "Fine."

Because Daddy refused to buy the cheesy war time merchandise in the department store, Mama had unearthed an old sleeping bag. It hung on the clothesline, airing out. Camp instructions said all Phoebe's other stuff had to be in a ditty bag, a large blue denim sack with white cord drawstrings, to be carried on the camper's shoulder like a sailor.

Phoebe stuffed her ditty bag with clothes and a book.

***

Mama and Sheila saw her off in Hollywood where the campers piled into the flatbed truck. Sheila was all bundled up in a winter coat and Mama tried to smile, but worries wrinkled her forehead. How come Mama splurged on her when she was so tight with money? Maybe Mama saw how miserable she felt about Charlotte Goren . . . how lonesome without Emiko . . . *Mama, I love you.*

Phoebe blew them a kiss and took a deep breath of the stale city air. The truck groaned to life and they were off. She did not look back. She was gonna have a wonderful time and forget that Mama had made a doctor appointment for Sheila, and that Daddy and Charlotte had weekend plans ahead for them for museums, Ice Capades, the Light Opera, and the zoo.

Phoebe's braids flew back in the wind. They climbed up the pass between Los Angeles and Bakersfield that became highway 99 north. On the Gorman hillsides, she searched for the springtime poppies that'd sprinkled the hills when she'd gone by on a Sunday trip with the family. They seemed like the same fields of poppies in *The Wizard of Oz*. Where were the poppies? She was stupid. It was July, not May.

Like a slow roller coaster, they snaked down the grapevine between split granite mountains. The long San Joaquin Valley stretched miles before them.

Phoebe took a lungful of air through her nose. Pungent manure mixed with sage.

She had a perfect spot right in back of the truck's cab. She glanced around. The other girls were either standing or sitting. One of them, a redhead, vomited over the side. Phoebe lowered herself to a sitting position and began to write in a notebook as best she could.

July 16, 1942

One of the other scouts is upchucking. Mrs. Rhor, our scout leader, also known as "Skipper," is a public health nurse. She's holding a red-haired girl by the belt of her shorts as the girl leans over the truck's side. Skipper is trying to duck the spray that shoots out of the girl's mouth, but some of it lands on her steel rimmed glasses and tanned face. Skipper pulls the girl in. Mrs. Rhor looks kind of disgusted, and she wipes her face and glasses with a towel. "What a bunch of sailors we have this time."

Phoebe stopped writing when she felt queasy. She had no intention of being car sick. Skipper grinned at her as if she heard the thought. Phoebe grinned back while all around her girls wailed. She'd been too excited to eat, so there was nothing to come up.

Skipper, Phoebe found out, never wasted time on the little stuff. If you broke your arm or leg, she'd take care of you, but otherwise, you were on your own. Right now, Skipper bent forward, peering through her glasses as the flat fields whizzed past them. She glanced at Phoebe's notebook and grinned.

They stopped to eat two hours later just before the turn off for Yosemite. In her sack, Phoebe found a peanut butter sandwich and an apple, and let Skipper pour her a lemonade from her big cooler.

Things changed as they started to climb into the mountains. Dusty oak trees had wilted in the heat. Then, getting cooler as they crept into the mountain, pines scented the air. Dark green fir trees outlined themselves against the low hanging sun.

Chipmunks scrambled across the road. All the girls cried, "Ooh!" as a caramel-colored deer with a white rear leapt from a clearing into the trees.

Phoebe's excitement grew when could see glimpses of water threaded through the trunks of trees. Bass Lake. The truck stopped. Throwing her ditty bag and bedroll on the ground, Phoebe jumped over the side. She felt like doing a war dance, but she stopped and just breathed for a second. How sweet and spicy the air was. *I'm free! I'm free! I'm free!* She hitched her ditty bag onto her right shoulder, the sleeping bag under her left arm, and followed the other girls up the sand and gravel beach. It even had a wooden pier just like in the movies! Rays of the setting sun made diamonds on the small choppy waves. On the other shore, Skipper said the trees Phoebe could see were Ponderosa pine with brown plaques of bark and Douglas fir. A large charcoal grey bird with white wing feathers held tightly to a branch. It was searching for something in the water. All the campers clustered together, watching.

"That's an osprey," Skipper said. "Watch now."

The bird flew up and then nose-dived into the water and resurfaced with a small wriggling fish in its beak. *Wow!*

Phoebe followed posted directions to the camping area, not talking to anyone. She should, Skipper said, because she was new to the group, but she couldn't.

At the campground, she saw World War I wood and canvas cots. She threw her sleeping bag under a sequoia tree onto a cot, and tucked her ditty bag under it.

Another sleeping bag thudded softly onto the cot near her.

"Hi, I'm Roselle Davis."

"I'm Phoebe Feldman."

"You're the one who wrote in a notebook." Roselle said, shoving her ditty bag under her cot with her hiking shoe. She had lively brown eyes and loose red ringlets that sprung over her forehead. She kept pushing her hair out of her eyes. She'd vomited over the side of the truck.

"You want a ribbon or a bobby pin?" Phoebe asked.

"Oh, thanks." She accepted a bobby pin and opened it with her teeth. "There. Much better. I lost mine in the wind when I barfed."

"When do we eat?" Phoebe asked.

"Don't you know? We scouts have to cook our own on an upside down grapefruit can."

"Oh. So that's what it's for." Roselle had made air holes near the top of her can with the sharp tip of a bottle opener. Phoebe would do the same.

"C'mon. We'll go get the food," Roselle said, starting toward a tent Skipper set up.

Soon, the grapefruit can placed over a fat candle was cooking a hamburger. In Phoebe's lap: a paper plate, an open bun with ketchup, mustard, and pickles and a couple of cookies. At her feet, a paper cup of milk. The food tasted delicious in the open air. Phoebe munched, enjoying Roselle's company even if they didn't talk because they were too busy eating. Phoebe didn't even mind washing the greasy grapefruit can under a spigot nearby.

The sun set, and it got chilly. Phoebe threw on a sweater. "A campfire would be nice."

Roselle said, "We can't have an outside campfire. War time regulations. Jap bombers might see it."

"Please don't say *Jap*."

"What? You a Jap lover?"

"Not all Japanese are our enemies."

"I get it. You knew someone."

Phoebe nodded, holding back tears. "Emiko was my best friend."

"Ew. How could you be friends with her?"

"We knew the whole family. My mother and her mother used to swap recipes."

Roselle's eyes closed, brow wrinkled, as if she had a bad headache. Then she changed the subject. "There's a rec hall with a fireplace. Maybe we can have campfires inside."

"Is that where the johns are?"

"I don't know. Let's go find them."

They discovered the bathrooms in a rickety building near the rec hall, with the toilets in a half circle without partitions or doors.

"Ugh. Do they expect us to use these?" Phoebe asked.

"Guess so," Roselle said pulling down her jeans. "The Boy Scouts use this camp sometimes. I guess they don't mind going in front of each other."

***

Phoebe wrote in her journal:

July 17, 1942

Even though we sleep next to each other, Roselle ignores me. She hangs around with some athletic girls, Bunny and Clarice. They love getting badges. I couldn't care less. I'd rather read *Caddie Woodlawn* or *Anne of Green Gables*.

***

Phoebe looked up from her journal to see Roselle in her bathing suit, looking over her shoulder.

"Don't write on a perfect day like this, Phoebe." Roselle closed the journal. "We're gonna try for the skin diving badge. You wanna come?"

Phoebe realized Roselle was giving her a chance to get in with her crowd. Bunny and Clarice, her two muscular friends, waited for Roselle a few feet away. "Uh, I thought I'd read this afternoon," Phoebe said. Not meeting Roselle's eyes, she said, "Um, if I go, what do I have to do?"

"We're rowing out to the middle of the lake. The water's eleven feet deep. We'll dive down and get one of the painted rocks Skipper has thrown in."

Phoebe's heart beat fast. She'd never been down deep before.

Roselle grinned. "C'mon. It'll be fun. Get your bathing suit on."

***

The sun warmed the lake near shore. Skipper sat on a red

and yellow canvas-backed beach chair. On her head a white Navy sailor's cap. Smoky glass pieces clipped to the frame of her specs hid her eyes.

Bunny, wearing a black one-piece swim suit which signified her professional attitude toward swimming, rowed them out to the deep part of the lake. The lifeguard, in another rowboat with a white rubber ring on a rope, hunkered down, trying to make herself inconspicuous.

"Last one in is a water rat," Bunny said, her bare toes hugging the gunwales as she dived in. Clarice followed her. Phoebe stood up and leaned over. She could barely see them in the cloudy swirl they made, grabbing red, blue, and yellow rocks.

Phoebe glimpsed Roselle's impish look in the instant before she pushed Phoebe into the water. Phoebe gulped air as Roselle dived in beside her and pulled her down. The others, clutching stones, shot up to the top. Roselle plucked a couple and left Phoebe. Phoebe could hold her breath for two minutes, so she began to search. Were there none left? She stirred up the mud on the lakebed with her fingers. Suddenly, she felt something brush her bare legs. A grey shape slid past. Phoebe panicked her way to the surface. As soon as her head broke, she yelled, "Help!" She scrambled to get into the boat, but was unable to hoist herself by her arms. The other girls hauled her in where she lay like a dead flounder, face upon the floor of the rowboat, coughing muddy water.

The lifeguard called, "Is she all right?

Roselle answered, "Yes."

Bunny said, "You chicken. You afraid of a bass?"

Clarice said in a mocking voice, "Oh, I'm so scared. There's a huge monster in Bass Lake."

They giggled.

Phoebe felt Roselle lay her towel on her as they rowed back. Phoebe groaned, her head spun, her stomach sick with humiliation. She was sure she was going to vomit.

"Shut up, you guys," Roselle said, and kept her eyes on the shore.

The others jumped out on the beach. Phoebe waited until Roselle had lifted her towel off before she dared to peep over the gunwale. She had no colored rock, therefore no badge for skin diving. Roselle probably wouldn't want to talk to her again. She almost wished she had been bitten by a monster fish.

Skipper looked down at her. "Sometimes fish can get large in lakes. They're harmless. Try it again in a few days."

When Phoebe dragged herself to her cot, Roselle had finished frying a piece of ham. A cloud of steam from burnt meat surrounded her grapefruit can and teased Phoebe's nostrils. Phoebe had never tasted ham. It smelled spicy, like pastrami. What did it taste like? Roselle didn't offer her a bite. Phoebe didn't feel hungry anyway. She was dead inside. Roselle didn't look at her. She didn't talk to her. Phoebe put her head under her pillow hoping for unconsciousness.

***

Skipper crunched up to her on the beach as Phoebe practiced getting into a canoe without overturning it.

"You okay?"

Phoebe nodded. She tried to board the canoe again in two feet of water and splashed into the lake instead.

Skipper laughed. "Hold both sides of the canoe steady while you board."

She grasped both sides of the wobbling canoe. What a relief. It worked. Phoebe dragged the canoe onto shore. Skipper was watching her, her arms crossed. Why was Skipper helping her? *Because I'm such a pitiful case?* Skipper's eyes hid behind her glasses. Skipper's mood was hard to read; she might suddenly crack a joke or bawl her out. It was 50-50.

Phoebe fidgeted with the bowline knot as she tied up the canoe. Should she ask Skipper? After all, the woman was a nurse. Still . . . oh hell. Out with it. Phoebe asked, "I can't go number two in those bathrooms. What should I do?"

Skipper said with a straight face, "Eat prunes." And she winked.

Gee, thanks! She'd been shocked to see campers sitting on the toilet passing the Sunday funnies to each other. "You need to get partitions and doors in those johns."

Skipper walked away, her hand waving goodbye.

Phoebe kicked a pebble with the toe of her hiking shoe. God. Even Skipper had deserted her. No fun. No friends. She read books instead of getting to know people. These girls were not sweet like Emiko. They would make fun of her if she told them her inmost thoughts. She knew she was not like the popular girls, but she wasn't a freak.

The freak arrived a few days after everybody else, by private car with a *suitcase* instead of a ditty bag, wearing big sunglasses and this silly white playsuit. Her brunette hair bushed around her temples. Instead of tennis shoes she wore old lady wedgies. The other campers stared at her with open mouths. Phoebe was sorry for Lisbeth at first and gave her a welcoming smile.

That's all Lisbeth needed. "I heard you're going to be on the program tonight at the rec hall."

How had she heard about that? Phoebe was memorizing the entire *Highwayman* poem in secret for the event. If she couldn't bring up rocks, she could do other things. She'd show them. Phoebe looked over Lisbeth's left shoulder instead of her eyes as she nodded. Maybe she'd go away if she was ignored, but no—

"I'm also interested in dramatics. I have a definite flair for acting. Even Herb Ruben thinks so. His father owns a stable in Malibu. We ride palominos every Saturday. Herb is a doll. But you should really know Ricky. Ricky is yummy. He has a yawl and enters the Cinco de Mayo boat race every year. He showed me his trophies in his bedroom one day when his mother wasn't home."

Phoebe shut her eyes tight and wished she could plug her ears, too. Who could care? Holding her hamburger patty, Phoebe noticed Lisbeth looking at her own raw meat hungrily. She followed Phoebe to her cot.

Lisbeth asked, "May I use your grapefruit can when you're done? I don't have one."

What a pest. Just like Sheila. Sighing, Phoebe said, "Okay, but you have to clean up."

After dinner, Phoebe, with Lisbeth sticking to her like adhesive, made her entrance in the rec hall. Roselle, Bunny and Clarice, chewing bubble gum took up front row seats. Every once in a while one of them would pop a big bubble. *Lovely. What an audience.*

Lisbeth sat alone. Nobody wanted to be near her.

Phoebe made it to the back of the performing area, knowing she had to live Lisbeth down, along with the skin diving incident. She felt no stage fright, just determination. This had to be done right or she might as well go home. She began taking deep breaths. She mouthed the opening lines.

The doors shut, the blackout curtains fell across the windows, and lamps came up on the performers. When Phoebe's turn came, she asked for lights out. She lit a candle, and stood behind it. She could hear the smacking and cracking of bubble gum from the front row. The hell with them! Her shoulders relaxed, her chin pulled her head back as she prepared to speak, demanding silently, *You will not laugh, you will listen to me.*

"*The Highwayman*, by Alfred Noyes." The rhythm and beauty of the first stanza gave her courage. She left her body as her voice invited them in, caught up in the beautiful tragedy.

The wind was a torrent of darkness among the gusty trees.

The moon was a ghostly galleon tossed upon cloudy seas.

The road was a ribbon of moonlight over the purple moor,

And the highwayman came riding—riding—riding—

The highwayman came riding up to the old inn door.

There was no sound in the big hall. Jaws had stopped

chewing. Feeling their engagement, Phoebe went on. She thrilled to the highwayman's burning kiss. She let her black braid fall over the casement. She pulled the trigger on the rifle under her breast. As the bullet-ridden highwayman lay mortally wounded in the dust with a bunch of lace at his throat, Phoebe's voice became a stage whisper:

And still of a winter's night they say when the wind is in the trees

And the moon is a ghostly galleon tossed upon cloudy seas

The highwayman comes riding up to the old inn door.

He knocks with his whip on the shutter, and who should be waiting there,

But Bess, the landlord's daughter, the landlord's black-eyed daughter,

Plaiting a dark red love-knot into her long black hair.

Phoebe snuffed out the candle. There was silence at first, then Bunny and Clarice began to applaud. Roselle, with tears in her eyes, jumped up on the stage and hugged her. But Phoebe was still in the poem. As she nodded and bowed, the words followed her to the cot and repeated themselves all night in her head. She saw the rapt looks on the girls' faces. The audience was going through it with her. They were crying. Phoebe felt a precious success in her expanding heart.

* * *

Phoebe said nothing as Lisbeth looked down at a letter from her mother and threw it in the trash. Any little thing would bring on one of her monologues.

80

"What's *your* news?" Lisbeth asked.

"Oh, my mother thinks the food is full of starch. She's afraid I'll get constipated. My dad wouldn't buy me a new sleeping bag because the wartime merchandise is so cheesy. He's still apologizing because I had to take a really old one we had lying around."

Lisbeth sighed.

Phoebe kept her lips pressed together. Where were the letters from all Lisbeth's boyfriends? Answer: There were no boyfriends. How sad. It was all a lie.

***

A day later, Phoebe found herself in Skipper's tent. Skipper was reading a report, and while she consulted it, she talked to Phoebe. "I'm glad you've befriended Lisbeth."

"I can't get rid of her."

Skipper clucked her tongue. "Now, now, Phoebe. I expect the stronger girls to help the weaker ones."

Did Skipper think she was strong? Oh boy.

"Lisbeth is an only child. Her father was gassed in the last war and is constantly sick."

Sick. Just like Sheila.

Skipper went on. "Her mother spends much of her time caring for him. Lisbeth can't make any noise or have friends over. It's no wonder she's out of step with these campers. I'm proud of you, Phoebe, for welcoming her."

I'm not nice. I can't stand her.

"Try to make a camper out of Lisbeth, Phoebe."

81

Phoebe swallowed. How could she explain that she had a shaky hold on her own standing? Lisbeth was an unnecessary drag, but under Skipper's admiring gaze, Phoebe could not refuse. It was not fair. Why did she have to reform Lisbeth on her vacation?

***

Later that day, Phoebe pushed Lisbeth into the shallow water, and taught her how to float on her back.

Lisbeth wouldn't shut up, of course. "I have an IQ of over 130. Mother is thinking of sending me to college early. What's your IQ?"

"I don't know," Phoebe lied. She knew she was average, normal, not gifted.

***

A few days later, after lunch, Phoebe pushed Lisbeth ahead of her toward the arts and crafts table. A jumble of colorful twine sat in the middle. A few of the girls were lacing lanyards out of the twine. They were long thick cords to hang around a person's neck for whistles or other objects.

"You're gonna make a lanyard for your mother," Phoebe said.

"I don't want to. I want to be with you," Lisbeth said.

Phoebe selected four lanyard twines, two white and two blue. "See, this is how you interlace them. See mine?"

"What are you gonna do?" Lisbeth asked, picking up the lanyard pieces reluctantly.

"Never mind. You just stay here and make your mother something."

Lisbeth began to lace the lanyard, a sullen look on her face.

The big baby. Phoebe hardened her resolve. "I have to think. Just leave me alone!"

Phoebe ran out of the craft area toward the lake, looking back once to see if Lisbeth was following. She slowed when she found herself on a shady path. Her shoes sunk into the pine needle forest floor. The quiet refreshed her. She could see the lake between the trees. Mushrooms' shiny brown caps grew scattered around the bases of trees. In a moist dell, she found a few late alpine strawberries. Camp rules forbade campers to eat anything without checking with Skipper first, but she couldn't resist, and each sweet secret bite thrilled her tongue. This was where the fairies lived. She'd seen a little green person once when they'd lived in City Terrace. He'd ducked behind a bush. She was afraid to tell Mama. Mama didn't believe in fairies. But Grandpa did. Zaada had told her of his encounter in Europe with the little people, who had spooked his horse one afternoon. She trod quietly now, so as not to disturb them.

The path led back to the lake, a short distance from camp. She sat on a thick branch out over the water and felt the tree swaying with the current. Pine trees perfumed the air—air different from city air, lighter, thinner, delicate air. She could see other Scouts swimming in the roped-off area, and heard their shouts. A stillness filled her body. All the knots in her muscles melted. She hummed *Jacob's Ladder,* the hymn they'd sung the night before, and climbed to heaven with eyes closed.

She had no idea how long she sat, suspended. Her arms and legs felt heavy and hard to lift.

She heard Lisbeth tearing through the forest in back of her before she saw her. "Phoebe! Phoebe!"

Phoebe turned around and squinted. Lisbeth was a sight running toward her with a letter in her hand, her hair flying all over, showing all her horse teeth in a big smile. Phoebe took a fortifying breath. Maybe one of her boyfriends did exist.

Lisbeth plopped down on the damp earth, pulling out the letter. "I'll read it to you!"

"I know. Yummy Ricky wants to go steady."

"Better than that!"

Phoebe threw her leg over the branch and jumped down, a constriction in her stomach. What could make Lisbeth so happy?

Lisbeth cried out, "Your father and my Aunt Charlotte just got married. I'm your second cousin now."

All the air seemed to leave her lungs. For a second, Phoebe couldn't breathe. "Oh no!"

"What's the matter? Should I get Skipper?"

A stomach cramp bent Phoebe over. "Stay away from me!"

"You think I'm weird. I know you don't like me, Phoebe, but—"

"Don't like you? I hate you!"

Lisbeth's eyes filled with tears.

Phoebe's hand clamped over her mouth. She didn't mean to say that. Oh yes, she did. Now she'd be saddled with Lisbeth forever. Daddy hadn't said one thing about marrying Charlotte

Goren. "What else does the letter say?"

Lisbeth reread the letter, her hand shaking. "Aunt Charlotte says she thought it would be a good way for us to meet."

Phoebe could just see Charlotte's stupid grown-up idea taking over her so-called mind. And Daddy let her do it. He didn't know anything about her if he thought this was a good idea. And whose idea was it to get married while she was at camp? A searing sense of betrayal made her shudder. She would never forgive him. Never. "Go away, Lisbeth!"

Lisbeth turned slowly, head down, and walked back into the forest.

Phoebe watched her go until she was out of sight. Then with a heavy sigh, she crumpled onto a rock, crying, her breathing slowing as it forged its way past the large dense mass that had become her heart.

***

Phoebe made one final entry in her camp journal:

July 27, 1942

Two women visited camp today. They've explored the rivers of Central America in their sailboat. I've never met women like them, so confident and unafraid of anything, tanned all over, with sun-bleached short hair. These *mariners* are always joking with each other. They pass lines to each other, tie knots on deck, and squint at the sky. They brought their boat on a trailer. They took us out on their *ketch*. I couldn't help it. I wrote a poem.

The big white ears of the sails
fill with wind and we're driven ahead
pelted by spray
laughing as we wipe our eyes
while the boat cuts a swath of white water
on the Persian blue lake.

They let me take the tiller. I was steering the boat! One woman put her hand on mine to help me with the tiller. She was so nice and patted me on the shoulder so I knew I was doing good. We all ducked when we *came about*. That's when the arm of the mast swings across the deck to tack against the wind. Tears come to my eyes remembering how I felt, sailing. I took in the clean air. I felt as if I could do anything with them as my teachers. If I could only go with them to Central America . . . .

***

That last night at camp the stars spread across the sky like silver sand. The black flags of fir trees waved against the yellow moon. At last Phoebe felt like Heidi on the Alm.

Chapter 9 - Joey's Problem

Phoebe jumped down from the truck bed with the rest of the Girl Scouts, coughing from the exhaust fumes of midtown Hollywood. Buses rattled by. Horns honked. She'd almost forgotten what it was like in the city. She'd left Bass Lake sadly, taking one last whiff of the bracing mountain air.

The other girls pushed past her on the pavement and while some disappeared into waiting automobiles, others huddled together giggling like babies. Her shoulders slumped. They had nothing to worry about, but she had troubles. Just the thought of Charlotte Goren as Mrs. Max Feldman weighed her heart down. And Daddy! That traitor. She dragged her ditty bag and bedroll to the bus bench, sat down and rested her chin on the upended roll between her knees. The streets were full of soldiers and sailors.

Where was Mama? With a sigh, she dug in her pocket for a nickel then lugged her gear into the public phone booth. Next to it was a stand where newspaper headlines announced that

Stalingrad was under siege by the Germans, and the Japanese now occupied the Carolinas, the Gilberts, the Marshall, the Marianas, and a portion of the Solomon Islands. She put the nickel into the slot and dialed.

"Hello," said Mama's voice.

"I'm back," Phoebe said.

"Phoebe! Sheila, she's home. It's Phoebe—my God, the time slipped away. You must be early."

"No. I'm late."

"Honey, I can hardly hear you. Tony's boys are moving in. They're clunking up the stairs with their big foot locker."

Phoebe said, "Mario! Oh my God!"

Mama hesitated for a second, then asked, "Did you have a good time?"

Phoebe thought a moment about Lisbeth and then answered, "Mostly . . . you gonna come and get me?"

"I'm almost out of gas coupons. Nobody there to give you a ride?"

Phoebe gaped at the receiver. "No," she said. Tears were coming. She'd forgotten, while she was away, how Mama had changed. She stared through the glass phone booth window at the milling crowds full of pickpockets, men dressed like women, and bums curling up in doorways. She shuddered. Did Mama forget this was Hollywood?

She heard Mama sigh. "All right. Where are you?"

"I'm at the corner of Santa Monica and Highland," Phoebe said with relief. She sat down again on the bench trying not to notice that the rest of the Girl Scouts were fast disappearing.

What would she do if she were soon all alone? *I'll kick anyone who bothers me.* She practice-kicked with her hiking boot then looked at her wristwatch. It would take Mama ten minutes. Bus doors whooshed open, then closed. Cars stopped before the arms of the traffic signals. As sun disappeared behind buildings, the crowds of people lost their individuality, becoming mushed together, their voices humming like the traffic.

A brown Ford stopped in front of her and the passenger door swung open. "Need a ride, girlie?" said a man's voice.

Her heart pounded. This was what Mama had warned her about. *Do not talk to strangers.*

Still, she couldn't help glancing into the car.

"Make up your mind," he said.

Behind him cars honked and a man yelled, "Get a move on." The car door slammed shut as the man pulled away.

A voice asked, "Was he bothering you?" A serviceman in his tan summer uniform and garrison cap reminded her of the USO soldier from Iowa they'd invited to dinner a month ago.

Is he looking at my tee shirt? She rounded her shoulders so her chest pulled in. Her breasts had grown that summer and she felt as though all men knew it. She hugged her sleeping bag to her chest. "No," she said. "My mother is coming to get me. Go away."

The soldier laughed. "Don't worry. I don't bother with San Quentin quail, but the Fleet's in and you better get out of here. And don't trust a sailor." He patted the top of her head as she ducked.

Mama better hurry up. A fog had settled on the upper

stories of the buildings. Even though she saw the sun through the haze, Phoebe shivered in her shorts. It would be night soon. Near the bench, above her head a blackout-shaded streetlight bulb flicked on, the color of lemon tea.

Then Phoebe noticed Roselle Davis shuffling toward her with her gear. *Her* mother must be late, too.

"I just called, but nobody's home," Roselle said. "I haven't any money for the bus. Would your mother . . . maybe?"

If Mama would . . . but Mama had that frantic sound in her voice. "Where do you live?" she asked Roselle.

"Silver Lake."

"That's not far. Okay."

"Oh thanks," Roselle said, shoving her gear next to Phoebe's.

Mama's green Chevrolet drove up as the fog lifted a little and the sunset peeked through.

"Let me do the talking," Phoebe said, and shoved Roselle into the back seat, her friend's gear after her, as she plunked into the front seat, and slammed the door. "Mom, you don't mind dropping Roselle off, do you? She lives in Silver Lake, okay?"

Mama said, "I'm not a chauffeur, Phoebe."

Roselle started to get out. "I better not."

Phoebe turned and reached for her, pulling her back into the car. "She hasn't any money for fare and even if she did, she can't drag a sleeping bag and duffle onto the bus, Mother." She wanted to add that Roselle had been decent to her at camp, but she was jerked back as her mother accelerated the vehicle and

90

said to Roselle, "Isn't your mother home? Doesn't she know you're coming in today?"

Phoebe glared at her mother for a second and then turned and gave Roselle a weak smile.

"It's okay. You can stop and let me out," Roselle said.

Mama asked Phoebe, "Where does this girl live in Silver Lake?"

Roselle told her in a meek voice.

"Don't surprise me again, Phoebe. I have a houseful of strangers moving in and I left Sheila with them to get you. Someday you'll know what it's like to be a mother and have thoughtless children use you for a chauffeur."

Phoebe fixed a frozen smile on Roselle. "We're almost there."

After Roselle ran from the car, Phoebe said, "I'll never, never ask you to do anything for me or any of my friends again."

"Don't be so dramatic, Sarah Bernhardt." Mama was silent for a moment, then she said in a bitter voice, "Do you know what your father has done?"

"He married that woman! I met her niece at camp."

"I didn't write you about it. I thought you should have fun. You know they actually wanted your sister at the wedding? Isn't the child unhappy enough? Sheila begged me to get her out of it."

Phoebe sighed. "Now Charlotte's our stepmother."

"Stepmother—*pah!*—I spit on her. Your mother is alive, Phoebe, very much alive. Look at me when I talk to you, you stupid kid."

"I have too many mothers!"

Mama gave Phoebe a blank stare for a second. "Oh, c'mon, let's not fight," she said, starting to drive again.

* * *

The raspy wail of a sax was coming from the upstairs window of their old Victorian house. *Mario.* Phoebe lugged her gear up the steps as fast as she could, stopping at the front door to straighten her tee shirt and plop her braids over her shoulders.

Mama spoke from behind her. "You primping for Mario? Be careful of him, Phoebe. Only sixteen but he's so cocky he thinks he's smarter than anyone else in the world. Walks around like the lord of creation."

Phoebe bowed her head.

"Understand I don't mean to talk bad about him. Can you imagine? Taught himself to play sax and clarinet."

Phoebe turned and gave Mama a big smile.

Mama said, "I put the boys in the one with the screened summer room. I had John install shutters so it wouldn't be cold in winter. I rented the other room, the one you liked at first, to a Mr. Green, a Hollywood writer. I told him you write a little too."

"You didn't."

"He wants to see something you wrote."

"No . . . "

"It's true."

Phoebe thought, this is how you used to be. You used to care about me.

***

In the living room, the deep voice of the sax belled from upstairs. Joey's scrawny legs thumped down the stairs pulling a big empty trunk on his way to the cellar. Tony dozed in the big wing chair.

Mama put her finger to her lips. "Shh."

What should I do if I see Mario? She realized she would bump into him every day. How could she stand to pass him in her bathrobe in the hall wearing a hair net? She looked up, hearing steps.

Mario was coming down the stairs. "Hi, Phoebe. How was Bass Lake?" Mario's voice, rich and deep, didn't sound like a boy's at all. His eyes were dark brown, his hair thick and brunette, and he was always laughing at something.

Amused, he said, "You're still wearing your greenies," eyeing her camp shorts and flipping one of her braids.

Phoebe's face was getting hot.

"Phoebe, show Joey where his trunk goes," Mama said, glancing from her to Mario.

Thanks Mama. She ran to the stairs so Mario couldn't see her face and grabbed a handle of Joey's trunk. She and Joey hauled it into the kitchen where the door to the basement was, and down the basement stairs. She had no fear of being with Joey. He was a big-nosed, pimply, skinny boy who never said anything good about other people, but he adored his big brother.

"You heard Mario playing?" Joey said. "He composed that."

"I'm sure. Uh, I guess you and I will be going to school together," she said.

"Heaven forbid," Joey said. "Stay away from me. You on one side of the street and me on the other."

She let her end of the trunk drop. Clunk. "I wouldn't walk to school with you and catch your cooties."

"Hoo—hoo!" Joey said, as Phoebe ran up to the kitchen, Joey following. He slammed the door, and elbowed Sheila. "Outta my way, Shrimp."

"Ouch!" Sheila rubbed her shoulder, and called after him, "You jerk!" Turning to Phoebe, she said, "I could just die. Him and that Tony are around here all the time now," she whispered, as if she couldn't talk out loud in her own home.

"I like Tony," Phoebe said. "He's sweet to Mama. He treats his sax and clarinet like they were his babies."

Her green eyes darting side to side, Sheila said, "Mama says he stays out all night and plays in a dive in the Negro part of town."

"Mario says that's where all the good music is."

Sheila continued, "Joey gives me the creeps. He screams in his sleep. Mama says he has nightmares because of something that happened in the Home. Yesterday he gets mad at Mama for asking something, and he smashes her sugar bowl, and Mama doesn't do anything about it. She just cleans up the sugar and broken porcelain without a word."

"Really? I would've kicked him," Phoebe said.

Just then Joey pranced into the kitchen, holding something behind his back.

"Ha, ha, ha. Look what I have?" He held up Phoebe's diary.

"Give me that, Joey." He's poked around in my room!

She reached up for it, but he kept the diary high and away from her as he began to read: "Oh Mario, your eyes are like melted fudge and your teeth are white as snow. Roses are red and soft to the touch. Mario, Oh Mario, I love you so much."

Mario stood in the doorway, a big grin on his face.

Oh no! Heat burned her cheeks and started down her neck and chest. She closed her eyes. She couldn't look at Mario. If she were only struck blind! Now *she,* really wanted to die. She touched her finger to her temple. *Die! Die!* Nothing happened. She was still there, caught like an insect in amber. *That Joey! It's all his fault.* She cried, "You dirty skunk. Give me that." Seeing red sparks, she yelled, "Argh," as she kicked Joey in the shins with her hiking boot.

He crumpled in surprise and dropped the diary, screaming, "Oooh. You goddamned bitch." He grabbed his leg, crying, "Jesus, Jesus." Then he limped out the back door and into the yard.

"What happened?" Mama asked, running in.

"Joey's gone crazy," Sheila said.

Mama switched on the blackout garden light and swept after him through the laundry room while Sheila and Phoebe sullenly watched from the screen door. Joey had torn a big frond off the palm tree and he'd begun to whip it around him in a circle as if he wanted to murder everything in his path while he screamed, *Jesus* and *goddamned bitch.* Phoebe glanced back, hearing someone in the kitchen. Mario was calmly pouring himself a cup of coffee. He gave her a wink, sat down and began to read the newspaper.

Sheila yanked on Phoebe's sleeve, and she turned around to see Mama approach Joey, who was still cursing and swinging that big frond. "Put that thing down before I have to take it away from you," Mama said.

Joey kept swinging and screaming.

"Put it down, Joey, put that thing down," Mama said, walking right into the path of the whooshing frond. Joey made the shrieking sound of a scared horse and stopped swinging just as he was about to hit her. For what seemed a long while, he held the palm frond over Mama, ready to hit her while his cheeks worked and his teeth showed. Then his face crumpled into crisscross lines and he dropped the palm frond and began to sob as if he were vomiting. Mama put his head on her chest and began stroking his hair.

The noise had awakened Tony. He stood, sleepy-eyed, behind Phoebe and Sheila.

"What's going on?"

At the fence, John, from next door, watched Joey and Mama with a concerned expression, and from an upstairs window, Phoebe heard a shade zip down. It was Mr. Green's window . . . Mr. Green, *the writer*.

Chapter 10 - Daddy's Offer; Mr. Green, Writer

Phoebe stretched out on her bed in her slip. Still morning and it was already suffocating, even with a lazy breeze swinging the screen door of her balcony back and forth. The house was quiet. Mario slept until eleven, and Joey would stay in bed until Mama forced him to get up.

Her new school clothes hung in the closet, a couple of plaid skirts and cotton blouses, and under them, new penny loafers. All her old sixth grade class was going to a different school. She knew no one at Virgil.

Then she heard Mr. Green's hair lotion and cologne bottles chime as he padded to the shower. If she had to go to the bathroom, she'd have to go downstairs because he spent some time there, coming out trailing wisteria-like scent to his room. Mama said he drank a lot of beer and wrote for Lux Radio Theatre. What was the room like now that he occupied it? Phoebe was curious. It was a room she couldn't enter anymore. Rooms. The room she'd shared with Sheila in their house before the divorce had murals painted on the walls. *Before the divorce.* Everything was measured before or after the divorce. Divorce. Marriage.

She laid her forearm across her closed eyes. *Marriage. Daddy and Charlotte.* She hadn't called Daddy since her return from camp. What was the use? He was different now. He belonged to Charlotte. The way Charlotte had fussed over him pleased him enough to marry her. She *should* call him, but why? He didn't deserve it. He'd married that woman while she was at camp and didn't let her know. Her lips trembled.

The phone rang in the living room. Phoebe grabbed a robe and ran to the landing. Mama picked up the receiver as Phoebe silently descended the stairs.

"Hi. I know. He didn't waste any time." Mama nodded and paced the rug. "She just walks right in and takes over. He's a fool. She handles him just like the old lady did. And what did I get out of it? Just two thousand dollars from the business and child support until the kids are eighteen. I was easy on him. I could have had alimony for life. Oh never mind." Mama dropped the receiver into the cradle.

"I guess you heard that," Mama said, seeing Phoebe.

Phoebe leaned on the banister, a dull ache between her breasts. "Forget Daddy."

"I wish I could, kid." Mama looked so alone, Phoebe rushed downstairs and took Mama into her arms and held her tight.

"We don't need his money, Mama."

"You're my right arm, Phoebe." Mama began to laugh and cry. "Who would've thought he'd marry so soon?"

The phone rang again. Phoebe disengaged herself and answered it. "Hello."

"So, Phoebe," Daddy's voice said, "How are you?"

She should hang up. She should scream, but to her surprise, the ache in her chest went away, and her eyes filled with tears.

"Are you there?" Daddy asked.

"Uh huh." Her eyes spilled over, and she wiped them with the back of her hand. Mama had disappeared.

"So you're back from camp and I don't hear from you."

"I'm sorry."

"Come down to the shop. I want to talk to you."

Phoebe's throat tightened. "When?"

"Can you get on the streetcar and come downtown now?"

"I guess so."

"I'll give you back the carfare."

"Okay."

***

Phoebe ran her hand along a glistening brown ermine coat on the dress form in her father's showroom. It was reflected in the long wide mirrors that made the showroom seem bigger than it was. She'd always been in awe of the showroom. Then she'd remember with pride that it belonged to her father, and she had a right to be here.

Phoebe had never longed for a fur. She felt sorry for the stretched skins of little animals nailed to boards. Her father's customers were movie stars and rich women. But now his shop belonged to Daddy and his life with Charlotte. Phoebe's saddle oxfords looked ridiculous in the mirror, so out of place. She hated him from the sore place deep in her chest.

She overheard Daddy and Uncle Leonard talking to Maury Levinson, another furrier, in the workshop.

Uncle Leonard said, "What do you want, Maury? So these skins are Canadian. The war is killing the fur business. Who can get Russian skins anymore?"

Her father said, "Russian skins are the only ones I'll buy. Maury's right. These are cheesy."

"I'm just trying to save you a buck," said Uncle Leonard.

"I don't use cheesy skins and that's that," Daddy said.

"All right, all right, but nobody will ever know the difference."

Silence. Phoebe could just see Daddy's stern face and Uncle Leonard's beaten-cur expression. Daddy wouldn't settle for second best. He'd designed a black caracul coat for Carole Lombard that she'd had with her when her plane crashed. Daddy had hand-sewn parts of it at their kitchen table.

In the full-length mirror Phoebe looked at herself and shuddered. Her legs were long and skinny, going up to a body whose hips were as wide as her waist. The skirt and blouse she wore made her body look like two stocky boxes. She turned sideways. A bump pushing at her blouse was an unmistakable breast. She rounded her shoulders and the breast disappeared. She sucked in her stomach and the breast popped out again. Right up against the mirror, she peered at her face. Maybe if she trained her nose enough, it would turn up all by itself someday. There was already a permanent crease behind the nose tip. She pushed it up until her face looked piggish.

"Phoebe!" Her father smiled from the shop doorway. With three big steps he walked over, took her face in his hands and kissed her.

He doesn't even know I hate him!

From the showroom door, Maury said, "This is not Phoebe, Max?"

Daddy nodded, smiling, looking at her, then away.

Maury pinched her cheek. "Little Phoebe, the blonda *shiksa*! You'll be looking for a husband for her soon, huh?" He nudged Daddy.

Phoebe gave him a smile of pale loathing.

Uncle Leonard came out with two bundles of skins. "See, side by side, you can't even tell."

"For God's sake, Leonard, I said no!"

Uncle Leonard shrugged and went back into the shop. He made no sign that he saw Phoebe. He never said hello to her. Every time he didn't say hello, she cursed him with smothered anger.

Maury eye-checked with Daddy, gave a nod and backed up into the workshop. The door shut.

Daddy stood at the window, his hands in his pockets, and looked down on the Hill Street traffic. "Charlotte tells me you met her niece at camp."

Phoebe blurted out, "You mean Lisbeth? I met her."

"Charlotte says she's a very intelligent girl."

You don't know anything. "She's kind of strange, Daddy."

Her father made an exasperated sound. "Lisbeth comes

from a very high-class family. They were all professionals in Germany. Charlotte's brother is in politics, her sister is a CPA."

So what? I'm gonna puke. Charlotte was talking through his mouth. Was there nothing left of him?

He spoke with his back to her. "When I met Charlotte, I began to mix with refined people. I began to recover from what your mother did to me. I feel human again.". "I want you to know that Charlotte loves you very much. She wants to do a lot of things for you and Sheila."

Oh no. Phoebe slumped into a chair and began to chew on a braid. *Keep talking, but it won't do any good.*

He still spoke with his back to her. "Your mother never loved me. I can see the difference now. But she can't help it. Her whole family is low-class. They all yell at each other. When I met your mother she and her sisters fought like alley cats. That's why I love Charlotte. She has control of herself. She's a lady. Nobody in her family fights. Never a cross word."

Phoebe sighed. He was a stranger. She touched his shoulder so he would turn and face her. She searched his face for any resemblance to who he used to be. Mama had become hard, but at least she was interesting. Daddy had become an ordinary bore.

Then Daddy announced, "If I could only have you and Sheila live with me, then I would be completely happy."

"Live with you . . . and *Charlotte*?"

"Why not? She wants you. She'd be better for you than. . . ."

I hate you. She closed her eyes for a second, her heart double-tripping. "I can't. I can't. Mama needs me." *How dare he ask?* As if everything was just hunky-dory. As if he hadn't married Charlotte when she was at camp.

He took out a handkerchief and blew his nose. "Stay with Mama then. I'll make a life for myself."

Mama was right. He was blind. All he had to do was reach out, hug her close, kiss her, and say he was sorry he'd been so stupid. But he didn't. He just stood there, blowing his nose, feeling sorry for himself. He put a few coins into her palm. "Here. Carfare."

"Goodbye, Daddy." He followed as her shoes trod silently across the showroom rug. Strange, but she felt sorry for him for a split second. Her arms rose on their own for a parting hug, but she caught herself and dropped them.

***

Phoebe ran into the house and up to her balcony. The sun beat down, throbbing with heat waves. Rivulets of perspiration ran down her forehead and into her eyes. She would not tell Mama what Daddy had proposed. Where was Mama anyway? The house seemed deserted. It was too hot on the balcony. Through the open door of her room, she called onto the landing: "Mama?"

Then she heard the tapping of Mr. Green's typewriter. Did he mean it when he said he'd look at her story? Excited, she dug through her drawers and came up with *My Life with Mother's Boarders*. Her manuscript written in pencil on lined school paper was her only copy. With the manuscript pressed to her chest, she approached Mr. Green's door and gave a timid knock.

The typing stopped. A chair screeched, and footsteps approached the door. Mr. Green's bleary gaze and hunched shoulders appeared as he opened the door. He was barefoot in his undershirt and slacks. He stared at her for a second, his pupils not focused.

"Mr. Green, are you all right?"

"Uh—uh—Phoebe?" He gave off a heavy odor of beer mixed with spicy shaving lotion.

She'd never been around drunks before. It was fascinating. Tony smelled like that sometimes.

"Yeah. I brought you something." She tried to see past him into the room. What did a writer's bedroom look like? "You must be really busy."

He opened the door a little wider, and said like a polite Englishman, "Would you like to come in?" The rumble of his voice was thrilling enough, but as she walked past him into the familiar room, she saw with delight that he'd decorated the walls with paintings, some of people in ancient gold and brown clothing, and some with modern splotches of red and blue paint. He'd put the big upholstered rocker Mama gave him near the window that overlooked the driveway. Just outside on the flower-pot shelf, she could see beer cans lined up. A writing desk with a typewriter sat in the alcove. Between the rollers was a sheet of paper with printing on it. It must be for the Radio Theatre! Next to the typewriter sat a bottle of beer, an ashtray, and a burning cigarette. He left the door open a little, put on a shirt, stubbed the cigarette out, took a gulp of beer, and settled in the rocker. He sat looking at her.

She discovered a small table with a large dictionary on it, and she flipped through some of the pages. "I love words," she said. "I collect them."

"Admirable," he said.

"I guess you want to know what I'm doing here."

"I was a little curious."

She held the story out to him. "You said you'd look at my writing."

He leaned forward to accept the manuscript. "So I did." He put the pages on the windowsill, which disappointed her a little.

"Let me know what you think, okay?"

He nodded.

"Your opinion means a lot to me."

He nodded again and fell back in the chair with his eyes closed.

"I'm sorry to have bothered you when you want to take a nap."

He jerked himself upright in the chair. "Huh? Oh, forgive me, my dear."

Phoebe looked out the window to the driveway, searching, and then turned to him, disappointed.

"Why were you looking out there?"

Phoebe knew she shouldn't, but the urge was irresistible. "I wanted to see the beer bottles Mama says you throw on the driveway."

He began to laugh and cough at the same time, and Phoebe ran to him and clapped him on the back. "Are you okay?"

He nodded with vigor, breathing normally again, and,

grabbing her hands, he kissed them. "What a refreshing young lady."

Her cheeks felt warm. She was blushing. *Refreshing young lady!* She felt like a princess. Only people who created stories could say such a thing. She couldn't imagine Mario or Joey kissing her hands. Mario kissing her? She was too scared of the thought. The closest Joey could come was to say, "Kiss my ass."

She observed Mr. Green in more detail. He was really old, maybe even forty. His sparse hairs were dull grey and black. He peered at her over his glasses with reddened eyes. His breath stank of alcohol and his toenails were a sick yellow. When he sat, a small pouch formed in his midsection. Yet his tobacco-stained fingers holding her hands were gentle, and she loved the way his shoulders hunched with weariness. He was almost as good as Van Heflin! She withdrew her hands and edged toward the door. "Thanks a lot, Mr. Green."

"For what?"

"For reading my story."

He looked at the pages she'd handed him, and nodded. "Oh yes. That."

"You don't know what being in the same house with another writer can do for a person," she said, and then wished she hadn't, but Mr. Green's eyes twinkled.

He gave a short bow. "Perhaps you'll inspire me," he said, shutting the door.

On gossamer wings Phoebe crossed the hall to her own room, humming the Cole Porter tune. With a fresh sheet of paper, she held the pencil ready. She wanted to write how it must feel to be in love . . . how it feels to have a colleague such as Mr. Green across the hall. She waited but nothing came. She fell asleep. At three o'clock the next morning, she lurched out of bed, dragging the sheet with her, the remnants of a sad dream forcing her to write:

THE PORCELAIN PRINCESS
I found her in an attic chair
a porcelain doll with glaz-ed stare
chipped nose, stone lips, cracked heart.
My tears fell on her dusty hair
My eyes they filled with her despair.
How did this mis'ry start?
Her stiff lips moved. "Attend my tale!
I pledged a knight my bridal veil
He promised to be true.
"But when he wanted more than one
My heart, it broke. I was undone
My hatred grew and grew.
"I took a knife, my anger blazed
I stabbed him while he watched, amazed
'I love you still!' he cried.
"'I love you too. What have I done?'
I staunched his wound, but blood did run
red-stained, I watched him die.
"Above me God had seen my crime
And filled with rue, I rust with rime

As stone a hundred years.
"'Look now! The sentence has run out
The stone, it melts, I move about,'"
she cried, in joyous tears.
The old Swiss clock struck five sweet chimes
I heard a rooster crow five times and
she was flesh once more.

by Phoebe R. Feldman, age 12

Chapter 11 - Mrs. Yachinflaster

When Phoebe tip-toed down the stairs late for breakfast, Mama was mopping the kitchen, wearing a threadbare housedress and old sneakers. "You've got bankers' hours," Mama said. "Wait 'til the floor dries. You're as bad as those boys lately."

Mama exaggerating again. Phoebe blinked in the morning light. She didn't care what Mama thought. Her brain buzzed with the poem. It was good. It was how she felt. She had buried *The Porcelain Princess* under quilts in the window seat of her bedroom where Joey wouldn't find it. She yawned, deliciously. She was unused to writing in the middle of the night. It felt daring. Writers did daring things.

Phoebe heard a knock at the front door.

"Oh hell," Mama said, parking the mop in the bucket with a splash. She wiped her hands down the sides of her dress. "Who can that be?"

Stan Silver's wife, Shirley, stood in the doorway wearing a black suit with a green velvet pillbox on her dark coil of hair. Across her shoulders lay a fox piece, with its shriveled head.

Why was she all dressed up in this heat?

Mama always said, *"Don't judge a person by their clothes, look at a person's heart,"* but her mother stared at Shirley's outfit for moment before saying, "Shirley! I'm in the middle of cleaning house."

Shirley walked right in. "I'll only stay a few minutes, Elaine."

Mama was already sputtering under her breath. The living room was a mess. Sunday papers and roller skates littered the floor. Cups and dessert dishes from last night stuck to the coffee table.

Shirley stood uncertainly in the middle of the rug until Mama said," All right, sit down, Shirley."

With her arms crossed in front of her as if to hide her housedress, Mama retreated to the kitchen.

Phoebe's gaze followed Shirley's slowly turning head as she studied their living room: the faded drapes, the smudges on the door, and the old fashioned wallpaper. Phoebe shrank back on the couch.

Mama plodded from the kitchen with a plate of cookies.

Phoebe caught Shirley staring at the yellow piano keys as Mama placed the cookies on the sticky coffee table.

Mama said, "You caught me on my busy day."

Phoebe straightened the uneven pile of *Saturday Evening*

Posts.

Mama tucked some stray wisps of hair back under her snood.

"I just took a chance and dropped in since I was in the neighborhood anyway," Shirley said, nibbling a cookie.

What a fib. She could see Mama trying to hold onto her temper as her eyes flashed back and forth and her hands kneaded the hem of her house dress. "Phoebe," Mama said, "get Mrs. Silver a glass of iced tea."

Phoebe brought the tea and overheard Shirley say, "Phoebe's gonna be a big woman." She felt Shirley's eyes measuring her. "My Cheryl is your age, isn't she?"

Cheryl. Phoebe's lips stretched in a forced smile. *Here it comes.*

At temple on Friday nights, Cheryl was the slim girl with glossy black hair cut in a perfect page boy fluff, dressed in fine wool pleated skirts and cashmere sweaters and wearing a tiny gold wristwatch with a chain guard. On top of that, Cheryl had a big brother and she was surrounded constantly by his friends,

Against Cheryl, I don't have a chance. Cheryl had only spoken to Phoebe once, when they were introduced at temple by Daddy during Oneg Shabbot.

Shirley was saying, "Cheryl is looking forward to school so much. Cheryl is a leader. I wouldn't be surprised if she runs for office."

Mama wore a tight smile. Mama never bragged about her or Sheila. She couldn't stand people who blew hot air about their kids. *Still, wouldn't it be nice if Mama could show us off a little.*

Phoebe took a big breath, waiting, but it didn't happen.

Shirley's voice droned on. "We figure if Cheryl holds an office in junior high, her name will be known. After all, high school is coming up. Nobodies don't get rushed for the best clubs, you understand."

Phoebe rolled her eyes. Shirley was an out-right social climber.

Mama regarded Shirley with a flat stare.

Apparently unaware of how many of Mama's rules against snobbery she'd violated, Shirley went on. "I think you should put Phoebe on a diet. The other girls can say hurtful things if she's overweight."

At Mama's nervous glance Phoebe closed her eyes, her face getting hot. "Well, you know, it's hard to fit Phoebe. She's in between sizes right now."

C'mon, Mama, admit it, I'm chunky, not exactly fat but not thin either. I hate it. She felt fat. She had to wear a woman's size sixteen because of big shoulders and a large waist.

"Cheryl's a size nine," Shirley said, drawing the fur stole over her shoulders.

That damn Cheryl. Phoebe bit her lip and sunk further into the couch. She stared at the elegant woman. Why was Shirley Silver visiting them? Was it because of something Daddy had mentioned that day she'd visited? He wanted her and Sheila to be with him. Did he send Shirley as a spy to see how they lived? If he could prove Mama was not providing a good place for her children, could he force them to live with him and Charlotte? Cold perspiration trickled down Phoebe's back.

To add to the embarrassment, Mario was descending the stairs with his clarinet case in one hand and his sax case in the other. His lips turned up in a sardonic smile when he saw Shirley.

"This is Mario Popela," Mama said. "Shirley Silver."

Mario bowed just a little, enough so you knew he didn't really mean it. He straightened up and stared *into* Shirley Silver like an x-ray while she posed with her chin on her fox piece. He *chuckled*. "I'm going to work. See you late. Take care." Then he strode through the front door.

"Has Mario got a job?" Phoebe asked.

Mama said, "Well, it's a music-playing job. Listen, a sixteen-year-old boy needs a little change in his pocket. And him, he could pass for twenty-one."

Phoebe closed her eyes, reliving the moment Mario diagnosed Shirley as if he were a psychiatrist. He wasn't afraid of the nasty snob. He'd taken her apart in a few seconds. He'd chuckled! He knew what Shirley was in an instant, and he'd chuckled. If only she could laugh at Shirley.

Joey stumbled downstairs in his pajamas, his hair sticking out every which way. He stopped as he saw Shirley observing him. He slicked down his hair and retied his pajama strings.

That was the difference between him and Mario. Mario didn't care what Shirley thought of him. Joey was about to run back upstairs when Phoebe asked, "Where is Mario working?"

Before Mama could stop him, Joey said, "Don't you know? Mario's working at the Bur-le-que on 5th and Main. He plays for the strippers." Then the goof-ball realized what he'd said and put his hand over his mouth.

Shirley sat straight up on the couch. "What kind of job is that for a young boy?"

Mama's blue eyes sparked. "Go get dressed, Joey. Then you and Phoebe water the Victory garden."

Phoebe hurried Joey to the kitchen where they pressed their ears to the door.

Shirley said, "Stan and I are worried about you. A woman isn't meant to be alone. Who would have guessed that Max would remarry so soon?"

"What do you want of me, Shirley? You want me to say I'm sorry I divorced Max? Well, I'm not. She'll find out, that woman, what it is to be married to a stone, to have to live like a stone. No matter how hard I work here, I wouldn't trade with her in a million years. I'm free of him—I'm free of all of it, Shirley. I'm free!"

Phoebe squinted through a crack in the door. Shirley put her glass of iced tea down in confusion. "I don't know what you mean, Elaine."

Mama sighed. "If you don't know, Shirley, you don't need to know."

Shirley shook her head as if she didn't understand, and then went on. "There's a nice man I want you to meet, Elaine. He owns a little watch repair business, and is very good-hearted, loves children! He's conservative, dresses nicely, has good manners, and he told me he wants to settle down, but he supports his mother, so if he married, he wouldn't want to put her in a home. Imagine, such a devoted son, forty-years-old and still so close to his mother."

Phoebe smothered her giggles with a dish towel as she saw Mama's horror-stricken face. "Not for me, Shirley!"

"Well, I just thought—" Shirley said, looking away from Mama and out the window.

It was quiet again. Phoebe heard the clock ticking.

Joey got bored and slipped upstairs again, probably to sleep.

"How much do you pay your colored gardener?" asked Shirley, still gazing out the window.

"I don't have a gardener," Mama said, looking out too. "Oh, that's John. He's pruning the trees for me. John lives next door."

"Next door! Didn't the former owners tell you when you bought the house?"

"The former owners were Japanese, and they were sent away, so nobody told me."

"Still, somebody should have, Elaine."

"Should have? I bought this house from the government very cheap, Shirley, and my neighbors are very nice."

Phoebe almost felt sorry for the woman as she paled and got up abruptly.

"I'm sure of it. To think you left a brand new stucco near us," Shirley said. "Aren't these old houses hard to clean, and ten rooms—with all that old plumbing!"

"I manage," Mama said through barely open lips.

Listen, Elaine, I really have to be going now." She pulled on a glove. "If you ever need anything, anything at all, I want you to call on Stan and me, all right?" Shirley touched Mama's hand.

"Stan and I were thinking, 'Couldn't Elaine find another way'? I mean, taking in *roomers!*"

"Look, Shirley, I do what I have to do. Max wouldn't part with an extra penny."

"Max is having a hard time now. Stan and I, we try not to take sides. I come here as a friend."

She isn't fooling Mama. She isn't Mama's friend.

Mama's eyes narrowed. Spit flew from her mouth with her reply. "Ha! Ha! Tell Max I'm patriotic. Tell him I keep roomers because there's a housing shortage."

Mama opened the front door, with a rigid arm.

"I wish the best for you, Elaine," Shirley said, looking as if she were leaving Mama shipwrecked on Devil's Island. She threw her fox over one shoulder and hastened down the stairs.

Mama waved and let the door slam. "Good riddance, Mrs. Yachinflaster."

Shirley was barely out of the door when the phone rang.

"Hello," Mama said, and then her hands clenched on the phone cord. "Max, don't send your spies over here. Don't act innocent. Who? Mrs. Yachinflaster, Shirley Silver." She eyed the ceiling, tapping her foot, then dropped the phone, and it dangled from its cord. After banging open a drawer in the dining room lowboy, she pulled out a creased paper. Back at the phone, she said, "You're responsible for this dental bill. I can't help it if you stuff her with candy on Sundays. Her mouth is full of cavities."

Phoebe circled in a frenzy. "No, no, no! I wish I were dead. I wish I had no teeth."

Mama said, "Are you kidding? She has rotten teeth all right.

Even I can see them."

Phoebe groaned, plopped on the couch and put a pillow on her face. Maybe she would suffocate. *No good. I can still breathe.* She flopped to one side and jammed a pillow over her ear, but she could still hear her mother. Phoebe jumped up, making a fist at Mama, and opened the lid of the window seat near the fireplace. With one eye on Mama, she stepped into the box and laid down, pulling the lid over her face. She heard the phone drop into the cradle, and closed her eyes. *Thank goodness.* She crossed her arms over her chest as she felt the lid rise.

"Come out of there, Phoebe."

Phoebe sat up slowly, her arms straight out ahead. "I am the bride of Dracula."

Mama's chuckle held a strain of impatience. "Don't start in on me."

"I am the walking dead." *Can't you see how I feel?*

"You are silly. I just got your father to do his duty." Mama pulled Phoebe up by her outstretched arms. "Did you water the Victory garden?"

Phoebe blinked.

"I thought not," Mama said. "That John from next door watches our string bean plants. I don't want him coming over here and watering. It's your job."

Phoebe hunched her shoulders. Mama had just changed the subject. Phoebe's misery over how Mama treated Daddy seemed unimportant to her. *If she loves me, she'll see how upset I am. Maybe she doesn't love me anymore. Maybe she just hates*

Daddy. "I don't care if John waters."

"Well, I care. I don't want him over here as if he owned the place." Mama gazed at the rug for a second. "John is nice and everything, but I just learned he had a white wife."

"No kidding?"

"He tried to make a pass at me."

"A what?"

"He tried to kiss me."

Phoebe's mouth dropped open. "Oh!" *Making a pass. That was a new one.*

"Phoebe, I wish him well, but that crossed the line. He's a nice man who's lonely. Don't ever let him in here while I'm gone. Keep the latch on the screen door."

"What if a person wanted someone to kiss her?"

"Who do you have in mind?" Mama asked.

Phoebe shrugged.

"If you're thinking about Mario, forget it. I see your big cow eyes looking at him. He's a selfish, egotistical boy. Some girl will break her back working for him, and then when he doesn't need her anymore, he'll desert her."

"You always make everything . . ."

"What? I tell the truth."

"I wish he liked me more. I'd kiss *him.*"

"You dumbbell. He'll take advantage of your stupid cow eyes." Mama appealed to the ceiling. "God, God, she doesn't even listen. All right. All right. I see you're a stone wall just like your father. You do everything the hard way. So this will be the hard way, too. Try to see ahead, Phoebe. Mario is a heartache. I hope you're wise to him." Mama frowned. "C'mon now, get going. You have a lot to do." She lifted Phoebe's chin and attempted a smile, then strode back to the kitchen.

Phoebe looked with longing at the window seat. She couldn't hide there anymore. She had to face it. With or without Mama's permission, she wanted Mario's attention.

Chapter 12 - Flashlight

Curled up in the oak rocker, with her black and white notebook in her lap, Phoebe could hear her mother calling, but she wasn't going to respond.

"Phoebe!"

In spite of her mother's voice knocking her pencil into a wiggle instead of a line, her writing was going well this afternoon. Tony was coming clear. She loved him because he listened to her, and he was a creative artist who encouraged others in their own creativity. He lived for music, from polishing his instruments to playing *Ramblin' Rose* for Mama. He was her mother's second chance to find happiness with a musician. Mama softened when she felt Tony's love. Phoebe knew Mama loved her then. *Tony brings love into our lives,* she wrote. There. She'd distilled it into clarity. (*Distilled,* new word.)

Mama's voice grated against Phoebe's ear. "Phoebe! Where is that girl?"

She reluctantly put her notebook under the quilts in the wooden seat.

Sheila said from her doorway, "Mama's looking for you to

help her. Tony's coming for dinner, and she's cooking special."

"She never asks you to take out the garbage, just me," Phoebe said.

Sheila's green eyes narrowed to slits. "You love Tony and I don't, and she knows it. Besides, I'm still sick."

Phoebe laughed, slammed the door in Sheila's face, and slid down the bannister to the landing, and then leaped the two steps into the kitchen.

Mama stirred the stew, added another teaspoon of salt and some pepper, and tasted it. "Mmm. I think some Tabasco sauce."

Phoebe handed her mother the small bottle.

"Where have you been? I need some help here. We'll be in the breakfast room because it's too hot to eat in the dining room. Set the table there, Phoebe. And open all the windows."

In the breakfast room, the windows ran across the width of the wall and looked out on a trellis with wisteria blossoms and a few black bumblebees. Wallpaper with big sunflowers glowed as Phoebe opened the windows. She then withdrew a white linen tablecloth. She shook out the cloth and let it fall like a parachute onto the table, giving off the scent of soap and bleach. *The table needed flowers.*

She peered anxiously at the wisteria blossoms and the bees. What if a bee stung her? That was a chance she'd take. *Tony is coming to dinner.* She grabbed scissors and dashed outside. The bees went on drinking nectar and ignored her, but she cut some blossoms with shaky fingers. Once back inside, she stilled her fast-beating heart by taking slow breaths as she placed the blossoms in a Mason jar filled with water.

From upstairs, she heard Mario practicing. The house rocked with Benny Goodman-like swing. Phoebe began to dance. She couldn't help it. And then she heard Tony say, "Something smells good." Phoebe ran into the kitchen and there he was, holding a straw-encased bottle of red wine. His eyes glowed as he looked at Mama, who wore a frilly white apron and whose cheeks were pink from the heat of cooking. Phoebe sniffed the savory stew aromas steeped in thyme, bay leaf, garlic, and braised cubes of beef bubbling in a big pot.

Her heart leaped as Mama smiled at Tony then added a sprinkle of paprika to the stew. Tony came up close behind her and kissed her neck. Mama turned, still holding the big wooden spoon. With her eyes soft and dreamy like a young girl, she murmured, "Wine and everything." Then she said to Phoebe, "What're you looking at?"

"She's learning," Tony said. "Aren't you, honey?"

Phoebe nodded.

Mama said, "Scat. Take this wine and put it on the table."

Phoebe didn't move. She watched as her mother put her arms around Tony's neck and they kissed.

"Oh for—get out of here," Mama said, after the kiss, and she and Tony laughed.

Phoebe put the wine bottle next to the Mason jar holding the wisteria blossoms just as she heard Mama announce, "Come and get it!"

There was a rumble of feet thudding down the stairs, and Joey stampeded into the room, knocking Sheila against the wall.

Sheila glared at him, but said nothing.

Phoebe tolerated Joey because he was part of Tony and Mario, but to show loyalty to Sheila, she said, "Watch it, Joey."

Tony came in singing, *Ramblin' Rose*. "How nice the table looks, Phoebe."

Even Daddy had never complimented her like that. *I love you, Tony.*

Mario ambled in as Mama entered with a big earthenware bowl of the steaming stew.

Phoebe had set Mario's place next to hers, and she sat with her elbow close to his, aware that with the slightest move she would touch him. His eyes were on the stew, though. He never looked sideways.

The minute Mama put down the oleo and rolls, Joey divided one, slathered the spread on it and put a whole half into his mouth, stuck his chin out to her and smiled with bread teeth.

Phoebe immediately looked through the window and, not willing to be distracted, she began to eat.

"Stop that," Mario said, turning to her.

Phoebe's fork was still in the air. "Stop what?"

"You scraped your teeth with the fork. It's like chalk on a blackboard."

Mama looked mildly surprised. "I've never heard of a fork scraping teeth before."

"Well, I hear it," Mario said. "Stop it now, Phoebe. I can't eat."

Phoebe couldn't eat, either. "I'm sorry, but I don't know I'm doing it." Very aware of all eyes on her, Phoebe took a careful forkful of stew.

"You did it again."

Tony said, "Mario has a very sensitive ear."

Phoebe threw her fork down. "I'm not eating with you!" She screeched her chair back and left the table. She ran up the stairs and landed on her bed, face down, sobbing. Surely Mama wouldn't let Mario get away with it. But she lay there for an hour and nobody came to console her or tell her Mario had been disciplined for being rude. She hadn't done anything wrong. Fork scraping teeth? Maybe Mama was right. He was a spoiled genius. He was a troll, grunting "Fork scraping teeth. Fork scraping teeth." And she was a little Billy goat trip-trapping across the bridge, just doing what she always did, and suddenly it was wrong and she was wrong, and nobody cared. Besides, she was hungry.

She crept out onto the second floor landing. Dinner was over. Tony was just below her, Mama in his lap, cuddling. *I need you, Tony. Drop Mama and help me.*

Sheila appeared on the stairs, bearing a bowl of stew and a roll. Phoebe grabbed the bowl, began to eat and whispered, "Thanks."

"I hate them," Sheila said in a muted voice.

Phoebe thought, *I should hate them.* Her outburst had meant nothing to them. Life went on without her. But Mario had been in the room and that gave it a charge of electricity. *What's more important, my pride or to be near Mario?* This new thing, this curiosity about Mario, aside from the exciting feeling she guessed was sexual, bewildered her. Phoebe thought, *Do I hate*

Mario and Tony?

She stared at Sheila for a long moment. It would be great to agree with her for once. She felt bruised deep inside. It would be easy to hate them. Mama had not stood up for her. Did she hate Mama? Oh God. This was so hard. How could a person love and hate someone at the same time? She dropped her gaze to the bowl in her lap. No answers there. Nothing seemed to help. She still wanted Mario's attention, but not that way! She still wanted Tony's love. *Tony, I forgive you for not saying something to defend me. Keep liking me. All I know is both of you make this house ring with music and excitement. Nobody has ever paid such attention to me, Tony. I need you. I crave you. I can't be mad at you. And Mario. You're strange and wonderful. I want to understand you even if I have to swallow words.*

Phoebe slowed her chewing. "Hate them?" she whispered back. "They're just different. I want to find out more."

"You're nuts."

Phoebe brought her empty bowl to the kitchen where Mama was now doing dishes. Mario was drying. Phoebe saw a glint of amusement in his eyes.

Trying to act nonchalant, Phoebe asked, "Where's Tony?"

"He went to work," Mama said.

"Oh." She sat on the steps and listened.

Mario said, "You know I was thinking, Elaine. I'm sixteen. If I apply to Juilliard now maybe the army won't get me."

"The army will get you if the war lasts," Mama said. She seemed to be in a good mood because she added, "Whatever happens, Mario, you'll make your way. You have something about you. Nothing will hold you back."

Mario regarded Mama from under his eyebrows. "You're all right, Elaine."

The peace between them made Phoebe take a long soothing breath. Maybe they'd be a nice family like Laura Ingalls Wilder's in *The Long Winter*. Phoebe closed her eyes. Aroma of roasted coffee beans. The iron stove's red glow protecting them from the roaring wind outside as the house shuddered on the freezing plain. The family huddled together. Gee. Mario would be her brother.

Phoebe sighed, content. Then Joey came in with two girls and two boys.

She could tell they were a rough foursome. The girls wore tight tee shirts, and red lipstick with thick mascara. The boys wore jeans and sleeveless tee shirts, and nudged each other as Joey introduced them. "Some friends of mine want to play a game. This here is Chuck, and that's Barry. And the chicks are Mady and Rhonda."

Chuck and Barry looked at their shoes and grinned. Mady and Rhonda stared impudently at Mario. Mario wore his inscrutable smile. (*Inscrutable,* new word.)

"What game?" Phoebe asked.

"Flashlight. Ya wanna play?"

"I don't l know how," Phoebe said.

"We'll teach ya," Joey said. "Come on."

Joey grabbed Phoebe's arm and led her and the giggling Mady and Rhonda, followed by Chuck and Barry into the living room and through the French doors into the library.

"Play nice," came Mama's voice.

The only things in the room were the bookcases that housed Mama and Daddy's collection of Charles Dickens and Mark Twain that they'd collected over the years with grocery coupons.

"See this?" Joey said, holding up a flashlight. "I turn off all the lights and everybody walks around in the dark. When I turn the flashlight on you, then you have to kiss whoever you're standing near."

Phoebe looked longingly toward the French doors. Out went the lights. She pressed against the wall. She heard the others laughing nervously. It was so black she put her hands on the wall to be sure it was there. Shoes shuffled across the rug. The occasional squeak of floorboards beneath were the only sounds. A body bumped into her and Phoebe heard a feminine laugh. Then out of the dark, a pair of rough hands grabbed her dress and yanked it up. Strong fingers began to pull down her panties. "Mama!" she began to yell, but someone put a hand over her mouth. She began to elbow and scratch him. The harder she fought, the more hands grabbed her legs and arms and brushed over her breasts. She bit someone's finger. He screamed, "Bitch!" Her body shook with outrage but also something else pulsed through her. Something that felt so good she tingled all over, and she was mortified to be feeling it.

The French doors opened. Someone came in. The silent tug-of-war for her underpants stopped suddenly. She ran for the door, shaking, when the flashlight illuminated her. Caught in its glare, she almost fainted. Mario was at her side. He smiled, leaned over politely, and put his lips on hers. She closed her eyes, counting double beats in her chest. She forgot the crazy fight for her panties, the rough arms holding her, the dirty hand over her mouth, and let herself feel Mario kissing her: a drop of water from a rose petal landed on her lips and went right to her heart.

He straightened up. And the flashlight went out.

In the dark Phoebe groped for the French door and finally grasped the knob. It was too much. The good and bad things all mixed together roiled her stomach. She bolted into the living room, trembling and out of control. A shrill giggle came from the library.

"What's going on in there?" Mama called from the kitchen.

Phoebe blinked in the kitchen light as she leaned against the door frame, breathing hard.

Mama gave her a sharp look. "I'll break that up." And she ran to the library.

Phoebe heard her say, "Everybody out—c'mon, out! Out!"

"Aw, gee, Elaine," Joey said.

Mama said, "I'm ashamed of you, Mario, letting this go on under my nose."

"We were just having a little fun," Joey said. "C'mon, let's play Kick the Can outside."

Mama said, "Play Kick the Can, a good, clean, healthy game."

Phoebe peeked into the living room as Mama slammed the front door on Joey and his friends. Next thing Phoebe knew, Mama was shaking her by the shoulders. "What's the matter with you? Are you okay?"

"I'm—I'm—" The vomit came up in her throat as she ran for the downstairs bathroom and, bent over the toilet, she barfed the contents of her stomach into the bowl. She could feel Mama behind her, worry in the air.

"You have a fever?" Mama put her cheek against Phoebe's forehead. "No. Here take some Milk of Magnesia. It'll soothe your stomach. You got yourself all upset."

I'm upset in a brand new way. Help me! Phoebe shook her head at the Milk of Magnesia. Mama was in love with Tony. Mama admired Mario. Phoebe sighed. She knew she was all alone.

"I don't want you sick for the first day of school, Phoebe. Go to bed."

Phoebe felt Mama's arms go around her, and then Mama shuddered, pulled away and looked down. Phoebe gave Mama a weak kiss on the cheek, and climbed the stairs to her bedroom, very confused. What was going on? Did Mama really understand? Maybe she did, but she wasn't willing to talk about it. If so, it was the first time Mama ever evaded an issue.

Phoebe crept into bed, and realized Sheila was there again. Poor kid. Afraid of imaginary lions. Phoebe pushed her gently to the edge of her narrow bed, but Sheila rolled back on her side and put her hand on Phoebe's stomach. It felt kind of good so she didn't move her again.

Phoebe was still lightheaded. When she thought of being in the flashlight's glare and seeing Mario, her body began throbbing like an engine. Her face burned. She must be pretty *horny* (new word). That's how Joey described it. Mama had told her when people did it, they got all excited like they were drunk. That's how it could happen. Then a man could put his penis into a woman, and she'd let him. Phoebe's forehead tightened. Nobody was ever going to do that to her. And yet, the velvety touch of Mario's mouth, and the way her lips came away heavy and tingling, with little alarm bells going off all over her body, what was that all about? She lay awake, staring into the dark, tracing a wondering finger over her lips.

***

Since the night of Flashlight, Phoebe had been nervous and unable to concentrate on anything. She wrote pieces of verse and threw them away. She tried to read, but her eyes strayed to Mario's room. She tried to avoid him, but met him on the stairs and stepped around him in the hallways. Afraid to meet his eyes at dinner, she passed the potatoes in a blur of fast-scanned faces.

Mario gave no sign he was going through the same discomfort. He laughed out loud as she skittered away from him, but she saw quick pleasure in his eyes when she dared look straight at him. They never mentioned the night of Flashlight. What confused her was that she looked forward to the sweet strain of bumping into him, even though she was embarrassed and unable to talk. What surprised her the most was he didn't use his chance to further humiliate her. It was all so wearying that she started Junior High with relief. At Junior High, among the orderly desks, the poised and impersonal teachers, she could forget herself and just be a student.

Chapter 13 – Laurie

Phoebe hated being late to the first day of school so she tried to hurry along, but the sanitary pad between her legs wobbled precariously. It was just her luck to start menstruating for the first time. Did it show? She'd worn a pleated skirt. Would it soak through and leave a blood stain for everyone to laugh at behind her back? Mama had reassured her that none of these things would happen. Phoebe carried more pads in a brown paper sack exactly like her lunch bag. What if someone opened the wrong sack? Once, at camp, a girl had used the cheesecloth off a pad for a doll's bridal veil. They'd all laughed at her.

Phoebe thought she was ready for her period because Mama told her about it, but Mama never told her how cramps hurt, that she'd feel edgy, and how uncomfortable it was to wear pads. So this was growing up. When her notebook slid a little from her hip, she changed it over to the other side and the shoulder straps of her new slip fell sideways, impeding her arm movement. Why couldn't they make wide shoulder straps like the ones she used to wear that didn't have to slide up and down? Phoebe put the notebook, the two paper sacks, and her purse on the sidewalk, and looked around to see if she were being observed. There was no one. Then, reaching for the strap's metal slide through the neck of her blouse, she pulled it up. One breast slid out of its satin cup. *The hell with it*, she thought. *Let it hang there.*

She resumed her walk to school, remembering how Joey had dashed out of the house ahead of her and crossed the street, not making eye contact. They walked in parallel lines until he began to run, leaving her by herself. He was probably already at school.

Phoebe smiled, recalling Mama's warning not to tell the Ezsha-Bubbe she was now menstruating. It was something about an Orthodox Jewish custom that required one to be slapped on both cheeks upon one's entrance into womanhood. "Don't worry," Phoebe had said, "I'll never tell."

Before Phoebe turned into the Junior High building, she bent down and rubbed the dust off her brown leather shoe with a tissue.

In the hall, a notice told her classes were being changed around and she should go to the library. She followed a scraggly line of boys and girls.

In the library, some boys at a polished mahogany table whispered to each other as Phoebe sat down across from them. A grinning boy wrote something on a sheet of paper then turned it around. It said, "You hard up?" Phoebe averted her face. She knew Joey used that phrase. She didn't know quite what it meant. It was something about sex. Not here, too. She rose and went to the rest room.

In the rest room mirrors, a girl put on lipstick with a broad red stroke, another adjusted her bra strap, and one stared at herself, brushing her long black hair.

"He's so cute!" said the first one, giggling.

"Not my type," said the second one.

"Who could care?" said the third, "I like high school boys."

If they would only talk to me. She hadn't had a girlfriend since they'd moved. But they flounced out of the restroom, ignoring her. High school boys! She had Mario, and wouldn't they be envious if they knew about Mr. Green?

Phoebe left the rest room and returned to her seat and glared across at the stupid boys.

They were now staring at a fat girl in a too tight sweater a few seats down from Phoebe. They nudged each other, and one boy got up, sat next to the fat girl and began to talk to her as if he liked her. She smiled shyly, and looked into his eyes, and she didn't see the other boys laughing and whispering behind their hands.

Even though the girl didn't know what was happening, Phoebe's throat constricted. Was she going to let those boys get away with that? She had to eat dirt at home, but now she could almost get back at Joey who was so like them. She punched the air with her rigid third finger at the boys. The hard-up one, in delight, let his finger rise in *increments* (new word) until it fully erected, but the others just sat there with their surprised mouths like o's. The fat girl turned around and gasped as she sensed what was going on. She gave Phoebe a blushing glance, grabbed her books, and hurried to the other side of the room. Phoebe's elbow hit the table so fast her arm knocked her lunch sack to its side. *Oh no!* Milk began to creep across the shiny surface. The boys took off to the restroom, laughing.

Phoebe turned the sack upright and observed the spilled milk for a second as if she couldn't believe what she saw. Then she heard a voice say, "Those awful boys. You poor kid!" Phoebe looked up. A girl with long chestnut curls focused on her milk flood.

"Quick, grab some paper towels," the girl said, "and pick up your notebook. It's gonna get wet."

Phoebe snatched her notebook and dropped it on a chair just before the milk got to it. She ran to the restroom and returned with wet and dry paper towels. The girl grabbed them and began to mop up the milk. They worked together, Phoebe brought more paper towels from the rest room, and the girl wiped the table with long efficient strokes until the table was dry and it gleamed.

"There now," the girl said, and turned to Phoebe. "I saw the whole thing. Somebody had to get back at those nasty boys. Good thing no teachers saw it." She giggled and offered her hand. "I'm Laurie MacDonald. What's your name?"

"Phoebe Feldman. Thank you."

They shook.

"I was just so mad," Phoebe said. "I couldn't stop myself."

Laurie's chocolate brown eyes laughed. "Don't apologize. They had it coming." Her pert, unusual nose swept from forehead to upturned tip without an indentation at the bridge.

She wore a flower-patterned dress. It crackled with starch when she moved.

Phoebe wanted to say she didn't usually stand up for others. She wanted to say she had to be goaded into action (*goaded*, new word). "I couldn't stand it. I felt sorry for the poor thing. She was so happy he paid attention to her."

"Just because she's fat and doesn't know she shouldn't wear a tight sweater that shows all her bulges is no reason to tease her," Laurie said. "I'm proud of you. I wanted to know you."

"Oh my gosh," Phoebe said. Why did she feel she didn't deserve Laurie's praise? Maybe because Mama always called her a coward?

"C'mon, they want to put us somewhere now," Laurie said, taking Phoebe's hand. Her grasp was firm and Phoebe found her own long fingers laced with the girl's short strong ones. She and Emiko had not held hands. Phoebe hadn't minded. Emiko was Japanese. They had their own ways. It felt pleasant, yet weird to hold another girl's hand like that, but Laurie was so friendly, Phoebe allowed herself to be led down the hall. The aroma of the girl's clean starched clothes, and her springy curls, felt familiar. Something about her friendly attitude, her old fashioned hair-do, the engaging way she had of being helpful reminded her of someone else. In Phoebe's mind, an image lay just below the surface. Who could it be? Then it came to her. Could she be so lucky?

"I hope we're in the same class." Laurie smiled wide enough for Phoebe to see the rubber bands on her braces.

At recess, Phoebe and Laurie sat on a bench. Laurie

crunched celery stuffed with peanut butter for her snack, and Phoebe bit into an apple.

"I've never been to public school before," Laurie said. "San Jacinto Hall was much better because I learned French, ballet, and horseback riding."

"Gee," Phoebe said. "That is better." The way Laurie reeled off her benefits didn't sound like bragging. It sounded like the matter-of-fact way a rich girl might say it. "You must be wealthy."

Laurie giggled. "Are you kidding? We live in a single, all three of us, Mama, my sister, Meg, and me. We have a Murphy bed for Mama and me, and Meg sleeps on a cot."

"So how—"

"Well, when my parents divorced, I was five and Meg was seven and Mama had to make a choice. If we lived with her, she couldn't work. So she decided to send us to boarding school and work full time. She's a secretary for the Board of Education."

"Did you say *divorce?*"

"Yeah. Daddy drank, you know. So never mention *a-l-c-o-h-o-l* around Mama. Daddy lives with Grandma."

Phoebe stopped chewing her apple. "I've got a divorce too."

"Oh kid, I'm sorry. But that makes us buddies, doesn't it?"

Phoebe nodded. Somehow the divorce looked less awful through Laurie's eyes.

Laurie continued. "Daddy comes to see us and takes us out for picnics and stuff. He's from Edinburgh, Scotland, and we have a family tartan. We go to the Highland Games sometimes. We're Baptist. What are you?"

136

"Jewish."

Laurie finished her last of her peanut butter and celery, and wiped her lips. "Oh. I've never met a Jewish person before. Is your church like the Baptist?"

Phoebe laughed. "I don't know. We all believe in God, don't we?"

"We do!" Laurie said. And her curls bobbed, and her eyes laughed and it was all Phoebe could do to keep from hugging her.

The bell rang and the girls got up.

"Let's play hop scotch at lunch," Laurie said. "Got a lagger?"

"I have two Bobby pins. I could hook them together."

"Okay. But I'm first," Laurie said.

**

They sat under the pergola at lunch. Laurie munched a ham and cheese sandwich.

"Jews are not supposed to eat ham," Phoebe said.

"Why not?"

"I don't know. Maybe because you can get sick if you don't cook it long enough?"

She looked at the sandwich with curiosity. "Could I have a teeny bite?"

"Sure," said Laurie, breaking off a piece.

Phoebe chewed the salty meat a while before she swallowed it. It tasted just as good as bacon.

"You know just after the divorce Mama brought home all the foods we were not supposed to eat. I call it *The Day of*

Forbidden Foods."

Laurie said, "Your mother is adventurous."

"She broke all the rules. Daddy had only one kidney; the doctors ordered him to drink gallons of water, to eat plain foods, and for protein, only chicken and fish. I never tasted a hot dog or a potato chip until after Daddy moved out. Then Mama came in with a big brown paper bag and spilled it onto the kitchen table: delicatessen and a pound of bacon. God, I ate so much I upchucked it all."

"You tell good stories," Laurie said, chuckling and chewing.

"We crowded around the bacon, wondering how to cook it. Mama pulled out the blintz pan and laid the strips down. It began sizzling and it smelled marvelous. Mama cooked the whole pound—"

Here Laurie stopped chewing for a second, and with her mouth partly full, said, "Nobody eats a whole pound of bacon."

"We did while burning our fingers and tongues. It was so good we couldn't eat it fast enough."

"Oh kid! How funny. You're so brave."

Brave? Phoebe somberly regarded Laurie, who now bit into her apple. She knew she wasn't brave about Daddy. She let Mama make fun of him. Laurie didn't know her, but maybe she could change. She took a big breath. Laurie was good for her. Phoebe said, "You don't feel horrible about your divorce like I do."

"What good would that do? My parents still fight. Meg and I always have to leave the room when Daddy starts to shout and Mama argues, but I don't let it bother me. What they do is their business."

Their business? Phoebe glanced down at her bitten fingernails. It had never occurred to her that she was not caught hopelessly in the tangle. "You don't know how nice it is to talk to you. My divorce seemed terrible. Like a mountain that fell on me. But you talking so easy about yours makes mine seem not so hard to put up with."

"You didn't ask to be born, did you, Phoebe?"

"No!" Laurie was right. Phoebe jumped up and swung her linked Bobby pins. "Let's play hop scotch." Her heart swelled. She could be free of them, both of them. Let them fight 'til they dropped. She'd have nothing to do with it.

On the hop scotch, balanced on one foot, Phoebe felt a menstrual cramp." Oh-oh. I don't feel so good."

"What's the matter?"

"I started my period. This is the first day, and I feel awful." Phoebe doubled over on the bench. "My stomach's twisted in a knot."

Phoebe felt Laurie's arm go around her shoulder. It was nice to have a friend again.

Laurie said, "When my sister Meg started, she thought she was bleeding to death."

"Your mom didn't tell her ahead of time?"

Laurie shook her curls. "Uh uh. Meg went pee and saw blood in the toilet. She was sure she was going to die. She lay on the couch all afternoon, crying, until we heard the elevator grinding up to our floor bringing Mama home from work. She explained it."

"Poor Meg. How could your Mama forget such a thing?"

"I don't know, except Mama doesn't like to talk about men and women things."

"Have you started?" Phoebe asked.

"Last June. Isn't it a pain?"

Phoebe nodded. "No wonder they call it *the curse*." She rubbed her stomach.

"You don't feel good. Let's not play anymore," Laurie said.

Phoebe nodded in gratitude. "Thanks again. You said you have an elevator?"

"It's really old and it bangs and groans going up four flights. I'm afraid it might quit working one day, and I'll get stuck."

"I don't have an elevator, but I live in a rooming house with all kinds of people in a big old place that my mother owns," Phoebe said.

"How weird." Laurie doubled over, laughing.

Phoebe laughed too. It was impossible for her to feel sorry for herself with Laurie around. Her energy seemed to burst from her in a spray. "Come over to my house tomorrow!" Phoebe said, and then felt herself turning red. *What if Laurie refused?*

Laurie's eyes twinkled. Her nose crinkled up. "Okay!" she said, blowing her apple-scented breath into Phoebe's face.

Phoebe hurried home from school with Laurie's name on her lips. She floated up the stairs and into the house.

"So, how was the first day of school?" Mama asked.

"Wonderful! Just wonderful! Guess who I met?"

"Clark Gable?"

"Better. I just met Anne of Green Gables."

Chapter 14 - Laurie Visits the Rooming House

At school the next day, Laurie whispered in Phoebe's ear, "See that girl over there? She's wearing a striped blouse and a plaid skirt. All her taste is in her mouth."

Phoebe giggled and absorbed Laurie's fashion advice. Girls in too-tight sweaters were supposed to be easy with boys. The most popular girls wore cashmere sweaters. Laurie had one pink cashmere. Phoebe had none. Girls who wore bright red lipstick were cheap. Laurie and Phoebe decided not to wear lipstick at all.

***

After school, Laurie went home with Phoebe. Her enthusiasm for the old place matched Phoebe's. She ran up and down the living room. "Oh, look, a big old fireplace."

"See, what did I tell you?" Phoebe said to Mama. "Laurie is like *Anne*."

Laurie crept close to the arched opening of the fireplace and then gave a giggling scream. "Eek! Look!"

A tiny mouse was balancing on a tennis ball. Phoebe and Mama ran to see.

Laurie clutched Phoebe's arm. "You have circus mice."

"Oh my God," Mama said, and she sped into the kitchen and came back with a broom.

Mama tried to bash it, but the mouse skittered away.

"Don't kill it, Mrs. Feldman," Laurie said. "He's so cute."

"I'm getting a cat," Mama said.

"Oh Mama," Phoebe said, and nudged Laurie into the kitchen where, on a counter, a large bowl held fruit. Honey cake and bagels with cream cheese sat on a platter. Phoebe said to Laurie, "Here, try a bagel."

Phoebe smiled as Laurie bit into the elastic, chewy bagel and licked cream cheese off her lips. "Mmm, that's good." She pointed to what looked like a built-into-the-wall oven. "Oh—you've got a dumbwaiter. We had one at San Jacinto Hall. When you were sick and couldn't come to meals, they sent your food up."

"We never use it," Phoebe said. "Except once Sheila and me, we put my turtle on it and shipped him to the second floor."

"You cuckoo."

"Now for the upstairs tour," Phoebe said.

They almost ran into Mr. Green, coming down in a cloud of spicy cologne. He took the stairs in a hurry and gave Phoebe a quick hello. She and Laurie hung over the bannister and watched him cross the living room and leave the house.

"He's the writer," Phoebe said, full of pride.

"No kidding?" Laurie yawned.

Phoebe, about to protest that Mr. Green worked for a Radio Theatre and deserved more than a yawn, found herself speechless.

Laurie turned to the semicircle of bedroom doors. "Now let me guess which one is yours."

Phoebe gave it away by eyeing her door, and Laurie started for her bedroom. Phoebe got there first and flung the door open, "Ta Da!"

Laurie rushed in, and Phoebe heard her say, "Gosh!" The screen door to the balcony squeaked, and Laurie said, "Do you know how lucky you are to have a balcony?"

Dusty English ivy and yellow dandelions grew together on the embankment below the balcony. Low in the sky, the sun backlit a row of palm tree silhouettes on the horizon. It was going to be an orange and pink sunset. Phoebe grinned from the doorway. "I know. I pretend here. If you won't tell anybody . . ."

"I won't tell. Cross my heart and hope to die." Laurie turned around so that she was also back-lit by the sun.

Since Phoebe couldn't see Laurie's features, it made it easier to share something she had never shared, not even with Emiko. Laurie had a divorce, too. Laurie would understand. "Okay. See, I imagine I'm this princess, and I wear a gold satin gown, caught up high under the bosom with a sapphire brooch." She heard Laurie sigh with rapture. "And I love this knight. I'm his Lady, but he's going off to the Crusades. He promises me he'll be back, but I know he won't. I'll never see him again. I know it when I look at him, and I think he knows it too, but we don't act silly and grab each other and cry. I have to be dignified and take care of the kingdom. He has to go to war. When he gallops away, I get this awful feeling. I think, *did he know I loved him?* But it's too late. He's gone and I will never see him again."

Laurie's voice, strangely dulled, said, "That's very sad."

"When someone you love goes away, it's the saddest, isn't it?" Phoebe said, going to the balcony railing. Now she could see that Laurie's eyes were moist. Her friend shook her head like a wet dog, refusing to cry. Phoebe saw a desperate, almost *madcap* (new word) lightness flitting across Laurie's face as if her *buoyant* (*buoyant*, new word) spirit refused to be dragged into sadness. "I don't want to think about that kind of stuff." With something like resentment in her tone, she said, "I don't *know* about you, Phoebe."

"Don't you pretend?" asked Phoebe.

"I used to."

"Like what did you pretend?"

Laurie said, "I can't remember."

Phoebe was discovering it was typical of Laurie to forget the past. She seemed to live for right now, with all these plans for the future. For instance, she knew she was going to be a nurse.

Laurie pushed up her sweater sleeve, yawned again, and strolled back into Phoebe's bedroom. She began to look around, examining the peeling wallpaper, the dingy windows covered with dust grey Venetian blinds, and the untidy stacks of books on the floor. "What a darling attic ceiling you have, and a wooden seat built right between the slanted walls. Don't you want to fix it up?"

"We have no money."

"It would sure look cute with pink flowered wallpaper and padding on the seat, with a pillow so you could read there. You could have organdy curtains and a hooked rug on the floor. On the bed you could have a careless arrangement of stuffed animals."

"Wouldn't that be darling?" Phoebe sighed.

"Then why don't you do it?"

"I can't sew."

"You can learn."

Phoebe looked at her shoes. "Mama wouldn't let me use the sewing machine."

"Why not?"

"Because I mess things up. Because I cracked an egg on the floor and she threw me out of the kitchen. I'm a *klutz*."

Laurie laughed. "A what?"

"You know, basically clumsy."

"Oh kid, we're gonna take Home Economics. You can learn at school."

"Maybe. I don't think I'd be good at it."

"What a pessimist," Laurie said.

"I know it." Phoebe stole a glance at Laurie, whose face was flushed with *consternation* (new word).

"But you can't be a pessimist, Phoebe. You have to *do* things."

Laurie was beating at her with words, trying to get to her, trying to lift the web of paralysis that kept her from trying.

145

Inside, Phoebe felt a little wisp of hope flutter. She paced back and forth. "I know—I know I should do things, but when I get ideas, I say, *Who do you think you are?*" Phoebe shrugged. "All I know is, I'm bad. I've done something awful. And I'm fat, and I have pimples. How can somebody like me do anything?"

Laurie sounded astonished. "Here I've been thinking you have this marvelous sense of humor. You're not afraid of nasty boys. You're not fat. You just don't hold your stomach in, and you have less pimples than I do. You get to live in this castle of a house with a balcony, and you're gonna write 'A' compositions." Laurie grinned. "Am I wrong?"

Phoebe took a deep breath. *Oh my gosh.* Phoebe felt herself growing taller and stronger.

With Laurie at her side, she could do anything.

Before waiting for an answer, Laurie slowly raised her leg to the dresser like a dancer at the barre. "Look at these thick ankles and my short legs. Put your leg up here."

Phoebe hauled at her thigh until by bending her other knee her ankle was soon parallel to Laurie's on the dresser. Phoebe's limb was long and slim, the ankle narrow. "I have much better legs than you have!"

"Together we'd have the perfect body," Laurie said. "My shoulders, neck and waist, and your hips and legs."

"Be happy with what God gave you," Phoebe said like her mother. Then she clapped her hand over her mouth. "I'm sorry, Laurie."

Laurie laughed and withdrew her leg from the dresser. "Don't be silly. It's true. Anyway, I proved it."

146

"Proved it?" Phoebe stroked her superior leg, after hauling it down.

"I knew you had faith," Laurie said."

Just because she *invoked* (new word) a familiar saying? Faith was what Mama had, what made her so courageous in the face of a hard life. "What's your faith like?"

"You mean being Baptist?"

Phoebe nodded.

"I go to Sunday school, study the Bible, and learn about the Lord's love . . . how Jesus died for me."

Phoebe cringed. *Not all that God stuff from Laurie!* "We don't believe in Jesus."

"That's too bad. Maybe you will someday. All you have to do is open your heart. Jesus understands."

"Mama says it's a lot of baloney. Jesus was just a man, and after he died all these fairy-tales were made up about him."

Laurie's brown eyes widened. "Jesus is my personal savior, Phoebe. When I need him, his strength is there for me."

Phoebe slumped onto her bed. She'd run out of arguments. "We were first," she mumbled at last.

Laurie put her arm around Phoebe's shoulder. "Of course you were. Christianity came out of Judaism. We also study Palestine and the Old Testament."

Laurie knew more about Judaism than she did. *Why did I ask anything about religion when I'm so ignorant?* Laurie had been surprised that she'd met a Jewish person yesterday. Oh God! She'd probably lose Laurie because she was a stupid know-nothing, and she didn't care to know about Judaism because

Mama made such fun of it. Moreover, Mama was against all religion, not just Judaism.

"You do go to your church, don't you?" Laurie asked, removing her arm from Phoebe's shoulder.

"Temple," Phoebe said. "I go once in a while where my father goes."

"Oh good," Laurie said.

"It's not good," Phoebe said. "It's boring. A lot of it is in Hebrew."

"Oh," Laurie said. "You need a translation. How do they expect you to believe something you don't understand?"

Everything Laurie said made sense. The divorce and now religion. Phoebe drew a ragged sigh. If she could only have Laurie's life. But like being a Jew, her life had been imposed on her, and like it or not, she was stuck with it. She raised her chin, clenched her teeth and smiled, trying to be a good sport.

"Oh kid, I wish you were Baptist. Christ is all forgiving. He's waiting patiently for people to accept his word. Then their troubles will be over."

Phoebe's smile stiffened. *Over my dead body.* It couldn't be that easy, but Laurie had swallowed it whole.

Laurie rattled on. "I'm gonna be baptized soon. That's when the minister lowers you into a tub of warm water and you're washed clean in the eyes of God."

"Clean? Clean of what? Laurie, are you dirty?"

"Oh Phoebe. Your sins, of course."

Phoebe covered her eyes with the back of her hand. She felt feverish. *Her sins. Of course.*

148

Laurie's voice ran over Phoebe's stunned reaction. "Our minister is very gentle. He talks to you all the time to help you be brave and then when the time comes, he baptizes you and you're not scared because he's there to hold you in his strong arms."

Being Baptist, Jesus, and the minister. They were all Laurie's. Suddenly she felt she was in Daddy's arms and she was sick, and he sang Jewish songs to her, and gave her orange juice. How old was she then? Four or five? Why was it Daddy and not Mama? Daddy kissing her, Daddy bringing her presents, Daddy and her on their hikes later on. Daddy telling her how Mama didn't love him, and Phoebe feeling sad for him, and telling him she loved him. Her eyes filled with tears.

"Don't cry, Phoebe," said Laurie's voice.

Phoebe brushed a tear away. She wouldn't cry. "I'm not crying. I just think you have a nice minister."

"You could meet him, Phoebe."

"No."

"Why not? Maybe you'd be interested in being Baptist?"

Oh hell, here it comes. She had to put Laurie straight. "I have my own religion, Laurie. Please understand. Being Jewish is something like a birthmark you're born with. You can't get rid of it even if you want to. And I don't want to. Not after what I've been learning. The Nazis hate us. Do you remember The Night of Broken Glass a few years ago?"

"Something in the papers. It happened in Europe, I think," Laurie said.

"My father thinks they plan to murder us. He won't let me

forget it. Kristallnacht, 1938. I'll never give up being Jewish."

"Oh, kid, forgive me. I just meant . . . I thought it would be like my aunt who became Methodist after being Baptist."

Phoebe laughed. "And how did she make out?"

Laurie's forehead wrinkled, then she grinned at Phoebe. "Mama won't talk to her."

Phoebe giggled and hugged Laurie. "See?"

Laurie said, "You have your religion and we have ours. What difference does it make anyhow?"

"Not here. We're all Americans."

They hugged.

"Do you have a room big enough to dance in?" Laurie asked.

"Mama's!" Phoebe led Laurie to the master bedroom, a huge space with bay windows.

"Our whole apartment would fit in here," Laurie said, and crossing the room, she peeked into the walk-in closet. "Oh my gosh. It's bigger than our bathroom."

Phoebe said, indicating the alcove in that room, too, "See this used to be a bathroom. They covered up the toilet space. The sink right there doesn't work anymore, but look at all the shelves! Mama loses things because there's so much storage space."

"Gee, kid, this is great." Laurie spiraled on half-toe across the room, her arms whipping her around, then bent like a slender tree in the wind.

"Gee, I wish I could do that," Phoebe said.

"All you need is the room," Laurie said, with a joyous leap. She landed lightly poised on the ball of her foot.

150

"Really?" Phoebe tried to leap and fell with a thud onto the floor.

Laurie was instantly at her side. "Are you okay?" She helped Phoebe to her feet.

"Teach me to dance."

Laurie brushed brunette curls off her forehead, smiling. "Okay."

Chapter 15 - The Laurie Effect

The ancient elevator clanged shut behind them as Phoebe and Laurie entered the apartment.

"Hang your sweater here," Laurie said, indicating a hook next to hers in the closet.

Stacked boxes labeled with their contents sat on a high shelf. Phoebe was sure if she opened the one marked, "Laurie's scarves, hats, and gloves," that's all there would be.

The MacDonald's apartment was clean and shabby, the threadbare side of the rug tucked under the couch. A potted sweet potato stuck with toothpicks resided near a horseshoe-shaped radio, the latter giving off fumes of furniture polish.

Laurie's older sister, Meg, smoking, played solitaire at a card table.

"Did you go shopping?" Laurie asked.

Meg slapped a card down, then regarded Phoebe with a lazy brown gaze. She drew her fingers through lank blonde hair, her shoulders rounded so far forward that her frowsy bathrobe revealed her breasts.

"Get into some clothes and do your chores," Laurie said. "You could say hello to my new friend, Phoebe."

Meg whined, "I'm sick. You go to the store." She nodded at Phoebe. "Uh, hello."

Laurie rushed Phoebe into the bare kitchen that smelled of soap and bleach. "Now I have to go to the store for her or we won't have dinner when Mama comes home."

"Do you have to make dinner?" Phoebe asked.

"Of course. Mama's too tired after work. But that darn Meg won't do her part."

Laurie opened the refrigerator revealing a couple of apples and a quart of milk in isolation on the spotless shelves. Laurie pulled a box of graham crackers down from a cupboard, removed exactly two sets of linked crackers, and placed one at each place on the kitchen table. She divided what remained of the milk into two small glasses.

Phoebe watched her precision with fascination. In Mama's kitchen, nobody measured anything. The littered counters always meant something delicious was in the oven, on the stove, or in the refrigerator. It was a place of floured breadboards, onions yellowing in oil, and steam hissing from hot pans plunged into cold water. Phoebe gaped at the two graham crackers.

Laurie bowed her head. "Thank you Lord for what we are about to receive. Amen." She raised her glass, "You can eat now."

Phoebe nibbled the graham cracker and sipped her milk. *That's why you're so slim, Laurie.* She felt envious and sorry for her at the same time.

***

A shirtwaist dress, made of navy blue polished cotton with a big red flower, hung from a hook on a hanger, drip-drying over the kitchen sink.

"That's Mama's dress." The label read Bullocks Wilshire. "She has to look good for work. Nobody ever knows we're poor." Laurie whisked away the glasses, washed them, and brushed crumbs from the table.

On the living room wall Laurie pointed to a framed picture. "That's Daddy." William MacDonald's eyes, turned-down at the outer corners like Laurie's, twinkled at the world. His sturdy physique exuded the same energy as his daughter's.

"He looks nice," Phoebe said. *Fun, like Tony.*

"When he's sober. I don't know how the two of them ever got together, except Mama was new in California. She's Irish from Iowa. She met Daddy at a dance, and he swept her off her feet."

Phoebe gazed at Mary MacDonald's photo next. She was a gentle-looking lady with prematurely grey hair, and a long, angular figure. "Meg looks kinda like your mom."

From her chair by the window, Meg gave a smothered laugh.

Laurie grabbed a small purse from a drawer, opened it and recited the shopping list. "A pound of hamburger, a loaf of bread, a jar of peanut butter, a head of lettuce, and a quart of milk." She withdrew a few dollar bills. "I guess I have to go to the store. Phoebe, wait for me. I'll be back in no time." She left the apartment with a wicker basket dangling from her arm.

Phoebe settled on the couch with *Vogue* magazine.

"How can you stand Laurie?" Meg said. "She and Mama won't put up with the least little mess."

Phoebe regarded Meg with distaste. She could smell the sour odor of her dirty feet. She held up the magazine to hide her face. "I won't talk about Laurie behind her back."

"You're a lot better looking than she is," Meg said. "She'll never get a boyfriend."

"Do you have a boyfriend?" Phoebe asked.

"Sure. Herbie. He calls me *Nutmeg* and I call him *Herbiferous.*"

"Amazing," Phoebe said, almost to herself.

"You wanna play Old Maid?"

Old Maid. Phoebe giggled as Meg cleared the solitaire game away.

***

When Laurie returned, she slammed the full basket of food down on the kitchen table. "Meg, you can't play with Phoebe. She's *my* friend."

"Why don't you ask her what she wants to do?" Meg said.

"It's okay, Laurie." Phoebe looked from Laurie's set face to Meg's sly smile. They were fighting over her! Pulses in her temple went *thud, thud.* She was nobody to fight over . . . or was she? Let them think she was okay. If she kept her mouth shut, maybe they would keep their good opinion of her. She flipped a braid over her shoulder to show them how *nonchalant* (new word) she felt. "I'm your friend, Laurie, but I don't see why I can't be Meg's, too."

Laurie let out an infuriated sound as she scooped up the cards, then folded the card table and said to Phoebe, "That's what she does. She's too lazy to go and get her own friends so she takes mine."

Meg ground her cigarette out so hard that it disintegrated into brown crumbs in the ashtray. "Take her. I don't care."

Phoebe glanced at Laurie. Her friend was almost in tears. Laurie needed her!

Then she heard the elevator come to a grinding halt outside.

"Mama's home," Laurie said and she pushed the flattened card table into the closet just as their mother entered.

Mary MacDonald wore a light blue suit, with a belt, and white heels. Her bag was blue leather and matched the suit. Her grey hair dipped in a wave at her forehead. She removed a pair of white gloves, and said, "Hello, girls" as she sorted the mail she held in her other hand.

"Hi, Mom," Laurie said, "This is my new friend, Phoebe."

Mary's voice was the coo of a dove, "Hello, Phoebe. What a nice name." She was Marmee straight out of *Little Women*.

With an angry look at Meg, Laurie said, "Meg didn't go to the store. And I had company, but I had to go!"

"You don't have to do Meg's chores," Mary said. "You girls must be more thoughtful. Why didn't you do your chores, Meg?"

Meg took a puff on a new cigarette and spoke to the rug. "I didn't feel good and Laurie nagged me so much I didn't want to go."

"I see." Mary turned to Phoebe. "Please pardon us, dear."

"I was just leaving," Phoebe said.

"I hope you won't think badly of us," Mary said, ushering Phoebe to the door. A scent of floral cologne emanated from Mary MacDonald's clothes and skin.

"Goodbye, Laurie. See you at school?" Phoebe said.

"See you tomorrow," Laurie said. "And don't listen to Meg."

***

Phoebe walked into her home after her visit to Laurie's apartment in a mood to criticize. Joey and Sheila were playing gin rummy on the piano bench, and Mario's feet stuck out from the end of the couch where he lay reading *War and Peace*. Nests of orange peels and crumpled napkins littered the floor. "God, Joey, is that all you can do, play cards?" she said, running into the kitchen.

From the living room, she heard Sheila burst into tears. "I didn't win—I didn't win—"

Mama stood surrounded by aromas of poultry seasoning and garlic, basting a chicken at the open oven.

Phoebe slammed the kitchen door. "You should make those pigs clean up."

"Listen, listen to her," Mama said, ladling drippings.

With the image of Laurie in her crackling stiff dress, Phoebe got down on her knees and tunneled into the cupboard beneath the sink. "Look at all this stuff." She began to throw rags, rusty scouring pads, empty mason jars, cans of cleaning solution, and a dusty whiskey bottle onto the floor. "There must be some here, somewhere."

"What are you looking for?"

"Starch."

Mama sounded amused. "Starch?"

"Yes, starch."

"What do you want with starch?"

"Don't you have any?"

Joey and Sheila stuck their heads in. "What's wrong with her?" Joey said.

Sheila pointed. "What a mess she made."

Phoebe backed out of the cupboard with a faded blue and white box in her hand. "Is this all you have. Just this teeny little bit?"

"What's got into you, Phoebe? You know I don't use much starch."

"That's just it. My clothes hang on me, limp—droopy—"

Joey and Sheila stared at each other. Joey made a slow circle with his finger near his head.

Phoebe turned in anguish on Mama. "Please . . .."

Mama pushed the chicken roaster back into the oven with her shoe. "God help me, it's a matter of life and death. Get off your knees, Phoebe. All right. I'm not against a little starch. But you have to starch your own clothes and iron them. I haven't the time for such things."

"Just get it for me, Mama." She began to put jars and cans

back into the cupboard. The faded blue and white box, however, remained on the drain board as a reminder.

* * *

"Okay, try it again," Laurie reset the needle for *In the Mood*. Phoebe moved her shoulders to the swing music and looked down at her feet. They refused to budge.

"Like this." Laurie twisted the ball of her foot this way and that, put her other foot in back and brought it forward. "One, two, three, four. Oh no, Phoebe. Listen to the music. Get some rhythm. Stand in back of me and do what I do."

Phoebe sighed. It looked so simple. She ran one foot at a time through the steps. There. That worked. Now put it together. In front of her Laurie's feet seemed to know what to do without her telling them. She had a long waistline from which hung a perky little *tush* and that *tush* now waved side to side in front of Phoebe.

"How're you doin'?"

"I'm trying."

Laurie turned and giggled. "Zombies dance better than that." She offered her arms to Phoebe like a male partner. Phoebe stepped in close and Laurie's arms encircled her. She felt Laurie's solid narrow body against hers. "Move."

Phoebe creased her forehead in concentration. She willed her legs to do the step, but she couldn't get the loose springy motion Laurie had. "You're not having any fun," Laurie said. "You move like a sack of cement. Let's work on your body."

Laurie made her bend over at the waist. Then with her palm

on the small of Phoebe's back, she pressed down, and let Phoebe spring back. Then she pressed again. It was like pumping an oil well. "Okay. Get up now. Work your ankles around and around. Yeah, like that. Now bend sideways as far as you can."

Phoebe could only go an inch or so either way. Her stiff body dismayed her.

"You're gonna be sore tonight," Laurie said. "But by tomorrow you'll be able to do more."

They sat on the floor and sang along to *Chickory Chick Chalot Chalot, I Used to Work in Chicago*, and *Three Little Fishies in an Itty Bitty Pond*.

***

That night, in Phoebe's bedroom, Mama rubbed mentholated ointment onto Phoebe's back. "Is this worth it?" she asked. "I never had any trouble dancing." Mama's eyes lit up. "Maybe I can still do it." Mama threw off her apron, shucked her shoes, and began to sing. *"Charleston! Charleston!"* She kicked up her legs like a wild woman, her arms swinging. *"Charleston! Charleston!"*

Sheila, in her pajamas, ran in from next door. *"Charleston! Charleston!"* Sheila followed Mama's steps until Mario appeared. Sheila gave Mario a dirty look and ran back into her room.

Mario joined Mama. *"Charleston! Charleston!"* They danced together like they were Fred Astaire and Ginger Rogers, until they both landed on Phoebe's bed, out of breath.

Everybody but me can dance.

"Pew! What's that smell?" Mario said.

"Mentholated ointment. Phoebe overdid it at school," Mama said.

Mario ruffled Phoebe's hair. "Take care, little one." He said to Mama, "That was fun, Elaine. You're a good dancer." And he left the room.

Little one. She was just a kid to him. She stuck her tongue out at the closed door.

Mama was in one of her good moods. She suddenly kissed Phoebe. "It all takes me back, honey. I was so full of life then. I used to go to Manhattan and look at all the lights. They shined down like stars. I felt there was no limit to what I could do. I had a good job, I was pretty—"

"You still are," Phoebe said.

"Yeah? Well, kid, I had a family who dragged me down. It wasn't their fault, really. They lived in Brooklyn in a cold water flat and Grandpa had to press suits for a living. You know what he was in the old country? A foreman of a rich nobleman's timber land. He rode around on a horse and made the peasants work. We lived in a castle. Grandma cooked for the workers and the family. She had an oven so big a lamb fit in it."

Phoebe rose up on an elbow. "Don't forget the part about the windows—"

"You love those fairy-tale windows—My bedroom window panes were shaped like diamonds, and when I opened them in spring, branches of white plum tree blossoms would be right there on the sill as if asking to be let in. In the summer I picked big juicy purple plums right from my window. My mother made tart plum jam and your Grandpa made *zwetchgenwasser,* schnapps."

"Schnapps?" Phoebe said. "What a thing to do to the poor plums."

Mama went on as if in a dream. "In America, there were no castles. We had to live in a crowded tenement. But Grandma Rebecca dug up the little square of ground below where we hung the wash from the fifth-floor window, and we had carrots, potatoes, turnips, beets, and onions. I remember—she carried mattresses up five flights of stairs. We called her The General. But my sister and I fought all the time. I had to get out of there."

"You did."

"You mean by marrying your father?"

"No. The Blue Baron."

Mama's eyes teared. "My family ended that."

"Now you have Tony," Phoebe said. "Marry him, Mama."

Mama's fingers parted Phoebe's hair. "Would you like that, Phoebe?"

"It's what I wish for before I can eat the tip of the pie."

It was a lovely feeling, with Mama being her softer self, asking her opinion, Mama's gaze upon her face. It was like before the war, before the divorce.

Then Mama smiled at her as if puzzled. "You're a funny kid. Goodnight."

After Mama left, Phoebe tried to sleep but couldn't. *Funny kid.* There it was again, *little one, funny kid,* but this time it meant *odd,* as if she was someone else's child. She lay wide-awake in the darkness, feeling her eyeballs becoming dry. Her

162

mouth felt dry, too. Why was it strange that she wanted Mama to marry Tony? Mama didn't want Daddy now. *I can talk to Tony.* She sank into sleep, longing for Marmee's soft lap, Marmee's soothing hand on her head.

***

Phoebe practiced her exercises and gradually she became more limber. Laurie was patient. "I don't have anybody else to dance with."

On the day she danced to Laurie's satisfaction they were in the master bedroom. *Tuxedo Junction* was on the turntable, and the music sounded so good, Phoebe just got up without thinking, and let it move her.

"Yea!" Laurie grabbed Phoebe's hands and swung her around, and they did the Lindy Hop all over the bedroom.

"Now for the waltz," Laurie said. "One-two-three, one-two-three . . . ."

Chapter 16 - The Facts of Life

When Phoebe heard Mr. Green click the bathroom lock, she crept into the hall and snuck into his room. Where was her manuscript? She glanced over her shoulder before she lifted his papers from beside the typewriter. There it was at the bottom of the pile. She was about to grab it and run when she saw he'd written something on it. *Funny and sad. Kid has talent.*

Phoebe froze. *Kid has talent.*

"Oh!" She heard the bathroom lock turn, dropped the manuscript back into place and ran from Mr. Green's room into her own with a fast-beating heart. She dropped onto her chair and remembered what she had written:

Mama felt sorry for this young couple, Bud Hilby and his pregnant wife. A 4F because of flat feet, he was also a drunk. His wife Wanda could barely walk she was so fat and in her sixth month. They lived in the library and breakfast room, now a small apartment. The French doors shook when he yelled at Wanda night after night as the brute beat his wife. Mama approached those French doors with a shovel as a weapon. She demanded through the door that he stop. He told her to stay out of it and called her an old bitch. Mama told him she'd call the police. He'd also called her an interfering *cunt* (new word).

When Mama kicked Bud and Wanda out, an old couple, the Crumpetts, moved into the library-breakfast room. Mrs. Alma Mae Crumpett smelled musty and had a prune face. She wore long dresses and carried a dingy lace handkerchief in the cuff of her sleeve. Sometimes her brown wig tilted, and you could see her grey hair underneath. Mr. Crumpett had had throat cancer and he'd lost his voice. Fixed-up by his doctors with a talk box that he operated by pressing a button on his chest, a mechanical voice with a background of static said, "I am Mr. Crumpett." He scared Sheila so bad she ran whenever she saw him. I figured he couldn't help sounding like the villain of a movie serial. This awful white dog with a head like a sheep guarded them. It wrinkled its forehead as if it could understand what people said and snarled when anyone came near its owners. Because they kept to themselves, the Crumpetts weren't too bad.

The *Yanskys* were bad. They descended upon us for a few horrible weeks. Mama called them locusts, I guess because they ate up our lives while they were with us, demanding things and fighting with each other. I hated them. Naturally, they came recommended by our so-called good friends. Mama threw me out of my room and I had to bunk with Sheila in Mama's bedroom to make space for them. I was so mad!

The husband, Ed Yansky, was Jewish, an unemployed boxer. Alice, Mrs. Yansky, was a dumb, skinny *shiksa-cup* nurse with peroxided hair, who seemed to have no opinions of her own, being so polite she sounded stupid. I have been called a *shiksa-cup* by relatives because I'm not good at snappy comebacks. My Uncle Leonard thinks he's so funny.

Alice's whole conversation was about how she'd been Shirley Temple's nurse in the '30s. We had to hear over and over about Shirley's doll collection that Alice had to take care of along with Shirley.

The third locust was an incredibly *kvetchy* four-year-old boy, Schloimy, who demanded everybody's attention by screeching above the grownups. They made me baby-sit and I literally had to sit on him to keep him from driving me crazy.

Shortly after they moved in, Alice began to drink. She was afraid Ed would hit her because she'd promised to stay sober. They had noisy fights. Mama tried to talk her out of getting drunk, but it was an ingrown habit, so Mama made her chew raw onions and pumped her full of black coffee to fool Ed, but it didn't work. Ed knew she was potted and slapped her around. It was getting worse and worse.

One evening, when Mama was trying to sober her up, Alice told Mama she was afraid he'd kill her next time since he was a boxer and threatened to beat her with his fists. She begged Mama to take her to her sister in San Bernardino. Mama told me to get Schloimy dressed. When they were ready and in the car, Mama said I was not to tell Ed where they went. And off they drove.

Soon after, Ed came home. Sheila and I sat on the piano bench, our knees knocking together as he lurched upstairs. We heard him cursing, opening and closing closet doors and then he raced down. He demanded to know where they'd gone. I answered him in my best *shiksa-cup* voice that we'd just come home from piano lessons and nobody was home.

He didn't believe me and tore back upstairs.

We could hear him ripping the drapes and breaking the room up. He was coming down again when I looked at Sheila. She was shaking and looked terrified.

When he shook his fist at us, she hid her face in my skirt. I remember his eyes like boiling brown waves and the spit in the corners of his thin lips like James Cagney's in *White Heat. If you know and are not telling—*

Sheila moaned. I told him he was scaring my sister. He loomed over Sheila demanding to know what she knew about his wife and Schloimy. Sheila trembled. Then he said he was going, shook his fist at us, warning us again if we knew and were not telling—and he left.

As soon as he was gone, I bolted the door and locked the windows. Sheila and I got into bed and pulled the covers over our heads. Sheila was afraid to go to sleep and I was determined not to.

We never saw the locusts again. The police told Mama that Alice took Schloimy to live with her in a trailer and became a prostitute to pay for her drinking. The Public Health Department took Schloimy away. Mr. Yansky disappeared. He never contacted our friends who'd sent him to us, either. I was always afraid he'd come back and get us. I began to dream of

Sheila's lions.

The bathroom door opened and she heard Mr. Green and his clanking bottles cross to his room. She peered at the back of his bathrobe disappearing through his door, not knowing whether to be mad at him for not telling her she had talent, or happy that he liked her writing.

***

It was an October Saturday. The sound of rain pelting down came through a window ajar in the kitchen. Phoebe ran in and slammed the window shut, turning to Mario who drank coffee heedless of the drenched curtains. "Are you crazy? There's puddles on the floor."

"So what? The kitchen needed airing out," Mario said in his maddening slow voice.

"You don't just let the rain in."

He leaned back in his chair like a pampered cat who'd just been fed. "Where is Elaine?"

"She went grocery shopping." She was alone with him. Phoebe's heart fluttered.

"I think I'll have a radish sandwich," Mario said, opening the refrigerator. He pulled out a couple of wilted radishes and sneered. "I guess these will have to do."

Radish sandwich? "Wash them. They'll freshen."

He grinned. "Good idea." He rinsed them in cold water.

"I've never had a radish sandwich," she said, settling in a chair to watch.

"Pop's favorite." He smeared the bread with mustard and mayonnaise. "You cut the radishes in half and lay them like cobblestones on the mayo and mustard, then lots of lettuce. Oh, I forgot, you have to have a blue onion."

"You *have* to?"

"You can't make a radish sandwich without Bermuda onions," he said, pulling out the crisper, then he shoved it back in disgust.

"What difference does it make?"

"God! What difference?" He walked around the kitchen with his hands in his pockets, muttering to himself. Then, with a sharp intake of breath, he said, "The difference between the real thing and an imitation." His curly black hair fell across his forehead and he flicked it back with annoyance.

He was like Daddy. He wouldn't accept second best. A little thrill went up her spine. "Then we have to get one." She knelt beside him as they searched the refrigerator, Phoebe acutely aware of his body next to hers. Way in the back, she found an old dried-up Bermuda onion wrapped in wax paper and held it up in triumph.

Mario snatched it from her and examined it. "Pretty old, but . . ." With a sigh, he took it to the cutting board and began to slice it. He laid the slices with care across the radishes.

Phoebe gazed at the profile of his short strong nose as he finished building the sandwich with lettuce and another slice of bread. He glanced at her, his eyes lit with satisfaction as he gathered it up, opened his mouth and his beginning moustache widened as he went *crunch*.

"Pretty good. Want a bite?"

Phoebe shook her head. If he got close, he would feel her trembling. *Then what would happen?* "I like sour cream and banana sandwiches on rye."

He chewed and winked. "You eat strange things. Fattening, too."

Did she look fat? Phoebe crossed her arms over her chest. "I'll just have an apple."

"That didn't make you mad, did it?"

She shook her head. She was almost in tears. He saw how lumpy she was. He'd stopped eating. He was looking at her breasts! She had to get out of there, or she was gonna scream.

He tipped back on the kitchen chair, licking the rest of the mayonnaise off his lips. "You're just right, really. In fact, give you a few years, and you'll really be fine, really something."

"I'm just a doll," she said, striking a pose. "Think I'll make *Vogue*?"

"I think you ought to measure yourself. You'll never make *Vogue*."

She stretched her lips in a false smile. "No?"

Mario roared with laughter. "You're much better looking than those scarecrows in Vogue."

Phoebe stopped smiling. The heat in her cheeks told her she cared too much what he thought. Yet was she going to let him have the last word? Was she gonna shrink away like a deflated balloon? She could play too. She went to a drawer and pulled out a tape measure. With an attempt at lightness, she put the tape around an ankle. "My legs are good, see, ankle, nine-and-a-half inches, calf, fourteen, thigh, nineteen, hips, thirty-five." She dropped the tape. "Oh, never mind."

Mario picked it up. "C'mon, let me help." He put his hands around her waist and pulled the tape forward.

Phoebe went rigid. Her arms stuck out sideways. His skin smelled fresh, like a minty aftershave. His curly head bent close as he thumb-nailed the tape and brought it to his eyes. "Hmm, waist, twenty-eight inches." As if holding in a laugh, he said, "Phoebe, my waist is thirty inches."

"No more!" Phoebe grabbed the tape.

Now he was laughing, a teasing roll of a laugh. "Really, Phoebe, give me the tape . . . ha, ha, ha, let me see." He tried to pry the tape out of her hand while she held it tight. She put it up and he jumped for it. She ran into the dining room and he followed. "C'mon, Phoebe, let me have it."

She held it behind her and he enclosed her within his arms, backing her up against the wall. His curls brushed her lips. His face was right up against hers. Then they stopped struggling. He stopped laughing. They looked at each other, eye to eye for a long moment.

"So this is what goes on when I'm not home," came Mama's voice from the door. She marched into the kitchen and slammed the groceries onto the table. Phoebe slunk into the kitchen after her.

Mario stood in the doorway. "We were just measuring—"

"Why do you want to do that?"

"It was my fault," Phoebe said.

"You stay out of this!" Mama said, and turned to Mario. "I

don't like it. Why aren't you busy taking out a girl your own age?"

He laughed. "Now look, Elaine . . . ."

"And you, Phoebe."

"Aw, leave her alone," Mario said. He picked up his sandwich and walked out.

"What does he think he's doing with a little girl," Mama said, banging cupboards and the refrigerator door.

Little girl! Doesn't Mama have eyes to see? I'm growing up.

The woody music of his clarinet wafted down from his room.

Phoebe said as she tilted her chin toward the sound, "He'll never come near me again."

"Good. You're so stupid. He could have done anything to you. It looks like we have to have another talk."

If it was anything like that last talk they'd had . . . . Last month Mama had found a book on white slavery in Phoebe's bedroom. "What's with this book, Phoebe?"

"Laurie and Meg asked me to hold it for them. They don't want their mother to know about it."

Mama had laughed. "Really? That woman goes to church and prays, but her kids have to hide things from her."

"At least when she leaves that apartment she looks like a million dollars," Phoebe said, looking at her mother's housedress.

"It's all on the surface," Mama said in a quiet voice.

She had hurt Mama's feelings. Why had she said that? She picked up the book with its cover of a half-naked woman cowering before a man with a whip. "Pretty *lurid* isn't it?" *Lurid* dropped from her lips like the oleomargarine color packet, orange and oily.

"Don't make fun, Phoebe. Do you know what white slavery is?"

"All the book says is the girls are kidnapped by dope fiends, kept as slaves, and have to have sex with everyone."

The corners of Mama's mouth, turned down in a grimace. "That's cleaning it up a bit. These girls are treated like animals, beaten, drugged into unconsciousness; they get diseases and die young."

"That's horrible!" The book hadn't said that. "Laurie and Meg, they wondered if they could talk to you about some things, Mama."

"The poor kids. Of course they can come to me. Why that lady-like hypocrite. All that church talk and her kids smuggling in books on white slavery."

"They'd have to knock me out before they could have sex with me," Phoebe said, shoving the book aside.

"That book is full of half-truths. You'll change your mind about sex," Mama said.

Phoebe looked out the kitchen window, remembering that day. She was still confused as she watched Mama, on a footstool, stacking cans on the shelves. She didn't want another "talk." She knew all about it. *I saw you and Tony.*

Mama turned to her. "Hand me that sack of flour, Phoebe."

Phoebe handed up the flour. *I saw you and Tony.*

She'd opened the door to her mother's bedroom one night

and there were Tony and her mother, both naked on the bed. Tony had his back to her so she could see his behind and his fat hairy back as he bent over Mama. She closed the door in alarm as Mama moaned and Tony grunted. Had they seen her? So that's what it looked like: two white worms twined around one another, rocking back and forth. She felt nauseated as she tip-toed away. In her room, she fought confusion. Her own mother! How could she? How could Phoebe even look at Tony again—she would see the two of them, naked, making those animal noises. *Tony!*

If this might mean Tony would stay with them, then what? Could she stand the memory of it? She'd rolled around bed, her eyes wide open.

She handed her mother a can of tomatoes. "I'm glad you love Tony, Mama."

"Yeah? Sheila's not so glad."

"Don't listen to her, Mama. She's a jealous kid."

"She can make my life miserable, Phoebe."

"Tony won't let her. Tony will win her over."

"What's so marvelous about Tony? He's no provider, you know."

Phoebe's throat tightened. "Have you had a fight with Tony?"

"Tony's a freeloader. He and his two sons are living high, wide, and handsome off of me."

"Doesn't he pay rent for Mario and Joey?"

"Not enough for what I do," Mama said.

"But what about love? When you love somebody, don't you

do for them?"

"What do you mean? What's love got to do with it?"

"You told me when people love each other, they become intimate. Like Tony and you."

"Tony is a dead end, Phoebe. He can't do anything for me."

"If you feel like that, how can you be intimate with him?"

Her mother suddenly looked drained. She turned away from Phoebe with a shrug.

"Women have physical needs. They need to have a man. You'll understand someday."

Phoebe shook her head. What was there to understand? Mama *had* to love Tony. And that rat Sheila was spoiling everything.

"My poor Phoebe," Phoebe heard Mama say as Phoebe rushed from the kitchen to her bedroom and out the screen door.

A few minutes under the overhang on the rainy balcony was enough. Phoebe slammed the screen door and barged into the big bedroom that Sheila shared with Mama. Her eight-year-old sister sat at the vanity looking at herself in the mirror. She wore Mama's yellow dotted Swiss summer dress from the '20s. She'd tied the wide sash around her middle with some of the fabric caught above her waist. Her face was too small for the large neckline flounce. In her hand was a lipstick. On the vanity: a box of loose powder, an eyebrow pencil, and a tube of mascara. "You better put that back where you found it," Phoebe said.

Sheila's green eyes narrowed. "You gonna tell on me?"

I can blackmail her. "Not if you do me a favor."

Sheila whirled around in her seat. She was also wearing Mama's t-strap dancing pumps, her feet shoved into the toes and the heel part bare. "What do I have to do?"

"I need you to lay off Mama about Tony," Phoebe said.

"I hate him."

"Why?"

"He smells like liquor."

"He's not like that guy with the pregnant wife. He's never got mean and beat anyone up."

Sheila shivered. "I'll never forget that."

"Me neither," Phoebe said. The two of them had sat on the upper landing of the staircase while outside the library, Mama pleaded with Bud Hilby to stop drinking.

"She always refers to us as her 'innocent children' when she wants to throw someone out," Phoebe said. In her mother's voice, she said, "*I have innocent children living here.*"

Sheila giggled. "Yeah."

"It worked," Phoebe said. "She didn't have to hit him with the shovel."

Sheila shivered. "I thought he was going to murder us." Her mouth screwed up as if she was about to cry. "You *like* all of this."

"No I don't."

"Yes, you do. You like vampires and Frankenstein too."

Phoebe said, "I like to be scared when it's safe, and Mama proved she can handle anything."

Sheila had not been comforted by Phoebe's faith in their mother. She'd crowded into Phoebe's bed that scary night, and dreamt of lions.

Now, on the matter of Tony, Phoebe said, "You have to know the difference between people, Sheila. Tony is good and kind."

Sheila painted her lips bright red then took a tissue and blotted it. "You love Mario. That's why you don't want Mama to throw them out."

"You little—okay, he has beautiful white teeth and an Italian smile, so sue me. Can I count on you to at least not say anything negative about them to Mama?"

"Boy, are you crazy."

"Promise me!"

"Well . . . okay," Sheila said, feathering her brows with the pencil. "If you don't tell on me."

"Better get that makeup back to Mama's dresser before she misses it."

"Do I look like Veronica Lake?" Sheila asked, pulling hair over one eye.

"Absolutely," Phoebe said, but Sheila looked more like the frail dancer in the Picasso painting over her bed.

Mr. Green appeared at the top of the stairs as Phoebe left the big bedroom. *Talent!* She gave him a big smile. "Hello, Mr. Green."

Chapter 17 - Lisbeth's Birthday Party

Descending the stone steps, Phoebe pulled her shabby coat close around her and stopped Sheila with her hand. "Charlotte's looking at us."

Phoebe could see that Charlotte's gaze from the passenger side window was directed not only on her and Sheila, but on the unruly ivy that hung over the retaining wall, over the crack in the stairs under their feet where crab grass grew, and up to the paint flakes over the front door of the rooming house. Phoebe took a deep breath and said to Sheila, "C'mon, let's get this over with."

Sheila took shelter behind her as they approached the car, and Charlotte rolled down the window.

"Hello, girls," Charlotte said with her false smile as Phoebe shoved Sheila into the rear. They sat shoulder to shoulder facing the indulgent expression Charlotte seemed to reserve just for children. She turned around to face the girls and tapped her red fingernails on the seat back.

Phoebe pulled her coat down as Charlotte stared at her homemade dress. "Max, we can't take them to Lisbeth's party like this."

Max belched, then turned to smile at them. "What's wrong? They look beautiful."

Charlotte sighed. "Maybe we should stop somewhere and buy them coats."

"Where could we find a store open on Sunday?" Max said.

Charlotte sighed loudly.

Sheila nudged her, and in disgust, Phoebe ground her teeth and scrunched down on the seat with her eyes closed. Phoebe raised her eyelids as she heard Daddy groan softly. He turned to them with a sickly grin.

He said, "They'll take off their coats as soon as we get in the door."

She couldn't look at him. He was knuckling under to her. How Mama would laugh. Why did he allow Charlotte to boss him?

Not long ago he had complained to Phoebe, "Oy. Does she know how to use my money—a new house, antique furniture, a swimming pool, and she even redecorated me." He'd stroked the soft wool of his new suit.

Charlotte continued to stare at the two of them like a mama owl. "Did your mother make your dresses?"

"Uh huh," Phoebe said, staring back, smoothing out her skirt. She tried to think of ways to shame Charlotte like Charlotte was trying to humiliate her. She was sure Charlotte wore a corset. She wheezed a little every so often; the stays pushed her fat up, making bulges over the back of her dresses. Thin dull brown hair barely covered her skull. Every week she emerged from the beauty parlor with curls that flattened in a day. Her skinny legs looked as if they couldn't support her heavy body. She also had a short neck that sank into her shoulders when she sat down. Makeup barely hid her colorless cheeks and heavy brows. Sometimes tiny powder flakes drifted onto her expensive suits. What made her so snobbish, so arrogant? Certainly not her appearance.

Daddy drove with a *morose* (new word) expression. He kept glancing at Phoebe and Sheila in the rear view mirror.

Charlotte's gaze slipped past Sheila's sulky mouth and dark-circled eyes to lock on her. "Did you get Lisbeth a nice gift?"

"Oh yes!" Phoebe said, nodding her head with vigor. She looked down at the present wrapped in old tissue paper ironed flat, and the bow Mama had scrounged from somewhere.

Charlotte asked, "What did you buy her, dear?"

Phoebe crossed her arms and looked out the window. "A book. A mystery."

"Oh," Charlotte said, "that's nice, but, you know, Lisbeth has a library full of classics."

Phoebe's lips stretched painfully in a smile, and said, "She's a very smart girl."

Charlotte's ringed hand fell over the back of the front seat. "She has an I.Q. of 130. Paula doesn't know which college to send her to. A girl with her potential . . . ."

Phoebe swallowed Lisbeth's *potential* like a lump of undigested meat. But then the memory of the frizzy brunette in white flapping shorts, sunglasses, and wedgies of a year-and-a-half ago, reminded her that in the world of thirteen-year-olds, Lisbeth had been an oddity. She smiled at Charlotte, nodding, agreeing, hating herself for it.

Sheila pressed her thigh against Phoebe's and Phoebe pressed back. Sheila was glaring at Charlotte's beauty parlor curls. Phoebe hoped Sheila also noted the hair growing out of a brown mole on the woman's cheek.

"Sheila and I are going to play in a piano recital next week," Phoebe said, in a cheery voice.

"At that ramshackle studio near you?" Charlotte asked.

Phoebe blinked back tears. She stared at her father's neck, waiting. If just once, Daddy would turn to his new wife and say, *Leave the kids alone. Piano lessons from that teacher are fine*, there would rise from Phoebe's heart a love sweet and powerful, but Max continued to drive in silence. If she could only pull his head around and say, "Look, It's me, Phoebe!" But she feared he wouldn't recognize her in front of Charlotte.

Phoebe recalled Charlotte's laughing, self-conscious words of a few weeks ago, "I'm not your wicked stepmother," but Phoebe had not laughed with her.

***

From the dining room, Phoebe heard Aunt Paula, Lisbeth's mother, say in the kitchen, "I make a pink cake every year for Lisbeth."

Aunt Corrine's voice said, "Why did you make a *pink* cake?" Aunt Corrine was Phoebe's new cousin Larry's mother, and more understanding than her sisters, Paula or Charlotte.

"How could I disappoint her?"

Corrine said, "She is growing up, Paula."

This idea appeared to be too repugnant for Paula to admit, and she muttered, "Where's my antacid? My ulcer has flared up. No, no, Karl, Tante Sarah brought her own food. You know she won't eat here. My house isn't kosher enough. Oh-oh, the baked Alaskas are almost ready. Quick! Get the children seated so I can serve."

Charlotte herded Phoebe and Sheila along with several other guests to the table.

Phoebe sat near Larry. His skinny body pulsed with held in laughter while he pushed his thick glasses up the bridge of his nose. "This is too hilarious," he said to Phoebe.

Phoebe nodded. She liked Larry. Although Larry's mouth usually hung open, giving him a dopey look, she found him intelligent. He told her he wanted to be a doctor.

Even though Lisbeth was now a teenager at fourteen, little-girl pink crepe paper and pink balloons decorated the room. All the cousins had been invited, even the toddlers. Larry cracked his knuckles and twisted in his seat. He had asthma. She could hear him breathing.

None of the children knew each other. Phoebe said hi to a girl on her right.

The girl asked, giggling, "Are you Lisbeth's cousin, too?"

"Sort of—by marriage."

The girl said behind her hand, "Her mother invited the five of us because we're in Lisbeth's English class."

182

Phoebe nodded in sympathy with the glum group. "Where is she?"

Then Lisbeth exploded out of the hallway into the dining room, her frizzy hair like a crooked wig, wearing a low-cut crepe dress and balancing on high heels. "Cousin Phoebe! How nice of you to come. Where is Cousin Sheila?"

Phoebe looked around. Where had Sheila gone?

"Remember Bass Lake and all the fun we had at camp?" Then to the group, she said, "Phoebe's my new cousin. We were great chums at camp, you know."

Phoebe felt as if a breeze had snatched up her dress and revealed her panties. The others grinned at her. She tried to ignore them as she pushed her gift forward. "I hope you like it."

Lisbeth waved her hand *a la* Tallulah Bankhead, taking the gift. She dropped it onto another table piled with presents wrapped in pastel paper. She spoke to the guests as if there were a cigarette holder between her fingers. "Thank you all for coming. Mother dear! Every year a pink cake and baked Alaskas, again?"

Somebody snickered.

Lisbeth said, "Marvin DeLong is taking me out for my birthday tonight. He promised to buy me champagne. I told him my mother wouldn't allow it, but he's such a rogue."

Phoebe looked down at her hands. Marvin DeLong did not exist.

The birthday girl gazed with disdain at the pink iced cake with its pink ballerina candles. Phoebe could see Lisbeth's bra in the low cut neckline as she bent over to examine it.

Larry's pale face reddened. The other boys smirked at Lisbeth. They seemed to know they could do whatever they wanted and she wouldn't react. Phoebe felt a swell of pity for her.

It was sort of like the fat girl in the library.

Aunt Paula, Aunt Corrine, and Charlotte could be seen through the partly opened door of the kitchen. Phoebe heard Corrine say, "Paula, you and Karl are too strict with Lisbeth. This place is not a home. It's half-museum and half-hospital. You ignore her because Karl is always sick."

Aunt Paula said, "What do you want from me? Pretend Karl wasn't sprayed with mustard gas during the First World War?"

Corrine said, "But she tells Larry you hit her with a fly swatter when she makes the slightest noise. All you care about is her intellect."

After hearing this, Phoebe sighed. How could she hate Lisbeth now?

The kitchen door swung open as Aunt Paula pushed out a hostess cart of baked Alaskas. Her big masculine face looked worried, but she said with forced cheer, "Here comes the surprise!"

At just that moment the door to the bathroom opened and Sheila appeared in the doorway. She started forward, then stopped as she was about to cross paths with Aunt Paula's cart.

"Come on, come on dear," Aunt Paula said, and pushed forward. "Don't stand there. I can't get by with you there."

Sheila paled, panic in her eyes.

With a huge sigh, Aunt Paula's words put ice in the air.

"Come in or stay out, Sheila dear. You're blocking the way and the baked Alaskas are melting."

They started forward at the same time. Sheila was jerky as if her joints had stiffened, and they collided. Sheila lost her balance and she fell on her face. The baked Alaskas slid off the cart onto Sheila's back, then slipped off onto the floor.

A jumble of voices gave high pitched commands. "Get the mop—there's a sponge on the sink- oh, they're ruined!" Aunt Paula's cat calmly lapped up the puddle.

Phoebe rushed to Sheila's side where she lay as if dead. "Sheila! Sheila are you okay?"

Sheila groaned and put a hand to her mouth.

"Bravo, Sheila, did that pink cake make you sick, too?" Lisbeth said, bending over the little girl. Lisbeth stood up, her arms crossed, smiling at the adults running back and forth. The children at the table sat numbed, with bent heads. A few looked out the windows as if Sheila were not lying in a mess of ice cream and meringue.

Phoebe ignored Lisbeth and guided Sheila to the bathroom as she dripped a path. Tears rolled down Sheila's cheeks as Phoebe peeled her sister's dress off and let water run over it. "What happened to you?" Phoebe asked.

"I feel sick." Sheila leaned over the toilet, coughed and vomited.

Phoebe wiped Sheila's face. "Gee, you are."

Sheila said, "Let's go home."

When Daddy came in, Sheila was sitting on the floor in a corner, in her panties and undershirt, her head down.

"Did you hurt yourself?" he asked.

Phoebe answered. "She's okay but she says she feels sick."

"I want Mama," Sheila said, not looking at Daddy. "Can we go home?"

Daddy spread his hands in a helpless gesture. "If she's sick, I'll take you both home."

Phoebe said, "Thanks."

"It's not fair. You'll miss the party, Phoebe," Daddy said.

Phoebe grimaced. "I'll survive."

Charlotte came in. "What happened, Sheila?"

Sheila gave her a hollow-eyed stare.

Phoebe spoke up. "She's sick. Daddy is taking us home."

Aunt Paula stuck her head in. "It was just an accident, Sheila. Come out now and have some cake."

"She's sick," Daddy said.

"Does she have a fever?" Aunt Paula asked, coming in, but she stopped just inside the door seeing Sheila's huddled shoulders and sullen expression. Paula exchanged a glance with Charlotte and the two women left the room.

"Your dress is still damp, but you'll have to wear it," Phoebe said to Sheila. "Daddy, we'll wait for you outside."

Daddy said, "All right. I'll get the car." And he left the room.

"You stole the show from Lisbeth," Phoebe said, shaking Sheila's dress. "Are you really sick?"

"I vomited, didn't I?" Sheila said, ambiguously, putting on her dress.

Phoebe heard Paula murmuring to Charlotte nearby and put her ear to the door. "I think that child is retarded. After all, she has a crazy mother."

***

Phoebe and Sheila sat quietly in the back seat, listening to radio music as Daddy drove them home. When he stopped the car in front of the rooming house, he waited as if reluctant to say goodbye. He glanced over his shoulder. "Wait a minute. I have the check."

Phoebe accepted the envelope.

He said, "There's something there for you, too. Buy yourselves what you like."

Phoebe said, "Thanks," in that stilted voice she always used since the divorce.

Sheila tugged at her coat, impatient to leave, but Phoebe couldn't take her eyes off the back of his neck. He was hunched over the steering wheel. Wasn't he going to say goodbye? She wanted him to say, *Don't go! You don't know how I've missed you,* but Charlotte had silenced his lips. He didn't know them these days.

An announcer interrupted the music on the radio, and Daddy turned up the sound.

Breaking News: The Struma, a ship headed for Palestine, has been sunk off the coast of Turkey by a Soviet sub. All 769 passengers, Romanian Jews, seventy of them children, were lost. The ship had been delayed by a promise from the Red Cross to take the children if they anchored off shore and waited.

Daddy pounded the steering wheel with his fists. Tears poured out of his eyes. "Why do they hate us so much?"

Phoebe put her hand on his shoulder. "Don't cry, Daddy."

He turned bewildered eyes on her. "They're killing us! The children! Why couldn't they wait? A Soviet sub? What were they doing there? What business is it of theirs? The boat was going to Palestine. They weren't hurting anyone . . . . The world has no use for us." He put his face on his forearm and sobbed on the steering wheel.

Sheila shrank against the rear seat, her cheeks sunken, her fingers in her mouth.

Phoebe leaned toward her father, and stroked his bald place. "Please stop, Daddy. You're scaring Sheila." *How dare he cry? Fathers do not cry.*

He took out a large white handkerchief and blew his nose. When he faced Phoebe again, furious words replaced his tears. "How come I can't have my children? These *furstunkener* divorce laws. I'm still your father! What am I supposed to do?" His face went grey, and his eyes looked wild.

Sheila, next to her, began to tremble.

Daddy, leaning over the back seat, brought their faces close to his so he could kiss them. "My *kinder*. Thank God you're safe."

188

Chapter 18 - Jack Ruchek; Heart Break

The new roomer's dense thicket of black hair almost brushed the ceiling. (Joey and Mario now bunked together in the adjoining screened room.)

Mr. Ruchek inspected the small bedroom with gloomy eyes as he rubbed his blue-black chin stubble. "Meals?"

"No," Mama said, "just linen and room."

He sat his satchel of jiggling perfume samples on the floor; his gaze measured the room. Then he turned to Mama, his eyes boring into her face. She barely came up to the second button of his vest. "I'll take it," he said, slid his fingers into his jacket pocket and put a few bills into her hand.

The atmosphere of the house was heavy with his presence as they went downstairs. After she shut the front door after him, Mama said, "He sure looked at me strangely."

"He gives me the creeps," Phoebe said. "I feel his hypnotic x-ray eyes on me."

Sheila said in a *tremulous* (new word) voice, "I'll be afraid to meet him in the hall."

"Heh, heh, heh," Phoebe said. "His sinister power has taken over our house. He may choke you in your sleep." She came for Sheila with outstretched hands.

"Oh for God's sake, Phoebe—you never laid eyes on him before, and already you have a story made up about him. It's all right, Sheila. He's just another roomer."

"When can we stop having roomers?"

"Do you want me to work in a war plant and leave you alone all day?"

Sheila looked down, her lips pressed tight.

"I think our roomers are interesting," Phoebe said. "I'm writing a novel and I'll make a million dollars and give it all to you, Mama."

Mama's lips turned into a thin smile. "You're a good girl, Phoebe. I could use more money, but don't write a novel, write a movie. They pay more."

"A movie?" Phoebe said. "I didn't think people wrote them. I thought the actors just . . . ."

"My dreamer," Mama said, yanking Phoebe's pigtail. Mama looked out the window, her eyes sad. "I hate Sundays. The hours drag by."

Suddenly, Mama laughed out loud and pulled off her apron. "Let's get out of here and take in a movie." She grabbed a brush and crackled it through her hair. "If we can find enough money, we'll get chili dogs, too. See if you can come up with some change."

Phoebe and Sheila ran up and down, looking for coins in kitchen drawers, ashtrays, the sewing box, and the glove compartment of the car.

"I've got five cents," Sheila said.

Phoebe said, "I have ten cents. That's enough to get me into the movies."

"And I have the rest," Mama said. "We have enough for a chili dog each."

Phoebe's heart rose to the ceiling. *Chili dogs! Wow!* "Hooray!"

She grabbed a sweater and they bounded out of the house, giggling. On the way down the stone steps, Phoebe turned back to admire the solemn face of the old house in the dusk, its second story brow already shading the veranda, and a prickle of fear clutched her throat. The house was now haunted by creepy Mr. Ruchek.

"Well, I'm glad we don't have to go to Union Station for fun today," Mama said. "I only go there because some of those people come from New York. They smell like New Yorkers, talk like New Yorkers, act like New Yorkers." Mama grabbed a tissue from her pocket and blew her nose. "I'll never forget taking you kids to Seventh and Broadway in L.A. the first time. What a hick town."

"Everybody could hear you," Phoebe said. "I was so embarrassed."

Mama grinned. "Well, when you've seen Manhattan—"

Sheila said, "All I remember was a donut and a malted milk."

"You poor kids," Mama said. "L. A. has no pizzazz, no style." She parked the car near the Alvarado Theatre. It was across the street from the Park and its stale pond, where rented electric boats cruised around. "I could cry when I remember New York," she said. "I let your father drag me to California away from everything that meant anything to me, all my friends and relatives. New York is full of excitement. Everywhere you can feel its heart beating. We had fast subways, not rattling trolley cars, good theatre, museums, not the burlesque and taco stands."

"L.A. has a museum," Phoebe said.

"I know," Mama said. "Full of mummies and dinosaur bones."

Phoebe and Sheila burst out laughing. Phoebe said, "What do you expect in a museum?"

"You kids haven't been to the World's Fair," Mama said, getting out of the car. "C'mon, let's see *The Great Waltz* and *The Constant Nymph.* Charles Boyer is supposed to be the big lover in one of them. Personally, I don't like him, but I guess he's a good actor."

Phoebe liked *The Great Waltz,* but Mama sat there eating popcorn and complaining. She especially hated Poldi Vogelhuber, the wife of a *philandering* (new word) composer. Poldi knew her husband was running around on her, but did nothing.

Mama whispered loudly in Phoebe's ear, "Moldy Poldi!"

Sheila giggled, "Moldy Poldi."

"Gey in dreart, go to hell, you limp dishrag," Mama said.

That did it. For the rest of the movie, every time Mama said *Moldy Poldi*, Sheila would scream with laughter. People shushed and poked Mama, but nothing could stop her. She and Sheila laughed so hard they breathed in gulps.

Phoebe watched Poldi thoughtfully. At the end of the movie, the husband came back to Poldi, begging her forgiveness. Why couldn't Mama and Sheila see that Poldi understood you can't force anyone to stay faithful, just as you can't force love. Poldi knew she couldn't fight her husband's nature. She could wait and hope he would recognize her. And he did, finally. Phoebe sensed the husband's independent spirit in Mario, and it made her a little afraid of him. She knew instinctively she must not cling to Mario or show too strongly that she admired him. He had to recognize her on his own. Mama and Sheila kept laughing, and Phoebe stared straight ahead at the screen as if she didn't know them.

A scene in the Charles Boyer movie, *The Constant Nymph*, has the young girl, Joan Fontaine, so glad to see Charles that she leaps on him, kissing him, then cuddles in his lap. It was how Phoebe felt about Tony, how she'd felt as she saw Daddy getting out of Uncle Leonard's car, home from work. How she'd run to him! Then, another scene made her catch her breath. Charles Boyer marries Joan's older sister, and the sister is jealous of Charles' attention to Joan. She scolds Joan about her relationship with Charles, accuses Joan of taking Charles' love from her. Poor Joan says she can't help loving Charles, but she's decided never to see him again. The sister mocks her, calls her a child. How could she know anything about love? Joan's face looks wistful. "I know everything about it," she says, sadly, and the sister takes it wrong, accuses her of having an affair with

Charles.

Phoebe suddenly bowed her head. All those hikes with Daddy where he poured out his grief to her about Mama, shamed her. Even listening to him seemed like a traitorous act. Then, later, she'd watch Mama's set face, trying to see her through Daddy's eyes as a malicious woman, but all she saw was her mother's pale blue gaze, her red rough hands, her shabby housedresses, and all she could feel was pity. It was as if Mama and Daddy each had hold of one of her arms and they were tearing her in two. What did they want? Was Mama jealous of Daddy's love for her, Phoebe? What love? *Where are you, Daddy?* With Charlotte. Charlotte had taken him over. *Will I never really see you as you used to be?* A searing yearning welled up in her chest. She had to get out of there. "I have to go to the bathroom," she said, jumping out of her seat.

"Take Sheila," Mama said.

Phoebe shook her head and hurried up the aisle.

The lobby couch was soft red plush. She sat, grabbed her knees and bent to shield her head with her arms. Then she sat back up because she felt someone was watching her. She looked into the gilt mirror on the wall. A man, standing in the shadows of a velvet drape near the rest room, stared at her. She stared back in the mirror. He smiled a little and walked toward her. Phoebe's heart began thudding. The way he put his feet out like a duck with his hands in his pockets reminded her of Daddy. Even his baldness was the same. *I wished for you and you came.*

He stood over her and took her hand. He wasn't Daddy.

Why had she ever looked at him? Uneasily, she said, "I'm going to the Lady's Room." She rose, but he blocked the way

His eyes, muted with a shy, tender expression, made her feel like stroking his cheek. She caught her hand rising and pulled it back.

He whispered, "Are you alone?"

"Let me by, please. Leave me alone. I thought you were someone else." She pushed past into the restroom, and his hand lightly squeezed her arm. His eyes were like Charles Boyer's, dark without a visible iris, kind, yet compelling. She used the toilet and washed her hands, viewing herself in the bathroom mirror. She was flushed. Her eyes had a dreamy quality. Tony called them bedroom eyes. What would she do if he approached her again? Darn it. She couldn't stay in the restroom. She opened the door a crack. It looked empty. She stepped into the lobby. Just as she was going to open the door to the auditorium, a voice at her ear said, "Tell me why you look so sad." And there he was.

She reached for the door handle. He took hold of her wrist, and as if it were the most natural thing, led her into the shadowy cover of the velvet drape.

"You poor child," he said in a soothing voice. "What is the matter?"

Nobody had ever asked her that, not Mama or Daddy. Her lips parted as if to answer him. She felt her eyes brimming, but in the next instant, an inward bell of alarm stiffened her. "Nothing. I have to get back." She turned away, but his hand rested lightly on her shoulder.

"Don't go."

It was a request so faintly uttered that Phoebe partly turned around. In the shadows he was a silhouette.

"That's right. Come here . . . to me."

She was close enough to see his face working strangely, and he kept repeating, "Poor baby, sweet child, beautiful, darling baby." His hands began to run up and down her blouse. Phoebe's breasts picked up under the thin material. She started to breathe in short gasps. *Get out of here,* she told herself, but her body wouldn't obey.

"Nice, nice, you're not afraid, are you?" he said, and drew her hand down to his open zipper. She felt something very warm, soft, but rigid. With horror, Phoebe drew back from the contact.

"I'm sorry, I'm sorry," he whispered in a fever.

Mama's face rose up in her mind. *Sex. It's like you're drunk. You get carried away. You don't know what you're doing.* Shaking, Phoebe ducked from under the drape and ran into the lighted lobby. She looked back. He reached out with both arms, looking distraught, but keeping himself behind the curtain. Then everything scattered in confusion as she ran down the aisle and took her seat beside Mama and Sheila.

"Where have you been? The movie is almost over," Mama said.

On the screen, Charles Boyer was looking down at Joan Fontaine lying on a couch. She lay as if in sleep, but Phoebe knew she was dead. She'd had a bad heart. Phoebe burst into tears as the house lights came on. Phoebe couldn't look at her mother. She'd done everything she shouldn't. She'd let him—oh God she'd *let him!* She'd pitied his pleading eyes so like Daddy's, and the feverish way he tried to reassure her. Why had she ever gone to the restroom?

"Good movie, but I sat too long," Mama said, crumpling a popcorn bag. "It's late. C'mon, Phoebe, it's only a movie."

Phoebe's hands covered her eyes. She trembled and sobbed.

"What's the matter with you? Get up. They're gonna throw us out."

Phoebe sobbed louder.

"It's only a stupid movie. Stop crying. It's all over. Don't make a scene."

"C'mon, Phoebe!" Sheila said.

"She's all right," Mama said. "She's doing the same thing she did when we saw *The Cat and the Canary*."

Sheila grinned. "Remember? She was so scared she was afraid hands would reach out from the curtains and choke her, so she slept with her head at the foot of the bed."

Phoebe barely heard Sheila. The whispery voice of the man kept saying, *Come here, sweet child.* Phoebe let out a moan and turned her back on Mama and Sheila.

People leaving the theatre smiled in sympathy with Mama, who explained, "She's all right. The movie had an effect on her."

Phoebe, crying uncontrollably, forgot where she was. Faces melded into one another. She couldn't hear what they said. A rushing sound filled her ears. Her hand clasped in Mama's, her legs unsteady and trying not to stumble, she allowed Mama and Sheila to lead her up the aisle.

"Let's get our chili dogs," Mama said.

"It's so late," Sheila said.

"We'll find a place open."

Outside the theatre, Phoebe took big breaths of the fresh air, and felt better, but in the snack shop, she couldn't eat her chili dog. A heavy secret slumped her shoulders. She avoided Mama's eyes. Mama would call the police. "I don't know what came over me," Phoebe said.

"I'm never going to the movies with you again," Sheila said.

Mama slapped the table. "If Phoebe wants to be a drip like Moldy Poldi, who are we to stop her?" Red chili crept like lava as she squeezed her chili dog's bun.

Radio static filled Phoebe's ears as she tried to listen to her mother. Both Mama and Sheila looked small as if seen from the wrong end of a telescope.

"Laugh at yourself, Phoebe. Don't take everything so hard."

Phoebe forced a grimace.

"You have to have a sense of humor or you'll be dead," Mama said. "Where are your guts, kid?"

More tears streamed out. Phoebe forced a sound, turned her lips up and began to laugh hysterically.

"She's laughing!" Sheila said, relaxing her anxious little face.

"Sure she's laughing," Mama said, putting her arm around Phoebe's shoulders, but Phoebe shrugged her off.

When they arrived home, Phoebe shivered to see Mr. Ruchek's light was on. Phoebe imagined that his grim face watched them climb the stairs from a window.

Chapter 19 - The Light Bulb Incident

It was on a Sunday evening, after Phoebe and Sheila came home from their visit to Daddy, that the strangest thing happened. Everything was normal at first, Mario sprawled out on the rug, face up, his hands locked over his stomach, listening to loud music. Tony dozed in the armchair, the paper over his face lifting with his breath. Joey played solitaire. Phoebe and Sheila, in their nightgowns, were climbing the stairs to go to bed. Suddenly a loud groan from the kitchen shook the air.

Phoebe heard a *pop!* Then came a crunch. Mama came running out of the kitchen holding a light bulb. "Get up, Tony and help me. I just wrenched my neck trying to screw in this damn bulb."

Phoebe and Sheila stopped and looked at each other. Sheila gave a frightened sob, and her legs disappeared up the steps. In distraction, Phoebe ran fingers through her loosened hair, wanting to follow Sheila, but instead, she crept down. She could feel her mother roiling up. What was bothering her now? Mario switched off the record player, packed up his platters, and Joey gathered his cards. They both followed Sheila.

From the bannister, Phoebe saw Tony pull the paper over him like an afghan. Mama ripped it lengthwise. "Ah-ha! Run away, all of you, disappear, or watch me suffer. That's all you're good for, the whole bunch of you!"

Tony opened one eye, then shut it. "What's the matter, honey?"

Phoebe bit her lip. She'd hoped this wouldn't happen. To Tony, if a woman was too *good* she sometimes became bitchy. What did he mean? Why did that make her bitchy? Her mother was a good woman. She shook her head, bewildered. Tony now cringed before her mother's rigid fingers holding a light bulb. *Do something, Tony.*

"C'mon, sugar, come to Papa. Tell me, what is it?" Tony said.

Mama's eyes narrowed as if she was trying to figure out Tony's intentions, and finding nothing to combat, her fury crumbled into a defeated shrug. She massaged the back of her neck, still holding the light bulb with the other hand, "If I need a light bulb put in, *I* have to climb up, while you all lay around and let me kill myself."

"Aw, baby, is that all?" Tony pulled Mama down on his lap and began to stroke her face, her arms. He tried to extract the light bulb from her hand, but Mama's fingers whitened around it.

Mama was still complaining. "You know, Tony, I'm not a strong woman. I don't ask for anything but consideration. You should teach the boys to help me. Why do I have to change the light bulbs?"

Tony listened with closed eyes. "You know I love you, sugar. Jesus, how I love you."

Phoebe mentally urged him. *No, Tony, no! Promise her you'll teach the boys to help!*

Phoebe stared at Tony's hands going up and down Mama's arm, and then his eyes opened a crack and his eyebrows went up as he saw her on the landing. He crinkled his eyes. "C'mere, Phoebe, c'mere, baby." Phoebe ran over and let Tony put his other arm around her, and it felt good to sit in his lap with her head nestled under his chin. "My girls," Tony said, and kissed them both on the forehead.

Mama leaped off his lap, brandishing the light bulb.

Phoebe jumped, too, but gave a sharp cry. A lock of her hair was caught in his shirt button. They tried to disengage her hair while she felt Mama glaring at them.

"Uh-oh," Tony said, glancing up at Mama's furious face. His fingers shook, and Phoebe's heart beat fast as they worked to untangle her hair.

Mama rocked back on her heels. "Oh boy, oh boy, why do I let you get away with that *schmaltz*? You think all that love-schmove stuff means a goddamned thing to me?"

Finally free, Phoebe jumped away from Tony. Mama was angry with her, and she didn't know why. She felt Mama's gaze on her downcast head.

"Phoebe, Tony's soft talk is like quicksand. Don't get caught in it." She held up the light bulb. "This is a sign of your great love—that you let me break my neck for you and those lunks you call sons." Tears gathered in her eyes. "My life is lugging garbage cans, scrubbing floors, and washing sheets and towels. Look at me, then look at my hands and keep your nicey-nice speeches. I spit on them."

Phoebe looked from Tony to her mother. Could Tony *understand* Mama's eruptions? *She doesn't mean it, Tony! Don't listen to how she talks! Love her anyway!* But Tony's expression had become veiled.

Mama spoke to the ceiling. "I'm a big fat sap, a sucker. You hear that, Phoebe? Your mother is a sucker!" She turned from Tony in a fury.

The steps began to shake and lumbering down the stairs came Mr. Ruchek. Phoebe backed away as his enormous shoulders hung over Mama. He looked down at her with his brooding eyes. Then, leaning over, he removed the light bulb from her fingers and walked heavily into the kitchen.

Phoebe and Mama tiptoed to the kitchen door and watched him crunch over the broken pieces of light bulb and he screwed in the new light bulb. Then, like a silent mastodon, he creaked up the stairs to his room.

Mama shivered and stared after him. "Well, how do you like that?"

"You must have woken him up," Phoebe said.

"He just put the bulb in and I didn't even thank him."

"Thank *him?*"

"It was very nice of him," Mama said, beginning to sweep up pieces of broken bulb. "He's really very nice."

A thread of fear wound around Phoebe's throat. Mama couldn't be serious. Tony's warm eyes were a comfort, but now dread took over. *Was Mr. Ruchek to be the one? Not Tony?*

Chapter 20 - The Crumpetts

After worrying about Tony's standing with Mama, Phoebe felt a weight drop off her shoulders to see Tony appear in the kitchen, cheerily humming *Cherokee*. Alma Mae peeked around the corner of her apartment door. Phoebe had almost forgotten the Crumpetts, they were so quiet, except for the nasty white dog, who growled when anybody went past their place. Alma Mae ducked back into her room.

Tony's eyes crinkled and he said softly to Phoebe, "Poor old soul." Suddenly his eyes looked merry, and he walked right up to their door and knocked. The dog began to growl.

Phoebe watched from the kitchen. She wasn't gonna get bitten by that dog.

The door opened. Alma Mae shyly said, "Yes?"

Tony asked, "Do you like music?"

Alma Mae nodded.

Behind her, Calvin's mechanical voice asked, "Who is it?"

"I'm Elaine's friend, Tony. I play the sax and clarinet. I'm about to give a concert in the living room. You're both welcome."

Alma Mae turned back to Calvin in a muffled request. Calvin's reply was a dull negative, but Alma Mae grabbed a shawl and said, "That would be lovely."

It seemed to Phoebe that Alma Mae had shed her age in a flash. Her cheeks turned pink; her smile erased some wrinkles as she took Tony's arm and cake-walked into the living room.

Tony turned on the record player, and with a big band backup, withdrew his sax from its velvet-lined case. It was a polished and well-cared-for instrument, and when Tony put his lips to the mouthpiece, *Ramblin' Rose* came rolling from its bell.

Phoebe and Alma Mae swayed to the music. Tony put his sax down carefully and held his arms out to Alma Mae. The old lady rose and curtsied, and they danced around the living room. Alma Mae's eyes danced, too, and she was light on her feet. Tony smiled down into her face.

Phoebe applauded as the music ebbed. "You're real good, Alma Mae."

"I knew tap and ballet as well in the old days," Alma Mae replied.

It was then that Phoebe noticed Mama, with a dish towel in her hand, watching them.

"*Ramblin' Rose* is our song," Tony said, going over to Mama, and he kissed her.

Phoebe held her breath. *Don't say anything awful, Mama.* Although Mama's face remained tense, she'd allowed Tony's kiss. That was a good sign. Mama didn't say anything cutting to

Alma Mae, either. Phoebe breathed normally again, grateful for this moment.

***

"I'm worried about the Crumpetts," Mama said, "I haven't seen them for several days."

Phoebe went with Mama to the breakfast room door. A growl issued from behind it.

Mama knocked. "Alma Mae? It's Elaine Feldman. Are you okay?"

There was no answer.

"Calvin? Are you and Alma Mae all right?"

The dog growled again.

"Oh God." Mama put her key in the lock and opened the door.

The dog showed his teeth in a grotesque grin. Beyond him, Alma Mae sat at the breakfast table, with bottle of a Dubonnet in front of her. She turned, swaying in the chair.

"Call off the dog, Alma Mae."

Alma Mae slapped her thigh and the dog trotted to her. She patted its sheep's head. "Where's Calvin?" Mama asked.

Alma Mae burst into tears and pointed to the library which they'd made into their bedroom.

Phoebe and Mama brushed past Alma Mae and her dog and raced into the library. On the bed lay Calvin, his face blue. Elaine put her ear to his chest. "I think he's dead."

"Oh, poor Alma Mae—" Phoebe said.

"Phoebe, go get Tony. He's been to medical school."

Phoebe ran back into the hall and called, "Tony! Tony!"

Tony came running in.

Mama put a shawl around Alma Mae's frail shoulders.

Tony took Calvin's pulse, listened to his chest, pushed the man's eyelids up with his thumbs and examined each of Calvin's pupils with a flashlight. "He's gone. From the look of him, he must have been dead a while. Rigor mortis has set in."

"Oh no—" Phoebe gave Alma Mae a sympathetic glance, then looked at Tony. He seemed to know what he was doing. His face had assumed a dignity she didn't know he possessed.

Tony said, "Poor fella. It's a miracle he lasted as long as he did. The cancer must've come back."

Phoebe noticed a new respect for Tony in her mother's voice. "You think that's what killed him?" She frowned at the half-full wine bottle.

"Could be," Tony said. "Call his physician. He has to pronounce him dead." He turned to Alma Mae. "Dear heart, who is Calvin's doctor?"

Alma Mae looked dazed for a moment, then bent her head and took another sip of the wine.

"Who is Calvin's doctor?" Mama persisted, but Tony stopped Mama with a look. He gently held Alma Mae's hand in his and said, "Calvin is no longer with us, dear. We need to contact his doctor."

Alma Mae nodded, tears running down her cheeks.

Oh, Tony. The old lady loved him, too. She cried soundlessly while Tony put his arm around her. Phoebe had laughed at Alma Mae in her faded dresses and her stockings rolled under the knees with garters, but not when Tony could hear. He always gave her a little bow as if she were royalty, and she'd curtsey in return.

The dog began to growl again. Mama shooed it away and said to Alma Mae, "Don't you know who Calvin's doctor is? Talk to me."

Alma Mae grabbed a chalk board and wrote, *I've lost my voice.*

Calvin had been unable to talk due to his gangbusters operation for throat cancer. And now, suddenly, Alma Mae couldn't speak either. Phoebe had heard of such things. People's hair turning white after a shock and such.

Mama poured Alma Mae a little wine. "Drink this, Alma Mae." The old lady guzzled the wine and hiccoughed. "You must know the doctor's phone number. Write it on the board."

The old lady shuffled to her tiny secretary and brought forth an address book. Her hands shook as she turned the pages. Mama took the number and went to the telephone while Alma Mae tottered into the library and crawled in bed with Calvin's corpse.

"Leave her alone for a while," Tony said to Phoebe. His eyes were wet.

The ambulance came and took Calvin's body away while Alma Mae slept off her Dubonnet.

***

"What am I gonna do with her?" Mama asked the air around her. "She's on Social Security, thank God."

Mama inspected Alma Mae's kitchen. "Nothing but canned vegetables, white flannel bread, and oleo. The only pot she uses is the little sauce pan."

Phoebe and Sheila wrinkled their noses at such little regard for food.

"She needs someone to care for her and that dog. Maybe I can find a person who will take over if I give her cheap rent."

Chapter 21 – Carmel; The Night Birds Sing

From inside the front door, Phoebe gawked at the young blonde girl who was holding a suitcase and a bamboo cage. She said to Mama, "I see you have a room for rent."

Mama said, "I don't think you'd be suitable," and she tried to close the door, but Joey, behind her, said, *"Hubba-hubba,"* and held it open.

Sheila, crowding in front of Mama, just stared.

The girl wore a soft grey suit with a lavender paisley scarf. Her makeup was flawless, and she had just the right shade of lipstick. A short fluffy haircut. She looked like the girl-next-door movie star, Teresa Wright.

"You wouldn't want this room," Mama said. "I'm renting it half-price—"

"But that's wonderful," the girl said.

"No, you don't understand. The reason I'm lowering the rent is because it includes the care of an elderly woman."

At that moment, Alma Mae appeared in a faded ivory and

mauve wrapper, her hair under a net, and holding a movie magazine. She took one look at the girl and threw her arms around her.

The girl gave a startled cry and dropped her suitcase.

Joey picked up her luggage and brought it into the living room.

Sheila led the girl into the house while Mama just watched, her arms crossed.

Alma Mae touched the girl's hair, ran her finger down the luxurious suit jacket and stroked the paisley scarf, her eyes misty. The girl's gaze fixed on the old lady's hands as they fingered her suit. She gave Mama a look of triumph as Alma Mae turned to Mama, nodding.

"Oh for—" Mama said.

The girl sat down on her suitcase and hung a cigarette from her lips.

Joey jumped up to light it for her. She took a long breath and smiled at Joey. Joey just about danced around the room.

"I've been on the bus for fourteen hours. My name is Carmel Lacy." She indicated the bamboo cage. "This is Rainbow, my chameleon. He brings me luck." She lifted the cloth around the cage revealing a green lizard looking at them.

"No pets," Mama said. "I'm sorry. I can't rent to you."

"But Rainbow is clean and quiet. He lives in his cage."

"What does he eat?" Sheila asked.

"Insects. He just loves cockroaches."

"Oh good. We have them," Sheila said.

"No we don't!" Mama said. "Sheila, are you running a fever?

You don't normally take to strangers." Mama looked closer at Carmel sitting on the suitcase, and said, "You're not an actress, are you?"

"Well, yes. This is Hollywood, isn't it? I was supposed to meet my agent, but we didn't connect, and when I got off the streetcar, I saw your sign."

Sheila's green eyes pleaded with Mama. "Everybody but you likes Carmel." She gazed at each of their faces to see who agreed with her, but Phoebe looked away. Alma Mae tugged at Mama's sweater, and Joey made big innocent eyes.

Mama sighed. "Well, I guess it depends on whether Miss Lacy wants to take care of Alma Mae."

Alma Mae scribbled on her chalk board. *I will take care of Carmel.*

Carmel's eyes moistened, and she said, "What a sweet person you are."

Alma Mae clapped her hands.

"She's really self-sufficient except she can't or won't speak since her husband died," Mama said. "Poor thing. She used to be a screen extra years ago."

Carmel nodded, giving Alma Mae a daughterly smile. "Thank you, I think I'd like to see the room, uh Mrs. . . . ."

"Feldman." With everybody else following, Mama marched into Alma Mae's apartment.

Mama had put twin beds in the library for the Crumpetts. Carmel placed Rainbow's cage on an end table, and her suitcase on the empty bed. "How much?"

Mama said, "Let's say we go week by week and see how it

goes. Half price. Five dollars."

Sheila skipped around, Alma Mae gave a joyful cry, and Joey grinned.

Mama told Joey to get lost, but Sheila stayed to help Carmel unpack. Phoebe ran around to the living room. She peeked through a slit in the curtains that hung on the French doors. Sheila was oohing and ah-ing as Carmel hung her clothes.

"Here, this is for you, Sheila," Carmel said, and handed Sheila a silver charm bracelet.

"Oh—it's darling," Sheila said, sliding it on. "It's all little animals. A giraffe, a horse, a lizard—"

"That's Rainbow. That's why I bought it." She held a satin nightgown up to her chin and removed Rainbow, putting him on her shoulder.

"He turned pink! What's that color?"

"Watermelon."

Sheila pointed to a small case. "What's that?"

"My makeup kit." Carmel clicked open the latch.

"Look-it! Lipsticks and eye shadow colors, and mascara—"

Phoebe shook her head. Sheila was going crazy. She'd never seen her so excited or with more color in her cheeks. Carmel indicated Sheila should sit at the vanity table. "I'll do your face."

With a look of ecstasy, Sheila sat down, then shyly looked in the mirror at Carmel. Sheila jutted her chin out while Carmel applied a cream. "This is concealer to hide the shadows under your eyes."

Sheila said, "I've been sick. Bronchitis. That's why Mama builds me up with milk shakes."

"A little green here on the eyelids will make your eyes stand out."

When Carmel was finished, Sheila admired herself in the mirror. "I'm beautiful . . . ."

Phoebe thought, *two of a kind*. Wasn't it just like Sheila to grab onto the beautiful actress and keep her all to herself?

"I have to go to sleep now, Sheila," Carmel said. "I can't have bags under my eyes tomorrow. I have an audition. Tell me to *break a leg*. That's show business talk for good luck!"

Sheila giggled. "Break a leg!"

"Goodnight, Sheila."

"Goodnight, Carmel."

Phoebe gave a surprised cry as Mama pushed her away from the French doors. "What do you think you're doing?"

"Nothing." Both sides of Mama's nose whitened, and it looked narrow and bony. She was still fuming over being forced to rent to Carmel by majority opinion. "You don't like her. Why? 'Cause she's an actress?"

"I don't like theatre people. They're all phonies."

"Gee, give her a chance. She's just off the bus from who-knows-where. She looks like Teresa Wright."

"No. She looks like someone else."

"Who?"

"My spoiled sister, Myrna."

***

Birds chirping in the middle of the night awakened Phoebe. She stood in the doorway of Mama's bedroom. Sheila lay sound asleep on her bed, but Mama jumped out of hers, grabbing the window sill with both hands, and shouted, "God damn birds. Shut up already! Don't you know it's night?"

Sheila rolled over and sat up, rubbing her eyes.

"See, you woke Sheila up!" Mama said, and dropped like a lump onto her bed.

Phoebe said, "They woke me too."

"I was already up with my eyes closed. I keep thinking about Carmel," Sheila said, and she popped out of bed and into Mama's. Phoebe crawled in after her, and they cuddled.

"The gang's all here," Mama said, squeezing herself between the girls. "You don't hear those birds in the daytime. Just at night in the *forschtunkena* upside down Hollywood."

"Don't the birds sing in the dark in New York?" Sheila asked.

"No, honey. New York is the middle of the world. Birds stay in Central Park where they belong, and only sing in the daytime."

Phoebe said, "I just remember a little bit about New York. It was so hot at night we slept on quilts on the fire escape."

Mama said, "Yeah. Those were the days. What else do you remember?"

"In winter, I wore a snowsuit. We built a fort and threw snowballs. I rode on the subway to Macy's. We bought dresses. Times Square with all the lights."

"The lights of New York are like no other lights in the world. I would stand there, *kvelling,* marveling at it. The subway's very fast. Here everything is so far away from everything else. You have to have a car."

"We have the movies here," Phoebe said.

Mama made a *derogatory* (new word) sound. "For whatever that's worth."

Sheila said, "Carmel has an audition. She's gonna be a star."

Mama laughed. "Sure. Sure. Dreamers with high hopes. Isn't my house full of lost souls whose dreams didn't come true? Take Tony. Wanted to be a bandleader like The Blue Baron, but got sidetracked into the medical profession, and then when he went back to his music, got bogged down somehow in a bad marriage. And Mr. Ruchek, selling perfume when he's really very smart. He's asked to use my car to go to Las Vegas. He has a deal cooking, he says. Should I lend him my car?"

"No Mama!" Both girls cried.

"The man wants to better himself," Mama said in a defensive tone.

"So does Carmel," Sheila said.

"Movie people! Not a real person in the whole bunch of them."

Sheila reached sideways above Mama's head on the pillow and gave Phoebe's hair a tug, and Phoebe tugged hers back. Mama was wrong. Her sister had suddenly come to life. It was nice to have talks in the middle of the night with Mama and Sheila. Phoebe yawned and wriggled her toes in luxury, stretching her arms up. "Mama, tell us again about Aunt Myrna. You said she was like Carmel."

Mama took a long breath, Sheila's head nestled under her chin. "Well there are parts of my life that weren't very nice. I was always fighting with my sisters, and Mama would hit us with the frying pan to stop it."

Phoebe and Sheila giggled.

"Myrna was the oldest and the prettiest. She looked like you, Phoebe. I was jealous of her. She had boyfriends and new clothes. I had to wear her outgrown dresses. You have no idea how good it was to buy my own with my first paycheck."

"You bought the black dress with the fringe!" Sheila said.

"Yes, Pushkela. It was the twenties."

Phoebe asked, "What happened to Aunt Myrna?"

"She caught the eye of a big shot, Sam Borkin, who managed a Chevrolet Agency. They got married around the same time I married your father. We kind of got pregnant together. We became better friends. But then the babies were born, Benjy and Phoebe. She went into a slump. She didn't want to take care of her own little boy. She hardly looked at him, and he was so beautiful. I used to take care of you, Phoebe and Benjy. Myrna wanted to party and travel like she was still a flapper . . . but the flapper couldn't flap anymore. She got more and more depressed. I was afraid for Benjy, but I should have been afraid for Myrna." Mama's voice shook. "Myrna drank oxalic acid, cleaning fluid. She killed herself."

Phoebe shuddered.

Sheila lay silent.

Phoebe asked, "What happened to Benjy?"

Mama's voice caught in a sob. "I wanted to take him, but Sam had relatives who took my Benjy."

Sheila yawned. "Carmel isn't like Aunt Myrna."

"Oh no? She doesn't live in reality, either. I'd hate to be around when she wakes up."

In the *ensuing* (new word) silence, the birds tweeted again.

"God damn birds. Got day mixed up with night. Hollywood! We need to get to sleep. Have good dreams, girls."

Phoebe said, "I love you, Mama."

"Me too," Sheila said.

"Sweethearts."

Chapter 22 - Rainbow

Phoebe munched Corn Flakes mixed with Wheaties and read cereal boxes as Carmel entered the kitchen. The actress wore a black suit, a small white hat with a veil, white gloves and a black purse. Her hair was tucked behind her ears, and she wore glasses.

"You look business-like," Mama said, taking a sip of morning coffee and shaking open the L.A. Times.

"I'm auditioning for a secretary part."

"Perfect," Phoebe said.

Mama gave her a *withering* (new word) look.

"For a second, Miss Lacy, I thought you were taking a serious position." Mama poured another cup of coffee. "Want a cup? I don't imagine you've eaten anything."

"Thanks. Alma Mae doesn't drink coffee."

Mama looked over the top of her newspaper. "Where you from?"

"A little town in Nebraska."

"Got any family?"

Carmel rolled the coffee cup between her palms. "Mother. Father. Brother." She rose suddenly. "May I use your phone to call my agent?"

Mama said, "The same one who didn't show last night? Sure. Help yourself."

Carmel went into the living room and phoned while Mama did the dishes.

"God, you're so sarcastic," Phoebe said. "You'll hurt her feelings."

"Really? If she has any."

"Didn't you warn Sheila and me about becoming involved with the roomers?"

"Shut your fresh mouth!"

Phoebe folded her lips in and clamped down on them with her teeth. *What a hypocrite.*

Carmel rushed into the room, excited. "The audition is still on. My agent missed the Greyhound and worried about me all night."

Mama indicated Carmel's outfit with a pointed finger. "While you're dressed like that, why don't you try for a real job?"

"This is a costume! You don't understand. I can be a girl-next-door, a school teacher, a nun—"

"Okay. Okay, I get it."

A look of uncertainty slid into Carmel's blue eyes. "Wish me luck?"

Mama glance at her for a second. "Luck. Luck." Mama let the soapy water out of the sink with a sucking sound.

Phoebe said, "Break a leg!"

"Thanks, Phoebe," Carmel said, slipping out the door, as Mama echoed, dully, "Break a leg."

Upstairs, Joey's trumpet squawked, making Phoebe wince.

Mama said, "He wants to be like his brother so Tony bought him an instrument."

The front door opened and closed. "Oh, here's Tony now."

Tony bounded into the kitchen, all smiles. "Who was that lovely creature I met on the steps coming up?"

Mama said, "You, too?"

Sheila appeared just then from the landing with the green eye shadow smeared to her temples.

Mama said, "What's that on your face? Take it off right now."

"I tried, but it won't come off."

"Use cold cream. Get upstairs. Do it now—"

Mama took another sip of coffee and glared after the retreating Sheila. "That new tenant is trouble. I'm too big-hearted."

Phoebe choked on her cereal.

"What? What?" Mama said.

Phoebe shook her head, chewing and laughing.

"Laugh, but you'll see. She'll get herself in trouble."

Tony poured himself a cup of coffee, dumping in sugar and milk. "Ah. What's her name?"

Phoebe said, "Carmel."

Tony sang, "Carmel sweet as candy, sugar baby, tastes like honey, that's Carmel."

Mama said, "You old wolf. She could be your daughter. Anyway, she's just an overnighter."

"I'll say she is," Tony said.

Mama slammed her coffee cup on the table. "I've had

enough of this!"

Sheila appeared, her face pink from scrubbing.

"There's my girl. Here's your egg milk shake. Don't forget your lunch." Mama handed Sheila a paper bag.

Sheila drank the milk shake, took the lunch, and left the kitchen.

"I worry about Sheila," Mama said. "She's so fragile. The doctor says she had a touch of TB."

"Wish I could get her to warm up to me," Tony said. "She never says hello."

Phoebe helped herself to a cup of cocoa. "Sheila's okay. You should do something about Joey. He's teaching Sheila how to swear and play poker."

Tony said, "He's at that awkward age, fourteen."

"His face is full of pimples," Phoebe said.

"I bought him a complexion brush," Mama said.

Joey hit another wrong note, and Tony's face contorted. He yelled upstairs, "Watch your fingering!" Then he shrugged. "I gave him lessons, but he has no musical talent."

"I don't know anything about music, but that sounds awful," Mama said.

Tony took Mama into his arms. "Aw honey, we have to give him time."

Phoebe crossed her arms, sullenly. *For what?* Sometimes, even she became impatient with Tony.

Mama said, "Can't you find something he's good at?"

"You're the best something that ever happened to him or me."

Mama sucked in her cheeks. "This is more than—"

"I go down to the club, and my mind is at ease." Tony rocked her in his arms. "I'm happy you came into my life." Tony began to sing *Ramblin' Rose.*

Phoebe swayed to the song. Tony kissed Mama. Mama patted her hair as she released herself from Tony's embrace.

"You'll be late for school, Phoebe," Mama said with a smile.

Phoebe gave Mama a hug. "I know, but it's nicer here."

Joey barged into the kitchen and snatched his lunch. Phoebe extended her hand and Mama gave her a bag lunch, too. Joey and Phoebe got stuck in the kitchen doorway, but Joey elbowed his way out before her.

"See what I mean?" Phoebe called back into the kitchen.

***

"She's coming!" Phoebe whispered from the window to where Joey, Sheila, and Alma Mae sat on the living room couch, looking glum.

The first thing Carmel said was, "I met a producer today. He liked my audition." Seeing the group on the couch, she said, "What's wrong?"

Sheila began to cry. Alma Mae held her. Joey's hands hung between his knees. Nobody looked at Carmel.

"Oh Carmel!" Phoebe said. "How can we explain?"

"Explain what?" Carmel started for her rooms.

Phoebe got in front of her. "No, don't go in there."

"Let me by, Phoebe. Wait. It's Rainbow, isn't it. What's happened to him?"

Joey moaned, Sheila sobbed and Carmel sank into Tony's chair.

"I'm sorry," Joey whined.

"It was an accident," Sheila said. She jabbed Joey in the ribs. "C'mon, you chicken. Scared to tell?" Sheila waited for a few seconds, and then giving Joey a scornful look, said, "Joey's always teasing someone. This afternoon he got this dumb idea to put Rainbow down Alma Mae's blouse."

"Is Rainbow lost?"

Sheila moved over to Carmel, taking her in her arms. "No, Carmel."

Carmel's fearful gaze searched Sheila's eyes. "Then what? Where is he?"

Joey slunk out of the living room. Sheila spoke to his disappearing back. "He thought he was so smart! Alma Mae looked like a wild woman—"

Alma Mae began to cry, snuffling into a handkerchief.

Phoebe said, "She leaped like she was on hot coals. And he was laughing. And then she picked up a hairbrush and started hitting herself on the chest where Rainbow was zipping up and down inside her blouse. Before we could stop her, we saw blood."

Sheila said, "Rainbow just stopped moving."

Carmel and Sheila hugged each other, both crying.

Phoebe brought out a shoebox and handed it to Carmel.

Carmel's hands shook as she opened it, then slammed it shut. With closed eyes, she said, "I just knew it. It was too good to be true. Rainbow was my luck. And now my luck is dead."

Chapter 23 - Night Act

A few days later, Phoebe stood in her doorway while Carmel and Sheila picked from a display of clothes that draped across Carmel's bed. "Sheila, I'm going out with a producer. He's taking me to the ballet. Help me decide what to wear. It has to be simple, rich, but understated, as if I had money, but not a show-off."

Phoebe bit her lips. Why didn't Carmel ask her? *They're two girlfriends, like Laurie and me.* Phoebe thought a minute. *Okay. Sheila can have Carmel.*

Sheila said, "Try this one." She handed Carmel a white, Grecian style dress. "It's that jersey material, but slicker. If you get a coffee stain on it, you just throw it away 'cause since you're so rich you have tons of dresses."

"Mm," Carmel said, "but it only covers one shoulder. I'd have to wear a strapless bra, and I hate them. Do my boobs droop?"

"Turn sideways." Sheila's eyes narrowed. "Uh-oh."

"No good? What about this light blue chiffon?"

"It looks like a ballet costume."

"Ya think? I guess it makes me look naïve. Tonight, I'm a woman, not a girl." She slid her arm under a black silk sheath. "What about this?"

"You'd look like Bette Davis."

Carmel grinned. "Yes. Bette Davis in *Now, Voyager*. Old money. Boston. Perfect. Thanks, Sheila."

***

A chauffeur stood at the door and said to Elaine, "I'm here for Miss Lacy."

Sheila, Joey, Alma Mae, and Phoebe gazed at the top of the stairs. In her black sheath, with pearl earrings and necklace, white gloves up to her elbows, clutching a black sequined purse, and her hair shining golden, Carmel descended like a princess.

Sheila sniffed the air. "She's wearing White Shoulders."

Mama whispered, "I know. The whole bottle."

"No, Mom. Just a dab behind the ears and in the hollows of her elbows," Phoebe whispered.

"Oh, pardon me," Mama said, closing the front door after Carmel.

Sheila ran to the window. "Oh, it's so exciting!"

"Where's she going?" Joey asked.

"I'm not supposed to tell," Sheila said.

Mama said, "Why not?"

"It's bad luck."

"Has she got you covering for her?" Mama asked.

Sheila turned from the window. "No. Her luck's dead. She needs all the luck she can get." With a green flash of her eyes, Sheila looked like a cornered cat. "You can torture me, but—"

"Oh Sheila, don't be so dramatic. I don't care where she's going or with whom. It's you and your involvement. She told you not to confide in me, didn't she?" Mama said.

Sheila's forehead developed lines. Her chin lowered to her chest.

Carmel confided in Sheila! What did Carmel have to hide?

"Hoo-hoo. What a face you're making. Let's go to bed," Mama said.

Sheila blinked as if she were about to cry but walked past Mama without a tear.

***

Phoebe tried to go to sleep, yet tossed and turned until she fell into a light doze. Then, waking up still in darkness, she crawled out of bed and crept through her bedroom door. She bumped into Sheila on the landing.

Sheila put her finger to her lips. "Shh." Phoebe followed Sheila as they tip-toed downstairs into Alma Mae's apartment. The old lady snored gently. An empty wine glass on the end table told them she would not rouse easily. Even the dog slept as they approached Carmel's bed. Carmel wore a pink satin eye shade. "Carmel, Carmel?" Sheila said, shaking her gently.

". . . Go 'way."

226

"I can't stand the suspense. Please wake up."

Carmel pulled off the eye shade. "Sheila? What time is it?"

"I don't know. The middle of the night. I couldn't sleep."

"I have to be up early. I have another audition." She plucked a half-smoked cigarette from the ash tray and lit it, leaning on one elbow. "Phoebe too?" She blew smoke from the side of her mouth. "Gee—"

"How was the ballet?" Sheila asked.

"Um. I need to sleep."

"You can't. You promised to tell me."

Carmel sat up and sucked on the cigarette, her arms around her knees. "Okay, sweetie. It was beautiful. *Swan Lake.* How do they dance on their toes that way?"

"What was the producer like?" Phoebe asked.

Carmel exhaled aloud. "Him? Kind of pudgy. Loves starlets, he said. Loves to show them off before they get famous. He said he was showcasing me."

"Does that mean you'll be famous?" asked Sheila.

"If they give me a chance to act. I'm very good."

"Do something!" Sheila said.

"Now?"

"Please?"

Carmel tousled Sheila's hair. "Okay." She got out of bed and turned her back to them. When she turned around, she was a different person. Her eyes raged. Her lips curled. She huddled over someone, talking to him or her.

"I told you I married you for something. It turned out it was only for this. This wasn't what I wanted, but it was something. I never thought about it much but if I had, I'd have known that you would die before I would. But I couldn't have known that you would get heart trouble so early and so bad. I'm lucky, Horace. I've always been lucky I'll be lucky again."

"We just saw that movie," Phoebe said. "*The Little Foxes—*isn't that where Bette Davis doesn't get him his heart pills and he dies?"

"Good for you, Phoebe."

Sheila looked from Carmel to Phoebe, her little face tense.

Don't worry, I'm not stealing Carmel. "Aren't you too young for that part?" Phoebe asked.

"I'm an actress. Fooled you, huh?"

Sheila nodded. Phoebe made no comment.

There was a knock on the door. "What's going on in there?" Mama called. The door opened and Mama's face peered in. "Sheila? Phoebe? What are you doing? It's three A.M. Miss Lacy, my Sheila is a very impressionable child."

Sheila said, "Carmel's a really good actress."

"Go back to bed, both of you."

"Don't be mad at Carmel. I woke her up," Sheila said.

Mama said, "Uh huh. The night birds woke me up and what do I find?"

Carmel's eyes glinted. "Yes, Mrs. Feldman, what do you find?"

Mama's finger wagged in front of Carmel's face. "Just watch your step, Miss Lacy. C'mon, kids."

Chapter 24 - The Artistic Code

Phoebe suppressed a giggle at Sheila's angry blush as Joey laid down his cards and smirked. "I got three kings and two deuces. All you got is a pair o' queens, two threes and a jack. Strip."

Sheila said, "You cheater!"

She threw her cards at Joey and jumped off the piano bench.

Tony bent over the upstairs banister, his sax in his hand. "Elaine, keep them quiet. I can't practice." Tony had been visiting them a lot lately. He always stayed in the boys' room.

Mama's head ducked out of the kitchen. "Joey, she's only a child."

Phoebe put the palm of her hand over her mouth to keep from laughing out loud. This was too good. Mama had missed the "strip" part.

Joey said, "God, Elaine, she's a spoiled brat."

Sheila screamed, "I won't take my clothes off!"

Mama barged out of the kitchen. "You playin' strip poker with a little girl? Tony? Tony! Get down here."

Tony rumbled down the stairs. "What's the matter with you, Joey? Have some sense."

Joey said, "Stop picking on me. She's just scared I'll see her cherry pits."

Mama grabbed Joey by his ear. "That's the limit! If he won't discipline you, I will."

Right then, Carmel walked like a model into the living room in a clingy lavender dress and what looked like real nylons. She slid past Mama and Joey to the front door. She withdrew a pair of long white gloves and began to crinkle one up, then drew it over her fingers and her knuckles. She gave Tony an intense look, and started on the other glove. Tony was hypnotized.

Mama dropped Joey. Joey's eyes bulged.

"Wow!" Tony said. "Gettin' hot in here. Where ya goin', doll face?"

Sheila said, "She has an audition."

"For what?" Mama said.

Carmel gave Mama a Mona Lisa smile as she slipped out the door.

Tony called after her. "Who do you know, Carmel, sweetheart? Gotta know somebody in this town."

"She's wonderful," Sheila said.

Mama shook her head. "Well, she certainly can hold an audience. I give her that."

Sheila threw her arms around Mama's neck. "She's beautiful and talented, a real actress."

***

Uh-oh, Phoebe thought as Sheila headed toward Alma Mae's apartment. Mama gazed after her. Sheila knocked on the door. It opened. In a hopeful voice, Sheila asked Alma Mae if Carmel was home. Mama gave a big sigh as they heard Sheila's steps dragging back. She appeared in the kitchen, a bewildered look on her face. "Where is Carmel this time? She was gone all last weekend. I miss her."

Phoebe glanced at Sheila. *Poor kid.*

Mama said, "I don't know. And none of your business, Miss Nosy." She put a piece of honey cake in front of Sheila. "Eat."

Sheila nibbled on the cake, her head down, her shoulders drooping.

Mama snorted in exasperation. "I told you not to get involved with the tenants. Remember that prize fighter and his family?"

"They were awful," Sheila said, scowling.

"Scum of the earth. And they were recommended by friends."

Phoebe let out a laugh. She remembered Schloimy, the little brat. And how his father had tried to scare her and Sheila.

Joey slunk into the kitchen holding a note. He said to Sheila, "Get lost, squirt." He stared into Mama's eyes.

Mama said, "Sheila, do your homework in the bedroom."

Sheila gave Joey a dirty look, picked up her books, and left the kitchen.

Mama grabbed the note and read it. "Fighting in the showers? Then ditching gym?"

Phoebe kept her eyes on her book, hoping they wouldn't notice her, and listened.

"Why do we have to take showers?" Joey asked.

"What's wrong with a shower?"

He eyed Elaine apprehensively, then sighed. "Don't ask."

"Joey, you can't skip gym. You won't graduate."

"That's all you care about."

"This note is for your father."

"Yeah. They sent notes before."

Mama sank into a kitchen chair, holding the note. "What has he done about it?"

Joey gave a humorless grin. "Nothin'."

"I see." Mama started to get up, but Joey said, "Don't tell him."

"He's your father. He should know."

Joey snatched the note back from Mama. "Don't you tell him. I'll—I'll run away."

Mama took Joey's hands. "What is it, honey?"

Why does she care so much about Joey? She never asks me what's wrong. It's so unfair. A sound like the ocean filled her ears.

Joey pulled his hands away. "Just forget it, Elaine."

"Why are you fighting?"

He banged his head on the wall a few times. "Just sign Pop's name and give me an excuse why I can't take gym. Say I have a bad heart, or something."

Mama stroked Joey's hair. "I'm not doing anything until I talk to your father."

232

Tony's footsteps sounded in the hall.

"Jesus, here he comes. I'm gone," Joey said, and he ran upstairs with the note.

Mama threw up her arms, shook her head, and then bent to baste the brisket in the oven.

Savory aromas of garlic and browned beef wafted out into the kitchen. Tony crept up to her, kissed the back of her neck, and said, "If you only knew how beautiful you look doing that."

Mama whirled around, the baster dripping. "I never know when you'll show up. I don't understand a musician's life. You sleep half the day." She pointed to a chair with the baster. "Sit down. I have something to discuss with you. About Joey."

Tony took a seat near Phoebe, kissing her cheek, and smiled. "Has he been teaching Sheila bad words again?"

Because Tony was near her, Phoebe felt daring enough to chuckle. Anyway, Mama was too distracted by now to send her away. She viewed Mama through half-closed eyes as Mama said, "No. A note came from school. He's been fighting in the shower room at gym. Joey says you ignored earlier notes."

"Oh that. Boys fight. Teaches him to be a man, defend himself."

No, Tony. There's something really wrong with Joey. Everybody can see it but you.

"Is that all you have to say?" Mama pressed her fingers into her forehead as if she had a headache.

"Sweetheart, what can I do? I tried to talk to him. He clammed up."

Phoebe kept her eyes on her homework. Her feeling for

Tony wavered a little. He seemed helpless.

"And you let it go?" Mama said.

Tony turned his palms up. "Maybe you can get him to talk."

Mama slammed the note on the table. "He wants me to sign this note and tell them he has a bad heart and can't take gym."

Tony looked surprised. "Son-of-a-gun."

Mama said, "I assume from your stunned answer that you won't do anything."

"Now don't make a big thing of this, Elaine."

"It is a big thing. You're his father. Did you know he also got rejected from band?"

Tony's head drooped. "He shouldn't have tried."

"Why . . .?"

"Because lessons don't help. He won't ever be anything but second rate."

Phoebe gasped. What a mean thing to say! She examined Tony's expression. It was the same one he wore when he and Mario discussed music, serious, hard, and *uncompromising* (new word). Phoebe moved away a few inches.

Mama slapped the pot holder onto the table. "I suppose you told him that."

Tony sighed. "Lousy players can get famous. Harry James puffs his cheeks full of air."

Mama said, "I get it now. Even if he makes it, he'll be a failure in your eyes."

Phoebe stole a glance at Tony. His lips barely moved. "That's right."

His own son! Just because Joey had no musical talent didn't

mean he couldn't do something else. But what? She had no idea. She felt appalled at first, and then began thinking about it. Tony couldn't love him the way he loved Mario. He was proud of Mario's talent the way Mama was sometimes proud of hers. She reminded herself that Mama gave Sheila more love than she showed her, but Sheila needed it. She was always sick. Wasn't Mama always referring to Phoebe as her right hand man? Nobody could call Joey that. Couldn't Tony see Joey wasn't healthy in his thinking? Who could love him at all? In spite of Joey's nastiness, Mama wasted her time on the idiot when love for his son should come from Tony.

Phoebe had to admit Tony seemed to enjoy pretty women and take pity on old ladies like Alma Mae. Phoebe loved him for giving Alma Mae what she needed. It was puzzling then that he should not try to help Joey, who needed him badly. Tony excluded Joey from the passionate love of music he and Mario shared. It was cruel, but she was discovering artists were uncompromising, and she felt in some way she belonged to that group, and she understood. But as a father to Joey he was disappointing.

The thought of Tony made her feel warm and precious. Tony had kissed her cheek! He called her beautiful. He listened to her about camp. She was not invisible to him. So what if his love was a waltz, not a symphony? It made her day brighter. She needed him, too.

Two extra morning stars
in the glass eyes
of a lost doll.

- Lowku by Clair H. Horner

Chapter 25 - Arabella Suffers; Joey's Plight

Exciting news from the radio put Joey's problems out of Phoebe's mind.

"November 1, 1943. A major operation began today to capture Bougainville, an island in the Solomons, spearheaded by Lt. General Vandegrift's First Marine Corps."

Phoebe bent over her homework, conjugating the Spanish verb, *ir*, Mama began to sing, *Happy Days Are Here Again*, as she pressed Phoebe's blouse. The rhythmic swoop of the iron brought a sizzle of steam from the sprinkled garment. All Phoebe worried about was how to talk in Spanish as well as she could read it. Her teacher had met her at her post as a Girl Safety one morning and asked, *"Donde va?"* and Phoebe hadn't been able to answer.

She glanced guiltily at Mama ironing her blouse. She and Laurie were on the committee to decorate the gym for the Sadie

Hawkins dance, and she hadn't gotten to the ironing. The Girls Safety had been Laurie's idea and that meant Phoebe had to be at school early to guard a gate.

Mama took the iron off the blouse for a moment to stare at Carmel, who'd just come in on her way to her room.

Carmel asked, "Did I get any mail?"

The look Mama gave Carmel!

"Did I get any mail?" Carmel asked again, breezing past Mama and out of the kitchen.

"No." Mama took a breath and said to Carmel's retreating back, "You were gone last weekend, too." She bore down on the iron.

Carmel stopped, turned around. "That's right."

"What do you do on weekends?" Mama looked up, still pressing on the iron.

Carmel said, "I pay the rent, Elaine. Stop harassing me." Carmel turned to Alma Mae, who held the door open for her. "At least *you* don't nag me, Alma Mae."

With a fearful glance toward Mama, Alma Mae admitted Carmel to their rooms.

Phoebe tried to return to the irregular verb, *ir,* but just then she inhaled a sharp burnt smell.

"Dammit!" Mama said, lifting the iron, and with it came Phoebe's blouse, a brown imprint stuck to it. Mama peeled the blouse from the iron, and threw it on a pile of rags. "You should be doing your own ironing by now."

"That's my favorite blouse!"

Mama said from the ironing board, "Then why am *I* ironing

it?"

Phoebe retrieved the blouse and held it to her face. "I guess it's ruined."

"Guess so," Mama said, yanking a sprinkled pillow case from the basket.

Phoebe hadn't told her mother that she was now a Girls' Safety and was decorating the gym. She couldn't tell Mama. What if Mama demanded she give up these activities so she could iron her own clothes?

They both looked up as they heard the front door slam. Through the open kitchen door, they saw Joey and Tony. Joey's feet pounded up the stairs.

Phoebe and Mama ran into the living room.

Mama took one look at Tony's sad expression and said, "Uh oh. What's the story?"

"He's taking it hard," said Tony. "The Junior Orchestra rejected him."

Sheila arrived from school, panting. "What's wrong?"

Mama said, "Go do your homework. I have to talk to Tony."

Sheila pouted. "I never get to be in on anything."

"Sheila!"

"Okay, okay," Sheila said, dragging upstairs.

Phoebe followed Mama and Tony into the kitchen, congratulating herself on being invisible. She'd just discovered the word *irony*. She sat on a stool against the wall, supposedly engrossed in her Spanish homework.

"Well, we tried," said Tony taking a seat at the table.

"Oh, try again," Mama said.

Tony said, "I knew lessons wouldn't work."

"You didn't give it much time."

"Yeah, well, some things were never meant to be."

Mama wiped the table down. "I don't believe that. Hard work—"

"—makes a drudge," Tony said.

"Let me talk to him." Mama called through the door to the stairs, "Joey!"

Phoebe pushed her homework paper aside and using a piece of scrap paper began to take notes, writing, *My Life with Mother's Boarders* at the top.

"Excuse me from this, please," Tony said, and he left the room.

"Hi!" Mama said to Joey who carried his trumpet.

"What do *you* want?" Joey asked.

"Nothing."

"Huh?"

"Do I have to want something? Come, sit down." Mama took the trumpet from him and put it on a chair. "So, how are the lessons going?"

"Oh hell. Is this gonna be . . .."

Mama put a piece of apple-cinnamon coffee cake on a plate and shoved it toward him.

He grinned and began to eat.

"Are they fun?" she asked.

"What?"

"The lessons."

"Are you cracked?" Joey wiped his lips with the back of his

hand. "Fun? Music is serious business."

Mama washed the plate. "Yeah, I know. Artists and all that."

Joey said, "When we were in The Home, Mario taught himself to play clarinet and sax."

"Why did your mother send you there?"

Joey contemplated while he scratched at a pimple on his cheek. "What did she care? She had a new guy. He didn't want Mario or me. And then, after a few years, Pop showed up and he bailed us out of that jail." With a furtive look behind him, he said, "I know Pop is disappointed."

"You don't think you can measure up to Mario."

Joey began to search his pockets. "Oh shit. I need a coffin nail. You got one?"

Mama dumped a cigarette out of a pack. "You shouldn't smoke. It's not good for you."

He lit up, and took a long draw. "I been smokin' for two years."

With her elbows on the table and her chin squared, Mama forced Joey to look her in the eyes. "What's eatin' you, kid?"

"Everyone thinks I'm nuts."

"I don't."

"Pardon me, but you don't count."

Mama grimaced.

"Hey, Elaine, get this. I dream I'm jumping on coconuts and they crack and all this goo comes out. Then it becomes a head. I can't stop it. While I'm jumping, it feels so good I don't wanna stop."

"That doesn't mean you're crazy. Fourteen is a hard time for kids."

"What do you want, Elaine?"

"What would you enjoy doing?"

"He grinned. "I'd like to screw Carmel.""

Mama sighed.

Joey finally saw Phoebe sitting on the stool and gave her a dirty look. Phoebe jumped up so he wouldn't kick her as he rushed past. "Outta my way, Pheeb." Joey hurried upstairs with his trumpet.

Sheila ran into the kitchen. "Mama, what's up with Joey?"

"The poor kid."

"You feel sorry for him?"

"His mother didn't love him, Sheila."

"No wonder. He's nuts."

Mama hugged Sheila and stroked her hair.

Phoebe felt a little ping of jealousy, then shrugged it off.

Mama said to Sheila, "He's just hurting. What a shame. He has nobody."

"Well, I hate him. I wish you'd throw him out."

Mama held Sheila at arm's length and looked at her carefully. "Whew! What started this?"

"All you think about is him and Tony."

"Tony and his mother botched his whole upbringing."

"You don't feel sorry for Carmel," Sheila said.

Mama said, "That one! Where is her big leap to stardom?"

"Doesn't she pay her rent? She gets jobs. Her big break will come soon," said Sheila.

"What kind of jobs? She creeps in here at four in the

morning or doesn't come home for whole weekends."

"Just wait. You'll see." With a sullen look, Sheila said, "I don't want to live with roomers. I wanna live in a regular house like we used to."

"There's a war on, honey. People need a place to live since they stopped building houses and started building airplanes and ships and tanks. I'm being patriotic. And I get to stay home all day and take care of you."

Sheila touched her mother's face, then she cuddled her doll. "C'mon, Arabella."

"Wait, Sheila. Come back here," Mama said.

Sheila turned.

Mama put her arms around Sheila's narrow shoulders. "You still have blue shadows under your eyes. Oh honey!"

"Please don't marry Tony and please let's move?"

"As soon as I can, all right, Sheila? The war is going our way for a change. I just heard on the news we're gonna take an island in the Solomons, Bougainville. Isn't that great? And Japan will surrender and we can sell this house and move. I promise, sweetheart."

Sheila's eyes squeezed shut. "Oh Mama!"

***

Phoebe had figured out what to say to her Spanish teacher should she meet her in the hall again—*Voy a la sala de escuela*—but she'd not encountered the teacher again.

One day, Tony, and Joey after him, clumped into the living room. Phoebe heard Tony say, "Get upstairs. And don't come down until I tell you to."

Sheila sat on the stairs, rocking her doll, Arabella. She was getting over another cold, with a flannel compress around her neck. She jumped up, the red satin bed doll to her chest, as Joey flew past her, his head down.

Phoebe joined Sheila and Arabella. "He's in trouble again." Phoebe pulled a small notebook from her pocket with a stub pencil.

Sheila nodded.

They listened to the scene below them between Mama and Tony.

"What happened?" asked Mama, turning off the vacuum cleaner.

Tony paced back and forth on the living room rug. He looked at Mama like a puppy caught peeing on the furniture. "He's been expelled."

Phoebe and Sheila gasped and stared at each other. They edged down the stairs a little so they could see as well as hear.

"Expelled? Why?"

"I don't know what to do. What should I do?" Tony asked, sinking into his favorite chair.

Mama sat opposite. "Start from the beginning." She took another look at Tony's face, went to the low boy, and poured him a glass of wine.

Tony took a sip from the wine glass and began to cry. "It's that woman I married. The kid was nothing to her, but I never had this trouble with Mario."

Mama said, "I'm getting frustrated. You hold Mario's

achievements up to Joey. The boy's jealous. Worse than that, Joey thinks he has nothing to offer. And the sad part is he worships Mario."

Tony said, "The *world* will worship Mario. I'm afraid Joey will end up in jail."

"God dammit! What the hell happened?"

"He got into a fight and broke a kid's jaw. He bit another kid on the leg."

Elaine asked, "What made him so mad?"

Tony emptied the wine glass. "I should've gotten him out of gym."

"All these fights take place in the shower room. Why?" Elaine asked.

"They gang up on Joey there. If the gym teacher hadn't pulled them apart—"

"How long will he be expelled?"

"I don't know," Tony said. "I can't afford private tutors. Should I send him back to The Home?"

Behind Phoebe and Sheila, Joey crept up to the bars of the landing rail and pressed his face against them. When his father said *The Home,* Phoebe heard Joey groan. She and Sheila turned. They saw his knuckles turn white on the railing, his eyes bulging.

Phoebe nudged Sheila. They both had heard horror stories about orphanages. Even Joey didn't deserve that, but to her surprise, Phoebe saw Sheila creep up to Joey, with Arabella in her arms. Sheila whispered in his ear, "Kids at school can be awful mean. Tony doesn't know what else to do."

Joey said in a hoarse whisper, "Shut your trap! What do you know, little Miss Prissy!"

Sheila recoiled from Joey, and snapped, "I bet she's gonna throw you out. Go back to hell where you came from!" Her lips trembled as she scooted back to Phoebe.

"Oh yeah?" Joey went after her and grabbed Arabella. He ran down the stairs into the living room with Sheila screaming after him, "No! No! Put her down! Arabella!"

Phoebe froze.

Tony and Mama sprang to their feet.

Sheila began to hammer Joey with blows. "Give me Arabella!"

With a snarl, he gave the doll's right arm a wrench, and he threw it across the room onto the couch. He grabbed the left arm like a chicken wing, and twisted it off. He ripped Arabella's legs from her body, with their black patent shoes, and chucked them into the open fireplace with Sheila yelling, "I'll kill you! I'll kill you!"

Tony wrung his hands.

Mama's face set and muscles in her cheeks jumped.

"Do something!" Phoebe said, running into the living room as Joey clawed Arabella's stomach, elbowing Sheila out of the way.

Sheila leaped up to grab what was left of Arabella as Joey showered handfuls of kapok onto the rug. She dropped to her knees, scooping the doll's stuffing into her arms, sobbing, "Arabella! Arabella!"

Tony said, "God dammit! Drop that doll."

Joey threw what was left of Arabella's body at his father and looked around in a frenzy.

Phoebe knelt alongside Sheila, helping her. "Oh Sheila!" Phoebe glared at Joey, who looked like one of the slack-jawed wild-eyed movie monsters who'd scared her so, but she wasn't scared now. She was burning hot mad. "You—you—murderer!"

Mama said, "Stop it, Phoebe." In a calm, quiet voice, she said, "Joey . . . Joey . . . it's Elaine. Remember me?"

"Uuh! Uuh!" Joey said, as if in a daze. He sank onto the couch, and began to rock, his hands dropped between his knees.

"Oh! Oh!" Sheila said, rising with Arabella's stuffing in her trembling arms.

Tony said, "I'll replace the doll."

"Thanks. Hear that, Sheila?" Mama said. She glanced at Joey, then Tony. "I can't do this alone. You have to help, Tony."

Phoebe put her arm around Sheila as they went up the stairs. Sheila's green eyes, clouded with *incomprehension* (new word), appealed to Phoebe. Then she gave a shuddering sigh and nestled against her sister. "Arabella's gone."

"Didn't you hear Tony? He's getting you a new Arabella."

Sheila pulled away from Phoebe. "I don't want a new Arabella!" Ragged sobs burst again from Sheila's throat. Then her head bent over the mess of kapok and she stumbled to the master bedroom.

After Sheila slammed the door, Phoebe crept downstairs. Joey was still on the couch, but now he'd curled up like a baby on his side, facing the back. He lay so still he could've been dead. Phoebe watched for a time to see if he was breathing. She'd seen

246

a dead person once, when Alma Mae's husband Calvin Crumpett had died. He'd turned blue. Joey was not blue. She would add *crazy person* to the list of characters for *My Life with Mother's Boarders*. Her novel was growing thick.

Tony and Mama were back in the kitchen. Phoebe couldn't help but hear.

"I want to help, but I don't know how," Tony said.

"Has he always been this difficult?"

"No. He was a cheerful baby. At eight months, he had surgery. He was prancing around the crib in the hospital. Didn't know anything had happened."

"What kind of surgery did he have?"

"His testicles hadn't descended, so the surgeon tried to bring them down."

Phoebe put her fist to her mouth to keep from giggling. *Testicles* (new word). She could just see Mama's eyes narrow as she said next, "Was the surgery a success?"

"Well, no. He was such an active little guy. He pulled the stitches out."

"So he still has undescended testicles?"

"Yeah, I guess. Look, Elaine, I was facing a nasty divorce. I had to pay that surgeon in any case. It was a bad time for me."

A moment of silence, then Mama said in a soft voice, "That's why he doesn't like to take showers with the other boys." Her mother's voice grew hard. "He's got nothing down there!"

Phoebe imagined her mother's expression, her lips pressed against her teeth. "You let him grow up that way?"

"The surgeon said they might come down by themselves.

Don't look at me like that, Elaine."

"Take him to a specialist," she said.

On the other side of the wall, Phoebe mouthed the words, *Take him to a specialist.*

"I think it's too late."

Phoebe peeked into the kitchen. Mama wrung the sink cloth as if it was Tony's neck. "How could you neglect your boy like that? All I hear from you is music, but the real things . . . nothing."

Tony said, "Music is real."

Phoebe ducked back as her mother saw her and angrily motioned for her to disappear.

"Be his father not just by biology. Take him to a specialist!"

"All right, Elaine. If you'll stand by my side. I love you so much, sweetheart."

It was quiet for a moment so Phoebe looked in again. Tony was kissing Mama. She went upstairs, smiling. Tony and Mama were in love once more.

***

Phoebe found Mama and Tony sipping coffee and admiring two plastic marbles in a cellophane bag. Intrigued, she asked, "What's that?"

Mama said, "They're doing miracles with plastic these days. My cousin owns a plastics' factory. They make plastic this and plastic that. It's the coming industry he says."

Phoebe picked up the bag. "What are they for?"

Mama said, "They're for Joey."

Tony looked at the open door of the kitchen. "Quiet. He might hear you."

"What's the big secret?" Phoebe asked. Then she saw Tony redden and she understood. "For his—"

Mama said. "You've been snooping around. I suppose you know about his problem?"

"I know," Phoebe said. "But I didn't spread the news around."

"It's so he'll stop fighting," Tony said. "They call them prostheses. They implant them in the scrotum."

Scrotum! "Ew! That's enough!"

"Phoebe, it's your turn to do the dishes," Mama said, handing her the sink rag.

Phoebe's nose wrinkled, but she took it, poured soap and a little Borax into the sink and watched it billow into suds as the water poured in. She played with the snowy mounds making mountains and valleys before sinking the breakfast dishes into it.

"Does he understand he'll never be a father?" Elaine asked.

"I don't think he cares at this point. He's just scared of the little surgery to place the implants."

Mama said, "I think if we explain this to the school principal, we can get him back in."

"He should go to a new school," Tony said.

"Tony, you're talking like a father."

There was a moment of silence. Phoebe thought, *Maybe they're kissing again.* She turned around. Her mother leaned toward Tony, her eyes dreamy.

"You know how romantic and even sexy that is?" Mama said.

" . . . Uh, no. Is it?"

Mama said, "It is to me."

"Makes you . . .? Not moonlight and roses?" Tony asked.

"That's for young girls or dummies."

"Well, hello sweetheart . . .."

"Get your sax, Tony. Play *Ramblin' Rose.*"

Phoebe pulled a crystal glass from the soapsuds and rinsed it clear. *Oh yes, yes.*

Chapter 26 - Alma Mae's Devotion

In the breakfast room apartment, a policeman cuffed Carmel's slender wrists while Phoebe, Sheila, and Alma Mae watched in horror. Carmel stared straight ahead as large teardrops rolled down her cheeks. Alma Mae wiped Carmel's face with a handkerchief, crying too. Phoebe watched, dry-eyed. Maybe Mama was right about her. Maybe she was right about the whole Hollywood crowd. The piteous expression on Carmel's face looked authentic. But wasn't that the way actors fooled you? Still it couldn't feel good to be handcuffed and hauled away like a criminal.

Carmel, escorted by two cops, went out the front door. "What did I do?" she asked in a plaintive voice.

"Prostitution, and possession of drugs," Phoebe heard the policeman say.

Sheila's mouth dropped open. "Don't tell Mama," she whispered to Phoebe.

"Are you kidding? Of course not," Phoebe whispered back, but no sooner had Mama dropped the heavy shopping bags on the kitchen table then Sheila moaned, "Two policemen arrested Carmel."

Mama kept a bread from rolling off the table. "What? When?"

"About an hour ago," Phoebe said, starting to put away the cans.

"What are they charging her with?"

Alma Mae wrote on her chalk board and held it up in front of Mama's face. *Prostitution and possession of drugs.*

Mama dropped into a kitchen chair, and put a hand over her closed eyes. "I knew it! That baby-faced hypocrite."

"It's a big mistake," Sheila said. "You have to help her—"

Mama said, "Sheila, Tony saw her with Luigi Carparella in the club last week. Why would she hang around with a Mafia guy if her career is going so good, as you keep telling me?"

"Mafia? What's that? If Carmel did something wrong, she didn't know it was wrong, Mama. We have to help her."

Phoebe said, "You could call the police station and ask about her."

Alma Mae nodded vigorously.

"Why should I? I have my own claim against her. She has deluded my young daughter into thinking a person can do anything to get ahead." Mama got up abruptly. "I'm going into that tramp's room and I'm fumigating it."

Mama didn't get far. Alma Mae stood at her door with her arms stretched sideways, her eyes fierce.

Sheila pulled on Mama's dress. "Please, call the police."

Mama's whole body sagged, and she said in a tired voice, "All right . . . ."

They followed Mama to the phone as she dialed. "Hello? This is Elaine Feldman. My tenant, Carmel Lacy, was taken into custody today. No, I'm not family. She hasn't called here. I don't know them. Of course. How much? Oh. Thank you, officer."

Mama hung up. "I've got to give up letting rooms. Maybe I *should* go to work."

Sheila asked, "What about Carmel? How can we get her out?"

Mama said, "Have you got $400 for bail?"

Sheila's eyes teared. "No."

Alma Mae ducked into her apartment, while Mama yelled at Sheila, "I'm packing up that slut. What a fool I was listening to you dreamers."

Phoebe was putting away the last can when Joey wandered into the kitchen, grabbed an apple from the shopping bag, and bit into it.

"What's up?"

"Carmel got arrested," Phoebe said.

Joey let out a long whistle.

"Stop it!" Sheila said, continuing to cry. "Oh, Carmel."

"I forbid you to mention her name," Mama said.

Alma Mae strode past them wearing a 1920's coat with a fur collar, a cloche hat, and carrying a worn out leather purse.

Joey said, "Where's the ol' bag goin'? Oh, her pension came. She must be out of Dubonnet."

Sheila's tears dried on her cheeks. She brightened. "See ya later."

"Where you going?" Mama asked, but Sheila was already headed down the stone steps.

* * *

Tony, Mario and Joey went out to look for Sheila after Mama called the police again.

"What do you mean you can't file a missing person's report?" Mama cried. "That child is loose on the Hollywood streets. Two days? Just enough time for some ax murderer to dispose of her body? Yes . . . we had an argument. We're a family. We fight all the time."

Mama slammed the receiver down. "What good are the police?" She hung onto Phoebe's shoulder, biting her lips. "Where would she go? She's punishing me, that's what. Because I didn't love that drug pushing prostitute."

"She followed Alma Mae out," Phoebe said.

"Why would she do that?"

Tony, Joey, and Mario came in. "No luck," Tony said. "We searched clear to Larchmont in one direction and Alvarado in the other."

"She's sulking somewhere," Mario said. "She'll be home soon." He gave Elaine a hug, then climbed the stairs. Joey shrugged and followed him.

Tony slumped into his chair. "Sheila fell in love with what she thought Carmel was. Poor kid."

The key scraped in the lock. It opened and Carmel, Alma

Mae, and Sheila came in. Elaine rushed to Sheila, "Oh Sheila, baby—where have you been?"

Sheila wiggled out of her mother's embrace. "Bailing out Carmel."

"How? With what money?"

Sheila said, "Alma Mae spent her pension check on Carmel."

Alma Mae beamed, holding her purse in front of her, but Phoebe peered at the starlet, who, without makeup, looked about seventeen. She wore the pedal pushers and tee shirt she'd been arrested in, her hair in a ponytail. It was easy to think her innocent of any crime.

"I'll pay back every penny, Alma Mae," Carmel said.

"You're packed. You'll leave today," Mama said.

"If she goes, I'm going with her," Sheila said.

"You'll stay right here."

Tony said, "Why don't you give Carmel a chance to explain?"

Mama opened her mouth but no sound came out. She looked from one face to another.

Phoebe grinned at her mother's struggle.

Then Mama, in a strangled voice said, "All right. Explain if you can."

Carmel took a breath and her words tumbled out. "They lied to me. The producer, the agent, and the man I met, Carparella. I guess being from Nebraska, they saw me coming. But I'm not a prostitute. I just thought . . . that's the way it is in Hollywood, so I . . . you know . . . I would never have continued. I'm so ashamed now. Please don't kick me out, Elaine. I have nowhere to go. I have no friends here but you. I've been sending money home to Nebraska, but now there won't be any more. I just need a place to stay until I can get a job."

"Say yes, Mama," Sheila said.

"Don't tell me what to say, Sheila." Mama said to Carmel, "You look like a Swedish milkmaid. I'd hoped you were a wholesome girl." Mama crossed her arms, her eyes sparkling with anger. "Prove to me you are fit to be around my daughters. I'll give you one more chance, fool that I am."

Carmel fell into Mama's arms, and said, "Thank you, Mrs. Feldman. Oh thank you—"

With a sweep of her arm, Mama brushed Carmel away. "Get off me!"

Carmel paled, uttered an "Ooo," and fainted on the rug.

Tony rushed to Carmel, lifted her and placed her on the couch. Phoebe overheard him whisper in her ear, "Nice work."

Carmel's lids fluttered. She sat up, then stood, holding onto a chair. "I need to rest. Please excuse me." She stepped through the kitchen door.

Sheila hugged her mother. "Thank you!"

Mama hugged Sheila back, but her eyes were muddled with worry. She said to Alma Mae, "I couldn't lose my daughter, could I?" She stared at the old lady for a second, as if realizing something. "What are you going to pay the rent with?"

Alma Mae gave a slight shrug as if she didn't understand the question, then *scuttled* (new word) to her apartment.

Mama sighed, and said to Phoebe, "It's my own fault. That

whore has me cornered. If she didn't remind me of my sister Myrna—"

"—who killed herself by taking poison," Phoebe said, with a smirk.

"Who you resemble, Phoebe. When I look at you, I see Myrna. I loved her, but I was jealous of her boyfriends, how Sam Borkin adored her, and then, with a beautiful little boy to raise, she goes and does a thing like that. Against life."

From the window, they heard the birds begin to twitter. Outside they were swaying the telephone line.

Mama said, "Shut up, you *cochkas*, you squawkers!"

Chapter 27 - Bobby Carver

A young man in an Air Force uniform stood at the door, hat in hand, letting in the summer heat. "I'm Bobby Carver, Glenda's boyfriend. Is she in?"

Sheila crowded in front of Phoebe. "There's nobody named Glenda here."

Bobby loosened his necktie. "When she called her mom, she gave this address. She said Glenda was in a little trouble."

"Carmel!" Sheila opened the door wide. "Come in."

"Oh yeah. That's her screen name. Sure hot today. Say, I'm feelin' a little . . . . " Bobby stumbled to the couch and fell onto it.

Tony, who was reading the newspaper, sprang up. "He's passing out—Elaine!"

Mama came rushing into the living room. "Who's that?"

"Never mind. Get a wet wash cloth and a glass of water. I think the heat's got him," Tony said. He removed Bobby's tie and unbuttoned his shirt.

"Oh my God!" Mama ran into the kitchen and returned with a glass of water and the wet washcloth. Tony blotted Bobby's neck and face and made him drink the water.

"I'm so sorry," Bobby said. "I was light-headed. Is Glenda—I mean Carmel at home?"

From the kitchen, Carmel, wearing a kimono, came into the living room. She eyed Bobby and crossed her arms. "What are you doing here?"

"I thought you were in trouble, so I—"

"Go away," Carmel said.

His arms reaching out, Bobby said, "Glenda, honey, I've come so far. Please say hello."

Carmel's foot in a pink satin mule stomped on the rug. "How dare you follow me here?"

Phoebe's gaze darted from Carmel to Bobby. This was better than the movies.

Carmel turned her back and stalked out of the living room.

Bobby jumped up and followed her with Phoebe tailing him.

At the door to Carmel's apartment, Bobby met Alma Mae, barring the way.

"She doesn't speak," Phoebe said. "Alma Mae, let him in. He's Carmel's boyfriend."

"Thank you, Ma'am." Bobby went past Alma Mae into the apartment.

The door to the library-bedroom was partly open. Phoebe could see what was going on past Alma Mae.

Bobby flung his jacket on Carmel's bed. "Is this Hollywood game over? Will you come back to Nehawaka and be my wife?"

Carmel said, "I shouldn't have called my mother. I just had a small setback. I guess I panicked. Go home."

"I'm stationed at Edwards Air force Base starting today," he said. "That's the good news Glenda—"

"Carmel! I don't call myself Glenda anymore."

"Okay, then. I missed ya somethin' awful, honey."

Phoebe took mental notes as she crept closer to the library door. Carmel was staring at his muscular arms, tan against the white tee shirt with his dog-tags hanging from his neck.

The starlet's nostrils flared as she took a breath. "You're gonna ruin everything. Please go."

Phoebe was not convinced Carmel meant what she said because she allowed Bobby to grab and kiss her.

She struggled against him weakly, at the same time rubbing her breasts against his undershirt. He kissed her again. This time he lifted her off her feet and gently placed her on the bed.

Alma Mae was on her second glass of Dubonnet. Phoebe thought, *Good.* She had this movie all to herself. The dialogue didn't match the action as Carmel said in a serious voice, "I'm a different person now, Bobby." It was not much of a protest as Bobby pressed her with his body, his pants still on.

"No you're not," he said, kissing her neck.

One leg came out of her kimono and wrapped itself around Bobby's narrow waist. Bobby gave a quiet groan. He unzipped himself and Carmel helped him get rid of the pants. Phoebe could see one peach colored breast revealed as the kimono slipped. She was just as lithe as he was with a smooth belly and a small waist. Her pelvis arched up and then all Phoebe could see was Bobby's buttocks as they went forward and back.

Phoebe felt a flutter of pleasure down low in her abdomen.

Now this was more like it. She'd read about this. She was all tingly and dizzy. Phoebe checked on Alma Mae. Her eyes were closed. Her head rested against the chair back, wheezing.

Carmel made funny little noises with Bobby whispering to her, "It's okay, baby, c'mon, c'mon—" The bedding fell onto the floor, and Bobby threw pillows aside.

Phoebe heard Carmel gasp. What was happening? Was she in pain, or did she like it?

Then Bobby yelped, and he fell, first on Carmel, laughing, then onto his back. Carmel's eyes closed. She put a hand onto Bobby's chest. He took her hand and kissed every finger separately. Carmel sighed.

Phoebe looked away. She shouldn't watch, but she couldn't help it. Her nipples had become stiff and were sending messages to her whole body with incredible aliveness. Thank goodness Alma Mae was still drugged with wine. Back to Carmel.

Her eyes half-open, while Bobby slid off the bed, the starlet regained her command.

She jumped up, tied her kimono and said, "Go home. Please, Bobby?"

With an all-gone feeling Phoebe thought: What happened? Where's the romance? Don't they love each other?

Bobby said, "You kiddin'? I came to take you home. Your mother said there was some trouble."

"I shouldn't have told her," Carmel said.

Bobby stood tall over her. "What kind of trouble you in? Answer my question."

Carmel lit a cigarette and blew the smoke at Bobby. "It's

complicated."

He sat at her vanity, playing with the tubes and jars. "Go on. I have all day."

"You may not understand," she said, speaking slowly as if to a child. "I'm an actress. That's all I want. If I don't get to act, I might as well be dead. You must believe that! And in order to get that chance to act I may have to do things, sometimes, before I get my big break."

"What things?" Bobby asked, accidentally spritzing himself with cologne and making a face.

"Just things."

Bobby spun around on the stool. "Things that are not right? Things against the law?"

"There's been some misunderstanding, but I'm out on bail."

Veins bulged in his neck. "What did you do?"

Carmel reached down to a pile of clothes on the floor and held up an ivory colored silk blouse. "Look how wrinkled this is. I have to iron it."

Phoebe nodded. Nice way to change the subject.

Bobby pulled the garment out of her hands and glared at it. "Where'd you get fancy duds like that? That costs money—"

She pulled the blouse back. "It's just a costume. They gave it to me to wear."

"Who gave it to you?"

"The studio."

"Oh." He tossed the blouse back on the floor and ran his fingers through his hair. "Just tell me. Why were you arrested?"

"I was about to get a screen test. Do you know what that

means?"

Bobby slicked down stray hairs that wouldn't stay put. "I guess I don't."

Carmel touched a lock of his hair that sprung up. "You still have that cowlick."

Bobby grasped her palm and kissed it.

Carmel wasn't gonna face him with the truth. *She's handling him.* Phoebe stifled an impulse to laugh.

They stayed for a moment with Carmel looking down at Bobby and his lips on her palm. Then Carmel said, "Hand me the makeup case over there."

"You have to put that stuff on your face?"

"It's for the camera. Otherwise, I look faded."

Bobby passed her the makeup case. "You look good to me the way nature made you, Glenda."

"Please call me Carmel." She edged him off the stool and sat down, beginning to pat on foundation.

"Sounds like a candy bar. I'm not funnin'. It's too different."

"Bobby, please! You're the only one who doesn't like my name. I'm different now, Bobby. Get used to it."

"Not down deep. Down deep you're the girl I love. Hey, you didn't answer me."

"Just be patient, Bobby." She expertly applied eye shadow and mascara, then lipstick, and turned around. "How do I look?"

Bobby slowly closed his eyes. "Just like a movie star."

Bobby, don't give in! Phoebe clutched the door knob, wanting to shake Carmel. *Rubbing his nose in it.*

She didn't seem to care how uncomfortable Bobby was, and

she went on. "That's right. I'm gonna be up there playing opposite Cary Grant, Jimmy Stewart, and Henry Fonda."

Bobby said in a faint voice, "What about me?"

Carmel said, "Aren't you going overseas? Or back to Nehawaka?"

Phoebe heaved with silent laughter. The looks on their faces! Carmel, haughty, *imperious*—what a great word—and Bobby, with his neck literally stuck out, stupidly stubborn.

"I'm a mechanic," Bobby said. "I fix airplanes. So far, I'm at Edwards. I may never get to the war. And I don't want to go anywhere without you. Now, tell me why you're in trouble with the police."

Carmel scratched the rest of the enamel off one of her fingernails. "I didn't know Classic Companions was that kind of set up. On my first date, I went to the ballet."

"Honey, I may be from Nebraska, but even I know that sounds phony."

"But I had an agent. I thought he was working for me. I trusted him. He said I could meet producers and directors and earn something at the same time."

"And you believed that?"

"I had faith in myself. All I needed was a chance." Carmel turned back to the mirror. "And then my luck died."

Bobby put his fingers in her hair and played with a curl. "Your luck?"

"Rainbow, my chameleon."

"I don't know what you're talkin' about."

"Oh never mind!" She twisted around and said, "You want

me to become a waitress?"

"At least it's honest labor."

Carmel put her head on the vanity. "Acting is also a job. Don't you see? I have talent. I'm gonna make it. I have to be where I can make contacts . . . try to understand."

Bobby said softly, "Did you bring shame on yourself?"

Carmel began to cry. "Why did you come here? To torture me?"

Bobby took her into his arms, crying with her. "Oh no, no! I only want to hear the truth."

Carmel pushed him away with a theatrical gesture. "Go home, Bobby! I'm different now. You won't want me anymore."

"Have you become a dope fiend too?"

Phoebe chuckled to herself. This was just like the melodrama Daddy took her to. *Dope fiend!*

Carmel was ready for him, though. "Bobby Carver, what a thought! That's the big mistake the police made. All I did was carry some packages to Mr. Carparella, one time. See his regular courier was sick. The police found the packages on me."

"Well, Missy, ignorance is no excuse. They're gonna get you for that."

Carmel's big blue eyes fixed on his. "What am I gonna do?"

"I don't know."

"Do you hate me?" Carmel asked.

"No, no, how could I? C'mere." Bobby held her close. "Okay, that's it. You're my girl for better or worse." He slipped a gold ring with a small diamond onto her finger.

Phoebe drew a sharp breath as Carmel looked at the ring.

"It's beautiful, Bobby, but I can't take it now."

"Why not? I'd do anything for you."

"Then you forgive me?"

Bobby nodded. "If you'd been captured by Indians and forced to marry a brave and I'd found you again, I'd take you back."

Carmel's lips quivered with held- in laughter. "It's exactly the same. You've saved me, Bobby. I'll be grateful for the rest of my life." She threw her arms around Bobby's neck. "But are you willing to show your love in one more way?"

"Oh honey, it's so good to have you in my arms again. Just name it and it's yours."

Phoebe pressed her face against the wall and held her breath. *Uh-oh.* But she couldn't stop watching them for long.

The tiny diamond of the gold ring caught the light as Carmel said, "Bobby, I'll be your wife if you help me find my true place in Hollywood."

Phoebe let her breath out.

The starlet's eyes glowed. Either she had convinced herself, or she had no shame.

"How's that gonna work? You'll be with me at the base."

Carmel brought Bobby's hand to the small of her back and made him pull her close as she snuggled up. She ran her finger over his ear. "Well, we can get married here, and if you buy me a car, I can go to Los Angeles when I'm called for auditions, and be home with you the rest of the time."

Bobby took her finger off his ear. "How often would you be gone?"

"I don't know. It would vary. Maybe I could be home on the weekends."

Bobby snorted, put his hands in his pockets and paced in a circle. "That's not even half the time!"

Carmel twisted the ring on her finger. "You want me to be your wife? I will be yours 'til death do us part."

"But this Hollywood thing—"

"We'll be rich, and I'll be famous. You want me to be happy, don't you?"

With her blue eyes eagerly searching Bobby's, and her lips pouted ready to kiss, Carmel rubbed her breasts against his will. He gave a long sigh.

At that point she had the nerve to remind him, "You said to name it and it's yours, didn't you?"

Oh shame, shame!

He set his jaw and crossed his arms. "Guess I did." Then his lips curved up and his hands dropped, and he said, "All right."

"Oh Bobby! You've made me the happiest girl in the world." Carmel fell softly into his arms and kissed him.

Phoebe made a mental note. *Never act like that to anyone you say you love.*

Then Carmel put on her form-fitting suit, the one that clung to her curves and had made Joey so crazy he'd whinnied like a stallion. She brushed her hair, and touched up her makeup. Bobby tucked in his shirt, and put on his uniform jacket. Phoebe woke Alma Mae, and they tiptoed to the living room where Tony drowsed in his chair, Mama was reading, and Sheila played solitaire.

Carmel and Bobby emerged from the apartment through the French doors. Carmel showed the family her finger with the tiny diamond and gold ring. "Look what Bobby's gone and done."

Sheila said, "Is it real?"

"Uh huh."

"Nothin' too good for my girl," Bobby said.

Carmel held up their clasped hands like a prize fighter. "Bobby thinks I should have a real chance. So I'm gonna marry him, live near the air base, but come to Hollywood to pursue my career."

"After we finish with the police, that is," Bobby said. "I'm gettin' Carmel her own car."

Phoebe examined her mother's expression. Elaine's gaze went from Carmel to Bobby and back again as if she couldn't believe it. Then a sneer spread her lips into an insincere smile. "Well, Carmel! You have a good man there."

With a fixed grin, Carmel said, "Thank you for your blessing."

Tony smiled at Carmel, a teasing, twinkling smile that she ignored.

"We're going out to celebrate. We'll be back for Carmel's things," Bobby said.

Alma Mae pitter-patted to her rooms and came back with an old autograph book clasped to her chest, and with reverence, placed it in Carmel's lap.

"You want my signature?" Carmel asked.

Alma Mae nodded.

Carmel turned the pages. "Oh my gosh! These are autographs of all the greats: Charlie Chaplin, Buster Keaton, Lon Chaney, and Lillian Gish! Thank you, Alma Mae, for sharing this. Now I *have* to make it, don't I?" Carmel embraced the old lady and signed the book.

Sheila ran to the door as Carmel and Bobby left. She went to the window and looked out.

Mama sat back in her chair, looking relieved. "Poor boy. That ring is through his nose. I hope he doesn't get her pregnant."

Sheila said, "She's going to have a career, and then, babies."

"Oh yeah? I hope she never has kids," Mama said.

Tony said, "Bobby's in love. He'll stick by her. Let's wish them luck."

"Luck," Sheila said.

"Luck-luck—" Mama said, as Alma Mae pressed the autograph book on her. "What is it, Alma Mae? You want me to read your autograph book?"

Alma Mae turned to a page and Mama read, "'Best of luck to a peppy little gal named Ginger LaTour. With your looks and talent, the world is yours.'" Mama's gaze met Alma Mae's. "Signed, *Charlie*. Charlie Chaplin?"

Alma Mae nodded.

"Wait a minute. Who is this Ginger LaTour?"

Alma Mae pointed to herself and curtsied to the family.

Chapter 28 - "The Turn of the Screw"

Phoebe huddled in bed with a cold. Even though the heater radiated warmth, she shivered, but when she drew the blanket over her, she was too hot. She squirmed, unable to find a comfortable position, unable to breathe through her nose.

The door to her room opened with Mario's knock. He carried a book.

Phoebe shrank beneath the covers. "Hi! Don't get too close. You might catch it." It was awful to look and feel miserable in front of Mario, the one person she wanted to look her best for.

"Sorry you feel bad," he said, offering the book. "Here's something to keep you from being bored."

Phoebe held a tissue over her nose so he wouldn't see her breathing through her mouth. She glanced at the book. *The Turn of the Screw* by an author she didn't know. How embarrassing. Why would he give her that sex book? She wouldn't look at it.

Mario sat down on the end of the bed and grinned. "It's a ghost story, Phoebe. It's pretty good, really."

"A ghost story?" she said, barely whispering.

"Yeah. It's all about these kids and they are being manipulated by the ghosts of two servants to do things that shock their new governess. The way they can't talk about sex is very funny. They use voluptuous language to dance around the subject."

Phoebe mouthed the new words, *manipulated* and *voluptuous*. "I like when you explain things," she said.

Mario patted her arm. "I see you like to read."

"I read *Gone with the Wind* in five days, locked in my room."

"You should read better books," he said.

There was no better novel than that, but suddenly she was ashamed to say it. He knew more than she did. He was sophisticated even though he was just four years older. If she defended *Gone with the Wind* he'd know how ignorant she was. And why did he call a ghost story funny? She was afraid to ask. She stared into his intense brown eyes where a small glint made her feel as if he were humoring her. Her gaze went from his black curls to his strong hands, to his smile that showed perfect white teeth. He had broad cheekbones and his nose was short so he wasn't classically handsome, but it didn't matter. He saw into people and he found something different in books than others. She thought, *I will never know anyone like him.* "Mama has a lot of faith in you," she said behind her veil of tissue.

"Elaine's okay! I admire her. But she's going to cripple Pop."

Phoebe sat up tall, dropping the tissue and exposing her dripping nose. "What do you mean?"

"She's not *for* him. A woman has to be *for* a man. He has a hard enough time battling the world. He shouldn't be pushed and nagged at home."

"But they're getting along real good. Didn't you hear him playing *Ramblin' Rose*?"

Mario shook his head. He sounded exasperated. "That doesn't matter. She really hates men. I don't know what happened to her in the past, but she's full of anger and it's going to crush him."

Her heart broke to hear him talk like that about Mama, but he was right. Phoebe had no idea what kind of man would please Mama. Her mother always found fault. *I can't lose Tony, but I pray Mama loves him. She's got to love him.* Her scalp began to itch, but she forced herself not to scratch.

"Pop's an artist. He's gentle and loving. It should be enough for her."

Phoebe said, "It won't be."

Mario's eyes narrowed, "No, it won't. I'm glad you understand."

Her hand slid along the covers toward Mario's, but something made her stop. She felt he wouldn't like it. All she could finally do was look at Mario's somber beauty and let him find her.

"You're a good kid. You're sweet. Do you know you're going to be beautiful someday, Phoebe?"

His gaze swept over her and into her and she felt so exposed she grabbed the covers and pulled them up to her neck. Her eyes stung and burned. She grabbed another tissue. Her temperature must be 104.

Through the covers he gave her arm a little shake. "Stay sweet."

Phoebe thought, *anything for you.*

"I've been drafted," he said suddenly. "I can't go to Juilliard yet."

"No!" The tissue fluttered to the floor.

"Don't worry. This war is going well for us. The Russians are beating the Germans back into the Carpathian Mountains. It should be over soon." He gave her that enchanting white grin that she had come to call, *The Italian Smile.* Everything would turn out all right for Mario. When he left, indelible traces of him remained in the air.

Chapter 29 - The Big Let Down

Phoebe wrote in her diary:

January 5, 1944

I'm so happy I forgot to write. My cold is gone. Mama and Tony are getting along good. Mario is taking me to the show today to see double horror movies, *The Bride of Frankenstein* and *Dracula.* He has a temporary deferment from the army, something about Juilliard. When he has to leave, he's going to try to get into the army band to avoid carrying a gun and shooting someone. That's another way he's different. He's not gung-ho wanting to kill Germans or Japanese. He hates the war.

I went to Laurie's church on Christmas Eve. It was okay with Mama. Mama's taken me to all kinds of other services. One time we even saw Mary Baker Eddy in person. She asked all those who wanted to donate to stand up and then they played *The Star Spangled Banner,* and everybody had to stand up.

People at Laurie's church are friendly. Nobody tries hard to convert you. It's just fun. There's a big map of Palestine on the wall in the children's department. They honor Judaism as the forerunner of Christianity. But they try to get people to join them and they have missionaries in other countries. Mama says Jews don't look for converts, and it's hard to be a Jew. Jewish people in our family tend to be morose. They complain over this or that injustice, but every time I meet a friendly person with positive ideas, he or she turns out to be Christian.

I hear that clubs in high school are separated into Jewish and Gentile.

Would Laurie go into a club that wouldn't rush me? She's awfully picky who she hangs around with, but there's nobody in the world as darling as Laurie when she's in a good mood. I've never had a friend who could sit on the pot and talk about boys, for instance, while she rolls toilet paper around her hand. We took a shower together and she's hairier than I am. She has to shave her thighs or it shows outside her bathing suit. She said I was lucky and pulled my pussy hair so I pulled hers. We ended up laughing on the bathroom floor. When I'm with Laurie, it's like when I'm with Mario. They're special people. Just being with either of them makes me happy.

Phoebe closed the black and white notebook and tucked it beneath the quilts in the storage seat of her bedroom. She welcomed the day on her balcony with a big breath of air. Sun dappled the bedspread this Saturday morning. On her way downstairs she heard voices coming from the kitchen.

"Maybe you don't want me to see where you work," Mama said.

Through a crack in the almost-closed door, she saw Tony hunched over his coffee cup. His forehead was wrinkled. "Why sugar, who said I don't? Anytime you want, you're welcome."

Mama's mouth worked into a nervous smile. "Then take me tonight. If I'm gonna marry a man, I need to know where he works."

Joy! Phoebe danced into the room. She kissed Mama's cheek and Tony's bald place.

"You're in a good mood," Mama said to Phoebe. Mama examined the backs of her hands. "Just look at me. These red knuckles and rough skin."

Phoebe beamed at both of them. "Rub cold cream in and put gloves on. I'll do the housework today. You need a day off, Mama."

Mama looked so surprised she almost dropped the coffee pot. "You're volunteering to help me?"

"I should do more." Phoebe went to the refrigerator and took out the orange juice. "Would you like some, Tony?" Tony would live with them. She'd be Mario's sister!

"No thanks, honey," Tony said, grinning.

"Well, I would like to take it easy today," Mama said, with a sideways glance at Tony.

Phoebe poured herself a glass of juice and drank it while her mother washed the breakfast dishes and Tony looked into his coffee cup.

Finally, Mama said, "Will you stay home and watch Sheila

tonight, Phoebe? I'm going to Tony's club."

Phoebe said, "Sure!" She began to wipe the dishes, doing a little two step, and taking peeks at Mama and Tony.

Mama pushed a lock of hair back from her eyes. "I'll need a shampoo. Do people dress up? After all, it's like a night club."

With his finger, Tony pushed his fleshy nose to one side and let it fall back again. "Anything you wear is fine."

"That doesn't help, Tony. Is it formal or informal?" Mama wiped her hands on her apron and touched her hair. "I'll put my hair up. If I'm gonna meet people—"

"This is L.A. Anything goes," Tony said, drained his coffee cup, pushed his chair away from the table, and walked out of the kitchen.

Mama waved a dish towel at Tony's retreat. "What do men know," she said, smiling with difficulty. "Well, Phoebe, should I polish my nails?"

"Do your toenails, too!"

"I'm gonna be real dolled-up." Mama's lips were trying to maintain her smile, but it was as if she couldn't believe she could be happy about anything.

A clumping on the stairs brought Joey into the kitchen. Mario entered after him, blinking and yawning.

Mama said, "Phoebe'll get your breakfast." And she left the kitchen.

Phoebe put two coffee cups on the table because that's what they always started with. She poured the hot coffee, filling the kitchen with a rich aroma. They would be her brothers! There would be someone in the living room who cared who she went out with. Tony or Mario would say, *Get Phoebe home before twelve,* in a stern voice. And the guy would know he better obey.

"Three, sunny-side up," Joey said. "Light brown toast."

One of Mario's eyebrows arched as he looked at Phoebe. He took a sip of coffee. "Pop high-tailed it out of here. Said something about the club."

Phoebe shrugged. "What do you want for breakfast?"

"Onion omelet."

Phoebe took the eggs out of the refrigerator and dropped bread into the toaster. She melted margarine in the iron skillet and broke three eggs into the pan for Joey. She put a lid on it and turned the heat down. She could sense questions in the air, but this was her secret. It was delicious.

After breakfast, Mario and Joey went upstairs. Phoebe tidied the kitchen, swept the floor, and then pulled the vacuum into the living room. Oh, first she had to dust. Under the kitchen sink, she found rags and furniture polish, but she couldn't get to it just yet. Her body commanded her to drop the rag on the coffee table and lie down on the couch. She arched her back so she could see only the twin peaks of her breasts. Then, sliding on her back, she twined her legs up the arm of the sofa. Such voluptuous, undefined cravings, such bubbles of rainbow sensations followed one on the other that she moaned. Then words formed. She became the protagonist and the antagonist.

"Ah, my dear you are exquisite tonight."

"Thank you so much, Reginald."

Phoebe squirmed on the couch, turning on her side, running her hands over her breasts and down her body.

"You know you enchant me. Marry me, you witch."

Phoebe cackled, "Heh-heh-heh. You'd better mean it. Don't cross me. I have powers, strange powers . . .."

"Darling, don't be a goose. I said, 'Marry me'."

Phoebe rose from the couch and looked at herself in the wall mirror. "I know your kind, Reginald."

"Come here, you vixen!"

Phoebe bent backwards over Tony's chair, fighting off Reginald, twisting and grunting. "How dare you?" she said in a husky voice. With her hands she pushed her trembling body up. She undid her braids and let her hair fall over her eyes and through the tawny strands she viewed herself again.

"Your words say no, but your body betrays you."

"You want me? I'm not sure I want you for a husband." *Husband*. What a boring word." With a giggle, Phoebe grabbed the dust cloth, and flipped it all over the living room furniture, ending with a powder puff on the mirror dulling her image. She wrote "marriage" in the mirror dust.

"Is that the way you clean?" Mama said from the bottom stair.

Phoebe smeared the word away. How long had Mama been watching? Her mother had washed her hair and it lay in flat little bobby-pinned whirls under a net.

"I'll do better. I'm just too happy for housework," Phoebe said.

Mama smoothed Phoebe's unkempt hair. "You're such a funny kid. Sometimes I wonder who you really take after."

"I don't care. I'm myself."

"I heard voices. Who was here?"

"I was just playing a game."

"You were leaping around, talking with a fake English accent."

It sounded so *tawdry* from Mama's lips.

"If you're making up things again about real people, just calm down. Life is not like a story."

Phoebe glared at her mother's retreating back. "Just take the fun out of it, why don't you?" she grumbled to herself. With nervous peeks toward Mama's exit, she squirted some furniture polish on the coffee table and began to rub. She vacuumed until the living room smelled pleasantly of ozone. The Seth-Thomas clock began to peal the hour, and she realized she had to eat lunch soon and be ready for going to the movies with Mario.

***

It was like a date. They walked to the Belmont, a big, ornate theater that had been built in the twenties. Mario didn't hold her hand, but looked straight ahead in a comfortable silence. She didn't care. She was planning a wedding. Would Mama wear a white dress? Probably not. She'd told Phoebe white was for the first time. Would they have a canopy? Would Tony stamp on the glass? She giggled. Mario would look handsome in a tux. Would Tony's band entertain afterwards? She would have to learn how to talk to Mario. Suddenly she blurted out, "Why do you play things I never heard of? I can never hum your songs."

Mario turned to her, amused. "Well, take a tune everybody knows, like *Danny Boy*. You already know that. Why should I play it that way again? I play the song in a new way."

She liked *Danny Boy* the old way and didn't mind hearing it again, but if she mentioned it, he'd ridicule her. Could she ever speak her own mind around him? She had to, so she took a breath and said, "I don't get it. It sounds nervous. You keep on going when you should have stopped. And it all sounds the same."

Then he said, "That's because you don't listen enough."

"Really?" Had she not listened well? He'd boggled her brain again.

Mario sighed. "Phoebe, you're a square, a hopeless square."

He'd hung a sign around her neck. Every time he looked at her, he would read, "hopeless square." He hadn't even laughed this time. Her eyes filled with tears, and she looked away. It was a good thing they'd arrived at the Belmont where she could simmer in the dark.

He bought them both big bags of popcorn and they sat in the balcony. The downstairs was full of kids, screeching and throwing wads of chewed gum at one another, but when the show started, a hush came over the audience. Phoebe already had goose bumps as the house lights dimmed. The first thing was a Donald Duck cartoon, which she enjoyed because he was like Uncle Leonard, who was always having fits.

Mario laughed, too, stuffing popcorn in his mouth.

Then, *The Bride of Frankenstein!* Phoebe watched, thoughtfully. The poor monster. He was alone in a strange world and needed a mate, but because she rejected him, he destroyed them both.

Mario was laughing.

"What's so funny?" she whispered.

He laughed harder.

She gave up.

Dracula, she had to admit, was melodramatic. Bela Lugosi stared holes through the screen. She heard a little kid crying downstairs. She'd never understood vampires. She'd tasted blood when she'd cut her lip. It was salty and smelled like raw meat. She guessed it was the lure of living forever that made vampires a public favorite. And all that stuff about being protected by the cross left her out. Mario enjoyed it immensely, laughing and laughing.

After the movie, they walked home and he took her hand, swinging it. This took away some of the sting from "hopeless square."

"Would you give up food, and drink blood instead to live forever?" Phoebe asked.

He chuckled. "Maybe. If there was something I couldn't do in a lifetime."

"The thought of never eating ice cream again would stop me."

"You haven't found your passion yet," he said.

His music is his passion, she thought. "Did you have any lessons?"

"A couple, but mostly I taught myself."

"Yeah, I know. And now you're playing piano better than I can."

"That old lady teacher of yours is way behind the times,"

Mario said.

She took her hand out of his. He was so stuck up! What could she say that would get his attention, interest him, and make him want to talk to her? She glanced furtively at him and said, "Did you hear Mama's marrying Tony?"

Mario stopped dead. "You're kidding—"

"What's so strange about it? They need each other." Under the intensity of his full attention, she began to tremble. She said, "I'm going to be your sister."

His back hunched and Mario examined his shoes for a few seconds. When he looked at her, his eyes reminded her of Dracula's, hypnotic, obsessed. "Are you sure?"

"I heard them talking in the kitchen. Mama said, 'If I'm going to marry a man—'"

"Nothing against you, Phoebe, but it's impossible."

"Why?"

Mario began to take long strides and she almost had to run to keep up with him.

"Never mind. Let's go home."

Phoebe scurried to keep up. "What do you mean? Mario, talk to me!"

Mario took the stone steps two-at-a-time, burst into the living room, and scattered Joey and Sheila's pinochle game on the stairs.

"Damn him," Joey said, holding up a king and a queen. "I almost had four marriages."

Chapter 30 - Tony's Club; Exodus

Joey followed in Mario's wake, picking up Pinochle cards scattered on the stairs. "What's with him?"

Sheila asked, "Is Mario mad?"

Phoebe said, "Yes."

"Did you make him mad?"

Phoebe shivered. "I didn't think he would get so upset."

They heard a loud knock on Mama's bedroom door. Then it banged opened.

Phoebe scrambled up the stairs and saw through the open bedroom door that Mama had undone her bobby pins and was painting her nails. Mario stood there.

"Hello, Mario," Mama said.

He paced in front of her, his shoulders tensed.

A blob of red enamel was about to fall off the brush as she held it mid-air. "What's wrong?"

Mario said, "You and Pop—are you gonna get married?"

Mama put her palm on the table and painted another nail

red. "I don't think that's any of your affair, Mario."

He gripped the back of an empty chair, facing her, and said in earnest, "I like you too much to let Pop do it."

Mama bent over her fingernails. "What do you mean?"

"He hasn't told you the truth. He can't marry you."

"And why not?" Mama raised her head, eyes wary.

"He's already promised to marry someone else."

Mama jumped up, knocking the bottle of nail polish over. A red stream oozed across the table. She let it flow, watching as if hypnotized.

Mario said, "I'm sorry, Elaine, but I thought you should be informed."

Phoebe's hands shook. No. Mario must be mistaken.

Mama touched her fingers to her mouth. Her lips trembled, but she raised herself up tall. "Well, now you've told me. Are you proud of yourself?"

"I'm sorry," he said again and turned to leave.

Mama laughed harshly. "Me too." Then her voice became softer. "How do you know?"

Mario hesitated at the door, his forehead wrinkled. "He knew Rosalind before he met you. If it was up to me, it wouldn't be this way." He went back to Mama, took her two hands in his and kissed them.

Mama pulled her hands away. "Then you should have kept your mouth shut."

"You wouldn't want that!"

"Why not? I thought he loved me. Now he's made me a sucker." She sank into her chair. "How can I . . . How can I . . . "

Mario strode out the door.

Phoebe cowered near her bedroom and heard Mama call after Mario.

"You men! You do what you want with a woman. Use her, wipe your feet on her, and then you come back with all your charm in your hands saying, 'Here I am again, sugar.'" There was silence for a moment, then Mama came closer, standing at the bedroom door. "It's not enough. It's not enough for me, Mario. You know why I take any money from Max? So he'll never forget me. He has to write my name on the check every month for as long as the kids are minors."

Mario stopped at the head of the stairs then he turned around and walked back. "I'm sorry for you," he said to Mama in a soft voice.

Mama said, "Don't be. I'm strong. I'm strong enough to get rid of parasites that are eating my food and living under my roof."

Mario said, "I just had to tell you the truth."

"I like the truth too."

Mario backed away from Mama and went to his room.

Why had Mario kissed Mama's hands? He'd said he liked her. Maybe he loved her? Sometimes Phoebe had wondered about the way Mario looked at Mama, his eyes taking her in from top to toe. They danced together like Fred Astaire and Ginger Rogers, seeming to know how the other would move. Then why did he make her so miserable? Did he want Rosalind to be his mother? After a few moments, Phoebe heard him playing *Danny Boy* on his sax as if he'd lost Danny himself.

Phoebe crept into Mama's bedroom. She lay on the bed, crying and kneading the pillow. Phoebe said, "Oh Mama, I'm so sorry."

Mama said, "Go away."

"No, I won't." Phoebe sat on the bed, massaging her mother's shoulders as she had the day Daddy left.

Mama suddenly stopped crying. She sat up and clutched Phoebe's sweater with her red fingernails. "Sweetheart, this is a lesson. Don't trust their promises," she said into Phoebe's ear.

The nail polish spill was drying on the table top. "If you give yourself to love, you're a fool." Mama sighed, and let Phoebe go as she sank back onto the bed.

"Ask Tony," Phoebe said. "Maybe Mario has it wrong."

Mama got out of bed and began to pace. Her eyes turned to slits. "I just want to see how long it will be before he spills the beans. I want to hear every lying word coming out of his mouth." Her hand went up as if shooing Phoebe from her. "Oh, I know you like him, Phoebe, but he'll break your heart, too."

Phoebe couldn't believe her ears. "Then you're not going to tell him what Mario said?"

Mama's eyes had a glassy look, like the bride of Frankenstein. "I'm gonna let him hang himself."

Phoebe inched off the bed. "Oh Mama, don't do that."

"Get out of here, Phoebe. I have to dress."

***

Phoebe sat on the stairs for an hour, going over her conversation with Mario after the movies. It was her fault. She'd caused this calamity. She'd wanted to impress Mario. The house was silent. Mario, Joey, and Sheila were nowhere to be seen. Phoebe pulled on a hangnail until it bled. Then she sucked it. What would she do without Tony? Without Mario?

Around supper time, Tony arrived, freshly shaven, wearing polished brown shoes, a sport coat, a tan shirt, and a bolo around his neck. "Anybody home?" he said in a cheerful voice.

"Tony!" Phoebe called from the staircase.

He placed a straw-covered bottle of Italian wine in her lap. "That's for dinner."

Phoebe stared at the bottle. Dinner. Nobody had made dinner. She couldn't eat anyway.

He laid a cellophane-enclosed orchid beside her. "That's for your mother."

"Great."

He frowned and sat beside her. "What's the matter, chickadee?"

"Oh Tony!" She hid her face in his sport coat.

"Where's Elaine?" He began to get up, but Phoebe pulled him down. "Don't go there."

"Why?"

"Just don't."

"She is going to my club isn't she?"

"Yeah, but . . ." Tears began to roll down her face.

Mario appeared at the top of the stairs, sax and clarinet cases in either hand. His lips tightened. He shifted his grip on the handles, came down the stairs past his father, drilling him with his eyes, and walked out the door. Tony gazed after Mario, his eyes screwed up. "Mario? Mario! It's cold as a tomb in here.

What's going on?"

"It's all my fault." Phoebe wiped the tears off her chin with the back of her hand.

Tony put his arm around her. "What is it, sweetheart?"

"Did you promise to marry someone before you asked Mama?"

Tony looked so surprised that Phoebe stopped crying. "Someone else? Your mother and I haven't told a soul about us getting married." He shook his head side to side. "You mean what she said this morning?"

"I told Mario—"

"Oh, I get it. That's why Mario gave me the dead-eye just now."

They heard Mama's bedroom door open.

Tony said, "Here she comes. I'll get this straightened out."

"Maybe you should go get Chinese food for dinner," Phoebe said. "Mama couldn't cook today."

"What a great idea—" Tony gave her shoulders a squeeze.

Mama appeared on the upper landing, and Tony rose with a wavering smile. Her hair in light brown waves framed her narrow face. She wore a black crepe dress with a drape at the hip and a gold necklace with matching earrings. Her well-shaped legs in a pair of nylons ended in black suede pumps.

"You look sensational!" Tony said, and then he hesitated.

He must have seen her tight smile and frozen fish eyes. "I was just about to go for Chinese take-out."

"Feed the kids," Mama said. "I'm not hungry."

"I'll be right back."

Mama sat on the couch looking straight ahead.

Phoebe tip-toed into the kitchen and began to take silver out of the drawer.

When Tony returned with the hot food, he said to Phoebe, "I'm not hungry, either, honey-child. You guys eat it."

Tony bent over Mama and cradled her stiff elbow in his palm as she rose zombie-like. He carried the orchid in his other hand as they left the house.

***

Breakfast was a gloomy affair. Tony, Mario, and Joey sat at the table as if they were prisoners. The silence was broken only by the clink of cups and an occasional sigh from Joey. Tony had slept on the couch in the living room and Phoebe had wakened him. Mario stirred milk into his coffee. Mama ladled a glob of oatmeal into each bowl. Phoebe's throat tightened. Sheila's eyes glittered as if she were enjoying their discomfort.

Elaine set the pot of oatmeal down on a trivet. Her words burnt stone. "You boys will move out today."

You can't do that— Phoebe thought. She stared at Tony, begging him to say something, but his face sagged, and he remained silent. Did he believe everything Mama said about him? Did he think he was a cheater and a bum?

Finally he said, "You sure this is what you want?"

Mario let out a sound of exasperation. "C'mon, Pop." He pushed his chair from the table. "I'm going up to pack. Joey?" Joey rose also, and they left the kitchen.

Mama began to stack the empty bowls. "You've left me no

choice. I was honest with you."

"Tony—" Phoebe said. What *could* she say? She was teetering on the edge of a precipice.

Tony put his head on the table. "Phoebe . . .." He began to sob.

Mama watched with no expression.

Phoebe got up and stroked his rumpled shirt. *Do something. Say something!*

In a dead tone, Mama said, "We shouldn't have let strangers into our home."

Phoebe looked at her mother with disbelief. "You're running a rooming house—"

She looked down at Tony's sparse greying hair. He'd stopped sobbing.

Mama spoke again. "I could never marry a Catholic. I see now how strong religion is."

Phoebe stared at Mama. The brave bacon eater? What a stupid reason to throw Tony and the boys out. "You're full of crap!" she screamed.

Mama winced.

Tony scurried out of the kitchen.

"You better take that back," Mama said.

"I won't! I hate you." It was happening again—like when Daddy left. To judge from the stony look on her mother's face, it would happen as it had before, with the same searing rip of skin from flesh. Phoebe's whole body had been hot with indignation, but now a cold feeling began to creep up her spine.

She cornered Tony in Mario's room. He avoided her eyes.

"What happened?" she asked.

Tony sat on the bed, his head bent.

She sat beside him, rubbing his back with one hand. "I caused all this," she said.

"No, no, you didn't, chickadee."

"Then please tell me."

Tony hugged her shoulders. "Sure. Sure. I know you'll hear her version. Here's mine."

Tony began to relate the events of the night before. He'd been having misgivings on the way to the club. She had been ominously silent on the road. Why wasn't she yelling at him? He hadn't thought through what he would say to her about Rosalind. Elaine's silence was unusual. He was afraid to speak, afraid to unleash her tongue. The look of grey triumph on Elaine's face, scared him.

He tried to look at his club the way Elaine would: a dive near the black ghetto on South Vermont Avenue, its old dry cleaner's logo still visible on its side. She wouldn't even be able to walk these streets alone. With a glance at her stony expression, he pushed the heavy red door in, and a pungent whiskey smell mixed with smoke greeted them.

Elaine coughed, dabbed at her eyes with her handkerchief and then entered with him. He waved at the members of his band as he steered Elaine to a table. She pushed his hand off her elbow.

Should he leave her alone? "I'll get you a Tom Collins." He gave the order to the waiter and sat down facing her. She hadn't said one word. When the drink came she stared at it. He wanted to explain about Rosalind. He loved Elaine. He was done with Rosalind, but she was proving hard to get rid of. Elaine was different from the women he usually went with. She cared about Joey and Mario. She'd saved his ass. He owed her a lot, but he didn't have the words to get through her barricade. He had to get up and join the band, but he sat there watching her frozen face and despaired. The good sex didn't matter one bit. Because now Elaine knew.

Rosalind thought she owned him. She assumed they would get married. He'd never proposed, but her little girl called him "Daddy." He'd been too chicken-shit to have a showdown with Rosalind.

He hated to see Phoebe so upset. She looked up to him, and he was letting her down. He loved Phoebe. He couldn't lose her.

"I have to start the show," he'd said to Elaine. "You gonna be okay?"

She took a sip of the drink as if she hadn't heard him. The musicians were warming up, Sammy on the drums, Flatbush on bass, Floyd on the horn. He had to go. He was glad Elaine was drinking. Maybe she'd relax. Maybe Mario hadn't told her everything. He'd have to explain. He got up, went to the stage and picked up his sax. He let the band start without him, letting the sax hang around his neck. He pulled at his damp collar.

"Hi Tony," the band's singer said in his ear.

"Felice, not now."

"What are you looking at, Tony?"

"I have a friend in the audience. Please Felice, be a doll. Go away."

Felice smiled into the crowd. "Oh, a lady." She winked. "Let's make it a good show then."

"Yeah," he said, getting rid of her with a light spank. He began to lead the band. Elaine's head bent over her drink. Jesus—everything he did was an indictment. He put the sax to his lips. It was the only safe thing he could do. He mentally dedicated the number to Elaine. Sammy hung loose over his sticks, Flatbush smiled automatically as his fingers raced up and down the bass. Through his sax, Tony blew a love song to Elaine. Would she know he was trying to reach her in the only way he knew? The sax cried high notes and groaned low. Love and fear belled out of his sax until the music ended, and he took a bow.

Then someone picked up his clarinet and began to play Arabian music. Felice, in baggy oriental pants hipped her way onto the stage to the shouts of, "Yea, baby!" She carried a long scarf. Who was messing with his clarinet? It was Floyd, hamming it up. Felice danced her way to Tony, lassoed him around the middle with her scarf and worked the scarf back and forth. This wasn't in the show. Damn Felice! The audience howled in drunken appreciation. Felice reeled him in, bent him backwards and kissed him while Tony stretched his neck around to see if Elaine was still there. She wasn't.

Tony pushed Felice away and ran off the stage.

Outside, he found Elaine pulling at the handle of the car door. "Sugar, wait!" When he got between her and the car she punched him in the chest. "Let me go, Tony!"

"At least let me explain."

"You want to explain? You humiliate me in public with that

294

woman and you want . . .."

She poised for another blow and then let her hand drop.

"Felice didn't mean anything. She often ad libs."

"Did she know I was in the audience?"

"Well . . . yes."

"What kind of promises did you make to *her*? Only a jealous woman would do such a thing."

"She wanted to see if you were a sport."

"I don't like those people. She's the lowest—"

"Let's sit in the car," Tony said, and they got in. "I know Felice isn't upsetting you, Elaine. What is it really?"

"Have you promised to marry someone else?"

"I love you."

"That's no answer," Elaine said.

"Rosalind? I don't love her. It's over."

"Not for Rosalind."

"I didn't want to hurt you. It will take a little time to get rid of . . . her. I never asked her to marry me. She assumed it."

"You just played with both of us. I took you in, you bum— you and your two sons."

"You made me the happiest man in the world."

"Naturally. You just lay around, taking, playing it both ways."

In desperation Tony sought for some way to reach Elaine, but he could think of nothing but trying to kiss her. When he drew her to him, she shouted, "Get off me, you old buck," and struck him in the face with her handbag. "You *schtick dreck*!"

Tony bent over, cradling his head in his arms.

Elaine went on. "Do you think I could marry anybody as low as you? What do I need you for? You humiliate me, show me what I could sink to. You know what? I'm glad Mario opened my eyes. You were a good experience for me, Tony, not to have again. You poor has-been. How could anybody tie herself up with you?"

"Shut up, Elaine," Tony said. "Shut up, please."

Tears rolled down Tony's cheeks.

Phoebe said, "Oh, God, Tony, she won't forgive you. I feel like I'm dying."

An hour later, Mario stood on the landing holding his suitcase and his instrument cases. Incredible. She couldn't believe it. Joey pushed past him down the stairs. He put his key on the telephone stand.

Mama stood near the front door, and when Joey saw her, he put his suitcase down, wrapped his arms around her, and laid his head sideways on her shoulder. She stroked his hair.

Mario uttered a cynical chuckle. Phoebe's breath stopped. Wasn't he going to say goodbye? Mario placed his key on the telephone table, and said as if he were going to work, "Well, so long."

Phoebe croaked, "Goodbye." How could he just walk away? He couldn't leave her. She wanted to kiss him. If this was really the end, who would blame her? Then she remembered a dream she'd had. She was a queen and the king was going off to war. They were dignified and each knew their tasks. Nobody cried. Nobody hugged. They talked with their eyes. She clasped her hands behind her and nodded as Mario walked out the door.

Her dignity left as soon as he did. A wave of nausea rolled across her stomach and she bent over. *No—No—*

Mama went back to the kitchen, passing Tony without saying a word, but all of Phoebe's resolutions broke loose. She put her arms around his middle and locked her fingers. "You can't go!"

Tony looked down at her. "I'd love to take you with me, chickadee, but—"

"Nothing is right without you," she said through clenched teeth.

"Let me go, Phoebe," he said, undoing her hands.

She grabbed his arm, almost pulling off his coat. "Don't leave. I'll go crazy."

"Oh, Phoebe."

"You don't believe me?" She shrieked an insane laugh.

Tony's brows knit. "I tell you what, you come see me." He lifted her chin with two fingers.

Phoebe nodded, eyes spilling acid tears. She clung to his arm until he had to peel off each finger to get out the door. She ran after him onto the porch. He got into the car, and as they pulled away, she crumpled onto the sidewalk.

Mama grabbed Phoebe's wrist when she walked in. "Don't lose any sleep over Tony. That louse had another woman and promised to marry her. Do you hear? That's your Tony."

Phoebe gave a cry and ran up the stairs.

Mama, inflaming herself with more anger, ran up after her. "And the rest of his life is just as shabby. He fools around with a slut named Felice, and that dive he plays in has a low crowd. I'm well rid of him, the whole bunch of them."

Phoebe said from the landing, "You don't care if you ruin my life. You're an old witch! You stink!"

"Don't you dare talk to me like that! And get that stupid look off your face."

You won't even let me have my feelings. Phoebe felt her face scrunch up into a hard knot, her fists balled. Mama would be sorry for this. She'd get back at her someday—

Then Mama softened. "Call me names but I know I've done the right thing. You'll see."

Phoebe broke into fresh tears. "You don't know—you don't care how I loved them. I loved them. I loved them!"

Chapter 31 - Ruchek's Business

It was as bad as it could get. Phoebe moped around the house, breaking into tears when she came upon Tony's chair. Mario's coffee cup reminded her of that rainy Saturday he'd measured her waistline, and Mama's anger when she caught them about to kiss, but memories were better than no Mario. She practiced the piano because she had to, but it was useless. All music had been driven from the house.

Laurie was no help.

On the phone, Phoebe sobbed. "I don't want to meet a cute blind date."

"We could double," Laurie said. "It's not the end of the world, Phoebe."

"It is!"

"Are you getting all gloomy again?"

"You don't understand, Laurie."

Laurie was silent for a moment. "Okay. This is what I see.

You're getting all wound up in your mother's life again. You're almost fifteen. You should be thinking about boys, dances, what clothes make you look good, and how to fix your hair."

Good old Laurie. She lived for the present. Boys! Phoebe had known two beautiful *men*, Tony and Mario. When she thought of the boys at school, her lips curled: stupid kids with acne who wouldn't even look at her. Not that she wanted them to . . . but that would soothe her ego. Laurie was probably right. Why was she, Phoebe, so against kids her own age? It seemed as if she were taking a step backwards. Or was she? Tony and Mario were a lot easier to know than the snotty girls at school or the handsome boys who ignored her. "Okay. What do you want me to do?"

"You idiot! Don't ask me! I'm not your mother. Just meet this guy. But I get the cutest one—uh, yours is kind of nice looking. We'll go roller skating and then have an ice cream soda."

"Please, no ice cream. It's as phony as the wartime chickory coffee we have to drink. You should have heard Mama scream at the poor kid selling ice cream cones the other day. Her mother and father had a candy store in Brooklyn, and they used nothing but pure cream, eggs, and vanilla."

"There you go again," Laurie said, "getting off the subject."

Phoebe had to smile. She couldn't stay unhappy around Laurie.

"All right, I'll meet him . . . Laurie, remember when we made a vow never to wear lipstick?"

"Yeah. But we were just kids then. I broke that vow. I'm

wearing Tangee on the date."

"Me too!"

Phoebe hung up laughing.

***

"I'm done with love," Mama said one Sunday morning in the kitchen.

Phoebe stopped scrambling her eggs and let them set. "What do you mean?"

"Our lives will be practical from now on."

"Don't you miss Tony and the boys even a little bit?" She shoveled the eggs onto a plate and sat down.

Mama settled across from Phoebe, a cup of coffee cradled between her palms. "I miss some things."

From her mother's dreamy expression Phoebe guessed what those things might be.

She pushed the scrambled eggs away from her in disgust. "You spoiled my life."

Mama stroked Phoebe's hand. "Stop being so dramatic, honey. I couldn't help what happened."

Yes you could. Phoebe pulled the plate of eggs toward her and began picking at them.

"What do you mean by practical?"

"I'd like to make money, not just for paying the bills each month, but real money."

Phoebe laughed. "You should have stayed with Dad then."

Mama shuddered. "That immigrant ignoramus?"

Phoebe sprang out of her chair. "Don't talk bad about Daddy!"

A few drops of Mama's coffee spilled. "All right. You're so sensitive."

"It hurts me when you do that!" Phoebe said. "And you don't even know it."

"Do I hurt you?" Mama asked with surprise. "I don't mean to. All I ever want is to love and protect you and Sheila. Why do you think I bought this rooming house in the first place? So I could be with you and not have to leave you with a key around your neck while I worked."

"Instead you bring all these weird people to live with us."

"Weird people?"

Phoebe shuddered. "Like that Mr. Ruchek."

Mama's lips smiled, but her eyes were hard. "Mr. Ruchek is a good salesman with a big firm. He's going places."

"What else do you know about him?"

"He's Czechoslovakian and has no family here. He's a steady worker, and he doesn't play around with women."

"Who'd want *him*?" Phoebe said. She watched, appalled as Mama's eyes became excited.

"He's someone I could work with, be partners with, you know?"

Phoebe stared, speechless, for a moment. "That's the worst idea you ever came up with."

Mama laughed. "My poor romantic little girl. Life is more than music and sweet words."

Phoebe eyed her date. Marvin Fisher was a skinny boy who looked as if he weighed less than she did. He wiped his nose frequently with a large, used handkerchief. Laurie's date, Harry Brillwoark, was a football player, with neck muscles bulging from his shirt. Laurie looked tiny next to him. Phoebe tried to make herself look smaller by bending her knees and rounding her shoulders, but Laurie gave her a thump on the arm, a signal that she had poor posture, and Phoebe straightened up.

Marvin looked past her left temple as he asked, "How do you like high school?"

She hardly knew how to answer. The high school in Phoebe's district wasn't in Laurie's. Aunt Ceil lived in Laurie's school district. Phoebe wanted to go to L.A. High for several reasons. It offered creative writing, had a swimming pool, and Laurie was going there. So Mama wrote Aunt Ceil's address on the registration. Phoebe now lived on Citrus Avenue, not Virgil, and she was painfully aware of the lie as she answered Marvin's question.

"It's not like Junior High."

They laced up their roller skates and wheeled around the oval. Marvin showered the air with cold germs as he sneezed. She didn't want to hold his hand and was glad he didn't offer it. Laurie skated backwards in a zigzag, smiling at Harry who plodded forward. *That's my girl!* Laurie had perfect balance with short strong legs, a small waistline, and narrow shoulders. That's why she could dance and skate better than Phoebe, who was top heavy, with long, thin legs, a short waistline, a belly, and large shoulders.

In the ice cream parlor, Laurie ordered a banana split. Harry's hand fiddled with his breast pocket wallet. Banana splits cost a dollar! Phoebe ordered a doughnut.

"Doughnuts are the worst thing you can put in your stomach," Marvin said, like a disapproving mother. He ordered vanilla ice cream.

"You don't know what they put in ice cream these days," Phoebe said, and caught Laurie's irritated look.

***

The next day on the phone, Phoebe and Laurie evaluated their first dating experience.

"Harry wants to see me again," Laurie said. "He goes to Dorsey. He also goes to my church."

Phoebe said, "That's nice. I hope I never see Marvin again."

"I did the best I could."

"Don't pick boys for me."

"Then you'll never date at all."

"That's fine with me."

***

A few weeks later, Sheila, cutting paper dolls on Phoebe's bed, said, "Mama told me I'm getting the bedroom next to the one with the screens."

"Really?" Phoebe answered. "Where's Mr. Ruchek gonna sleep?"

"In Mama's room." Sheila clapped her hand over her

mouth. "Oh no! *Mama's room!*"

"I don't believe it!" Phoebe leaped off her bed and upset Sheila's paper dolls.

"Watch out—"

"Cut your paper dolls somewhere else—" Then Phoebe helped Sheila pick up the mess.

"I'm getting bad dreams again," Sheila said. "The lion . . . ."

Mama appeared at the bedroom door with Sheila's dress on a hanger. "Come help me, Sheila. What are you looking at, Phoebe?"

"Is he around?"

"Who?"

"Mr. Ruchek."

"No, Jack is working. You'd think people would hold off buying luxuries like his perfume, but they're making money in war plants, and they can't spend it fast enough."

Phoebe said, "*Jack?* You call him by his first name?"

Mama grinned. "Why not? He and I might go into business together. I've always wanted to work with a man, be his helper so we could get ahead. Jack has so many good ideas."

Sheila grabbed Phoebe's hand and squeezed it.

"Sheila's getting nightmares again," Phoebe said. "She crawls in bed with me. That man scares her." The image of Mr. Ruchek's hair growing up from his forehead like a stiff blue-black brush with five o'clock shadow on his rectangular cheeks, made her shiver. Phoebe tried to make wide circles around him and his black case of perfume samples. *What did her mother see in him?* Now she wanted someone who earned a living. Why

305

didn't she go back to Daddy? Of course, she couldn't. Daddy was married again, but Daddy had a heart; he was someone who could cry. Now it was as if Frankenstein's monster had taken up residence with them.

It was quiet and the rooms clanged with emptiness. No Mario practicing. No Joey slamming doors. The big house closed in on itself in mourning.

Mama said, "Sheila, Mr. Ruchek means you no harm."

"Why is he living in the big bedroom now?" Phoebe asked.

Mama's smile was strained. "We're working on a project together and I just thought it would be simpler, you know, for easy communication. Anyway, this project may be just the ticket. I won't have to take in roomers anymore. I'll be able to send you to college, buy you clothes, take vacations. Wouldn't you like that?"

Sheila nodded uncertainly.

Phoebe said, "I don't want anything from that man."

They all froze as they heard Mr. Ruchek clumping up the stairs, his steps shaking the furniture.

"He's home. You two stay in your rooms," Mama said. She straightened her blouse and smoothed down the pleats of her skirt. A blood vessel pulsed at her temple. "He's not used to children," she finally admitted.

***

Phoebe was done crying. Now the long pull of sadness filled her days. Sheila was the only one who understood. For once, they agreed on something: they both hated Mr. Ruchek. They couldn't go into Mama's room anymore while he was home. Noises issued from that bedroom at night. In the morning Mama appeared at breakfast, in her bathrobe, distracted, her hair mussed. She served Jack first and ate with him.

Mama spent hours typing papers for Mr. Ruchek in the big bedroom. Phoebe did not disturb her. From what Phoebe could see through cracks, the room had a filing cabinet and a desk now, and the bed was usually unmade. This was not like Mama. Phoebe began to think of living with her father and Charlotte.

***

One day, months later, Mr. Ruchek said he had to go to a company conference in Las Vegas and needed Mama's car. He left his old Ford coupe that had a rumble seat, for them. The rumble seat was fun. Mama tooled along at forty miles an hour. Phoebe and Sheila sang songs, while the wind whipped their hair back.

Mama made telephone calls to Mr. Ruchek every night. Phoebe watched her mother getting more and more nervous after each phone call.

"He sounds drunk," Mama said.

Phoebe gazed at the ceiling. For once, her mother didn't reprimand her for her expression. Mama was too nervous, too worried to notice. Phoebe knew it was no use, but she said, "I wrote a poem. They're gonna publish it in the school newspaper."

Mama's eyelids fluttered at the telephone. "You getting good grades?"

"Of course."

"I have to take Sheila to the doctor. She has dark circles under her eyes again."

"No wonder," Phoebe muttered under her breath.

"What did you say?"

"I said Sheila-has-galloping-consumption-and-may-die."

Her mother nodded.

Phoebe sighed as the phone rang and her mother grabbed it. "Hello, Jack? What? No! Are you all right? Oh my God! I'll wire you the money to come home."

Mama dropped the receiver into the holder. "Jack has had an accident with my car. It's all smashed up. He wasn't hurt bad." Her eyes dulled. "He didn't even say he was sorry." She put the back of her head against the wall and rolled it side to side. "I don't have car insurance." Mama grasped the bannister and pulled herself upstairs.

"Don't send him money, Mama," Phoebe said, as the bedroom door slammed shut.

***

Mr. Ruchek came back without Mama's car. She emptied his stuff out of the master bedroom and put him in Joey's little room. Mama's eyes were reddened, her house dress hung from her shoulders. Her hands shook as she poured Phoebe's morning orange juice.

"You don't look so good, Mama. Are you all right?"

"I'm sick." Her eyes darted to the kitchen door as it trembled from Mr. Ruchek's heavy footfall.

Mama sunk into her chair and put her elbows on the table, holding her coffee cup to her lips as if to shield herself. Jack Ruchek walked in, and Phoebe froze. He lumbered to the coffee pot, poured himself a cup and silently sipped, staring at both of them.

Phoebe jumped up. "I'm going to see if Alma Mae is okay." But she sat back down again as she heard Mama's next words.

"What are you doing about getting me another car?" Mama said, her voice hard.

His lips stretched sideways. "That piece of junk?"

"Not when I loaned it to you. It's junk now."

He said, "You messed up my papers when you moved my things. You better go straighten them out or we'll both be out of business."

Mama lifted her head. "I used to be an executive secretary for a big import export firm in New York." Then she rose and went upstairs.

Mr. Ruchek said, "She's got spirit, your mother. Okay kid, fix me some breakfast."

"I can't. I have to check on Alma Mae."

"I said fix me some pancakes, bacon, a couple of eggs, and make another pot of coffee."

"Uhh, "Phoebe said, looking around for an escape, and seeing none. "How do you like your eggs?"

***

A few weeks later, reports of the Allies and American troops routing the German army was the only good news. Mama wouldn't talk to Jack Ruchek, yet she took his rent money. The tension in the house replaced the sad silence, and Sheila and Phoebe hung on to each other.

One day as Phoebe came in from school, Mama was ironing in the living room, her back to the fireplace. By the way she bore down on the iron, Phoebe knew something else had happened. Her mother looked up. "I'm getting rid of Jack."

Phoebe wanted to say, *it's about time.* She flopped down on the couch and flung her books on the coffee table. "What's going on?"

"That skunk—" Mama ripped the pillow case off the ironing board, folded it and passed the iron over it once more. "He's no business man. He gambled away his money and mine in Las Vegas."

Phoebe's heart lurched. "You gave him money?"

"I was investing in a company we were building."

"He was supposed to get you another car. What happened with that?"

"He says I can use the Ford."

"Is that why you haven't thrown him out?"

"What am I supposed to do without a car?" Mama said.

Phoebe decided not to show Mama her published poem in the school newspaper. Laurie had proudly let her mother see it.

The living room shook as Mr. Ruchek entered. Phoebe grabbed her books and retreated to the dining room.

Tony's old chair groaned as Jack squeezed into it.

"Just destroy the furniture too," Mama said, ironing with fury.

He lit a cigarette and watched Mama like a lion watches its nervous prey.

"So when is this business deal gonna pay off? Are they making you head of the company yet?" Mama's laugh, full of scorn, seemed to make no difference to Mr. Ruchek's stoic expression. Her arms were rigid as she picked up the iron and slammed it down.

"Ever since you threw me out of your bedroom, you've been sore. I told you these things take time," Mr. Ruchek said.

"I don't think there is a business."

"Then what have you been typing all these weeks?"

"That's what I want to know."

He snubbed out his cigarette. "I need more money."

Mama's laugh became hysterical. "More money? You think I'm a bank?"

"If you don't want to lose the initial investment, you'll fork it over."

"I don't have it." She lifted the iron, gave Ruchek a poisonous grin, and slipped another pillow case on the board.

"You can take a loan out on the house."

Phoebe gasped. The nerve!

Mama must have thought so too because she said, "You're a con artist."

His eyes blazed. "Nobody talks to Jack Ruchek like that."

Mama put on her *piteous* act. Phoebe would have laughed if she didn't think her mother meant it this time. "You took advantage of me, a little, weak woman, with two innocent children!"

Ruchek laughed. "Took advantage of you? You thought you hit the mother lode!"

Mama gestured with the iron. "Get out of my house! What do I need with an elephant like you. You weren't even good in bed!"

"You bitch!" Mr. Ruchek shot out of Tony's chair, almost knocking it over, and advanced on Mama.

Phoebe closed her eyes.

Mama's hoarse shout rang to the ceiling. "I said 'get out'!"

When he raised his fist to sock her, she slammed the hot iron into his face. Blood spurted. He screamed, put his hands to his nose and, bellowing like a bull, he ran out the front door. The burnt copper smell of seared blood on the sputtering iron filled Phoebe's nostrils. It was quiet for a moment.

Phoebe peeked out the window. Mr. Ruchek had disappeared.

Phoebe ran to Mama, pulled the iron's cord from the socket, and put her arms around her mother. "Are you okay?" Mama eyes were blank as she helped her to the kitchen. It was hard to take in what had just happened. Her mother, speechless, in a daze, with Jack Ruchek's blood drying on the fireplace mantel.

Phoebe poured Mama a cup of hot coffee, with plenty of cream and sugar. "Here. Drink this."

Mama obeyed, guzzling the coffee. Phoebe could feel Mama eyeing her.

"My brave Phoebe," she said. "You didn't fall to pieces."

Phoebe's scalp tingled. Praise from Mama! Mama wasn't afraid of anybody when you got her good and mad.

Sheila and her school friend, Carol Song, sauntered through the front door. Carol wore a sign around her neck: *I'm Korean.*

Sheila poked her head into the kitchen. "Carol and I are playing in my room," Sheila announced, apparently not sensing the situation.

Phoebe watched the two girls climb the stairs. Carol leaned over the bannister, and with a quizzical smile, looked back at them.

In a few moments, Mama seemed back to normal. She sprung up and climbed the stairs, and returned dragging Mr. Ruchek's belongings in garbage bags. Mama lugged them outside, and with a grunt threw them down the stone steps in front of the house.

Chapter 32 - VE Day Celebration

March 26, 1945

Dear Diary:

This awful war is coming to an end. Today, General Patton crossed the Rhine River. Mama was so excited, she yelled the news up the stairway. We danced around in the kitchen and feasted on waffles, hot chocolate, and marshmallows for breakfast. Maybe now Mama will stop taking in roomers and we can live like other people, except I kind of like the daily dramas as they say on Grand Central Station. Signing off for today.

***

April, 13, 1945

Mama brought in the paper. The headline was such big news, it took up the whole page. It said, "Roosevelt dead." I felt as if Daddy had just died. Roosevelt has been president all my life. Mama said Harry S. Truman was being sworn in. Who is he? I want Roosevelt back. Mama told me Roosevelt was sick, that he looked as if he hadn't had a good meal for months. He was skin and bones with big dark bags under his eyes. She said anybody could see he was dying. They pushed him in a wheelchair to where he sat with Churchill and Stalin. He wore an old sweater. She said he'd given his life for us. I am so mad! I don't want anybody else for president. Mama laughed and said, "Aren't you gonna give poor Mr. Truman a chance?" How can anybody ever replace President Roosevelt? Signing off.

Phoebe stood at her mother's bedroom window. People were celebrating VE Day below, but she didn't feel like running all over the place, kissing strangers. Mario wouldn't be drafted now, thank goodness. Behind her in the hall, Mr. Green's door opened, and his slippers flip-flopped on his way to the bathroom.

Mama called upstairs, "I'm taking Sheila to the clinic. I hope I can get through the traffic. You be okay alone for a while?"

"Sure. Think I'm a baby?"

Phoebe heard the front door close, and she started back to her room. When Phoebe shut the screen door to her balcony, she turned and gasped. A large bug was crawling slowly across the floor, blocking her exit from the room. She froze. It had a little white face, and a green and orange body, and was as long as her thumb. Was it poisonous like a black widow? *Oh God, it's ugly. Looks like it came from space, and I'm trapped with it.* She fought panic. Joey loved bugs, even played with them. Ugh. Then a rattle of bottles. Mr. Green was coming out of the bathroom. "Help!" she cried, keeping her eye on the bug.

Mr. Green poked his head into her room. "Are you all right?"

"No! A bug has me hostage."

Mr. Green peered where she pointed and shook his head. "Wow. What is that?"

"I don't know."

"Step over it and come out."

"I'm scared to. What if it crawls up my leg?"

"Then leap over it."

"Hold out your hand," Phoebe said.

Mr. Green, also staring at the bug, took her hand. Their hands made a bridge over the slow moving bug. "You want me to smash it?" he asked.

The bug had just reached her favorite chair. What if it hid some place and she couldn't find it? How could she sleep? She took a breath, and using his hand, leaped to Mr. Green, then turned and saw the bug disappear under her chair's heavy skirt. She gave a huge sigh. "If you could please put a stick in front of it and get it to climb on, maybe we could throw it outside."

"Anything for a damsel in distress." Mr. Green disappeared into his room, and returned with a ruler and half a glass of beer with a few cigarette stubs in it. On his hands and knees, near the chair, he shoved the ruler at the bug and enticed the Martian thing to walk onto it.

"Ew!" Phoebe said, as the bug's head came out from under the chair. Withdrawing the ruler carefully, Mr. Green dumped the bug into the beer. The white baby face stared at them as it tried to climb the slick walls of the glass.

"Welcome to earth," Phoebe said.

Mr. Green laughed, and took the bug to his room. Phoebe ran after him. She stood in his doorway while he shook the bug down into the beer. "It's a merciful death," he said. "I think it's a potato bug, but I've never seen a green and orange one before." He stuck his arm out the window, and dumped the beer and bug onto the driveway. Then he turned his attention to her. "Would you like to come in?"

In all her fantasies about the remote Mr. Green, she'd never thought of getting any closer to him. He was a *writer*, as close to godliness as a human could get. But he'd never talked to her about her manuscript, and she wanted it back, so Phoebe entered. The very air was sacred because this is where he wrote his radio scripts. His typewriter was still in the alcove, with a pile of papers beside it. She casually walked to it. *My Life with Mother's Boarders* looked up at her. Dare she ask? A note paper-clipped to it said something. Did she really want his opinion?

She forced her gaze around the room, enjoying the alcove, the spacious window, the coolness of it in the warm afternoon. She said, "You have a good bedroom. I used to live in it." Idiot. What was she thinking, speaking to him in that way, as if they were equals. Then she glanced down at the note. She picked up the manuscript. It still said *the kid has talent*. So what. "I was wondering all these months if you'd read it." Her heart thumped. She felt hot and cold, elated but uneasy.

He took a swig of beer from a quart bottle and set it down. "It was funny and sad. I love those touches like how they warmed up their canned peas in a water bath—that was so good. And, my God, those two old ladies, the Ebberly sisters feeling sorry for your mother because you were Jewish: 'You may not believe in Jesus, but we respect the divinity in you, Mrs. Feldman!'" He laughed and said, "I got a kick out of it 'cause I'm Jewish."

Mr. Green was Jewish? He reminded her of a character in a tropical movie, unshaven in an old bathrobe as he reached for a cigarette and lit it, using the glass for an ash tray. He didn't look Jewish. He had one of those long pointed noses like English aristocrats. He didn't sound Jewish. He talked high-falutin'. He didn't act Jewish. Phoebe had never met a Jewish drunk. In her father's home, wine was used for sacramental purposes. Schnapps was for men to drink in tiny glasses on special occasions. Mr. Green was like a scholar who'd not lived up to his promise. He was the title of a movie she'd seen, taken from Shakespeare: *The Fallen Sparrow*.

Phoebe edged toward the door with her manuscript held close to her chest. Mr. Green blew smoke toward the open window. "They're going crazy out there."

"Everybody is kissing everybody," Phoebe said.

"That's natural. They're glad the war's over."

"Thanks for saving me from the bug."

"Couldn't let him crawl up your leg, could I?"

Phoebe giggled. She noticed his red-rimmed eyes. The acrid beer smell made her wrinkle up her nose. She began to feel a little nervous. It was time to leave.

"Where you going?" Mr. Green asked.

"Back to my room. I'm writing today."

"Oh, I forgot. We're writers."

"That's a funny thing to say. You forgot? You forgot you're a writer?"

"Yeah. Working for that Radio Theatre makes you forget."

"You're lucky."

"My child, I'm not. I don't have the freedom you have, for instance." He pulled his bathrobe up around his chin. "Go on, get out of here."

Phoebe had a sudden urge to take him into her arms like a mother and soothe him. She put the manuscript down and stroked his back.

He took her hand and kissed it. "We writers have to stick together. No matter what they do to us. You know I've been watching you. You interest me."

Phoebe withdrew her hand. "Why?"

His laugh sounded like a cry of despair. "You're young. You still have choices."

"Don't be silly. Just get dressed, stop drinking all that beer, and get to work," Phoebe said, and because she sounded like Laurie, she bit her tongue.

"Ha, ha, ha. I deserve what I get," he said. "Come, sit beside me."

An alarm went off in Phoebe's head. Much as she was fascinated by Mr. Green, she wasn't going to get any closer. "Mr. Green, I have to leave now."

He poured beer into a clean glass and offered it to her. "Call me Corville. Have a sip. Don't be scared. It will relax you. I want to get to know you better."

Beer was supposed to be mild. Her father drank it on occasion; she'd eat the pretzels. Wonder what it tasted like? Her mother would kill her if she found her here, drinking beer with Mr. Green. With one hand on the doorknob, her other hand laid her manuscript onto an end table and reached for the beer. She took a breath, put it to her lips, swallowed, and coughed. It went up her nose and tasted like bitter medicine. "It's awful."

"It's an acquired taste. Try another sip."

The second swallow, which she accomplished by holding her nose, went down better. Her head felt light. She giggled. Mr. Green began to look younger, almost dashing. *Corville, mon ami, take me into your arms and smother me with kisses.* She took a few more swallows.

He held his arms out and Phoebe walked into them. "I feel so nice," she said.

"That's 'cause you are nice," he said. "But I heard you crying. What's wrong?"

"I love Mario and he's gone," she said and began to sniffle.

"Poor child."

She put her arm around his neck and nestled there. It felt so good. So normal. She forgot he was Mr. Green, the writer. "Do you love somebody?" she asked.

"I do. But you wouldn't be interested."

"I would too! Have you written about her?"

"My novel waits for me to finish it. But I have to earn a living."

"Why can't you do both?"

"I have writers' block."

"What's that?"

Mr. Green began to weep.

Why was he crying? She laid her hand on his shoulder the way she did when Daddy cried, feeling as if her words made him sad, and Phoebe hugged him tighter. Again, she asked, "What's writer's block?"

"You are everything I'm not," he said, his voice soft, his breath coming in little gasps. "If I could just—" He touched the outside of her blouse, put his palm on her breast and began to massage it. Little tingles going from her breast and down her back mingled with her dizziness. What was happening? It didn't matter. Something was opening up down below and it began to make her warm and breathe fast. It was a marvelous feeling. She leaned against Mr. Green as he put his free hand on her other breast, rubbing, groaning.

A firecracker's blast jolted both of them. Mr. Green's hand flew away from her breast. Glass splintered. Mr. Green ran to the window. "They're throwing beer bottles onto the street now—"

The craziness outside roared in Phoebe's ears. She crossed her arms over her tingling breasts. Her whole body was shaking. Then a siren screamed. The police. Mr. Green stepped back from the window with a fearful look.

Phoebe stared at him as he turned his head away. She straightened her blouse, put a stray bobby pin back in her hair. She grabbed her manuscript, touched her burning cheek and could smell her own beer breath. "Oh my God!"

"I suppose you're gonna tell your mother," he said, still not looking at her.

"I tell her everything." Then she remembered how she'd not told Mama about the man in the movie house who'd exposed himself to her. Even though she'd been disgusted, she'd felt pity for him.

Mr. Green faced her, his eyes bulging. "I didn't mean to—oh please don't tell her."

Phoebe cupped her forehead in her hand. *I have to tell.*

"She'll call the police. I'll be arrested. I'll lose my job! It will ruin my life!"

"You got me drunk and then—" Her head bent over the manuscript. She'd never felt that good in her entire life. Like she was flying in dreams. So this is what Carmel and Bobby enjoyed together. It was why Bobby had followed Carmel and would put up with anything to be with her. It was what made Mama dreamy for Tony. She was ashamed of her thoughts, but now she understood.

"Don't be afraid of me," he was saying. "Sex is good. It's sweet. When you respond to me I want to love you. Don't let them kill what you have so naturally, so beautifully. I'll never forget it, even if you tell Elaine, and I go to jail. But you can make your first decision as a maturing young woman. You can remember it as a gift to me and yourself."

She knew what Mama would say to that. He was saving his own skin with pretty words, but she was not her mother. She ran to him, tears streaming down her face, and he held her like a father, and they cried together.

Chapter 33 - The End of Corville Green

Phoebe stepped into the hall from Mr. Green's room, just in time to hear her mother call, "Phoebe? We're home."

Mama said, coming up the stairs, "Everybody's in the street. We almost didn't make it." She rested at the top.

Phoebe tried to rush past Mama, but Mama stopped her.

"Honey, what's the matter?" Mama grabbed Phoebe and turned her chin up. "You've been crying." She sniffed Phoebe's breath. "Beer?"

"Leave me alone."

"You've been drinking beer?" Then Mama glanced at Mr. Green's door. "You've been drinking with *him*?"

Phoebe shut her eyes at the shocked look on Sheila's face. "It's VE Day. People are doing crazy things. We were celebrating."

"I'll give him celebrating." Mama knocked on Mr. Green's door.

Mr. Green's voice sounded weak. "I'm sick, Mrs. Feldman.

Please go away."

Mama shouted, "You giving my daughter beer?"

Phoebe got between her mother and the door. "Leave him alone—"

"You shielding him? That louse!"

"He said I have talent!"

"Talent? You fell for that old line?"

"Please, please don't bother him! He has writer's block."

Mama's laugh hit high *incredulity*. "He's contributing to the delinquency of a minor. Writer's block my ass." She yelled at the door. "You hear me in there? I want you out by tomorrow." She turned to Phoebe. "What else happened?"

Phoebe ran to her room. "Nothing!" she screamed as she slammed her bedroom door. Behind the door Phoebe heard Mama say to Sheila, "Honey, go lie down. You look exhausted."

She heard Sheila's door close.

Phoebe buried her head in her pillow. She could feel blood throbbing in her temples. Had he taken advantage of her? Like Mama thought? But she'd enjoyed it. All the more shame. She'd liked it. Would she go looking for more? The idea made her shudder. Grownups knew the power men have over women. It was like candy. Mama wouldn't let her eat candy because it was rotting her teeth. Was sex the same? What would happen next time?

When her mother barged into her room, Phoebe was biting her nails. "You always think the worst," Phoebe said.

Mama sat on the bed. "Oh honey, it's just what experience has taught me."

Phoebe could see she was worried because of the way her gaze darted back and forth and how she clasped and unclasped her hands.

"So, are you alright? He didn't do anything else?"

Phoebe laughed out loud. "I can take care of myself."

Mama's shoulders slumped. "You used to tell me everything. He's such a strange duck. I-I've wondered about him. I almost thought he was a *fagele* until he started bringing women in there."

"What's a *fagele*?"

"You know—men who like to do it with other men."

"Not him."

"How do you know that?" Mama said, her eyes narrowing.

Phoebe's heart almost stopped. "Just 'cause he's a gentleman and a writer doesn't mean he might be one of those."

Mama took her by the shoulders. "Look at me! Did he touch you?"

Phoebe looked straight into her mother's eyes. "Touch me? He's very sad. His story is very touching."

Mama sighed. "Look, Phoebe, I've had a hard day. The doctor says Sheila's bronchitis is a spot of TB. She has to rest and get nourishment or she'll end up in a sanitarium."

Phoebe hugged her mother. "We have to get her well then."

Across the landing, Phoebe heard Mr. Green's door open. Phoebe jumped up and strode into the hall, Mama right after her.

Mr. Green pushed his suitcase from his room with his feet. In his arms he carried his typewriter. His coat hung on him. The brim of his fedora hid his eyes.

"Leaving already?" Mama said, in that deadly way she had.

"I don't want to be where I'm not wanted," he said.

"Don't forget. You owe me half a month's rent."

He put down the typewriter, withdrew a few crumpled bills, and threw them onto the floor.

"You piece of filth. I should report you to the police," Mama said, bending to pick up the money.

His mouth worked as his grey eyes searched Phoebe's. Phoebe gave one small shake of her head.

He tipped his hat.

Mama opened his bedroom door as he worked his way down the stairs. She returned with several bottles of beer. "Here. You forgot this." She rolled the bottles down the stairwell.

Phoebe ran back to her room and threw herself on the bed. Where would he stay tonight? She could see Mr. Green shuffling around the streets of Hollywood with his typewriter in his arms. In a way she was glad he was gone. He stirred her up. Who knew what she might have done if that firecracker had not surprised them.

She heard her mother enter the room. "Well, that's that."

"You always get rid of people I like," Phoebe said.

"That's not true. I got rid of Mr. Ruchek."

Phoebe saw a hot iron crushing a man's nose. She hugged herself. "How could I forget?"

"What went through Green's mind, playing around with a child."

"He thought of me as another writer."

"Oh yeah. So he could get you drunk?"

"He didn't force me. I wanted to taste it."

"You could have asked me. I'd have given you a taste."

"You weren't there."

She felt her mother looming over her, as Mama said, "I guess—I—have to do this. I forbid you to enter any renter's room from now on."

"That's stupid."

"*You* are stupid, Phoebe. You're stupid, naïve, and headstrong. You need limits."

"That's the kind of rule Charlotte makes. Like a teacher."

"Too bad."

"You can't order me around. Look what *you* do—"

Mama flushed. "You little snot-nose. You've always been a fresh kid. These are the times I wish I had a strong man around. He wouldn't let you talk to me like that."

"You-you-*you're* always talking to me like that. You don't care what I think."

Mama said, "I'm trying to keep you from making big mistakes."

"Ha! You never ask me what *I* want." Phoebe stood up, face to face with Mama. "You always say I'm your right hand. Well, see what you can do without it—" Phoebe pushed Mama aside and ran downstairs.

Mama ran after her. "Where you going?"

Phoebe grabbed the phone and dialed feverishly just as Mama caught up with her. "Hello, Daddy? This is Phoebe. If you still mean it, come get me."

Chapter 34 - Caught Between

Phoebe crouched in her room as she heard her father barge through the front door. She heard him say in a trembling voice, "Where is she?"

Mama said, "You could've knocked."

He bounded up the stairs.

Phoebe was having misgivings. Now she'd have to live with Charlotte. She'd have to give up L.A. High. She'd lose Laurie.

Her father came into the room, took off his hat, and sat next to her on the bed. His cheeks sagged, but his eyes were shiny. "Phoebe. You called me."

Phoebe's eyes filled with tears as his arms went around her. She hadn't realized how she'd missed him. She began to sob. "Daddy—Daddy—"

"Phoebela."

A trace of the sour chemical they used on the furs clung to his coat, and she could detect his lemon-scented aftershave.

You're here. It's you. Enveloped in the safety of his arms, she relaxed.

"Phoebela, what happened?"

"Nothing."

She pulled out of his grasp and began drying her tears.

"Nothing? I don't hear from you for months like a daughter should phone a father and now you call me like a fire alarm and you say, 'nothing'?"

He rose, put his hands in his pockets and began to pace.

"I had a fight with Mama."

"*Nhu*? That's all? Nothing else happened?"

Mama stepped in. "Don't baby her. She became hysterical, that's all."

Phoebe stared at her parents. They were actually in the same room. They were talking to each other. It was a miracle. "Gee, Daddy, I'm sorry—I shouldn't have bothered you. It's a long drive from the valley."

"I come if you need me."

Phoebe looked down at her hands. He'd always been there, been just a phone call away. She'd judged him harshly. Had she come to think of him as her mother did? Other people loved her father. *He's a saint, a saint,* said his friends. *He takes care of his whole family: his mother, his sister, his hellish ex-wife, and his ungrateful children. He treats Charlotte like a queen. He's an honest businessman, and he's devoted to the Temple.* He was also her knight of *The Porcelain Princess*, and the King who went away to war expecting her to be strong.

"Well, you comin' with me?" he said, as she looked up.

She felt Mama's eyes intent on her.

He said, "You can come with me right now. Charlotte will fix up the spare room."

"That's very nice of her. Tell her thank you."

"Phoebe's not going anyplace," Mama said. "We just had a disagreement, that's all."

Phoebe shrunk into herself. Just a disagreement? "It isn't just that we don't agree, Mama," she said. "We always see the same things and think about them differently."

"What are you talking about?" Mama said.

"Let the kid say something for a change," Daddy said. "Phoebe is also part of me. I'm not surprised she thinks different from you."

Mama flinched. The skin around her mouth turned white. Silence.

Although Phoebe was grateful that Daddy had spoken up for her, she gave Mama a sympathetic glance. It must have been hard for her to live with him because she'd been a flapper, an American girl with a high school education, married to a greenhorn. A greenhorn with little schooling. He was trying, though. He'd recently taken up an interest in opera, *Carmen*, for instance.

Phoebe's mind was thinking up new ideas by the second. *I'm different from Daddy, too. He's old fashioned about women.* She couldn't stand to be what Daddy wanted her to be, a sweet young girl, obedient to his wishes. While she was glad he took her part, what she'd said to Mama about Corville Green could not be said in front of Daddy.

330

It had to do with her experience in the movie theatre. How could she tell them a man had exposed himself to her? She'd felt sorry for him and thought for a second he was Daddy. And how could she explain she'd allowed Mr. Green to get her drunk and touch her breast? Daddy didn't know what she'd learned in these years at the rooming house. *I still can't get over losing Tony and Mario.* Grief made her footsteps heavy, but it had also made her kinder to Sheila, even though her sister was sometimes a brat. She was also beginning to understand how the raw hurt in her mother caused her uproars.

Had she ever been *young and carefree?* Her father had no idea of what she was like. For instance, he didn't know she was writing a novel about the roomers, describing their lives in merciless detail. Mama knew but dismissed it as scribbling. Neither one of them had ever asked her what she wanted. Everything was thrust upon her. She was trapped between them. What could she say? What could she do?

She gazed miserably from Daddy to Mama, each with their different expectations and fought an impulse to run out on the balcony and throw herself off. Given permission to speak for the first time in her life, she twisted her body this way and that, unable to say a word.

Phoebe was shaking her head slowly back and forth as Sheila opened the adjoining door. "I thought I heard Daddy—" Sheila fixed upon Daddy as if seeing a ghost. "It *is* Daddy."

Daddy scooped Sheila up in his arms. "She's like a little pigeon. I can feel her bones. Mamila, you don't eat enough."

"She's sick," Phoebe said. "But we're gonna make her better, huh, Mama?"

"She's had a bad bout of bronchitis," Mama said, warning Phoebe with a glance not to say more.

"I don't remember she had such dark circles under her eyes," Daddy said. "I'll bring her carrot-coconut juice." He put Sheila down next to Phoebe on the bed.

Daddy shifted his weight and ran the brim of his hat through his fingers. "So, uhm—"

He looked at Phoebe.

Outside, the noise of the VE Day celebration was beginning to wane, and the crowd dispersed.

Mama stared through the screen door. Her lips trembled. For once she seemed to have nothing to add.

"Daddy . . . I can't go," Phoebe finally said. "I have too much to do here. I'm sorry I worried you. I'm Mama's right-hand man." *And you have Charlotte.*

Daddy indicated the room with his chin. "You tell me this is what you want?"

Mama came to life, and was about to speak, but Phoebe caught her eye, and she remained silent.

"It's my job," Phoebe said. *Living with Charlotte would stifle me. She would want me to be a debutante, a Jewish American Princess like those snotty girls who snub me. I would never meet a Mario, a Tony, or even a Joey.* These thoughts hung in the air. Daddy looked bewildered. Phoebe knew the King was going off to war and she needed to do her part and be strong. She got up and hugged him. "Be happy. It's okay."

He sighed and turned away. "I'll get Sheila some juice," he

said over his shoulder to Mama, and he walked out of the room. Mama followed Phoebe as Phoebe ran to the landing.

The door shut downstairs.

Mama put her forehead against the wall. "The big boob," she said in a sad voice.

Chapter 35 - Remek

Phoebe grabbed Mama's letter, reading it as Mama came running into the kitchen. Mama cried out, "I can sponsor my family to come to the U.S.! Uncle Hindl is still alive! See, here's his picture."

Phoebe snatched the sepia photo of a skull-capped patriarch from her hands. Hindl looked like a more filled-out version of his brother, David, Phoebe's *Zaada,* or grandfather. Phoebe remembered David as a skinny, blue-eyed, white-haired, magical story-teller, who would take Phoebe to beer halls with him when she was five. She remembered the free lunch on the counter: potato salad, juicy knockwurst smeared with mustard, sauerkraut, garlic dill pickles dripping with brine, and crusty bialys.

Zaada's friends placed her on a tabletop and said, *"Tonze! Tonze!"* and clapped as she gave her Shirley Temple tap. They ran their hands over her blonde curls in a kind of wonderment, nodding to each other and saying, "She'll do all right in America."

At home, her Zaada's varicose leg veins, wrapped in ace bandages, had felt a little creepy whenever she cuddled with him, but it didn't matter. She adored him. When he died, it seemed as if all of Brooklyn turned out for his funeral. The photo distorted as Phoebe's eyes brimmed. This man, Hindl, was her Zaada David's brother.

Sometimes, I wish we'd never left New York. On hot Brooklyn nights we slept on the fire escape on soft featherbeds. Mama would read to me from Heidi, Child of the Mountains.

Mama was saying, "And I'm sending for your second cousins, Jerome and Barish and their children. Hindl says they married Polish Christian women, Marya and Irina, and took their names to hide from the Nazis."

"You say there are little kids, too?" Phoebe said.

"I'm getting to that," Mama said. "Irina has Freddy. He's five. They think Marya's child, little Winnie, is Hindl's, but Jerome is raising her as his own."

Sheila's forehead wrinkled. "Why do they think Uncle Hindl is Winnie's father?"

"He was protecting the women while the young men fought." Mama winked. "They must have got kind of close."

Sheila scowled.

Uh-oh. Sheila was figuring it out. "Never mind," Phoebe said. "It's their business."

Mama gave her a funny look, and Phoebe shrugged. Could she help it if she was burdened with all kinds of things she shouldn't know at her age?

Mama said, "Do you want to hear the best part or don't

you?"

Phoebe said, "Oh, I thought you already gave us that."

Mama went right on, breathlessly. "Hindl has an eighteen-year-old son, Remek, by his Russian wife, Olga. Remek fought in the Underground alongside Jerome and Barish. They lived in a sewer for three years. They've all ended up on Cyprus in the Displaced Persons Camp." Mama waved Hindl's letter. "That's how I found them."

"Wow!" Phoebe said. "An eighteen-year-old cousin."

Mama closed her teary eyes and shook her head. When she opened them again, she'd changed to her visionary self, the one Phoebe loved. "Ah, Phoebe, Sheila, imagine . . . our brave people will be coming here to make a new life. We'll have a family again. You'll see who you come from." Her blue eyes shone and her lips turned up in a smile.

Phoebe caught her mother's mood. They would be the kind, noble, gentle people she was sure she belonged to.

***

Phoebe stared at eighteen-year-old Remek, as did Mama and Sheila. He stood at the train station in his belted jacket. He held a leather grip with straps. He resembled Mama a little with a narrow face, fine light complexion, slender figure, and soft red lips. His eyes were blue and shy.

Mama hugged him for a long time.

His cheeks pinked up a little in embarrassment.

Then Mama held him at arms' length, and said, "Are you hungry? I made matzo-ball soup, latkes, and roast chicken."

Remek smiled. *"Danka."*

The word, *aristocrat* kept repeating in Phoebe's head. A *young prince, shabby but dignified.* On the ride home, his skinny wrists, sticking out two inches from his frayed cuffs, lay calmly in his lap, but he jerked at loud traffic noises, and his cheeks trembled.

At home, Phoebe saw his big smile as he gazed up at the old Victorian house, and he began to climb the stone steps with them. Once inside, Mama went right for the kitchen, and they followed her.

Phoebe sat across from Remek as he methodically ate whatever Mama placed before him: golden chicken soup with fluffy matzoh-balls sprinkled with parsley, a quarter of a roasted chicken that he attacked with his fingers, grinning in spite of his stuffed cheeks. Whole latkes with lacy crisp edges, drenched in applesauce and sour cream disappeared into his mouth.

"So, tell me, Remek," Mama said, after she placed coffee and a piece of apple cake in front of him, "How is it you are the first to arrive?"

He gulped coffee, then picked the cake up in his fingers and took a bite. "There was a list. I am young . . . ah, much better than a woman or an old man. Hindl said, 'You go now. We will come next.'"

Better than a woman or an old man? Phoebe looked at Mama, astounded.

Remek was blissfully picking up cake crumbs with his fingertips. Mama's hand rested lightly on the top of his head for a second, then she said, "I would think you'd send the women, children, and old people first."

"No. I make ready for them. I see if you have place for them."

Mama said, "Even if I didn't have room, I'd put them up." She removed the cake plate from under Remek's fingers. "So how was it in the D.P. Camp?"

"Better than to be with the Nazis. But still the people dying, sickness, not enough medicine, not enough food, little water. Everybody want to come to America. Soon, Hindl and the others come to your California."

"I welcome them," Mama said.

Phoebe put her chin in her palm and rested her elbow on the tablecloth. *He's not shy. He speaks pretty good English, too. His accent is so cute. Wait 'til Laurie gets a load of him!*

Sheila had chosen to sit as far away from Remek as possible at the end of the table where she appraised him with narrow-eyed scrutiny.

Sheila's scared of everyone.

Remek looked up from the meal, wiped his lips with the napkin, and smiled. *"Danka."* He loosened his belt. His gaze followed Mama's aproned figure as she placed dishes in the sink.

A tingle went up Phoebe's spine. *Please don't look at my mother like that.* She reached into the sideboard for a pack of cards. "Wanna play Casino?"

Remek tilted his head. "Cassi no . . . ?"

Phoebe slid the cards hand to hand like a waterfall. *Thank you, Joey.* "If you don't know how to play, I'll teach you."

A dimple appeared in his thin cheek as he said, "It's nice for

338

me to find such beautiful cousins in America."

Mama bent to hug him, but he wouldn't let her straighten up and pulled her into his lap. He began to kiss her. She pulled away, laughing. "No—no, Remek. That is not how to thank me."

He answered by cupping one of Mama's breasts in his hand and slobbering on her neck.

Sheila's eyes were shocked cartoon blanks.

Phoebe dropped the cards. "Stop that, Remek!"

He ignored her and started in on the second breast.

"What's the matter with you?" Mama shouted, fighting his hands at her blouse.

Phoebe tried to pull Mama away from him, but then he dropped Mama, and his hands were everywhere on her as she slapped, pinched, and finally had to bite his lip when he tried to pry open her mouth with his tongue.

Mama now held a mop like a ramrod in front of her. Remek grinned and pushed it aside.

Sheila screamed and ran from the room.

"This is not funny! Now stop it, Remek," Mama said, and Phoebe hid behind her. "In America, we don't grab women."

He looked puzzled. Then he smiled. "So we will dance."

"Dance?" Mama shrieked.

"Dance with him. Maybe he'll cool down," Phoebe said, and began to drum a tango rhythm on the table while Remek and she sang, "Da da *dah* dah- da dada dah."

"Oh, for God's sake—" Mama said, but she allowed him to lead her off into the living room.

He was a marvelous dancer. They took a breathtaking turn

around the floor. Mama followed his lead like a professional, but soon his hands were creeping up and down Mama's back and she was slapping him again. "Run, Phoebe, get John from next door!"

"I'm not leaving you!" Phoebe shouted, pulling on Remek's shirt. "Stop it!" She felt the shirt rip in her hands.

Remek stopped suddenly and dropped his hold on Mama.

Phoebe saw his bulging red-veined eyes.

Mama brandished the mop again.

He put his hands in the air as if Mama had pulled a gun on him. "Not in America?" He seemed truly bewildered. "I thank you for your kindness." Remek examined his torn shirt. "I don't please you?"

"You would please me if you took the dirty dishes to the sink," Mama said. "You could wash them. You could mop the floor. That would please me."

"But you don't have a man," he said. "You need a man."

Two high spots of color appeared on Mama's cheeks. Had she become aroused by Remek? Or was Mama embarrassed? She was unsure. To Phoebe, Remek's behavior was as disgusting as a puppy's, who thinks your leg is his girlfriend. Thank goodness Sheila had missed it. Then she saw Sheila hadn't. Her pale face was at the living room window.

"What do you expect?" Mama said after Remek went upstairs, rubbing his swollen lip and fingering his torn shirt. "He lived in a sewer for almost three years."

Chapter 36 - The Survivors

September 15, 1945

Dear diary,

The rest of the family has arrived. Stooped and grey, Great Uncle Hindl looked so much like Zaada, I hugged him. His huge Russian wife, Olga, took over the kitchen, cooking with pails of boiling water. She cried happy tears, kept kissing Mama with her toothless gums, and nodded at everything we said because she didn't understand much English. Still, Olga tried to learn. It seemed she used her short wide nose to sniff the air for English words. Olga wiped her hands on her apron, crossed her arms and shook her head a lot, laughing and crying. Mama said that's what war does to people sometimes. It unravels them. Maybe that's Remek's excuse.

Goodnight.

***

Phoebe glanced in at Remek as he scrubbed the bathroom floor. The memory of his assault on her and Mama, fresh in her mind, had made her dodge him for days, but Remek hadn't bothered either of them since, and now he looked like a boy prince again, doing common labor. He was Mario's age, but oh, what a difference. Instead of Mario's quiet command of any space and refusal to even wash dishes, Remek's fragile body, out of place behind a mop, doggedly pushed it, panting. *He's too weak to do heavy work.*

He turned and leaned on the mop, smiling. "Cousin Phoebe. You see, I learn very fast how to be in America."

Phoebe kept an eye on the door to her room in case he tried anything, then smiled back. If he was going to be nice, then she would be too. "You didn't know our ways. It was a mistake," she said.

He pulled out a handkerchief and wiped his forehead. "You forgive me?"

"If you really mean it, Remek."

His eyes pleaded. "I work for Elaine. You see. I good worker."

Phoebe shuffled her feet in uncertainty. Was she was going to trust him again? *Be careful.* She would not introduce him to Laurie. Yet his command of the dance floor was still a vivid image. She yearned to master the tango. If he would teach her—

With his eyebrows raised, as if he could read her thoughts, he asked, "You like to dance?"

She blinked rapidly while barely nodding. *Don't get him*

342

started again. With her gaze on her bedroom door, she half-ran across the landing, flung the door open, flew in, and slammed it.

***

September 20, 1945

Dear Diary,

The house is crowded with relatives. Uncle Hindl's two sons, Barish and Jerome and their wives, Irina, and Marya, are here now with their children, Freddie and Winnie. Barish and Irina have Freddie, who is about five, and Marya and Jerome have Winnie, who is four. They've turned the whole house upside down. Sheila is constantly complaining about them. Mama can hardly get into the kitchen. Olga cooks stews and soups all the time to feed them. And do they eat! Like it's the end of the world. I take notes because when will this opportunity ever come again in my life? To be face-to-face with actual survivors of the Holocaust as they now call what happened to Jews in Europe.

If I thought the roomers were interesting, these people beat all. I'm the only one in the family thrilled to watch them, listen to them, write about them. Mama is getting more upset day by day. This is more than she imagined would happen when they got here. But I love it!

Remek showed his importance as the first to arrive, so when they came, he escorted them to the closet under the stairs where they were to put their valises. He indicated the living room floor where they spread out their musty sleeping bags. He put Marya in charge of rounding up dirty clothes, and explained to her how to run the washing machine and the wringer. The washing machine has been running non-stop since they got here.

Marya wears a flowered kerchief, and from under her dirndl dress, black leather shoe tips show. She speaks to four-year-old Winnie in Polish, and the child answers back. My stupid American brain is amazed the child can speak Polish! I laugh at myself being amazed. Winnie giggles at her mother, with mischief in her blue eyes. Yellow curls tangle around her face.

Irina, Freddy's mother is having a hard time keeping her five-year-old son from destroying the living room. Mama and I watch, dumbfounded, as the kid scrambles over the couch with his shoes on. Irina screeches at him in Polish, but he doesn't listen. He's a sturdy little kid, and his straight golden locks gives him the look of a Hitler youth. When he spots me, Freddie points his hands like a machine gun. "Ech-ech-ech-ech!" Irina turns to Mama, apologetically, shoving a strand of hair out of her eyes. "Forgive him. He a child." She pulls a heavy green sweater around her thin shoulders and calls, "Barish!" Her husband bounds into the living room. I can't understand what she says to him but the intent is clear. *Get this kid off the furniture.*

With curly black hair, Barish, whose *whip-thin* body shows the *tensile* strength of a dancer, (fancy new words) bows to Mama. Then he grabs Freddie by the waist and puts him on the floor. With a threatening finger, he scolds the child, but Freddie grabs his finger and shakes it like a hand. Barish slings the boy onto his shoulder, tickling him, and Freddie screams with laughter. I'm eating it all up. Mama's jaw sets. I know she was trying not to say anything. Earlier, Mama told me Barish used to play flute duets with Anna, her cousin, who'd perished in the holocaust.

Peace has made me think of Emiko again. I'm still trying to get over what we did to the Japanese people on Hiroshima and Nagasaki. But it did end the war and kept a lot of our troops from dying. Still . . . I wonder if Emiko is okay. Will I ever see her again?

All for now.

***

Phoebe shut her diary as Winnie bounced into her room, chattering in Polish. Marya was right behind her. "What's she saying?"

Marya's eyes showed her concentration as she attempted an answer as she'd been taking lessons from Remek. "She happy to be in California. She wants to see Mickey Mouse."

Phoebe applauded. "We'll go to the movies!"

Marya explained this to Winnie in Polish. Winnie jumped into Phoebe's lap and kissed her. *What an adorable child.*

Later that day, out of curiosity, Phoebe followed Marya, who was carrying Winnie to the upstairs bathroom. The shower was going constantly as one relative after another went in and out of it. Freddie, pulling off his clothes on the way up, pushed between them. In the shower, the children scooted between the adults' legs as Barish and Winnie's father, Jerome, sang European folk songs at the top of their lungs. The bathroom floor was a heap of twisted towels as Jerome stepped out of the shower, naked.

At the open doorway, Phoebe said, "Oh. Pardon me—" She ran for her bedroom.

With a towel around his middle, Jerome stuck his head out of the bathroom. "It's okay! Don't be afraid. We cousins."

Was he also a sex fiend like Remek? He was nice looking with light brown curls, a muscular chest with a scattering of hair. He had Remek's red lips. He turned to the children behind him. *"Sha, kinder, sha."*

Winnie and Freddie were quiet for about two seconds, then they started flushing the toilet over and over and screaming with excitement as the water swirled down.

The old couple were the last in line for the shower, but with no hot water left, Olga filled pails of water, heated them on the stove, and then emptied them into the tub downstairs. Mama helped Olga with Uncle Hindl's bath. When Olga'd toweled him off and got him into pajamas, Hindl appeared in the living room in a robe, his wet grey hair slicked down.

Phoebe and Mama checked on Olga in the bathroom. She'd lowered herself into the scummy water, humming a lullaby.

"Here, Phoebe," Mama said, lugging another bucket of hot water off the stove, "Give her a warmup."

Olga crossed her arms over her large breasts as Phoebe came in with the steaming pail, and asked, "Are you cold, Olga?"

The old lady's eyes shone with tears as Phoebe dumped the water into the tub. "Good . . . girl . . . so good."

The children and their parents fell asleep on their living room bed rolls.

In the dining room, Phoebe watched Uncle Hindl sip tea with a lump of sugar between his teeth. Mama and Sheila sat near him and Mama asked if he knew what happened to the others.

The old man turned his watery gaze on Mama and his chin dropped. In a mournful voice, he said, "*Alla toit.*" Everyone dead. "*Alla toit.*"

Mama bent her head. "We had forty relatives."

"Remek has a friend, Joseph. He's coming to us," Uncle Hindl said.

"Where are we going to put him?" Mama said.

"He's not our relative," Sheila said.

"Should we leave him in the D.P. Camp?" Hindl asked.

Mama said, "Of course not."

Phoebe leaned forward. "What's he like?"

Hindl laid his hand on Mama's and sighed. "He's not right since the war," he said, in Yiddish.

"You talk of Joseph?" Remek asked, coming into the room in his pajamas.

Uncle Hindl waved his hand in dismissal, but Remek went on. "Joseph is bitter. He saw too much."

"Too much?" Phoebe said.

"You must understand. He is my age, but he will never be young anymore," Remek said.

Uncle Hindl got up, slowly. "I go to sleep." And he left the room.

Phoebe turned to Remek. "Tell me about Joseph. I can take it." She shivered in anticipation. It would be like Bass Lake when the Girl Scouts told ghost stories over the campfire.

The dining room candlelight flickered across Remek's face. His gaze went from Mama to Sheila to Phoebe. Remek hadn't ever looked this sober. He didn't speak for a long time. When he did, he looked at his hands.

"We were in school together," he said. "He didn't go into the forest with us when the Nazis came."

"Why?" Sheila asked.

"He had a Catholic girlfriend. She hid him, at first."

Mama said, "Maybe Sheila shouldn't hear any more of this."

"Go, Sheila. This is not for you," Remek said.

Mama nodded to Sheila. "I think it will give you more nightmares."

"Yes. Go to bed, my little cousin."

Sheila rose in reluctance. "You better tell me in the morning, Phoebe." Sheila went upstairs.

Remek resumed. "When we came back to the city after the war, they were punishing collaborators."

"I heard they shaved their heads," Phoebe said.

Remek's eyes gleamed. "Yes, they did that. But Joseph did more."

Mama glanced at Phoebe. "Should Phoebe hear this?"

Remek shrugged. "She's old enough."

Phoebe leaned toward Remek. "Tell me—"

"Joseph's parents begged him not to be . . . uh . . . how you say, *serious* about this girl. She was Catholic. It could go nowhere, but he was in love. He risked his life to be near her. She hid him at first. Soon, she was tired of him and asked him to

348

leave. She didn't want to be caught hiding a Jew, she said. Where could he go? '*Gey in dreart,*' she told him to his face.

"What does that mean?" Phoebe asked.

"Go into the earth . . . to your grave . . . ?" Remek asked, looking to Mama.

"It's an idiom. *Go to hell,*" Mama said.

"Gee," Phoebe said.

"He hid in basements, always with the worry he'd be found. It was winter. Soon there was no food in the town. A Nazi officer wanted Joseph's girlfriend. He fed her, and gave her a fur coat. She went to live with him. This made Joseph angry. He risked his life to be with her, and she went off with a Nazi for a few potatoes and a fur coat. All around him Christian people were sent to concentration camps for little things like being disrespectful to a Nazi officer. People were starving, freezing, and she would walk by on the Nazi's arm, in her fur coat, her cheeks covered in makeup, her lips painted red. People in the town hated her. To Joseph, she was evil. He became like a wolf, with icicles in his beard, growling to himself what he would do to her if he had the chance." Remek took a sip of wine.

Phoebe and Mama were silent. Mama clutched her hand.

"Poor Joseph," Phoebe finally said.

Remek gave a mirthless chuckle. "He was getting more crazy by the day. He began to talk to himself. His hands curled as if around her neck."

"You don't have to finish the story," Mama said.

"You do—" Phoebe said, grabbing Remek's arm.

Remek put a hand to his forehead. "I have to, Elaine. I have

349

to . . . not . . . have it . . . inside me anymore."

Mama got up. "The war made people depraved. Why should I listen to this?" She walked upstairs. Mama's voice drifted down to them. "Don't come crying to me that you have nightmares, Phoebe."

Remek squeezed Phoebe's hand tight. "So comes the victory. They are punishing collaborators. Joseph comes back, jumps into the house where she was kept by the Nazi. The Nazi had run away. Joseph beat her. He raped her. He broke her neck with his bare hands. He threw her out of the window into the street. The town people tore her body apart."

Remek uttered one sob, released Phoebe's hand, and turned away from her. "Joseph is not himself anymore."

"He's coming here?" Phoebe asked. "Is he dangerous?"

Remek patted Phoebe's hand. "Joseph is only dangerous to himself. He lives it over and over." The candlelight made his features move. Tears glistened on the panes of his cheeks.

Phoebe could hardly wait. She'd already titled the story: "Joseph, the Werewolf."

Chapter 37 - Joseph, the Werewolf

September 30, 1945

Dear Diary,

Joseph arrived last week. He's a dismal bundle of rags. He won't look anyone in the eye and sleeps on the window box near the fireplace.

Mama is about to tear her hair out. She says Joseph smells bad, but he won't take a shower, or remove his rags. He's like a horror writer's monster. I take notes from as far away as I can. What does he smell like? Like the inside of a sour garbage can, with overtones of putrid, rotting meat. When awake, he stares straight ahead, and jumps at noises. If Remek, Jerome, or Barish don't check on him, he pees or does number two in his pants, adding stinking dreck to the rest. For the first few days, the whole house smelled so much that Mama put her foot down. Either he gets cleaned up, or the whole bunch of them has to go.

Later:

Joseph finally had a bath. I watched Joseph struggle with Barish and Jerome, twisting and tearing at them with his skinny arms and kicking with his sticks of legs. He bit them but then his disgusting green teeth began to drop out of his mouth. They wrestled him to the downstairs bathroom and threw him into the tub, rags and all, dumped laundry soap all over him, and turned on the tap. Oh, the inhuman shrieks! Barish and Jerome yelled in Yiddish, "It's for your good, Joseph!" Wet clothes hit the floor with a smack. Through a crack in the door, I saw Barish scratching a toilet brush across Joseph's back. A germ-filled toilet brush! As he scoured, pink skin started showing beneath the grey layers of dirt. By now Joseph was crying, begging for help. His back was bleeding in places. I began to feel awful for the poor guy. Jerome took the toilet brush over and Barish rubbed soap suds into Joseph's hair and scalp. Then they dunked him back into the filthy water. Joseph spurted water as the plug swam up, and the tub drained.

"Not clean yet, Joseph," Jerome said. He plugged the opening and ran the tap again.

"Have *rachmunus off mine cup*," Joseph whined.

"Pity you?" Barish said. "You will not get us kicked out. We will shear your scales like a carp."

Joseph mumbled a prayer, bending back and forth. "Let me stay dead. Let me stay dead."

"Sing, '*Ich leben*,'" Barish said. "I live! I live!"

The Joseph who emerged from the second scrub looked like a starved plucked duck. After Barish and Jerome wrapped him in towels and shaved him, they pulled soft cotton trousers over his legs and a tee shirt onto his shoulders.

Joseph stared at himself in the mirror. *"Himmel."* His eye sockets were dark crater holes with lead bullets at each center. His cheeks sucked in. His clothes fit as if on a hanger, with elbow and hip points holding up his tee shirt and pants. He looked up to Jerome and Barish as if they were the United States army of liberation. Then he almost fainted. They had to support him out of the bathroom. Poor crazy guy. I flew upstairs with my notebook.

***

October 2, 1945

Dear Diary:

Barish, Jerome, and Remek found an old commode at the Goodwill and talked Mama into buying it for Joseph. They put a sheet curtain around it near Joseph's bed. They potty-trained him as if he were a two-year-old. They wouldn't let me watch, but I put my eye to a rip in the sheet.

Barish said, "We give you a bath every day if you don't learn to use this." He demonstrated by placing his behind on the commode.

I couldn't help laughing.

Joseph looked like a scared Charlie Chaplin scrunched up on the window seat, his eyes darting from Jerome to Remek, and he gave a shuddering sigh. His shut his eyes, and he nodded.

Jerome and Remek shook hands and then hugged.

More delicious details later. Signing off for tonight.

***

"It's been two weeks. How long will they stay?" Sheila wailed. "I can't have my friends over anymore."

Mama held Sheila close to her chest and stroked her hair. "Remember what they've been through. We can't just throw them out like renters who don't pay."

Phoebe closed her eyes. *Oh yeah?* She pushed her French toast around on the plate, then arched an eyebrow, curious to see how Mama would take some new dirt. "Listen. On Sunday, I heard this moaning in the living room, and I hid on the stairs and saw them *doing it.* Jerome, Marya, Barish, Irina, and Remek, all piled up together while the kids jumped around, laughing. You would have thrown them out right then, Mama."

"Throw out Aunt Olga and Uncle Hindl too?" Mama asked.

"No, but—"

"They're happy to be free. They just show it in that way. I'm more worried about Joseph."

Phoebe nodded. "That guy's crazy. He hides in a corner, grabs his food and gobbles it. He hasn't said one word to us."

"I wouldn't want to be his psychiatrist," Mama said. "Well, they have two weeks to find another place. I've already told them they have to leave and it's not because they have sex in the living room. I can't afford them. The Jewish Agency has to help them now."

Sheila said, "I'll never forgive you, Mama, for letting them stay with us."

"Oh Sheila, can't you think of it as a big adventure?" Phoebe said. "What other kid in your class has such interesting relatives?"

"You like freak shows!"

"Stop it, you two," Mama said. "How would you feel if you'd almost died, but suddenly were given a new life and found yourself in paradise? Yes, I said paradise. You may think East Hollywood isn't so nice, but they can't get over the flowers blooming in winter, the food in the stores, the clean bathroom."

"They almost broke the toilet flushing it again and again," Phoebe said.

"Have some tolerance," Mama said.

"Do they have to *do it* in front of the kids?" Phoebe asked.

"I will speak to them," Mama said.

***

The relatives made no move to leave or contact the Agency. Finally, Mama took Uncle Hindl aside in the kitchen.

Phoebe watched and listened, under the cover of her geography homework.

Olga came into the kitchen and began chopping onions and carrots for vegetable soup. She added a marrow bone to the pail of water on the stove, as well as smashed garlic cloves, cut up celery, salt and pepper, and a pinch of paprika. It started to smell savory as it heated, and she added sliced potatoes to the pot.

Mama set a glass of tea in front of Hindl and spoke in Yiddish. "It's been two weeks. Our family needs to be alone again. Do you understand?"

Hindl's hand shook as he brought the tea to his lips. He'd been praying and still wore his striped *tallis* shawl over his shoulders. He nodded in answer to Mama's question.

When Hindl didn't say anything, Mama asked, "What can the men do here to earn a living?"

"They were in the hotel business. With food. They cooked the food."

"Maybe they could be caterers," Mama said. "I gave you the phone number of the Jewish Agency."

Hindl nodded and hunched his shoulders.

Phoebe vigorously erased a line she'd drawn on her map.

"Well?" Mama asked Hindl.

Hindl explained to Olga in Russian. They looked at each other, sighed, and he rose. Mama followed them into the living room where they began to pack. Phoebe turned the flame down low on the soup and joined them.

Mama said, "The streets are not paved with gold in America as you can see. I've made it too easy for you. You have to work!"

Olga began to wail.

Drawn by Olga's cry, Jerome, Marya, Barish, Irina, and Remek crowded into the living room. It seems they knew by Hindl's slumped shoulders they'd been ousted. Silently, they followed Hindl to the closet. He packed, and they watched him snap his suitcase shut. Remek, looking stricken, got the broom and began to sweep ashes off the rug.

Mama took the broom from him.

He cried, "I help you. I wash dishes. I mop floors."

Phoebe shut her eyes. She couldn't listen to this. But she did, and she opened her eyes again.

Olga said, "We . . . love you, Elaine . . . America . . . Elaine . . . love . . . you understand?" She looked bewildered and wiped her nose on her apron. She drew Phoebe into her cardigan sweater and embraced her, filling the close air with garlic.

"You good girl . . . so good . . . talk to old lady."

Olga's fleshy arms felt safe, her breasts inviting pillows. Phoebe realized she'd missed being hugged. It felt so good. Like Olga was her grandmother. And Olga had just told her how she'd made her happy. Phoebe lingered at Olga's chest as if she floated in warm honey. Then she pulled away, realizing something. *What am I doing? I'm not so good. I'm taking notes, storing it all away. Your whole humiliating experience.*

Look at Mama, standing there with her arms crossed. And Sheila—peeking out from behind Mama. Sheila has cruel eyes. She's gloating. The relatives don't look sad now. They just accept their fate. Am I the only one suffering?

The young people waited for Uncle Hindl. His temple veins bulged from under his fedora. A cryptic smile lifted the corner of his mouth. "We go . . . everybody."

Remek, Marya, Irina, Barish, and Jerome rolled their sleeping bags and stuffed clothes into cardboard valises with surprising swiftness. The grownups herded a suddenly quiet Winnie in her hand-me-down from Sheila. Freddie pushed hair out of his eyes as they left the house without even being allowed to use the bathroom. Lastly, Joseph scuttled out, clutching his blankets and pillow.

"You don't have to leave before lunch," Mama said. "Where will you sleep tonight?"

Remek called back, "We are all right. We sleep in barns, in fields, in the snow. This is California. Warm here."

Mama ran through the front door, and stood there, holding a dishtowel against her chest.

"It's against the law to sleep in a park. I didn't mean you had to get out today. Let me get you a hotel."

Phoebe joined her, waving goodbye at them as they straggled down the street. *How do you feel, Mama? You have to take credit for this.*

But Mama stared straight ahead, then said, "What am I going to do with all that vegetable soup?"

Phoebe said, sarcastically, "Donate it to The Salvation Army."

"Fresh mouth. I'm not hard-hearted. Would I have sent for them if I was? What touchy, proud people. Now I ask you, Phoebe, is it sensible to go off without eating? Who knows when they'll get a good meal like that again. They didn't give me time to tell them I'm planning to sell this house."

Phoebe's head jerked up, ready for a fight. She said, "I love this house. Don't sell it—" and she plunked down on the porch swing. "Why?"

"I'm tired of renters. I was an executive secretary. I think I'll go to work again."

Her eyes stinging with tears, Phoebe felt her cheeks contort. *How can she do this to me?*

"Phoebe. Dammit. Wipe that look off your face," came

Mama's voice.

"I won't."

"Then get out of my sight."

"You take away my home and everybody I love!"

Mama shot her a furious look. "Get that expression off your face!"

"No. I'll be any way I want to be!"

Mama's face softened. "C'mon, buck up, kid." It's not the end of the world."

Mama sat on the swing next to Phoebe and put her arm around her shoulders. Phoebe shoved Mama away. *You can't even feel bad? Gey in dreart, Mama.* Phoebe clenched her teeth. "I hate you."

"So you hate me today. So what? You'll love me tomorrow."

Phoebe suddenly got up and flung open the front door. "I'm going with them—"

Mama jumped from the swing. "Don't be crazy."

Phoebe ran into the house and up the stairs. She pulled out her suitcase, and had begun to fill it with her underwear, her heart pounding, when she saw Mama in the doorway, grabbing both sides of the door frame.

"Put that suitcase away."

Phoebe glanced at her mother's face. "No." She continued to fill her suitcase with clothing. From the storage seat, she plucked her novel and threw it into the suitcase, and she was about to slam it shut when Mama lurched at it, throwing the suitcase on the floor. Half the clothing and the novel fell out. Phoebe furiously grasped the clothing and novel and threw them back into the suitcase. "Get out of my life!" she screamed.

"You stupid kid! You can't follow them."

Phoebe shoved Mama toward the door. "Get out! Get out!" She had a spurt of strength and she used it to batter Mama through the door. She had no lock so she set her back to it, holding Mama at bay. "I'm going, and you can't stop me!" she cried.

"What's the matter with you? They had to leave anyway," Mama said.

"No they didn't. We could have found a way. But you're so mean—"

"I am not mean, Phoebe. I'm practical. You should know that by now."

"You slay me," came Sheila's voice. "I think you're just like them."

"Shut up, squirt!" Phoebe said, imitating Joey. Tears ran down her cheeks and onto her neck. She was caught, stuck! She looked toward her balcony. If she could grab the suitcase, climb over the balcony, drop onto the embankment, she could escape.

Mama said, "Come on Sheila, let her stew for a while." Mama stopped pushing at the door.

As soon as she thought Mama had stopped trying to break in, Phoebe made a run for the balcony. Mama and Sheila were right behind her.

On the balcony, Phoebe peered over the railing. Below her a dense leathery covering of English ivy could break her fall. Mama and Sheila tore through the screen door as she pitched her suitcase over the railing. Before Mama could get to her, she plunked herself on the railing as if riding a horse, feet dangling. With a sideways lurch she could drop into the ivy. That seemed to stop Mama from grabbing her. Phoebe looked down, then at Mama, who held Sheila's hand.

Mama's face was white, her lips a line. "Get down from there."

"No." Phoebe crossed her arms and looked at the ivy embankment.

"What do you want?" Mama asked as if she was being blackmailed.

"Don't sell the house. And bring them back, or I'll jump."

Mama laughed as if Phoebe were being absurd. "You think you can scare me, you little snot nose?"

Sheila squirmed in agitation. "You want to kill Mama?" she screamed.

"Nothing can kill her," Phoebe said, and jumped.

She landed on her suitcase, with one leg under her. A sharp pain jagged from her left hip to her toes. A rat scuttled past her under the ivy, and she reared up with a cry, trying to stand, but could only get to one knee. *The great escape. Now I've broken my leg.* She began to sob.

The front door banged open and Mama and Sheila stood on the stone steps. Sheila was crying.

"You idiot!" Mama said. "Can you walk?"

"No. My ankle is swelling up."

"Can you move your toes?"

"Yes."

Mama ran back into the house and reappeared with a mop.

"Get hold of this and use it like a cane," Mama said, and she shoved the mop toward Phoebe.

Phoebe grabbed the mop but could not rise to standing position using it. She flopped back down onto her suitcase.

"Call the doctor! Call the doctor!" Sheila pleaded.

"I guess I'll have to," Mama said. "Of all the stupid tricks—" She strode back into the house.

Sheila said, "I'm coming over there to keep you company." She started to pick her way through the ivy on the embankment slope.

"Watch out for the rats," Phoebe said.

Sheila stopped, frozen. "Where?"

"Under the ivy. One zipped by me."

Sheila scrambled back to the steps.

Mama came out and said, "They say it's not an emergency. They want me to take you to the clinic in the morning. They won't come here unless you're dying. This stupid war."

Phoebe groaned as Mama waded through the ivy. When Mama got close, she picked up the mop and hooked Phoebe's hand onto it.

"Get up on your good foot. Lean on me."

Phoebe rose shakily, resting her weight on Mama's shoulder. The ankle throbbed and had swelled to twice its size. She hopped through the ivy, using the mop as a cane. She couldn't navigate the stairs, but suddenly John from next door was there, his brown face wrinkled with concern. He picked her up, took her into the house and set her down on the living room couch. Mama put a pillow under her ankle, and an ice bag on top of it.

"I heard it from next door," he said, grinning. "You two ladies having a quarrel, I mean."

"Well, thank you, John. Do we owe you anything?" Mama asked.

"No—no—jus' being neighborly." He turned to Phoebe. "You listen to yo' Mama, hear?"

Phoebe's cheeks got hot. *You don't know anything about it, John. Why is Mama automatically right? Look at Mama, smiling at him.*

Phoebe sulked and stewed, and cried helpless tears. She searched every part of the room. In the corner, the window seat where Joseph slept reminded her of the time she'd felt so miserable she'd crept inside and risen as the Bride of Dracula, her arms stretched before her. Next to that, the big fireplace nobody used was where the little mouse had surprised Laurie by balancing on the tennis ball. And the mantel still seemed stained by Mr. Ruchek's blood. Her first kiss had been in the library just beyond the French doors when they played Flashlight. This was her castle, her memories, and Mama was going to sell it. Fresh anger charged through her.

Mama gave her two aspirin and a glass of water. "You'll sleep down here tonight."

Mama treated her like a buck private who'd gone A.W.O.L. Phoebe sighed and took the pills.

Phoebe said, "I wonder where Tony is tonight." Just the thought of the short man with the big nose playing his sax made her fight tears. Tony would joke her out of feeling bad. Where was he?

"I heard he and Joey lived with his sister, Bella, for a while," Mama said. "I lost touch with Bella. I'm sure Tony has another woman. Even though he's not much to look at, he has a certain charm."

Phoebe could not bear it—the way Mama dismissed Tony. "You didn't know when you had it good!"

"Listen! Listen! You don't know anything about that loser. Keep your trap shut."

"I will never be like you when I fall in love," Phoebe said, rising up on one elbow.

"Oh boy, I can hardly wait. You're a pushover for a few pretty words. I'm afraid for you, kid."

Phoebe let herself down on the sofa again. *What's the use? Mama is Mama.*

Mama would never be Marmee of *Little Women*, but who else's mother would buy a house and fill it with Hollywood characters that she could write about? That's why she loved Mama. *I'll learn to live without sweet mother kind of love, but love is flabby compared with my commitment to be a writer.*

She watched with amusement through the windows as the night birds lined up on the telephone wire and began to call to each other. She felt the birds, the house, the characters she'd written about in *My Life with Mother's Boarders* slipping away like attic relics. She'd hoped to live in this house forever. The house Mama wanted to sell. To Mama it signified rusty plumbing, a leaking roof, and endless sheets and pillowcases to wash and iron. The night birds irritated her. She'd said, "Singing all night. To them everything is upside down like crazy Hollywood."

Phoebe pointed to the telephone wire where the birds swayed back and forth, cackling and crowing. "Mama, the birds are singing in the daytime for a change."

"Wouldn't you know it? Just when I was getting used to birds singing at night."

Phoebe chuckled, but Mama laughed loudly. "At least I don't have to look at them."

Mama leaned over Phoebe and drew the drapes across the window. She sighed and indicated Phoebe's ankle with her head. "Does it hurt bad?"

"Only if I move it."

"Next time, think before you leap." Mama stroked Phoebe's face with her red rough hand.

Phoebe saw a little smile raise Mama's lips.

Mama got up, walked to the bookcase in the dining room, picked something out and came back to settle on the couch near Phoebe.

She held a blue book. It was the one with the inlaid silver letters for the title. It was old and the cover loosened from the body of the book. Phoebe knew it had an inscription on the first blank page. It said, "To Phoebe on her fifth birthday. I hope you enjoy this book as much as I have. Love, Mama." There were many dog-eared pages. Phoebe had read it for herself a few years later, but the memory of the first time Mama read it to her on that long ago birthday was the one that now brought tears to her eyes. Mama had sat close to her on top of the feather quilt on the fire escape in Brooklyn. While Phoebe rested her head against Mama's chest, Mama had begun to read in the mellow night air and Phoebe felt like a newborn kitten, safe, happy, and loved.

And now, here was Mama, with creases lining her face from all they'd been through, saying, "Would you like me to read to you from *Heidi?*"

"Like when I was little?"

"Yeah."

Oh Mama! *Your voice reading in the darkness with only a flashlight to illuminate the pages.* She reached over and gave Mama a kiss on the cheek. Mama cleared her throat. Then she opened the book.

Phoebe lay back on the couch cushions, waiting.

GLOSSARY

Alla toit: All dead

babela: little child, baby

bialys: a flat hard roll covered with onions and poppy seeds blintzes: thin rolled filled pancakes

cochkas: squawkers, in this case birds

Danka: thank you

dreck: stool

dulieben: live

Esha Bubbe: Grandmother who made you eat ess a bissel: eat a little

fagele: homosexual man

furstunkener: stinking

Gey in dreart: go to hell

himmel: heavens

kinda, Zetzin Zee : Children, sit down

kinder: children

kvelling: either extreme satisfaction or marveling

latkes: potato pancakes

Mamila: little mother

matzoh-balls: dumplings for chicken soup

mischugena: crazy

Mrs. Yachinflaster: Elaine's name for Shirley Silver

Nhu: well

rachmunus off mine cup: Pity me

Sha: Be quiet

Shabbos: Sabbath

schmaltz: fat, schmearing Elaine with flattery

Schtick dreck: piece of shit
Shiksa-cup: dumb like a gentile girl
tallis: prayer shawl
tonze: dance
Zaada: Grandfather
Zayagit: very good
Zwetchgenwasser: schnapps

Acknowledgements

I would like to express my gratitude to Stanly Kurnik and Renata Hirsch, who, in the 1950s, had faith in the unformed protoplasm that I was and helped me write with honesty. I would like to thank *The HayWire Writers' Workshop* without whose help I could never have finished this series of novels: Joshua, Madeleine, Hilary, Cindy, and Joe. I would also like to thank Stephanie Bartlett for her wise comments on my manuscript, Tom Romano for his editorial feedback and artistic contributions, and Rosalind Press, my publisher, for putting it all together and making this possible.

About the Author

Ruth Wire is an award-winning published poet, an award-winning screenwriter, a produced playwright, and published short story writer as well as a published lyricist.

In Los Angeles, she attended writing workshops, won a poetry slam, and first became published in prose and poetry. "Letting Poetry Happen" was taught in Ashland Schools as a Poet in the Schools. She put together a Writers' Faire at The Ashland Windmill Inn in the late '70s to give writers a chance to be heard and sell their books. She created two theatres in Ashland, Oregon, New Playwrights Theatre with Bradford O'Neil, and Studio X Experimental Theatre with Scott and Peggy Avery in the 1980s. She began a workshop for writers, HayWire, in 1995.

Ruth Wire grew up watching her parents tear each other apart and has spent the rest of her life putting the pieces of her heart back together. She lives in Ashland, Oregon where she is the President of Ashland Contemporary Theatre Board. She continues to mentor HayWire Writers' Workshop.

Phil G. Loveless, published author award winning poet, playwright.

The writer draws us into the story of a divorced woman buying a boarding house, a great concept for bringing the story a wonderful cast of characters that commands our attention. With all the emotions of people thrown together we close the book knowing we have witnessed real life and love.

Tim Kelly – Editor, Actor

This book is a delight for anyone who grew up in the war years of the forties, or just wants to gain a feel of this very special time in our history. This is a truly authentic peek into a young girl's journey into adulthood written cleverly without a single misstep. A true pleasure that must be read and enjoyed.

Made in the USA
Columbia, SC
11 November 2021

48796320R00204